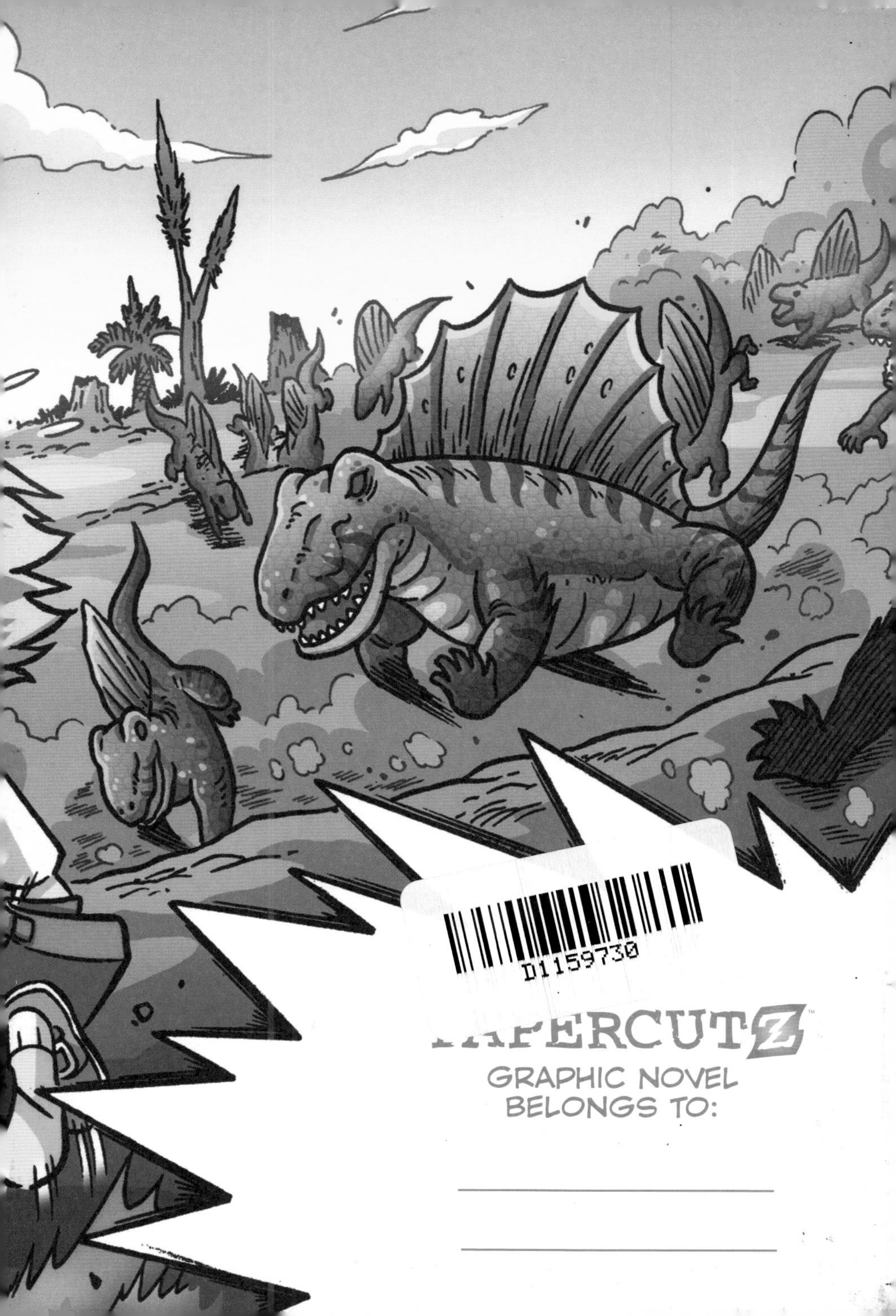
APERCUTZ
GRAPHIC NOVEL
BELONGS TO:

DINOSAUR EXPLORERS

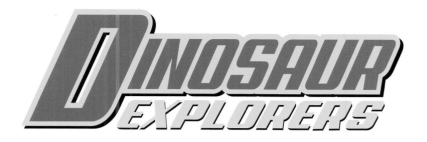

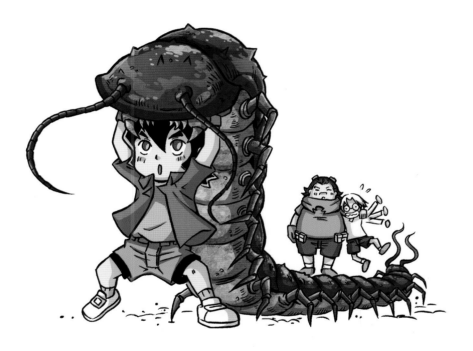

PAPERCUTZ

#3 PLAYING IN THE PERMIAN

© 2018 KADOKAWA GEMPAK STARZ
All rights reserved.
Original Chinese edition published in Malaysia in 2011
by KADOKAWA GEMPAK STARZ SDN. BHD., Malaysia.
www.gempakstarz.com

All other Editorial material © 2018 by Papercutz.
All rights reserved.

REDCODE and ALBBIE—Story
AIR TEAM—Comics
REDCODE & SAMU—Cover Illustration
MAX—Cover Color
EVA, MAX, FUN, SENG HUI —Color
KENNY CHUA and KIAONG—Art Direction
ROUSANG—Original Design
BALICAT & MVCTAR AVRELIVS—Translation
ROSS BAUER—Original Editor
GRANT FREDERICK—Editorial Intern
JEFF WHITMAN—Assistant Managing Editor
JIM SALICRUP
Editor-in-Chief

ISBN HC: 978-1-5458-0162-8
ISBN PB: 978-1-5458-0163-5

Printed in Korea
November 2018

Papercutz books may be purchased for business or promotional use.
For information on bulk purchase please contact Macmillan
Corporate and Premium Sales Department at (800) 221-7945 x5442

Distributed by Macmillan.
First Papercutz Printing.

DINOSAUR EXPLORERS

#3 PLAYING IN THE PERMIAN

REDCODE & ALBBIE – WRITERS
AIR TEAM – ART

NEW YORK

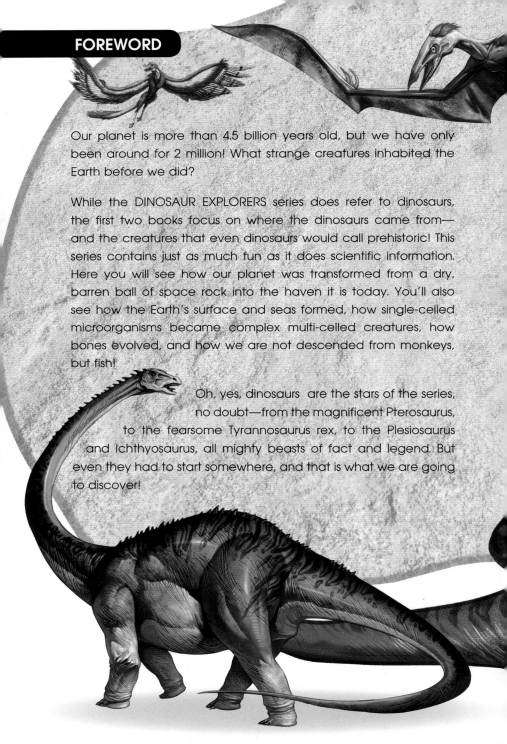

Our planet is more than 4.5 billion years old, but we have only been around for 2 million! What strange creatures inhabited the Earth before we did?

While the DINOSAUR EXPLORERS series does refer to dinosaurs, the first two books focus on where the dinosaurs came from—and the creatures that even dinosaurs would call prehistoric! This series contains just as much fun as it does scientific information. Here you will see how our planet was transformed from a dry, barren ball of space rock into the haven it is today. You'll also see how the Earth's surface and seas formed, how single-celled microorganisms became complex multi-celled creatures, how bones evolved, and how we are not descended from monkeys, but fish!

Oh, yes, dinosaurs are the stars of the series, no doubt—from the magnificent Pterosaurus, to the fearsome Tyrannosaurus rex, to the Plesiosaurus and Ichthyosaurus, all mighty beasts of fact and legend. But even they had to start somewhere, and that is what we are going to discover!

And once we are done with dinosaurs and their beginnings, we can find out what happened and what life forms were around after the dinosaurs. We will take a look at the Cenozoic era, with creatures such as the Icarus bat, the sabre-toothed cat, and the woolly mammoth.
With great stories and science that will wow your friends and teachers, this DINOSAUR EXPLORERS graphic novel series from Papercutz is something not to be missed.

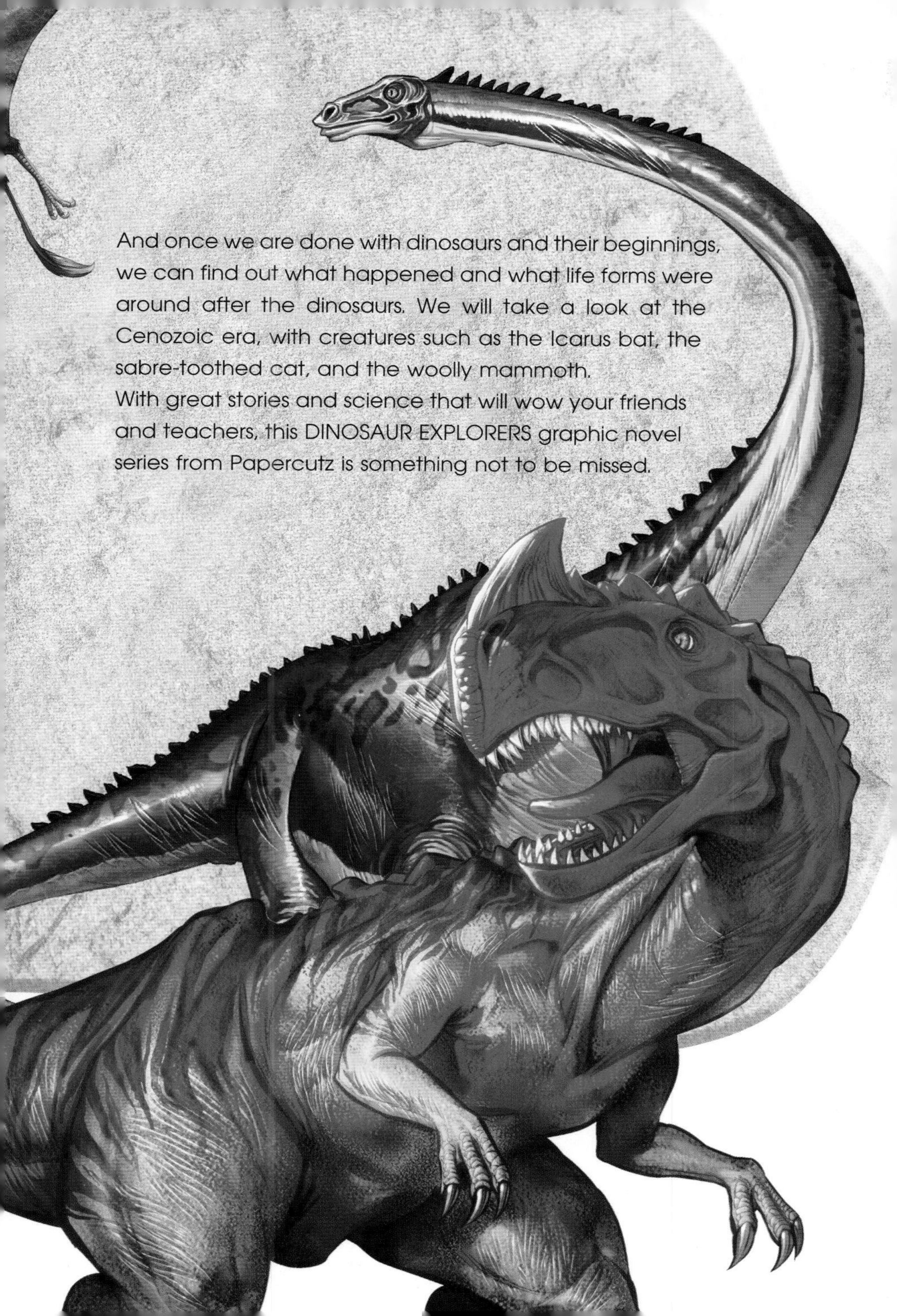

How the Earth was Formed

We know the Earth is the third planet in the solar system, the densest planet and, so far, the only one capable of supporting life. But how did that happen?

1 The Sun's formation

Way, way back, there was a patch of space filled with cosmic dust and gases. Slowly, gravity (and a few nearby exploding stars) forced some of this dust and gases together into clumps–the gases formed into a massive, pressurized ball of heat which became the Sun, while the dust settled into planets, the Earth being one of them.

2 Formation of the Earth

As the Earth formed, its gravity grew stronger. Heavier molecules and atoms fell inward to the Earth's core, while lighter elements formed around it. The massive pressures from the external material heated up the Earth's interior to the point where it was all liquid (except for the core, which was under so much pressure it could not liquify). These settled down into the Earth's 3 layers: the crust, mantle, and core.

While we cannot say for sure just when these dust clouds solidified to form the Earth, nor when they came into being in the first place, we can tell that they took place more than 4.5 billion years ago.

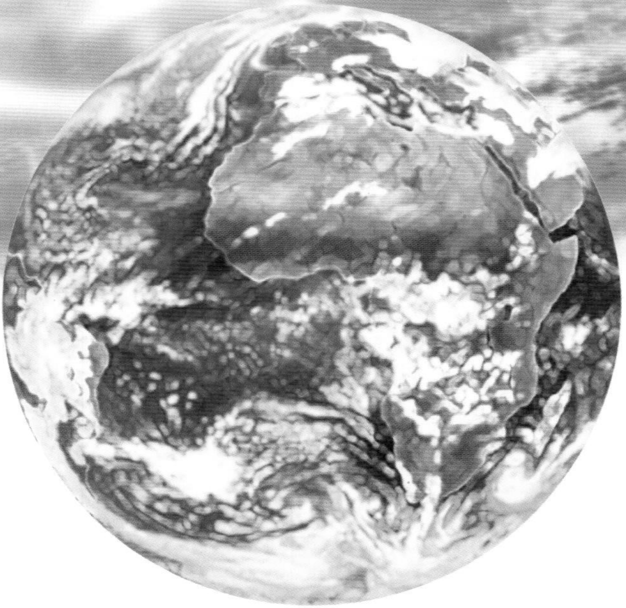

6 The Earth today

Even now, our Earth changes with time; its tectonic plates still move about on the lava bed of the mantle, pushing and pulling continents in all kinds of directions.

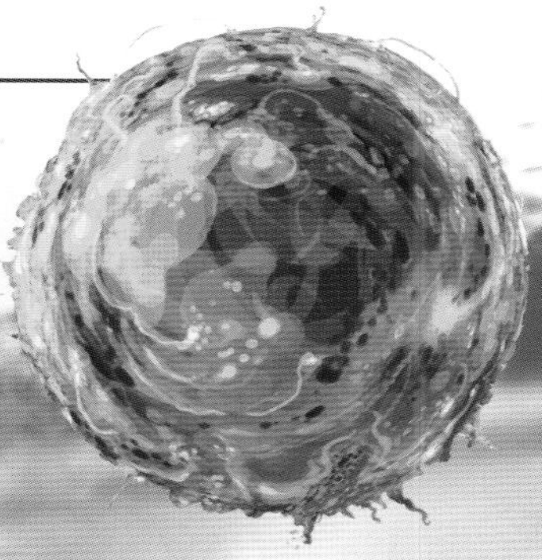

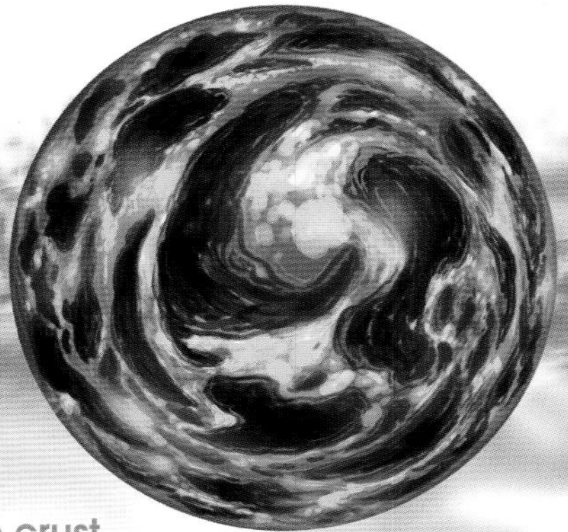

3 The crust

The crust was created around 4 billion years ago, as cooled, solid rock floating on the molten lithosphere merged. Even today, as the continental plates shift away and against each other, some of this rock and molten material might still change place.

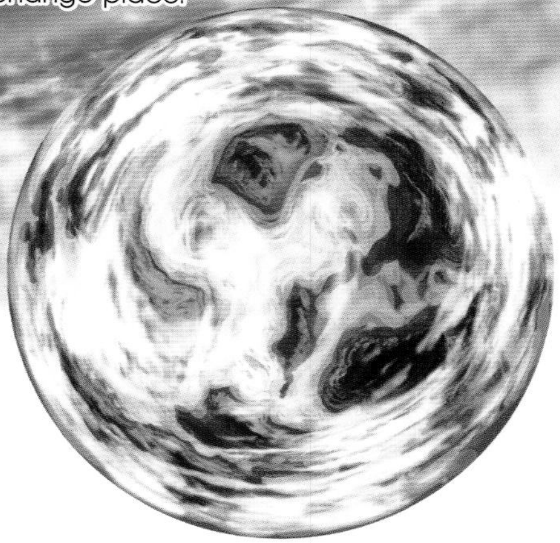

4 The formation of the atmosphere

After our crust solidified, volcanic gases formed our atmosphere. The cooling surface allowed the formation of water vapor and bodies of water.

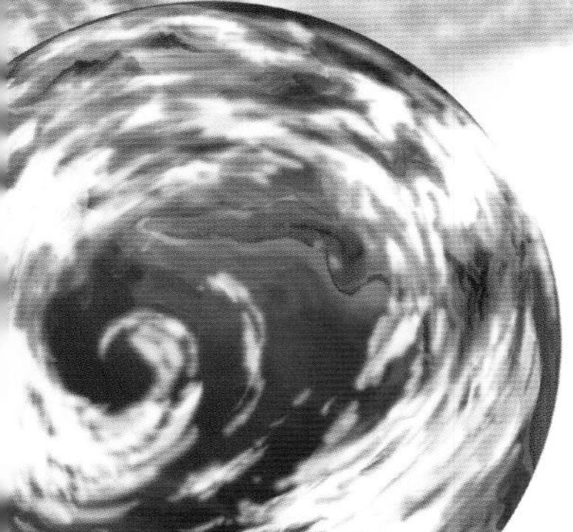

5 Land forms

Around 3.5 billion years ago, several land masses rose above the global ocean, giving rise to the continents we know today.

Geological Time Spiral

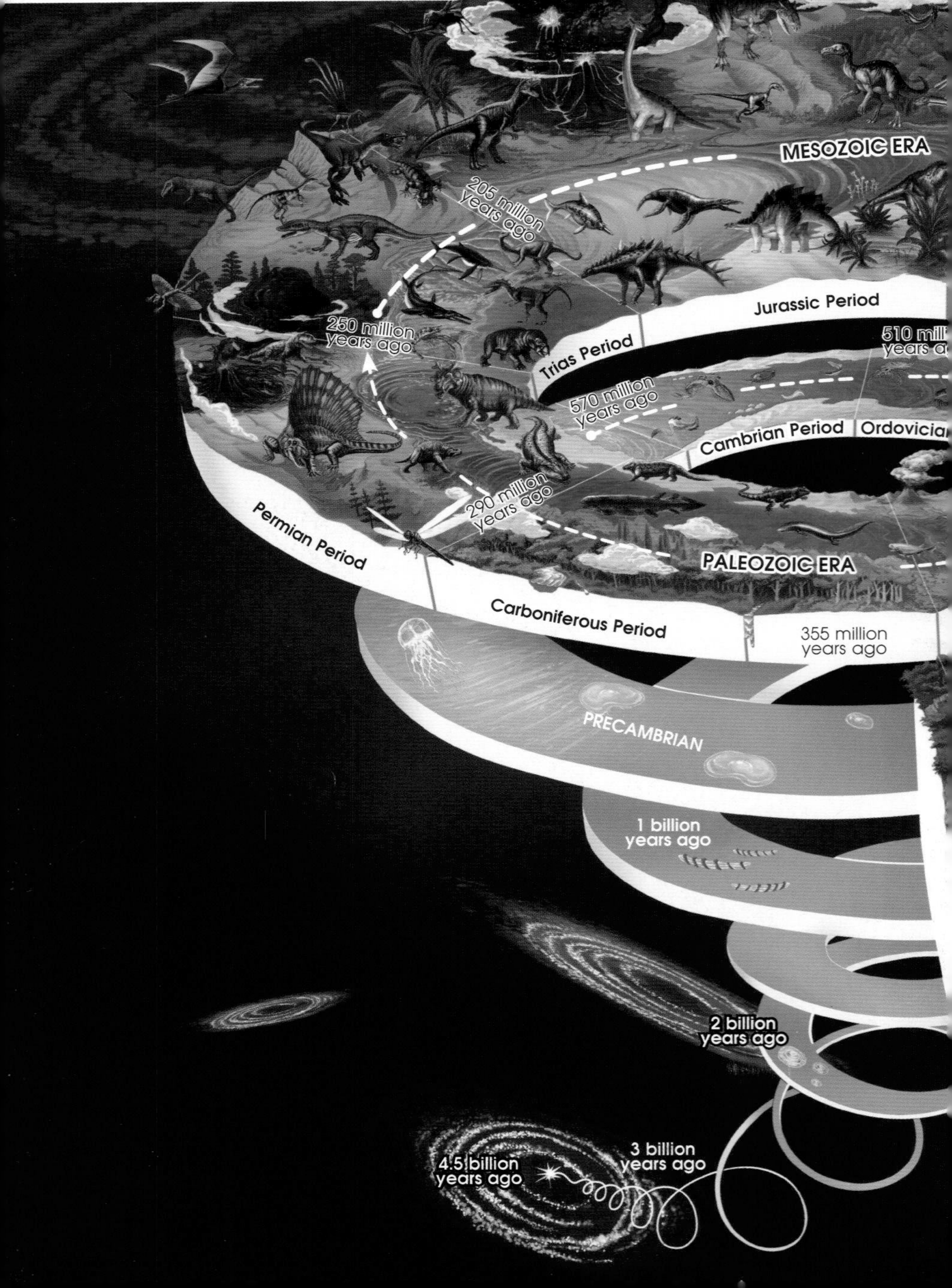
MESOZOIC ERA
205 million years ago
250 million years ago
Jurassic Period
Trias Period
510 milli years a
570 million years ago
Cambrian Period
Ordovicia
290 million years ago
Permian Period
PALEOZOIC ERA
Carboniferous Period
355 million years ago
PRECAMBRIAN
1 billion years ago
2 billion years ago
3 billion years ago
4.5 billion years ago

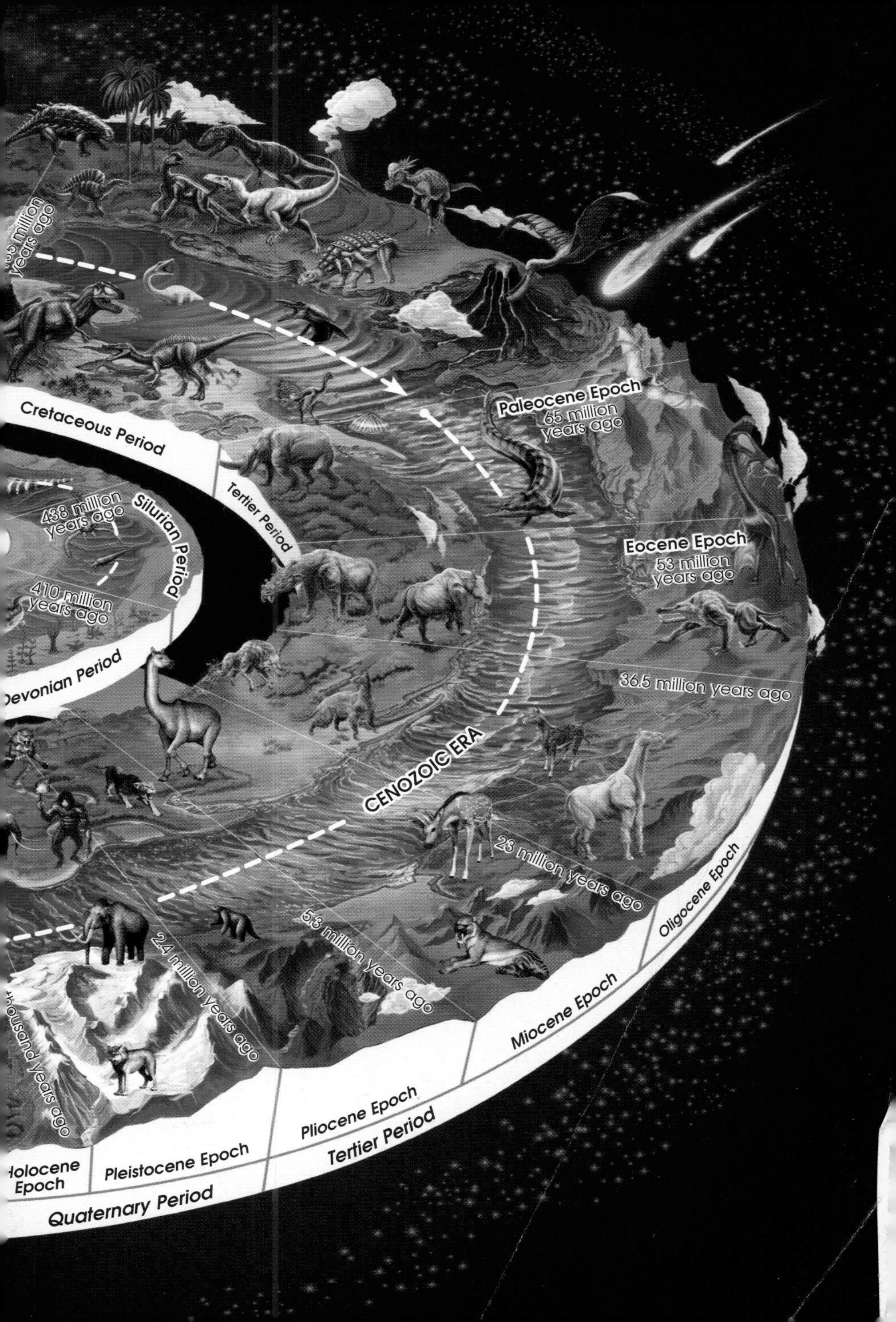
million years ago
Cretaceous Period
Tertier Period
438 million years ago
Silurian Period
410 million years ago
Devonian Period
Paleocene Epoch
65 million years ago
Eocene Epoch
53 million years ago
36.5 million years ago
CENOZOIC ERA
23 million years ago
Oligocene Epoch
5.3 million years ago
2.4 million years ago
thousand years ago
Miocene Epoch
Pliocene Epoch
Tertier Period
Holocene Epoch
Pleistocene Epoch
Quaternary Period

GEOLOGIC TIME SCALE

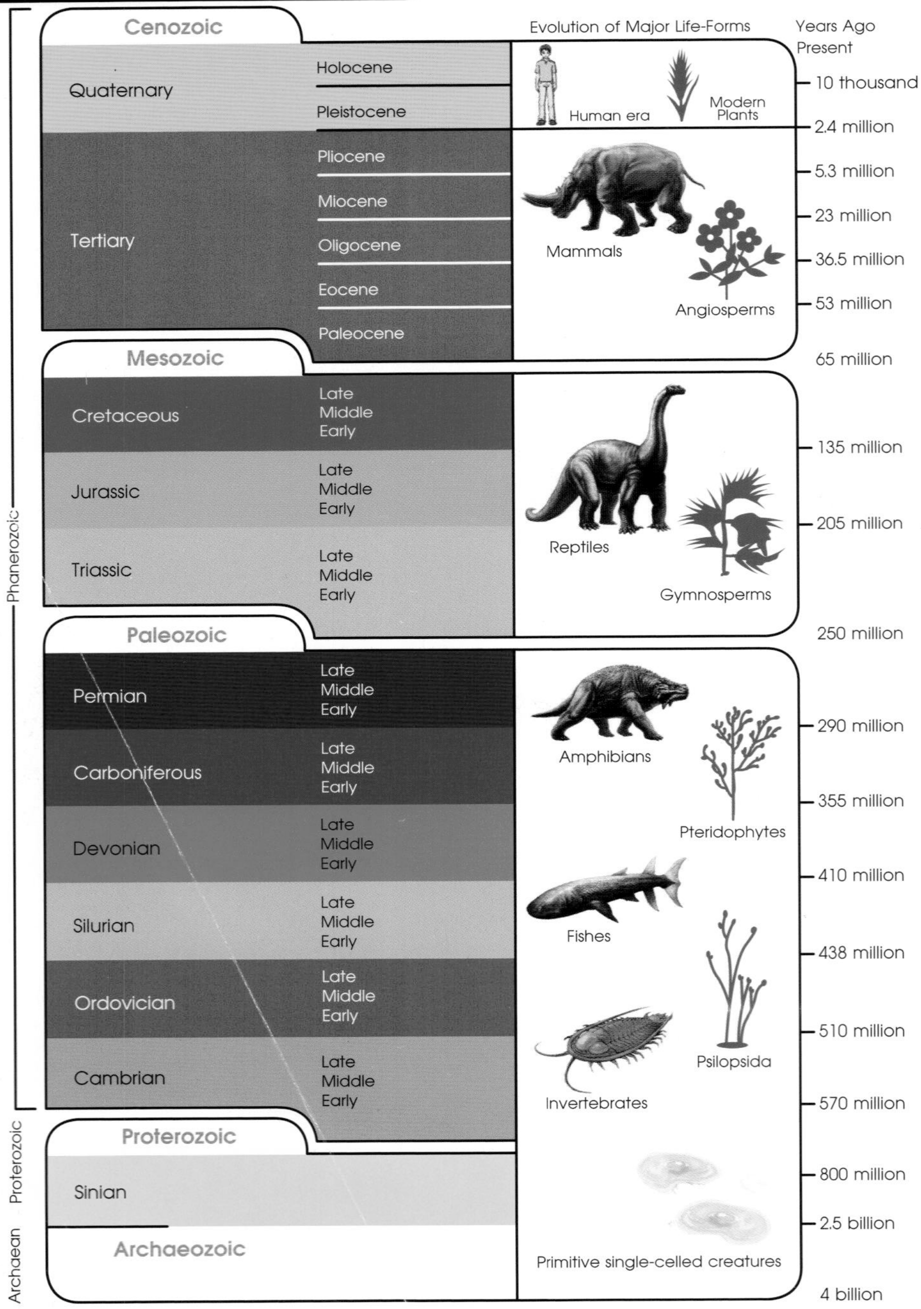

			Evolution of Major Life-Forms	Years Ago
Cenozoic				Present
Quaternary		Holocene	Human era / Modern Plants	10 thousand
		Pleistocene		2.4 million
Tertiary		Pliocene		5.3 million
		Miocene		23 million
		Oligocene	Mammals	36.5 million
		Eocene		53 million
		Paleocene	Angiosperms	65 million
Mesozoic				
Cretaceous		Late / Middle / Early		135 million
Jurassic		Late / Middle / Early	Reptiles	205 million
Triassic		Late / Middle / Early	Gymnosperms	250 million
Paleozoic				
Permian		Late / Middle / Early		290 million
Carboniferous		Late / Middle / Early	Amphibians	355 million
Devonian		Late / Middle / Early	Pteridophytes	410 million
Silurian		Late / Middle / Early	Fishes	438 million
Ordovician		Late / Middle / Early		510 million
Cambrian		Late / Middle / Early	Psilopsida / Invertebrates	570 million
Proterozoic				
Sinian				800 million
Archaeozoic			Primitive single-celled creatures	2.5 billion
				4 billion

Phanerozoic — Proterozoic — Archaean

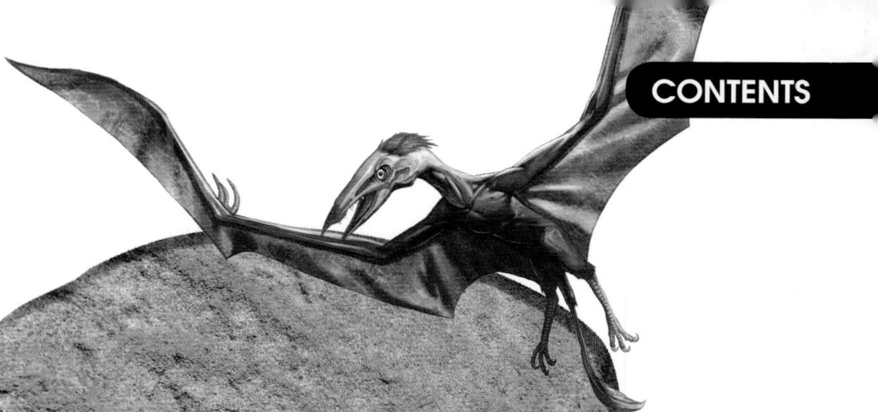

CONTENTS

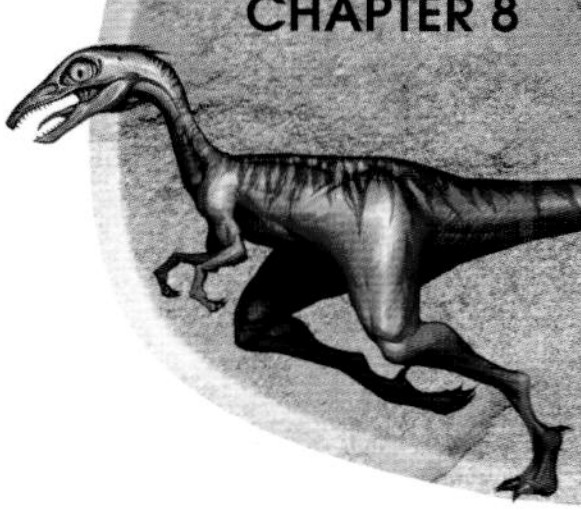

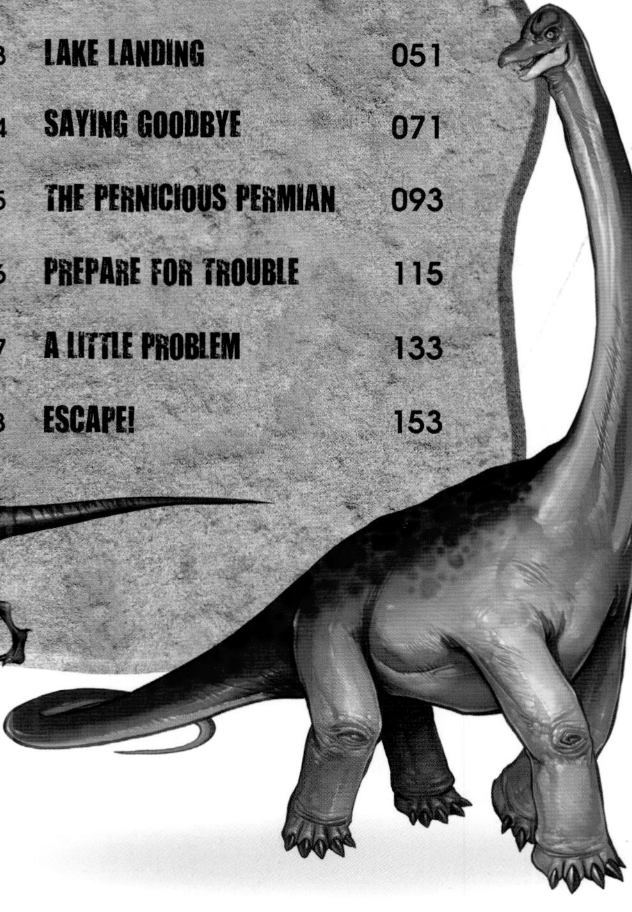

Cast

Sean (Age 13)
- Smart, calm, and a good analyst.
- Very articulate, but under-performs on rare occasions.
- Uses scientific knowledge and theory in thought and speech.

Stone (Age 15)
- Has tremendous strength, appetite, and size.
- A boy of few words but honest and reliable.
- An expert in repairs and maintenance.

STARZ
- A tiny robot invented by the doctor, nicknamed Lil S.
- Multifunctional; able to scan, analyze, record, take images, communicate, and more.
- Able to change its form and appearance. It is a mobile supercomputer that can store huge amounts of information.

Rain (Age 13)
- Curious, plays to win, penny wise but pound foolish.
- Brave, persevering, never gives up.
- Individualistic and loves to play the hero.

Dr. Da Vinci (Age 60)
- A professor at the National Scientific Research Institute.
- A genius inventor.
- Highly knowledgeable, loves adventure, but lazy by nature.

Diana (Age 30)
- Research-based Administrator, the Doctor's helpful assistant.
- A mature, beautiful, and capable lady.
- Good at problem solving.

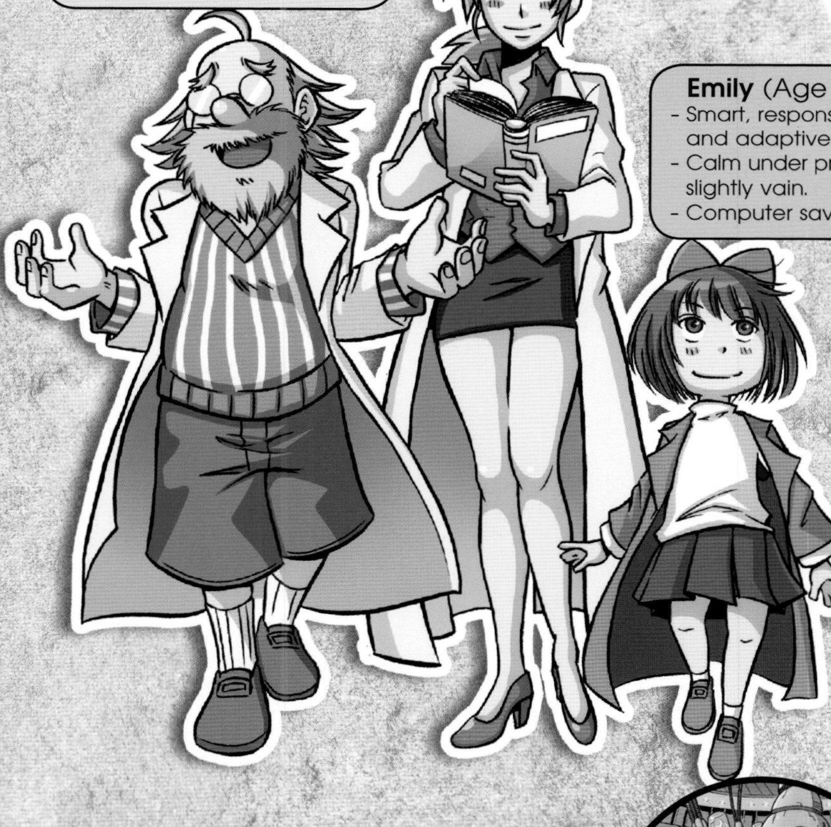

Emily (Age 13)
- Smart, responsible, and adaptive.
- Calm under pressure, slightly vain.
- Computer savvy.

Particle Transmitter
- One of Dr. Da Vinci's most important inventions.
- Able to teleport the team to any period of time and space to execute their missions.
- Able to send urgently needed items to the team at any time.

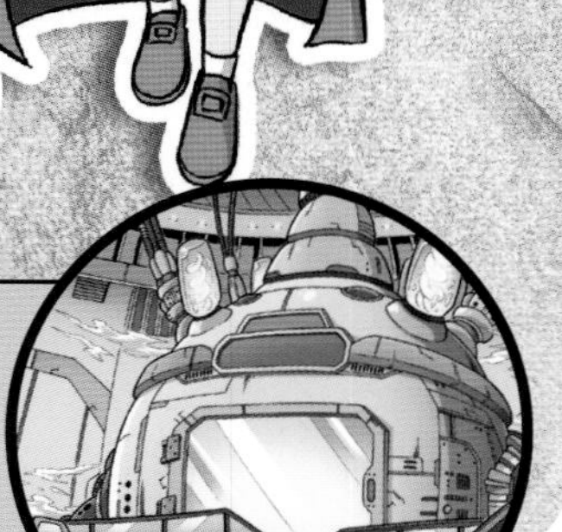

Sent plunging 570 million years into Earth's past due to an earthquake, the Dinosaur Explorers found themselves caught short as they struggled with energy shortages and enemy surpluses! Because of a lack of energy, they must hop through time in short jumps to make it home!

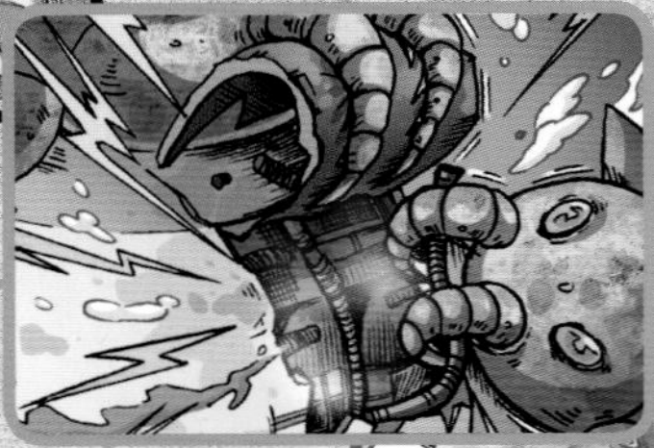

Cambrian

Ordovician

Silurian

Devonian

Carboniferous

Permian

Triassic

Jurassic

Cretaceous

Tertiary

Quaternary

But that is easier said than done, especially when they enter the Ordovician! An expedition to collect research materials became a little harder when giant enemy prawns tried to eat them! And things weren't made easier by Rain's close call!

Though they managed to escape, another jaunt through time brought them close to the jaws of the ferocious Ichthyostega — a creature that might have been a newcomer to land, but an expert at eating people! And that was not the only danger in the Devonian! Good thing our heroes managed to jump out of time, in time — or have they?

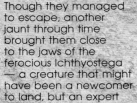

CHAPTER 1
DOOM BUGGIES

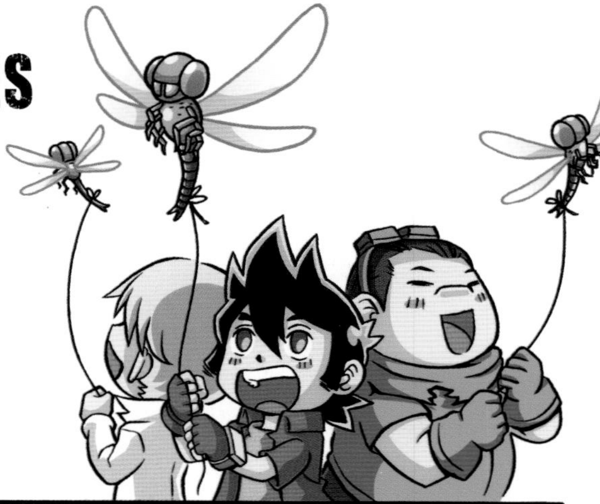

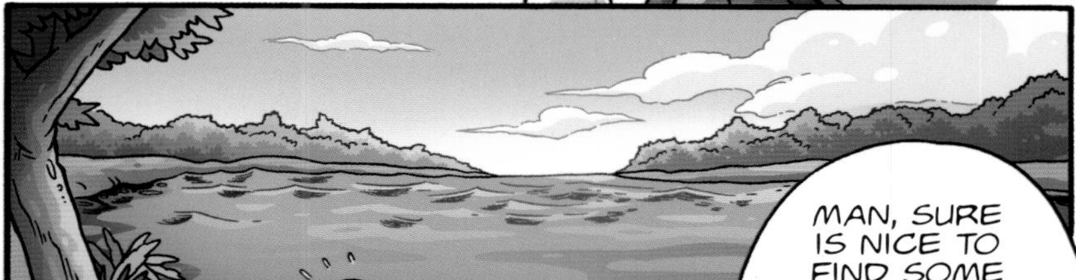

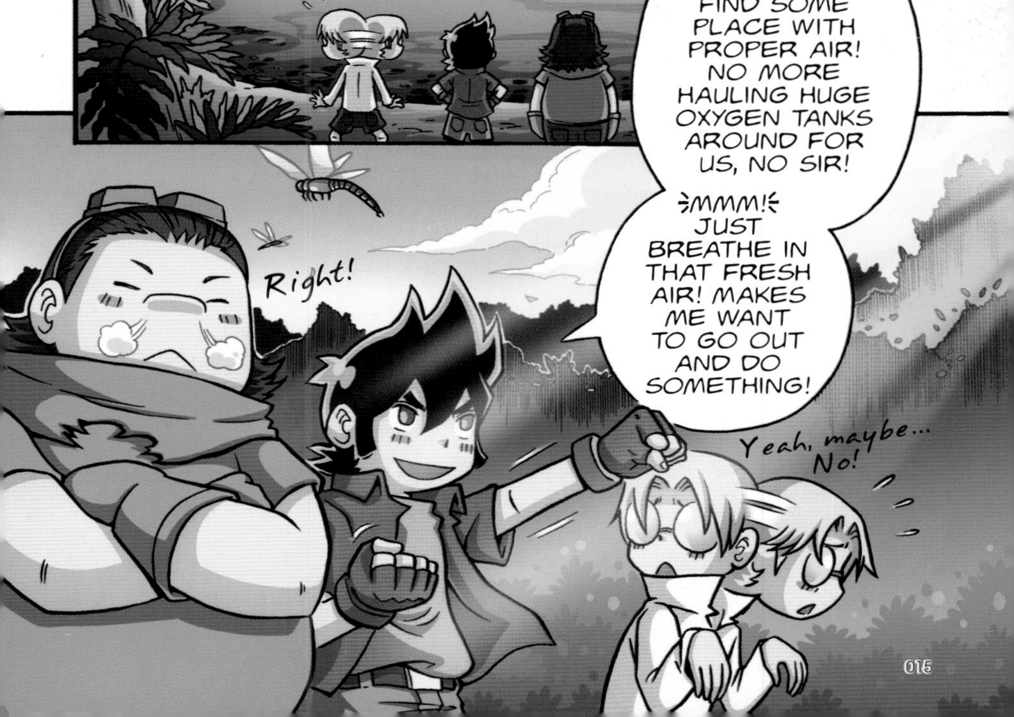
MAN, SURE IS NICE TO FIND SOME PLACE WITH PROPER AIR! NO MORE HAULING HUGE OXYGEN TANKS AROUND FOR US, NO SIR!
MMM! JUST BREATHE IN THAT FRESH AIR! MAKES ME WANT TO GO OUT AND DO SOMETHING!
Right!
Yeah, maybe... No!

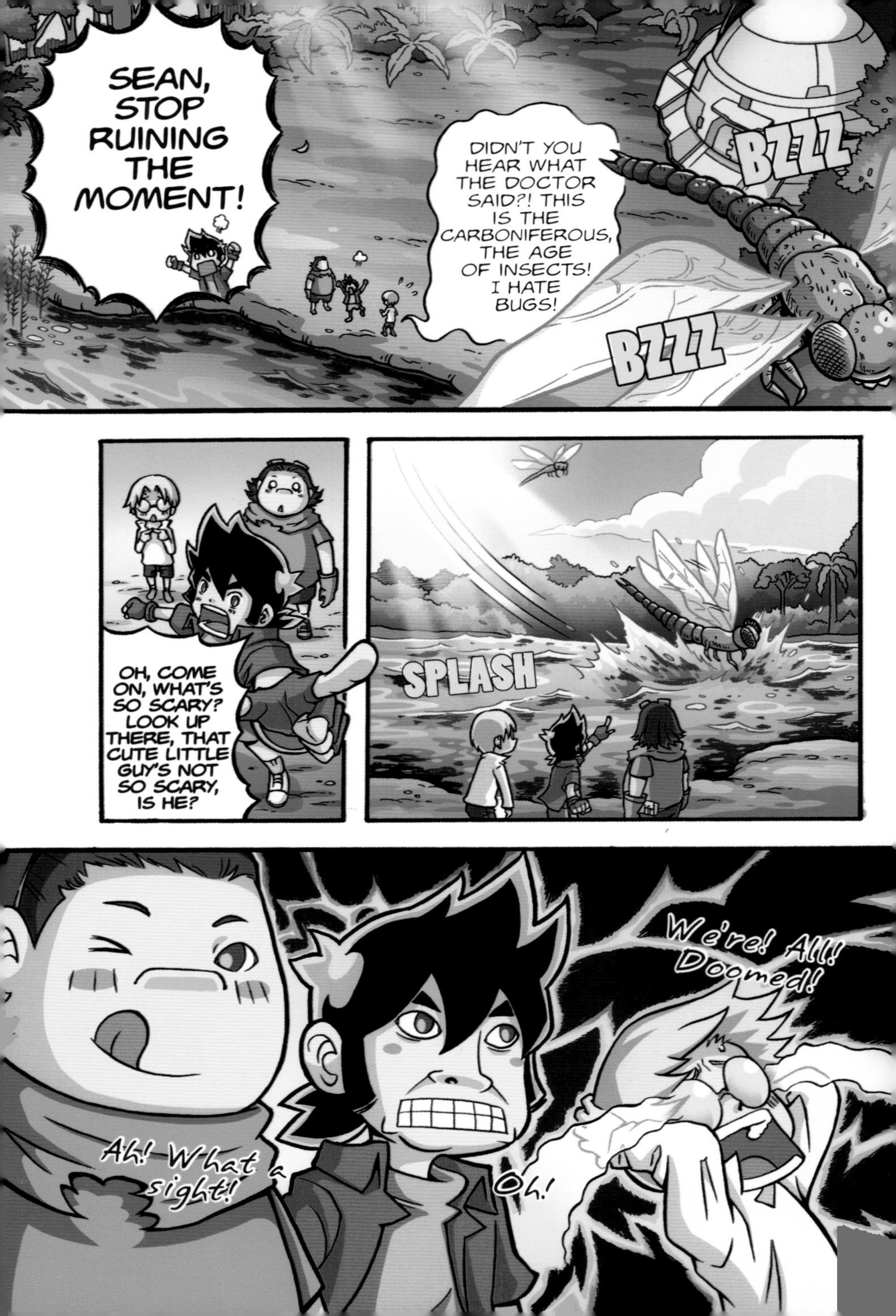
SEAN, STOP RUINING THE MOMENT!
DIDN'T YOU HEAR WHAT THE DOCTOR SAID?! THIS IS THE CARBONIFEROUS, THE AGE OF INSECTS! I HATE BUGS!
BZZZ
BZZZ
OH, COME ON, WHAT'S SO SCARY? LOOK UP THERE, THAT CUTE LITTLE GUY'S NOT SO SCARY, IS HE?
SPLASH
We're! All! Doomed!
Ah! What a sight!
Oh!

HOW CAN YOU BE SO CALM?

UH, WELL I THOUGHT I WOULD PRETEND, TO REASSURE THE READERS.

RUN BACK INSIDE AND HIDE THEN! I CAN HANDLE THINGS!

Huh?

DOCTOR DA VINCI TOLD ME TO GIVE YOU THESE.

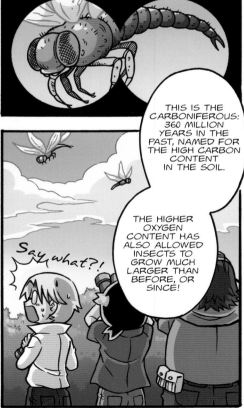

THIS IS THE CARBONIFEROUS: 360 MILLION YEARS IN THE PAST, NAMED FOR THE HIGH CARBON CONTENT IN THE SOIL.

THE HIGHER OXYGEN CONTENT HAS ALSO ALLOWED INSECTS TO GROW MUCH LARGER THAN BEFORE, OR SINCE!

Say, what?!

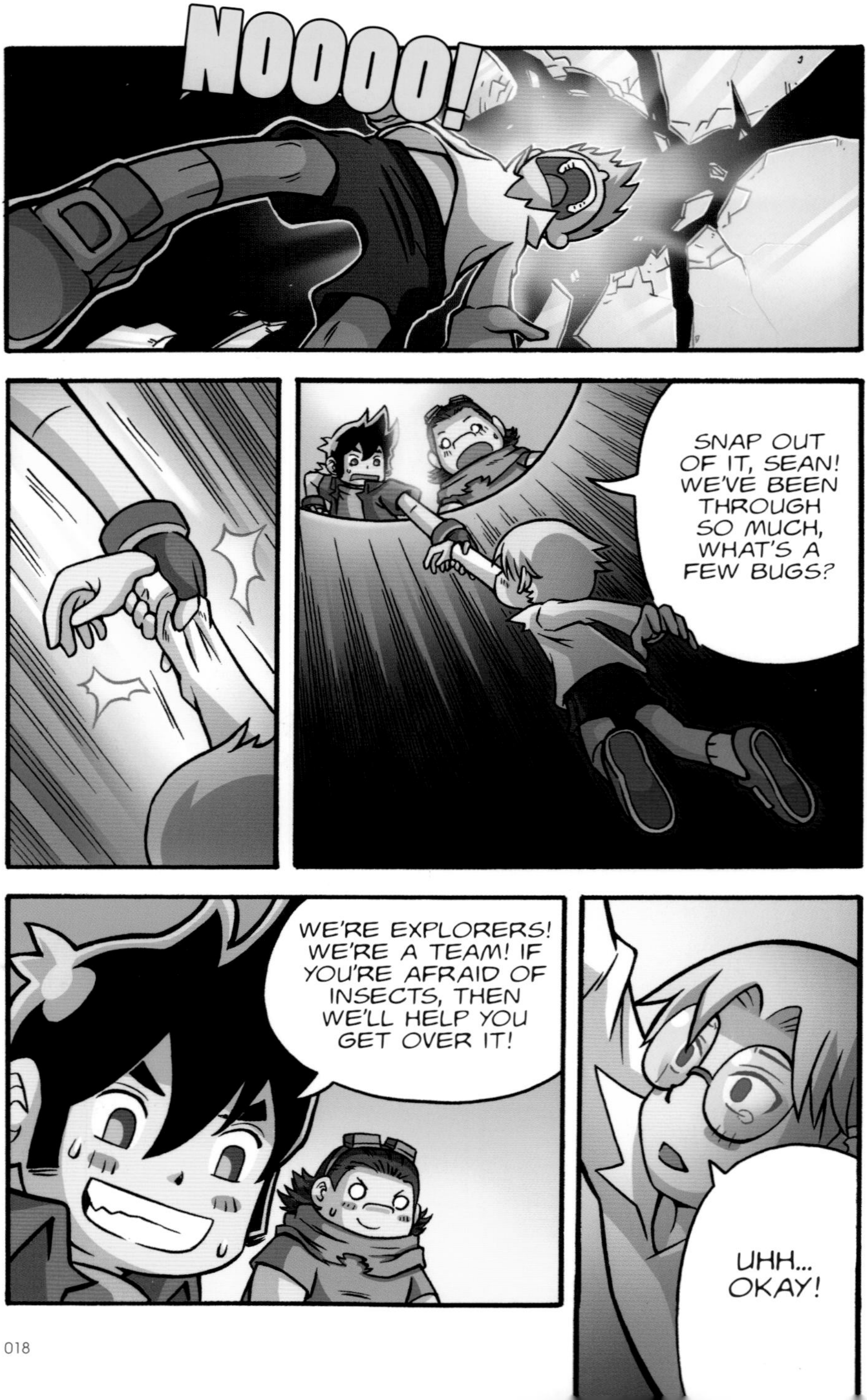
NOOOOO!
SNAP OUT OF IT, SEAN! WE'VE BEEN THROUGH SO MUCH, WHAT'S A FEW BUGS?
WE'RE EXPLORERS! WE'RE A TEAM! IF YOU'RE AFRAID OF INSECTS, THEN WE'LL HELP YOU GET OVER IT!
UHH... OKAY!

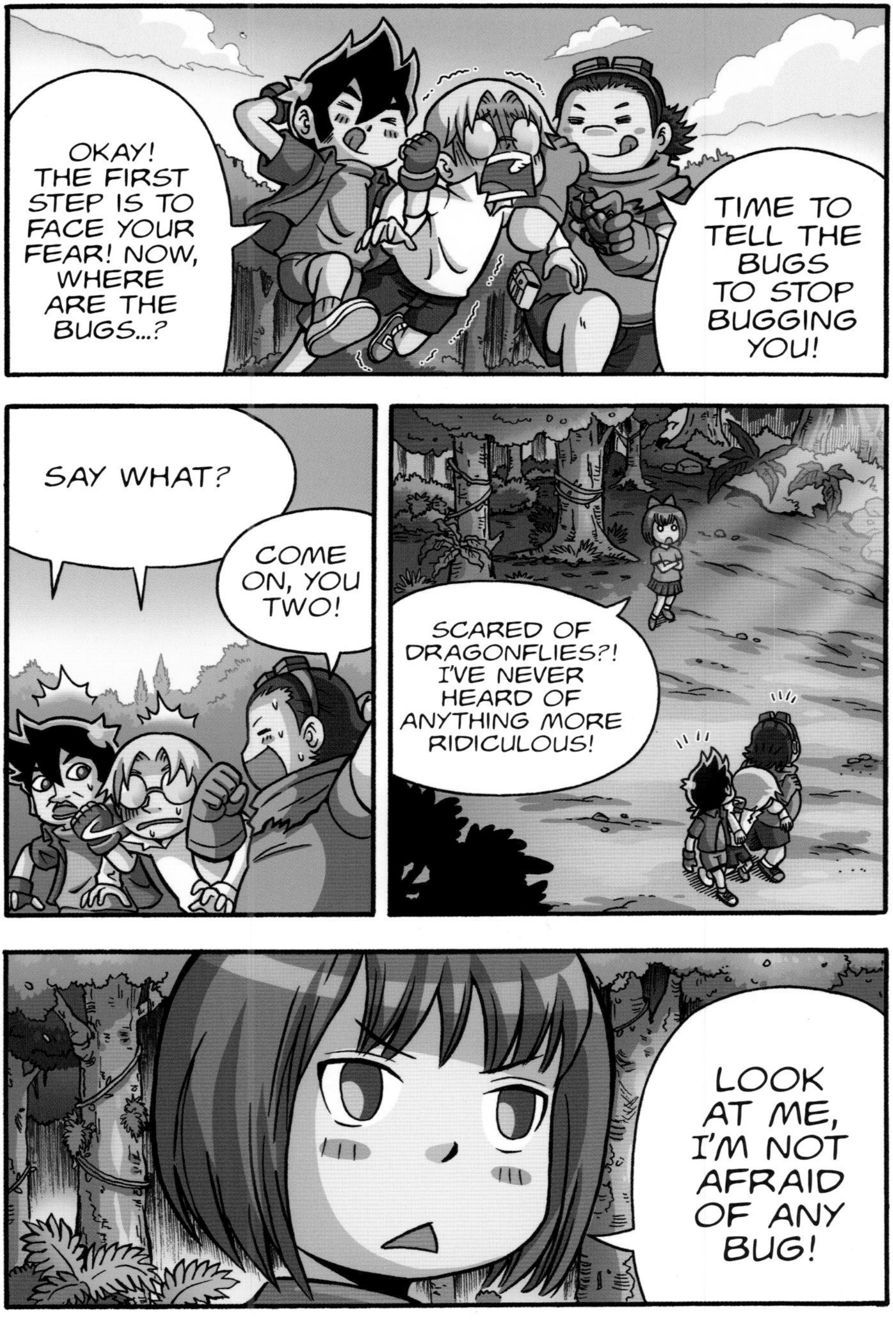
OKAY! THE FIRST STEP IS TO FACE YOUR FEAR! NOW, WHERE ARE THE BUGS...?
TIME TO TELL THE BUGS TO STOP BUGGING YOU!
SAY WHAT?
COME ON, YOU TWO!
SCARED OF DRAGONFLIES?! I'VE NEVER HEARD OF ANYTHING MORE RIDICULOUS!
LOOK AT ME, I'M NOT AFRAID OF ANY BUG!

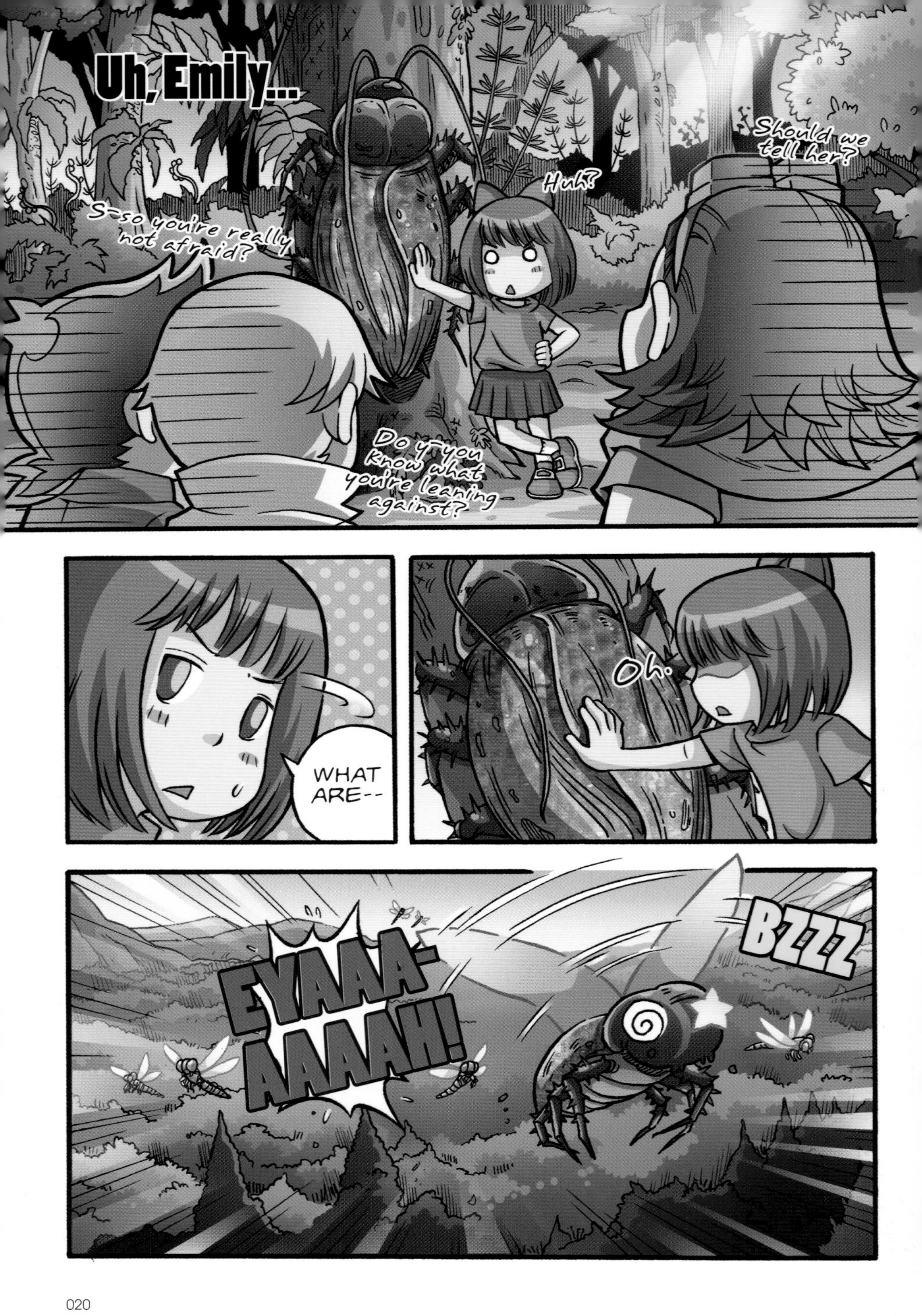

Uh, Emily...
S-so you're really not afraid?
Huh?
Should we tell her?
Do y-you know what you're leaning against?
WHAT ARE--
Oh.
EYAAA-AAAAH!
BZZZ

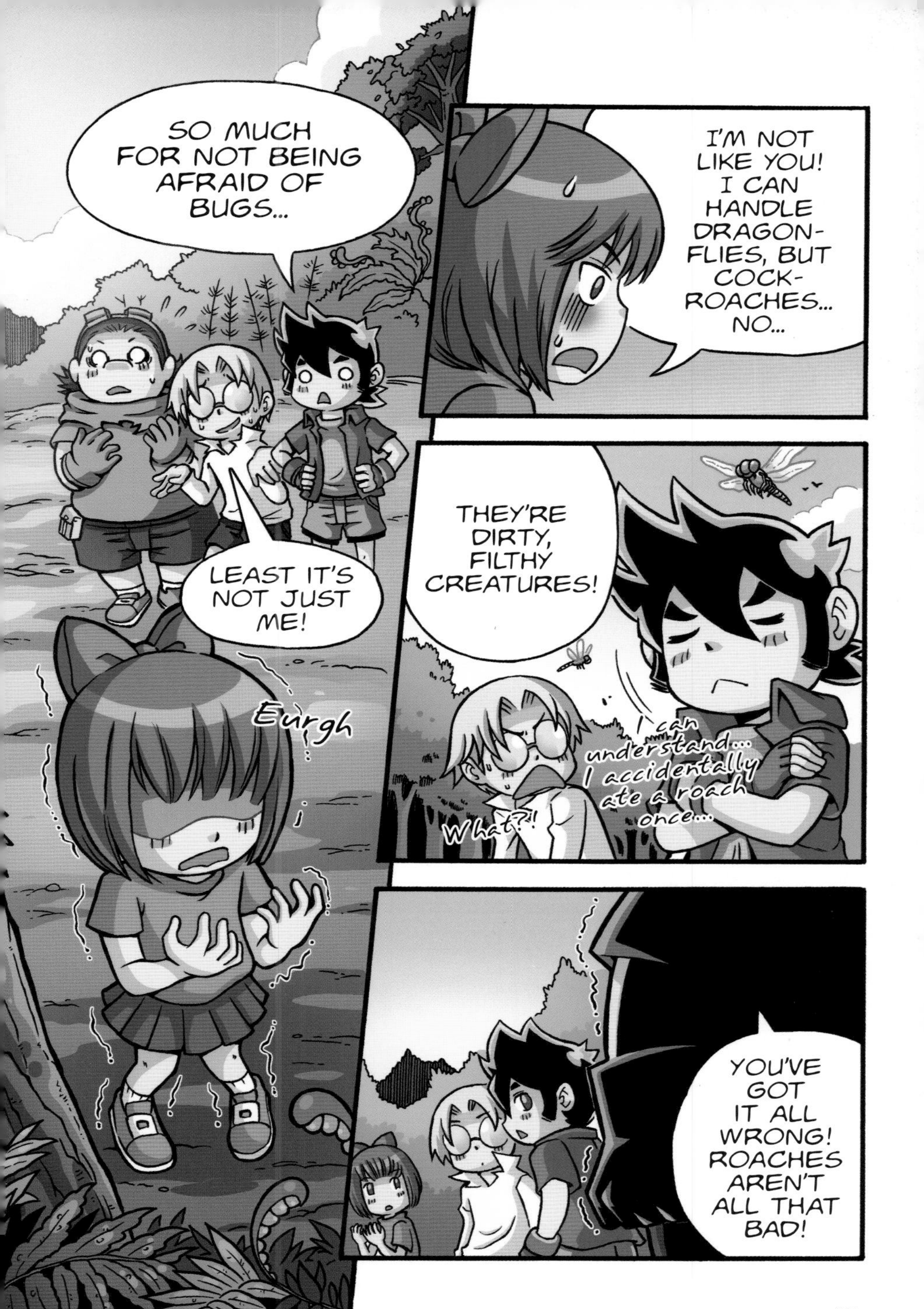
SO MUCH FOR NOT BEING AFRAID OF BUGS...
LEAST IT'S NOT JUST ME!
Eurgh
I'M NOT LIKE YOU! I CAN HANDLE DRAGON-FLIES, BUT COCK-ROACHES... NO...
THEY'RE DIRTY, FILTHY CREATURES!
I can understand... I accidentally ate a roach once...
What?!
YOU'VE GOT IT ALL WRONG! ROACHES AREN'T ALL THAT BAD!

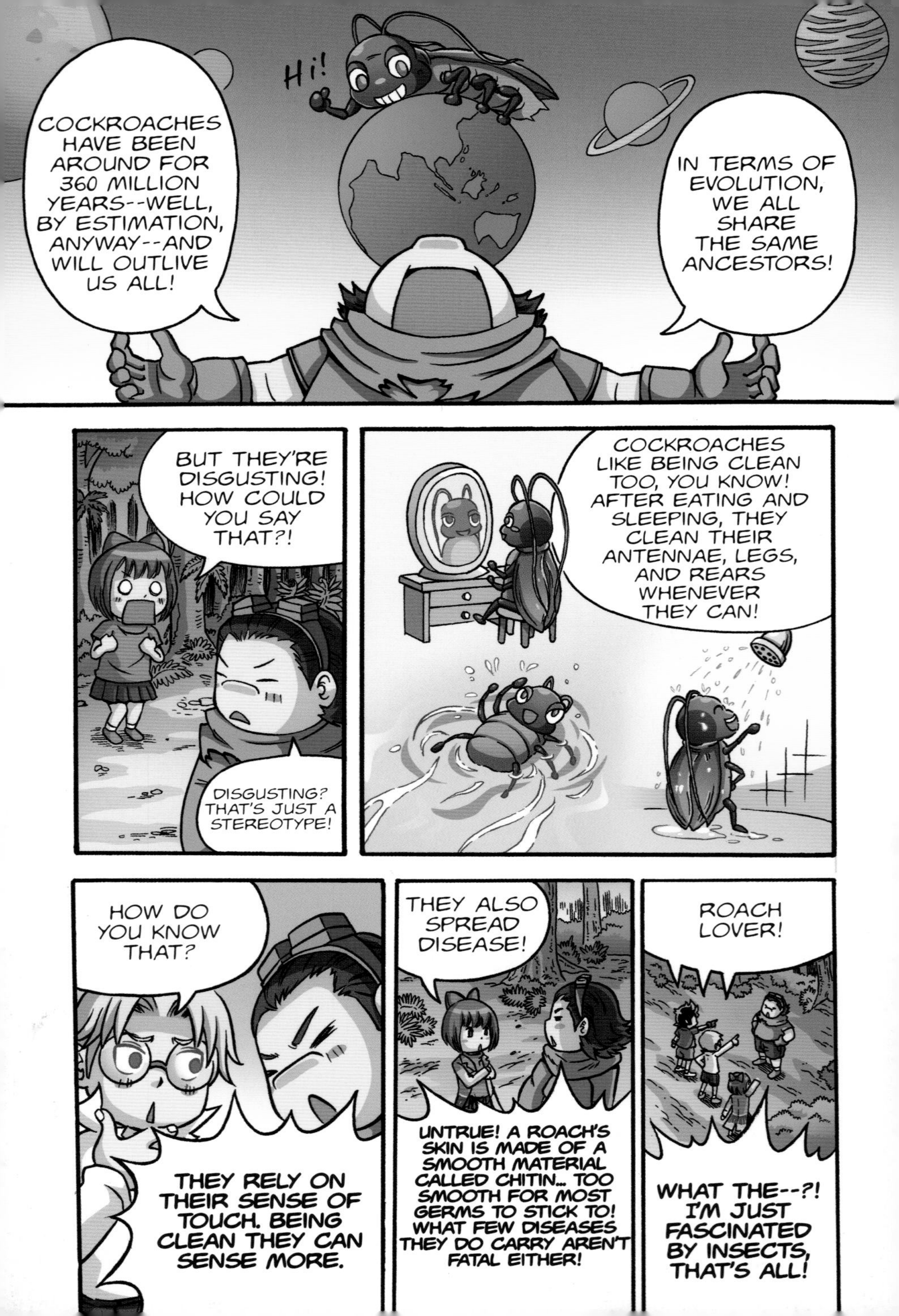
Hi!
COCKROACHES HAVE BEEN AROUND FOR 360 MILLION YEARS--WELL, BY ESTIMATION, ANYWAY--AND WILL OUTLIVE US ALL!
IN TERMS OF EVOLUTION, WE ALL SHARE THE SAME ANCESTORS!
BUT THEY'RE DISGUSTING! HOW COULD YOU SAY THAT?!
DISGUSTING? THAT'S JUST A STEREOTYPE!
COCKROACHES LIKE BEING CLEAN TOO, YOU KNOW! AFTER EATING AND SLEEPING, THEY CLEAN THEIR ANTENNAE, LEGS, AND REARS WHENEVER THEY CAN!
HOW DO YOU KNOW THAT?
THEY RELY ON THEIR SENSE OF TOUCH. BEING CLEAN THEY CAN SENSE MORE.
THEY ALSO SPREAD DISEASE!
UNTRUE! A ROACH'S SKIN IS MADE OF A SMOOTH MATERIAL CALLED CHITIN... TOO SMOOTH FOR MOST GERMS TO STICK TO! WHAT FEW DISEASES THEY DO CARRY AREN'T FATAL EITHER!
ROACH LOVER!
WHAT THE--?! I'M JUST FASCINATED BY INSECTS, THAT'S ALL!

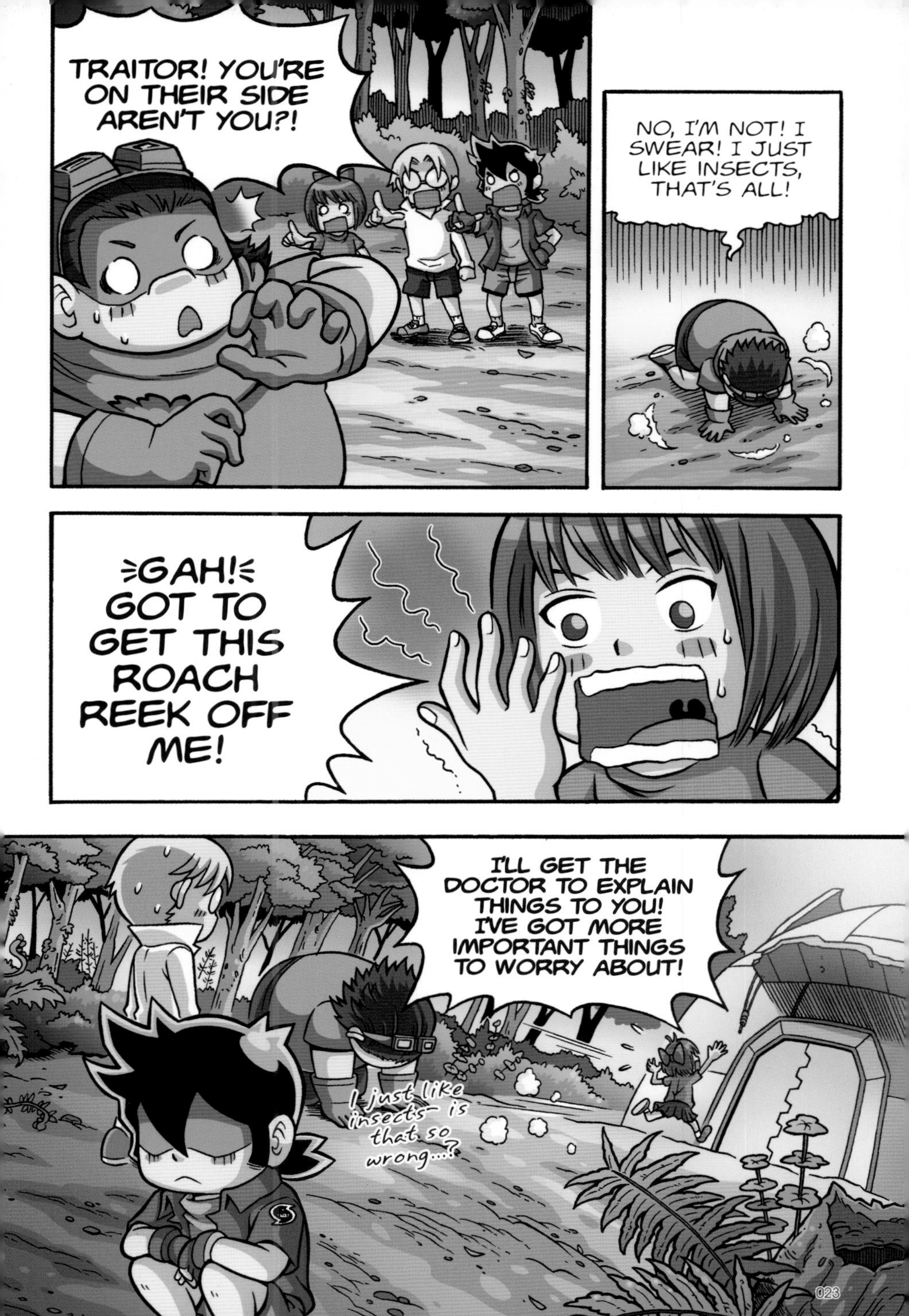
TRAITOR! YOU'RE ON THEIR SIDE AREN'T YOU?!
NO, I'M NOT! I SWEAR! I JUST LIKE INSECTS, THAT'S ALL!
GAH! GOT TO GET THIS ROACH REEK OFF ME!
I'LL GET THE DOCTOR TO EXPLAIN THINGS TO YOU! I'VE GOT MORE IMPORTANT THINGS TO WORRY ABOUT!
I just like insects—is that so wrong...?

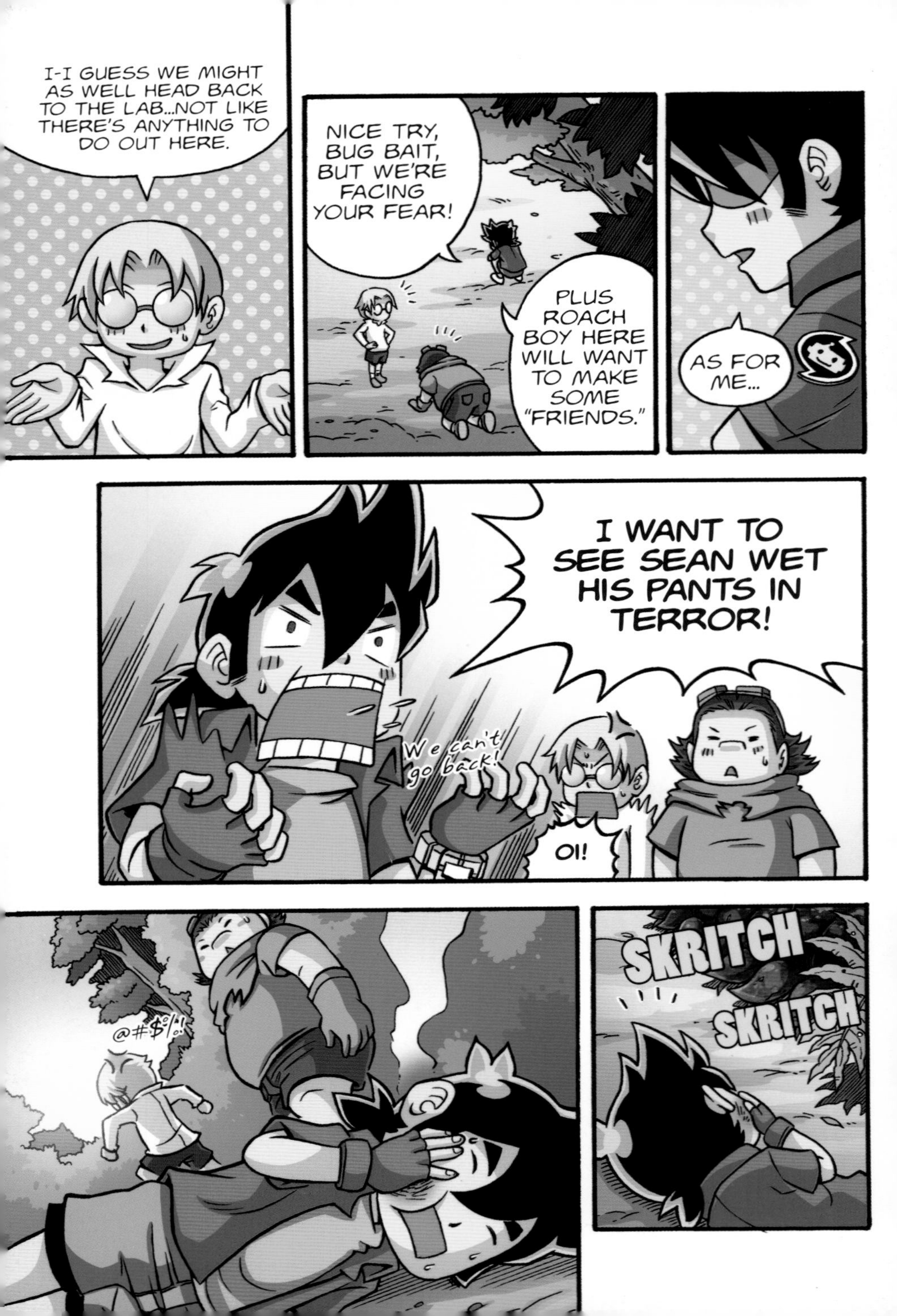
I-I GUESS WE MIGHT AS WELL HEAD BACK TO THE LAB...NOT LIKE THERE'S ANYTHING TO DO OUT HERE.
NICE TRY, BUG BAIT, BUT WE'RE FACING YOUR FEAR!
PLUS ROACH BOY HERE WILL WANT TO MAKE SOME "FRIENDS."
AS FOR ME...
I WANT TO SEE SEAN WET HIS PANTS IN TERROR!
We can't go back!
OI!
@#$%!
SKRITCH
SKRITCH

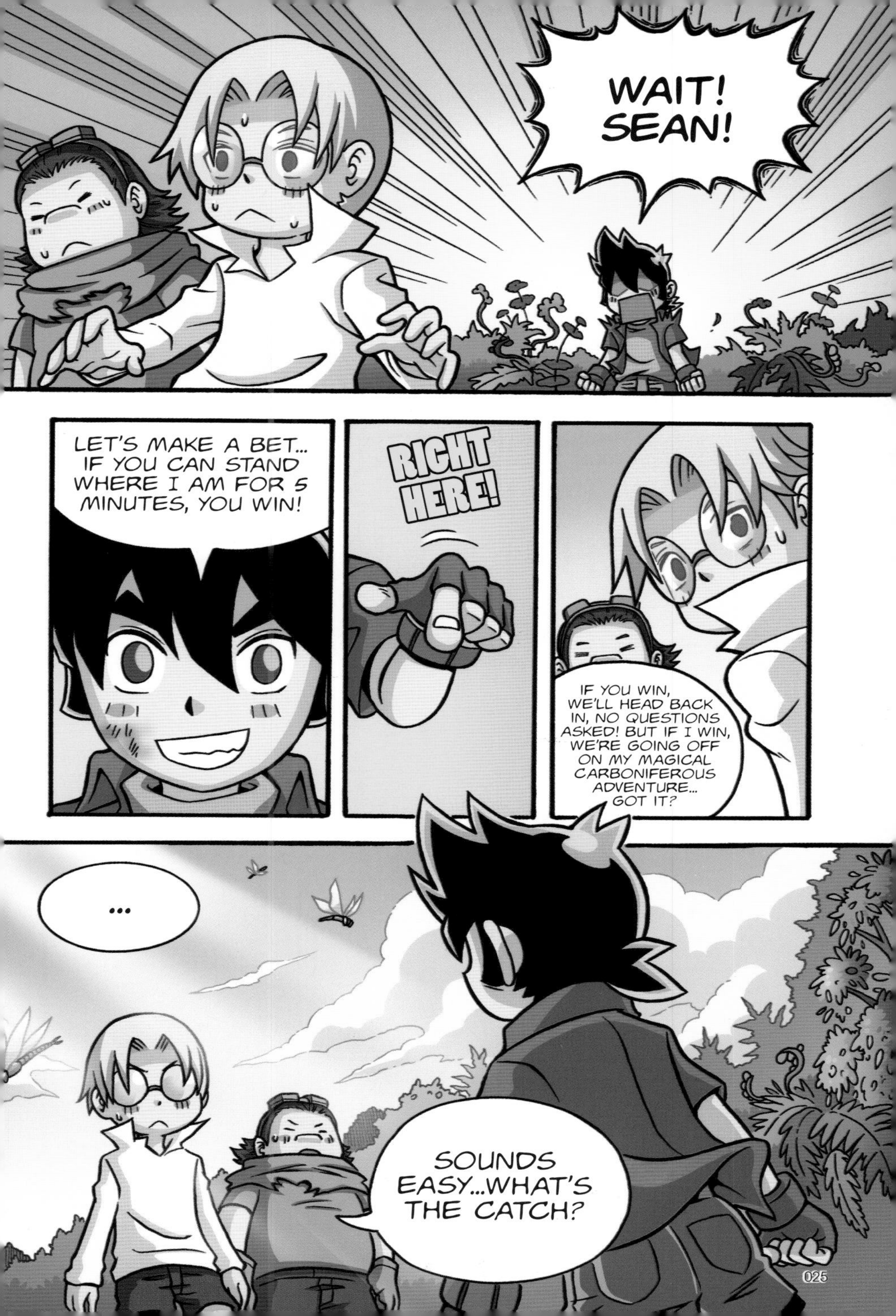
WAIT! SEAN!
LET'S MAKE A BET... IF YOU CAN STAND WHERE I AM FOR 5 MINUTES, YOU WIN!
RIGHT HERE!
IF YOU WIN, WE'LL HEAD BACK IN, NO QUESTIONS ASKED! BUT IF I WIN, WE'RE GOING OFF ON MY MAGICAL CARBONIFEROUS ADVENTURE... GOT IT?
...
SOUNDS EASY...WHAT'S THE CATCH?

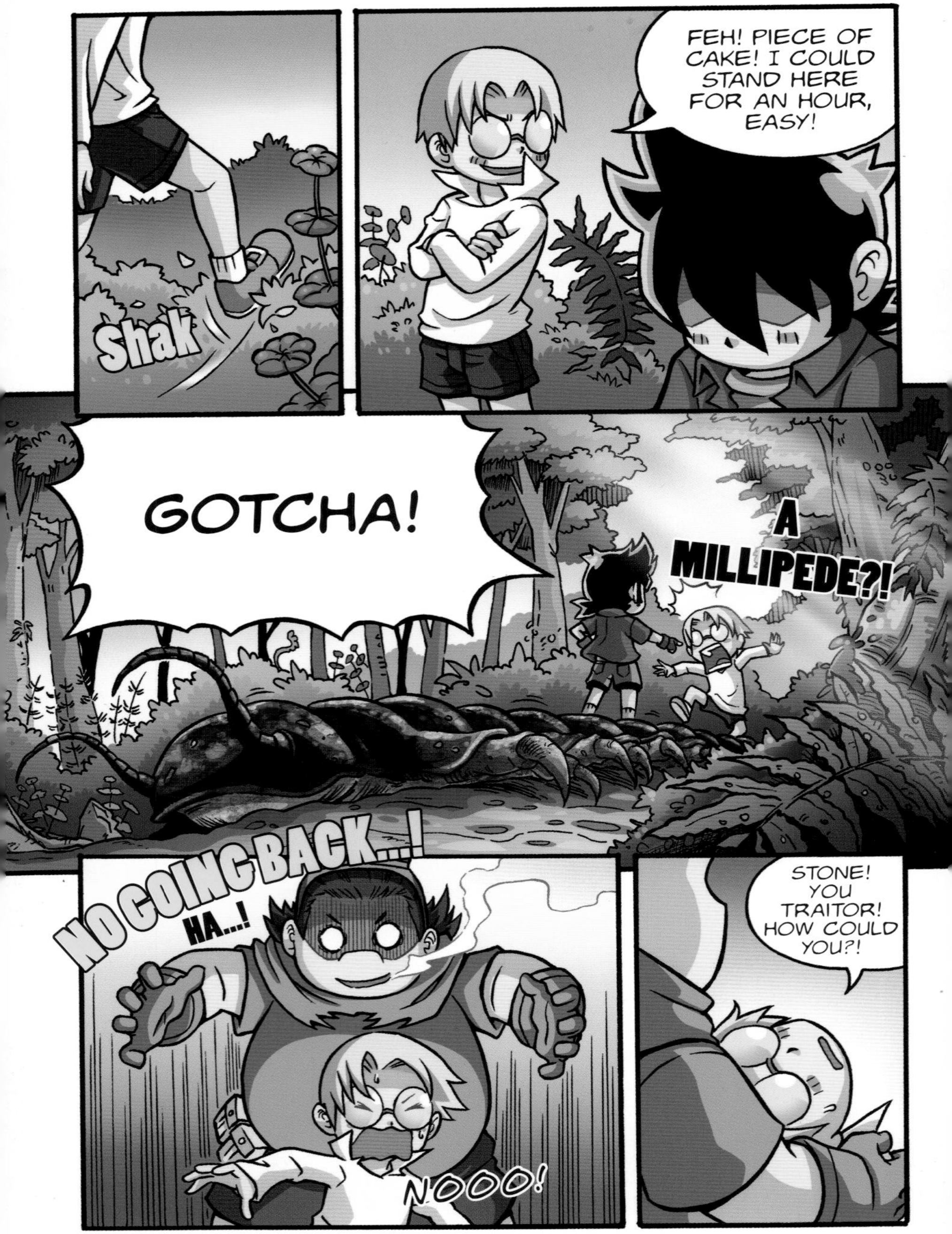
Shak
FEH! PIECE OF CAKE! I COULD STAND HERE FOR AN HOUR, EASY!
GOTCHA!
A MILLIPEDE?!
NO GOING BACK...!
HA...!
NOOO!
STONE! YOU TRAITOR! HOW COULD YOU?!

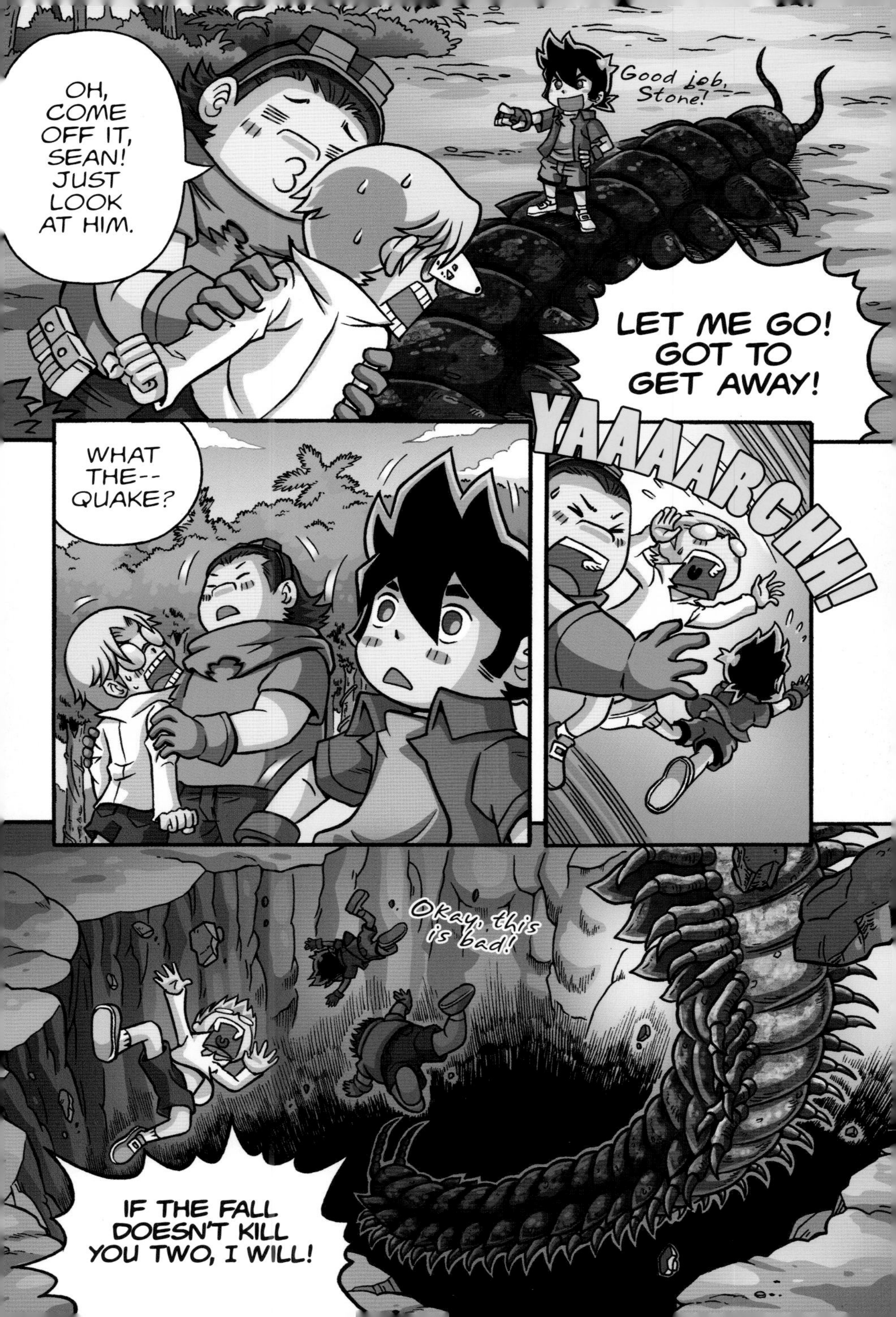

OH, COME OFF IT, SEAN! JUST LOOK AT HIM.
Good job, Stone!
LET ME GO! GOT TO GET AWAY!
WHAT THE-- QUAKE?
YAAAAARCHH!
Okay, this is bad!
IF THE FALL DOESN'T KILL YOU TWO, I WILL!

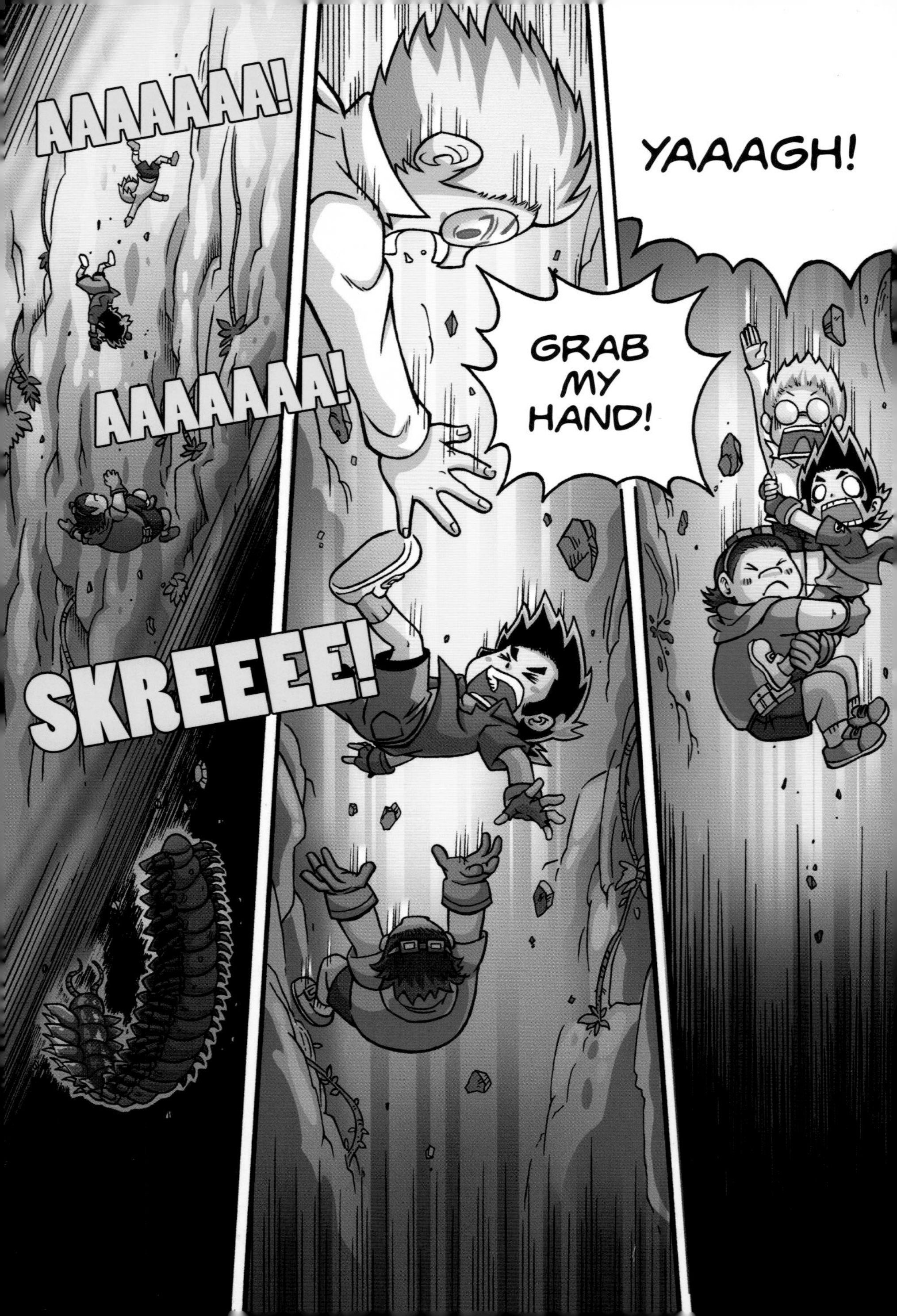
AAAAAAA!
AAAAAAA!
SKREEEE!
GRAB MY HAND!
YAAAGH!

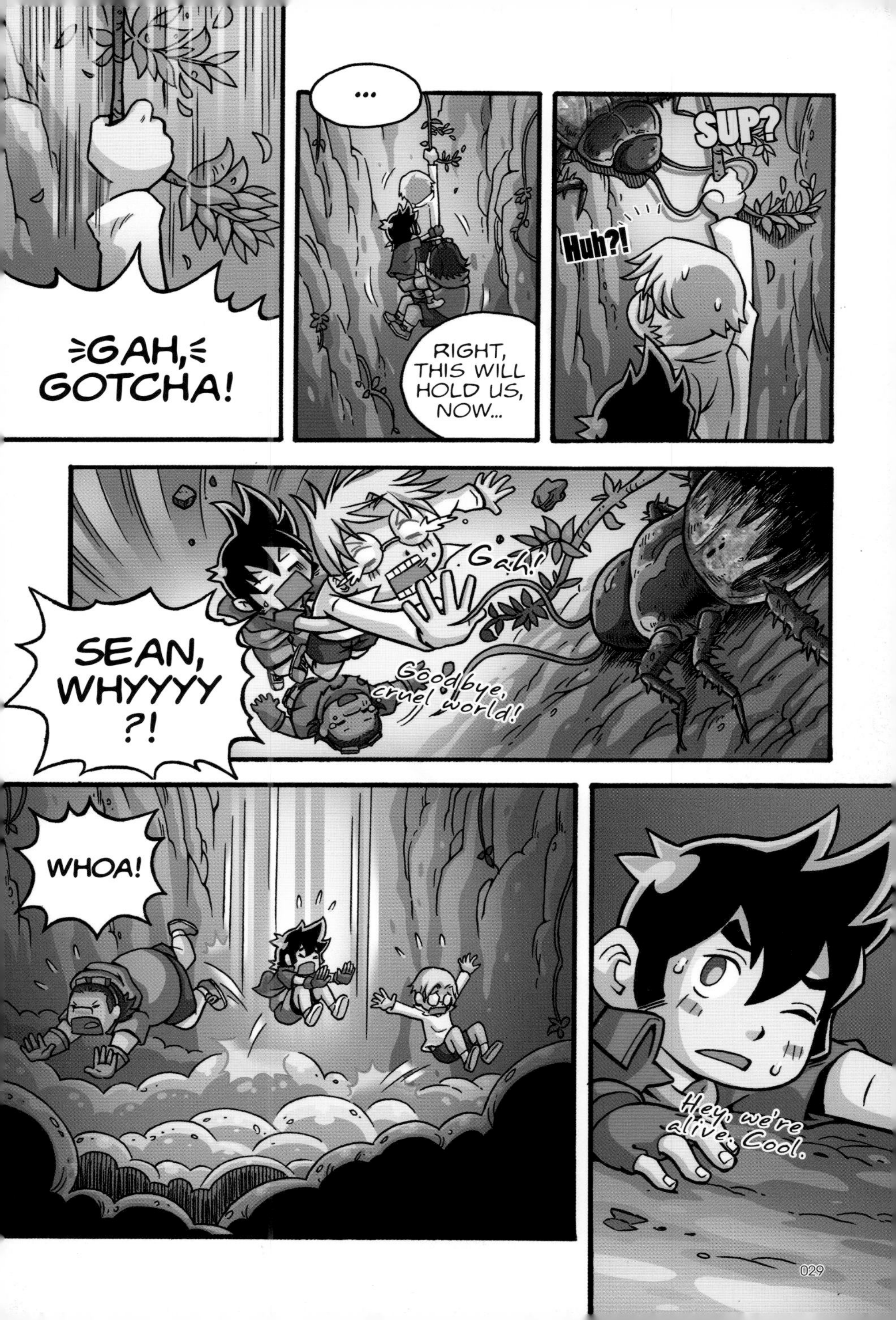
GAH, GOTCHA!
...
RIGHT, THIS WILL HOLD US, NOW...
SUP?
Huh?!
SEAN, WHYYYY ?!
Gah!
Goodbye, cruel world!
WHOA!
Hey, we're alive. Cool.

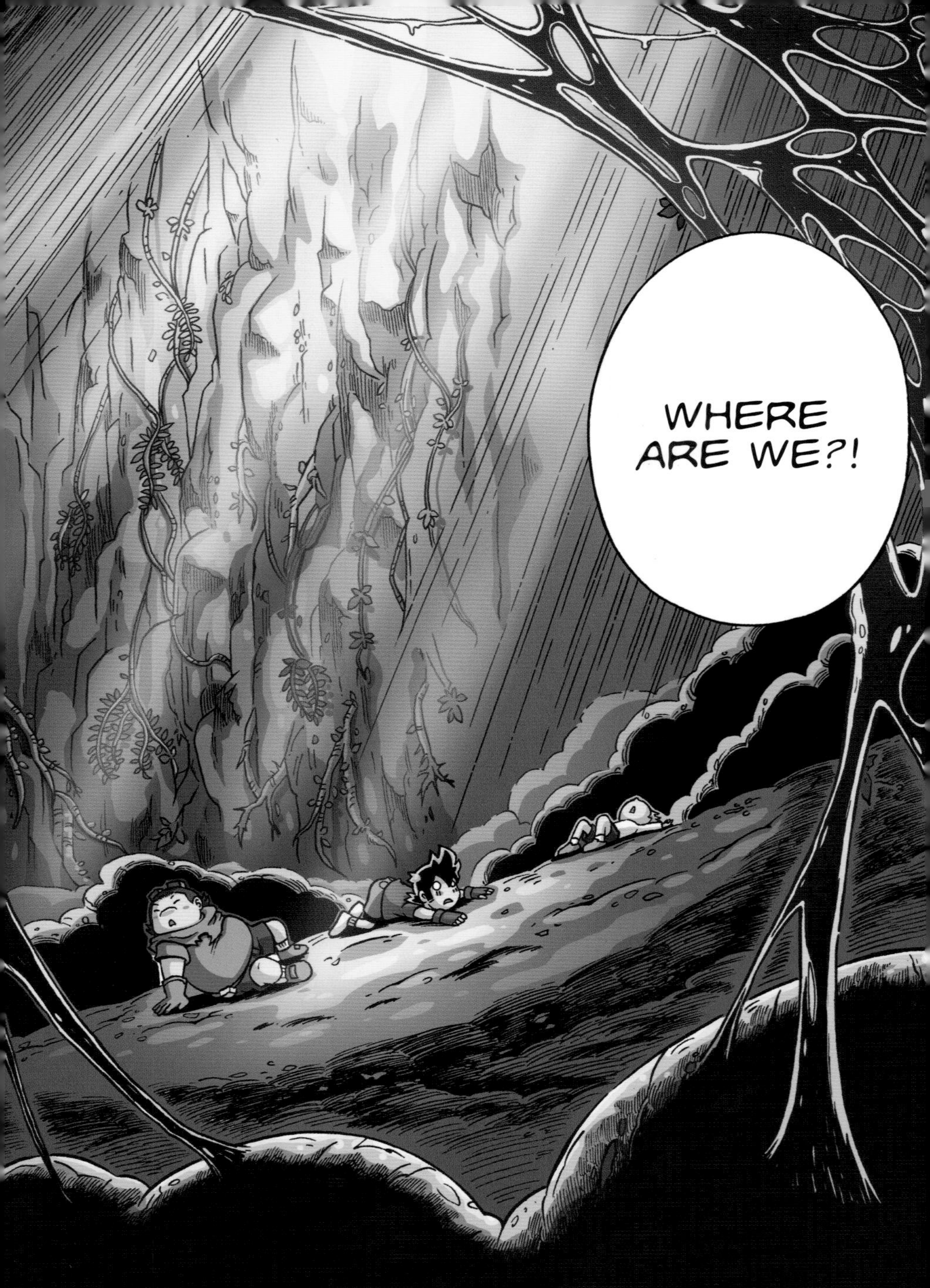
WHERE ARE WE?!

CONTINENTS OF THE CARBONIFEROUS

In the early Carboniferous, the continents of Laurentia in the north and Gondwana in the south were the only continents. These two supercontinents started moving toward each other in this era, with Gondwana approaching the South Pole.

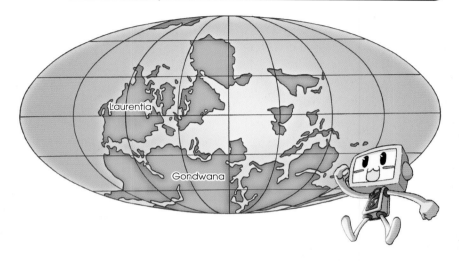

Laurentia

Gondwana

What was the Carboniferous?

The Carboniferous began 359 million years ago and ended 299 million years ago (lasting a total of around 60 million years). It was a wet and humid time, perfect for plants, and its high oxygen content allowed for the evolution of huge insects. Much of its plant life ended up buried underground, where the vast pressures of the Earth turned them into coal, a form of carbon, which gave the Carboniferous its name!

What was life like in the Carboniferous?

Land animals were mostly arthropods and amphibians, which spread widely in the vast swamps and forests the warm, humid climate promoted. Fish known as actinopterygii were the primary form of large marine creature at this time.

What's with all the monster bugs?

It was believed that the large amounts of oxygen present in the Carboniferous (due to all the plant life) boosted insect metabolisms dramatically. The high oxygen content also promoted an increase in the size of insect tracheas, which allowed them to take in more oxygen at once, helping their growth.

CARBONIFEROUS PLANTLIFE

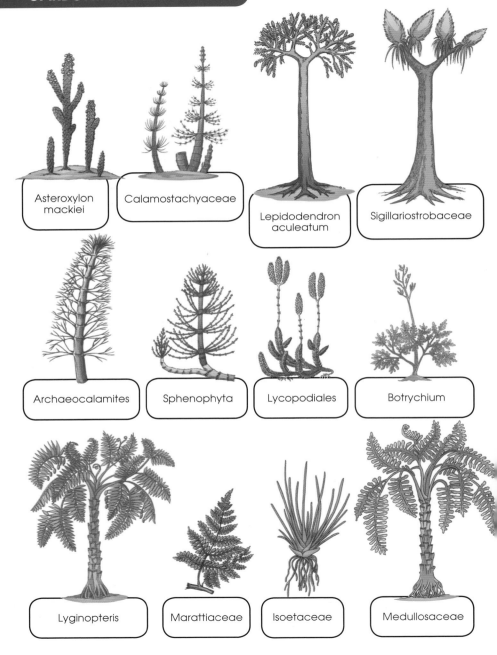

Asteroxylon mackiei

Calamostachyaceae

Lepidodendron aculeatum

Sigillariostrobaceae

Archaeocalamites

Sphenophyta

Lycopodiales

Botrychium

Lyginopteris

Marattiaceae

Isoetaceae

Medullosaceae

CHAPTER 2
SPIDER? I BARELY KNEW HER!

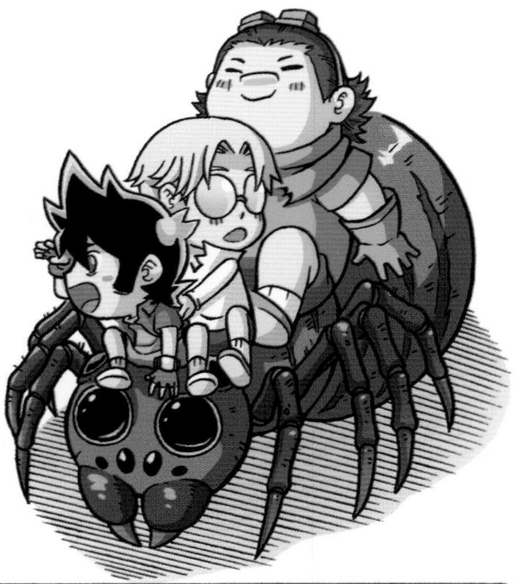

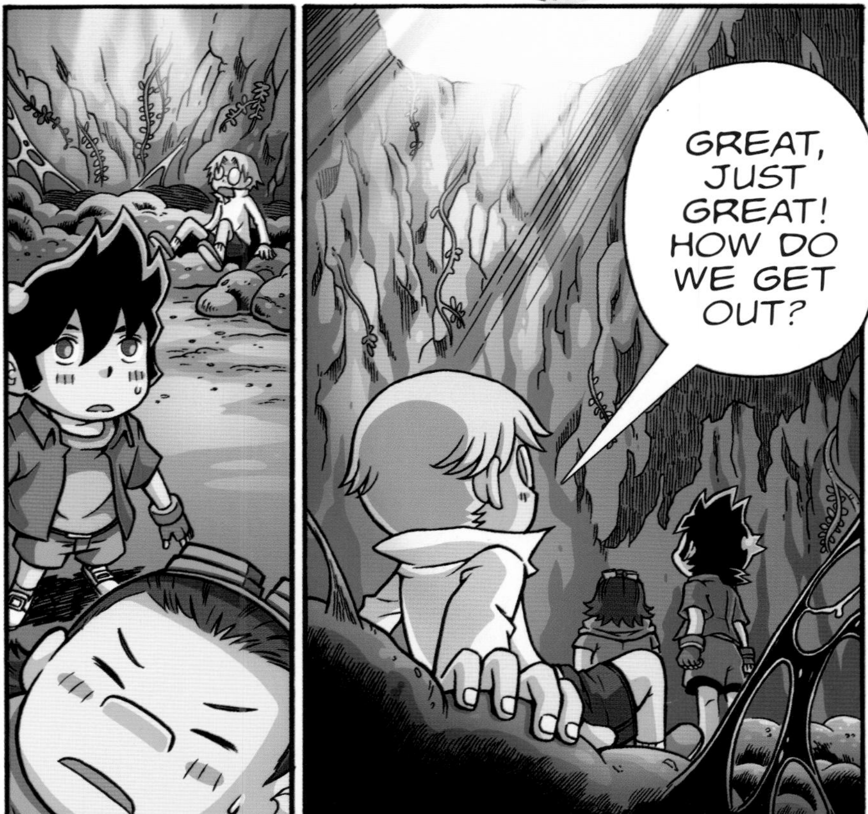
GREAT, JUST GREAT! HOW DO WE GET OUT?

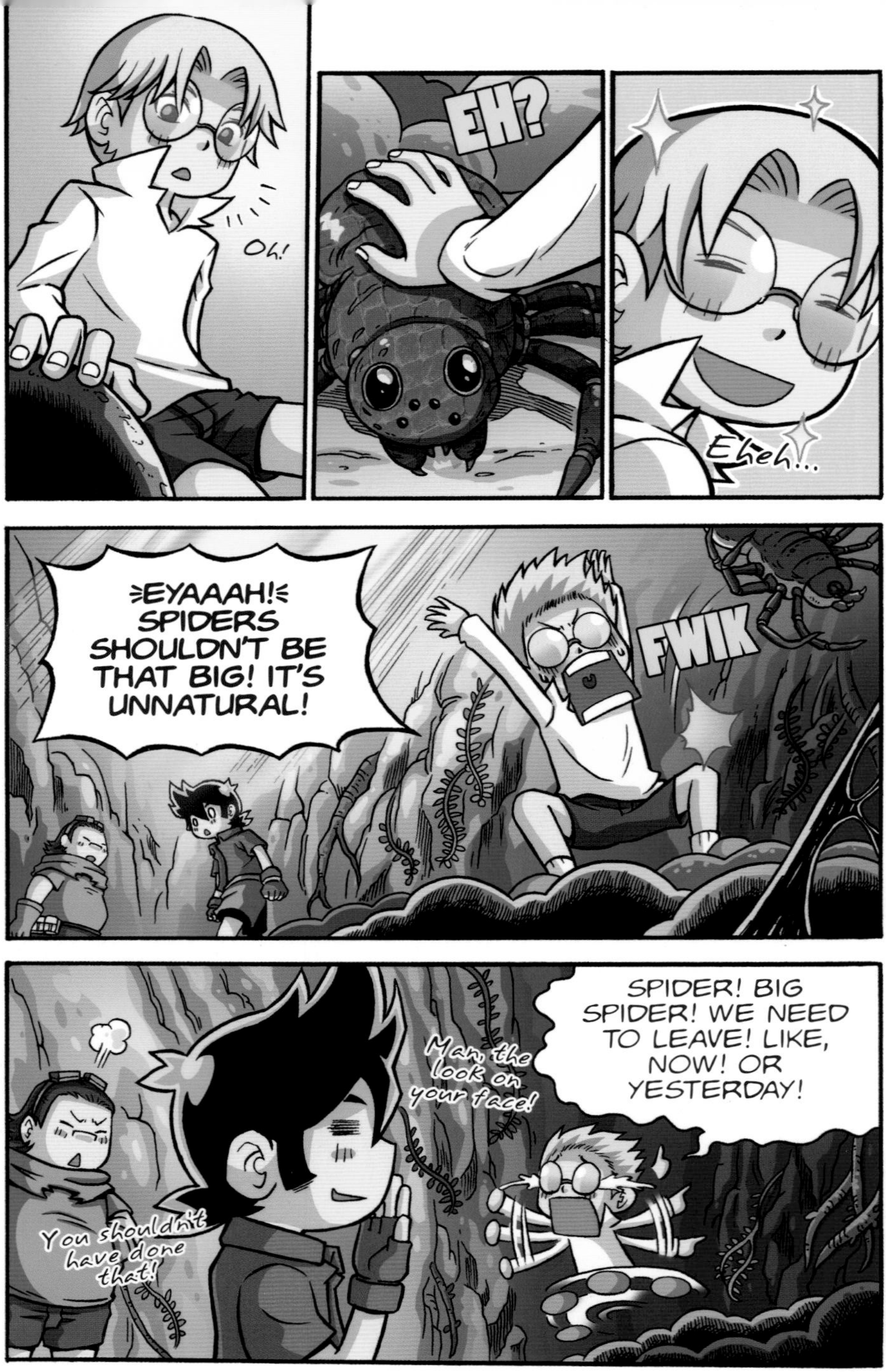
Oh!
EH?
Eheh...
EYAAAH! SPIDERS SHOULDN'T BE THAT BIG! IT'S UNNATURAL!
FWIK
Man, the look on your face!
SPIDER! BIG SPIDER! WE NEED TO LEAVE! LIKE, NOW! OR YESTERDAY!
You shouldn't have done that!

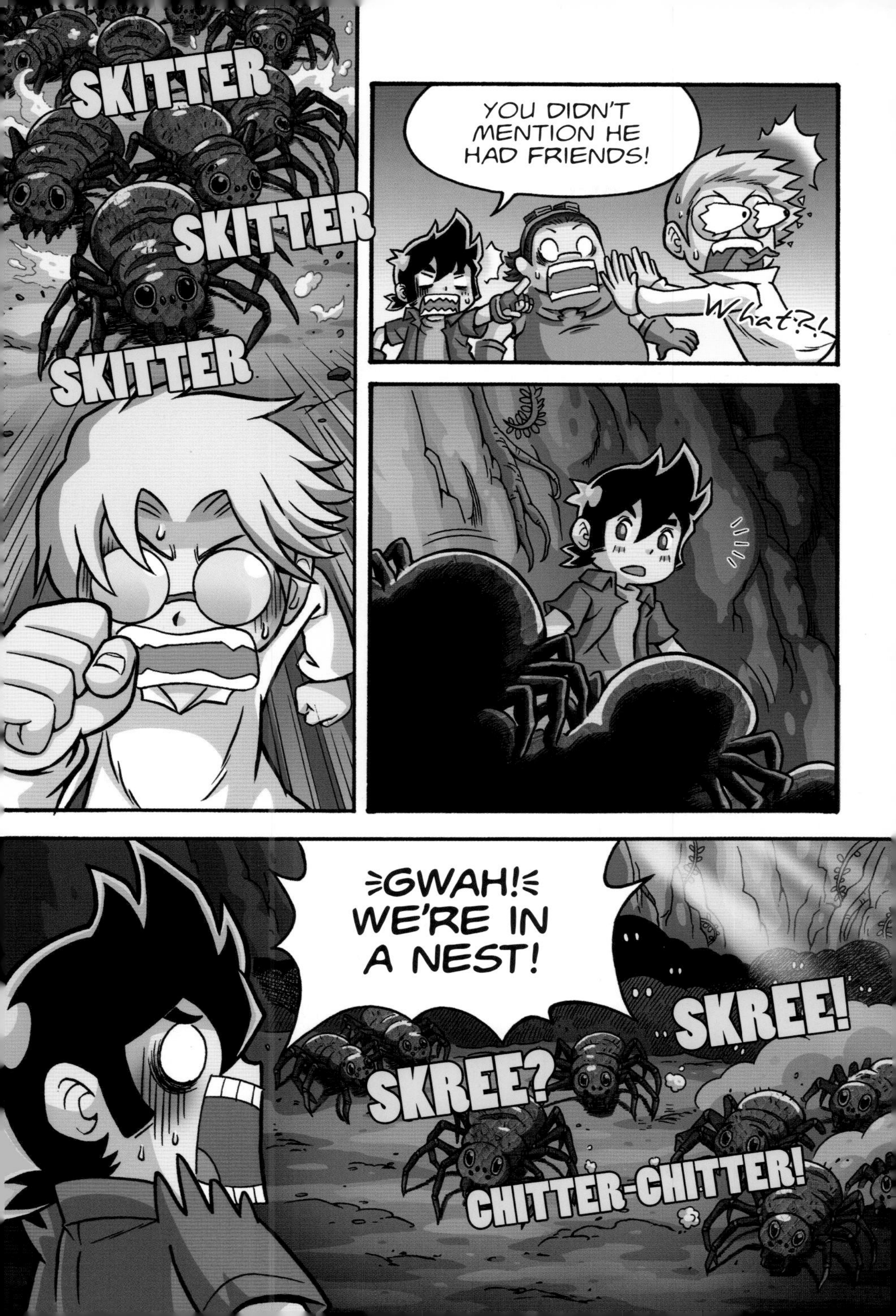
SKITTER
SKITTER
SKITTER
YOU DIDN'T MENTION HE HAD FRIENDS!
What?!
GWAH! WE'RE IN A NEST!
SKREE!
SKREE?
CHITTER-CHITTER!

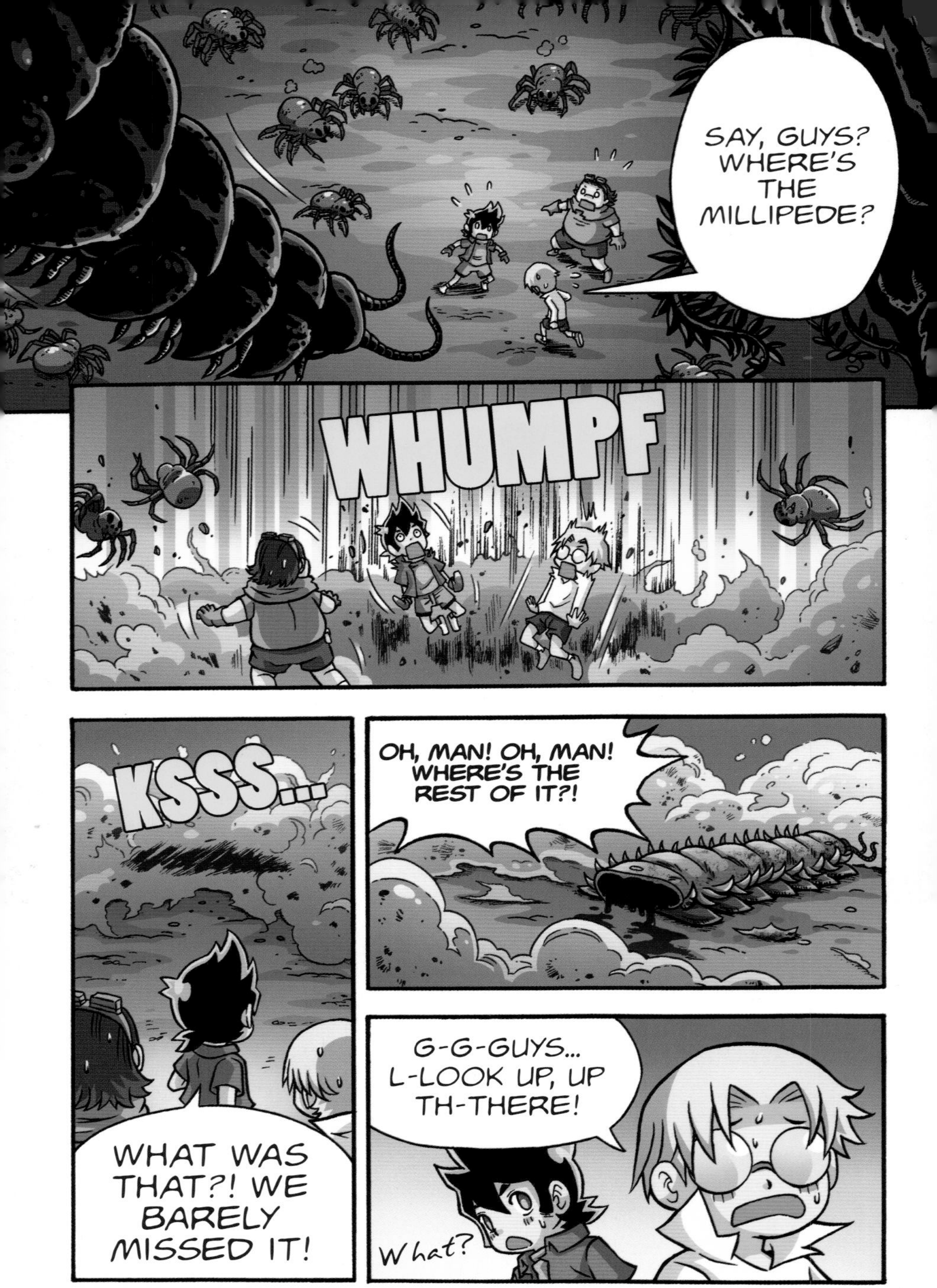
SAY, GUYS? WHERE'S THE MILLIPEDE?
WHUMPF
KSSS...
OH, MAN! OH, MAN! WHERE'S THE REST OF IT?!
WHAT WAS THAT?! WE BARELY MISSED IT!
G-G-GUYS... L-LOOK UP, UP TH-THERE!
What?

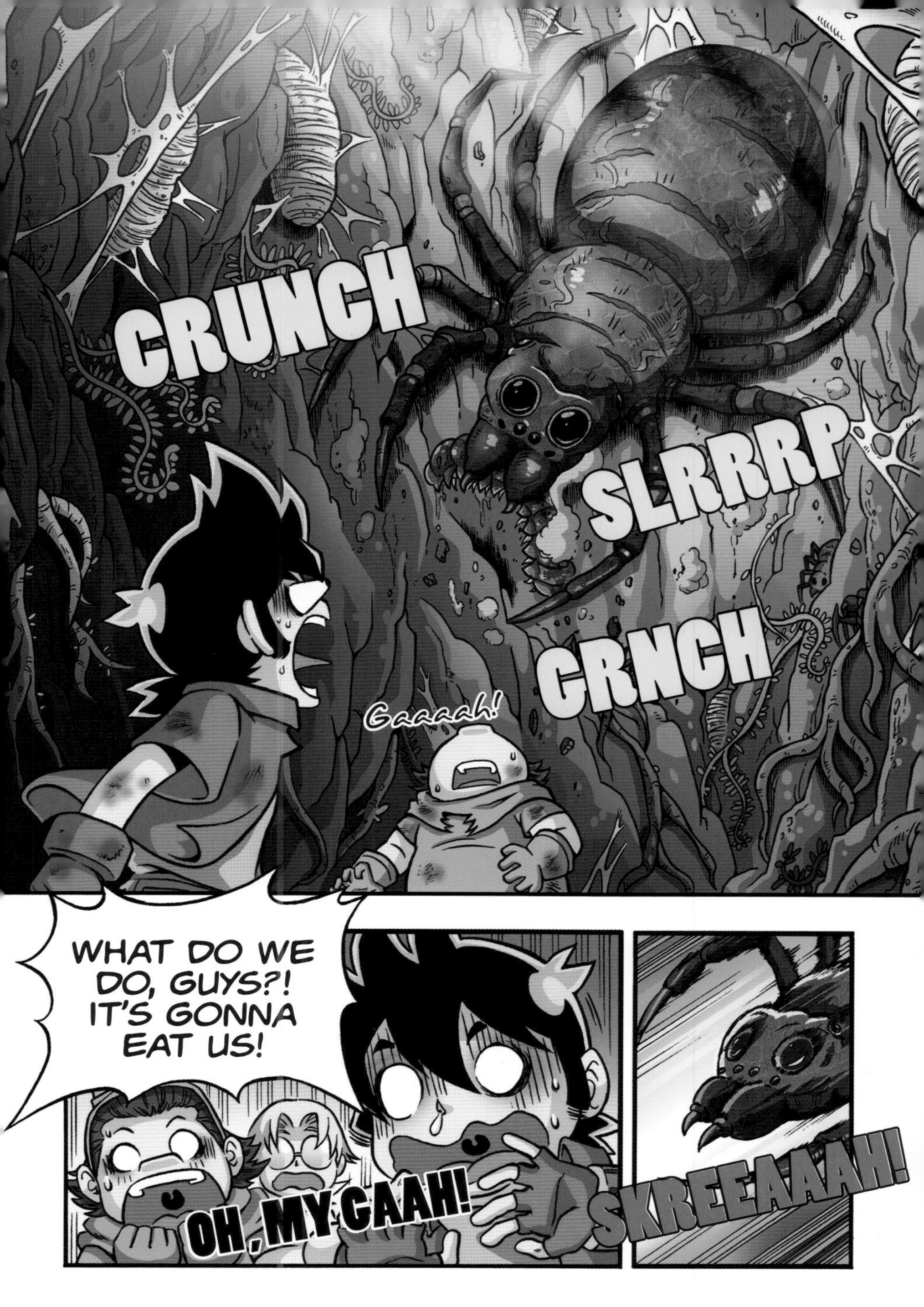
CRUNCH
SLRRRP
CRNCH
Gaaaah!
WHAT DO WE DO, GUYS?! IT'S GONNA EAT US!
OH, MY GAAH!
SKREEAAAH!

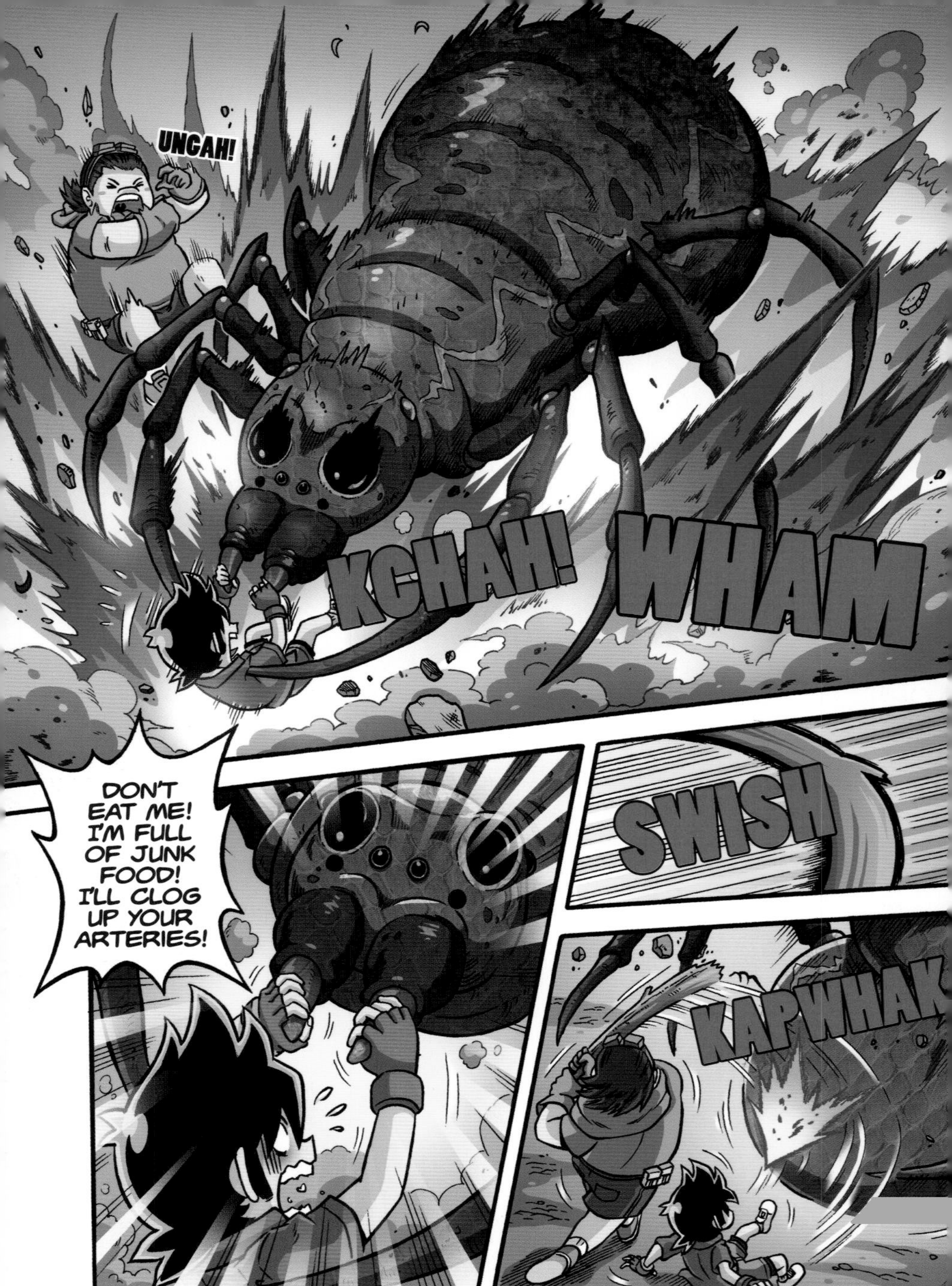
UNGAH!
KCHAH!
WHAM
DON'T EAT ME! I'M FULL OF JUNK FOOD! I'LL CLOG UP YOUR ARTERIES!
SWISH
KAPWHAK

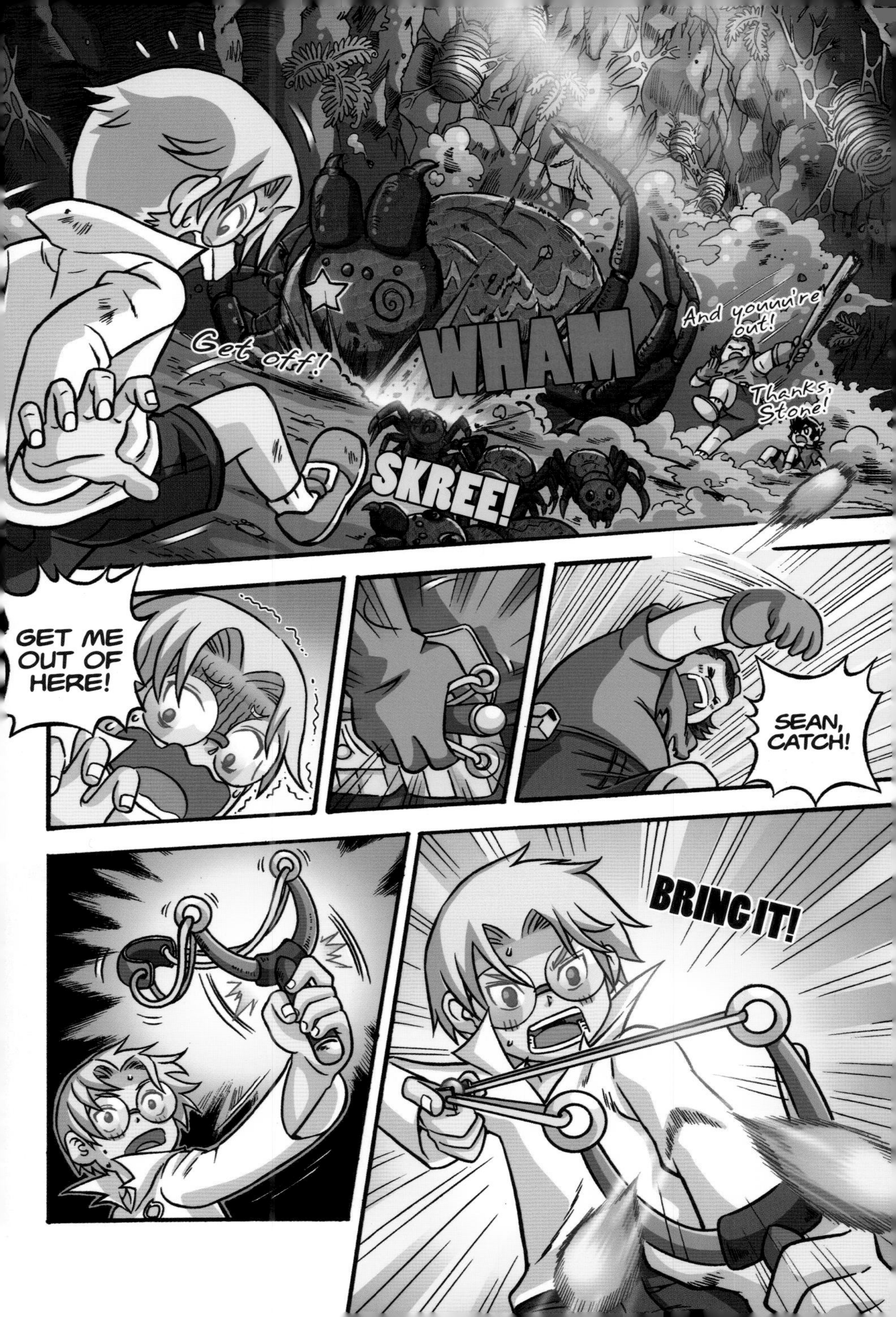
Get off!
WHAM
And youuu're out!
Thanks, Stone!
SKREE!
GET ME OUT OF HERE!
SEAN, CATCH!
BRING IT!

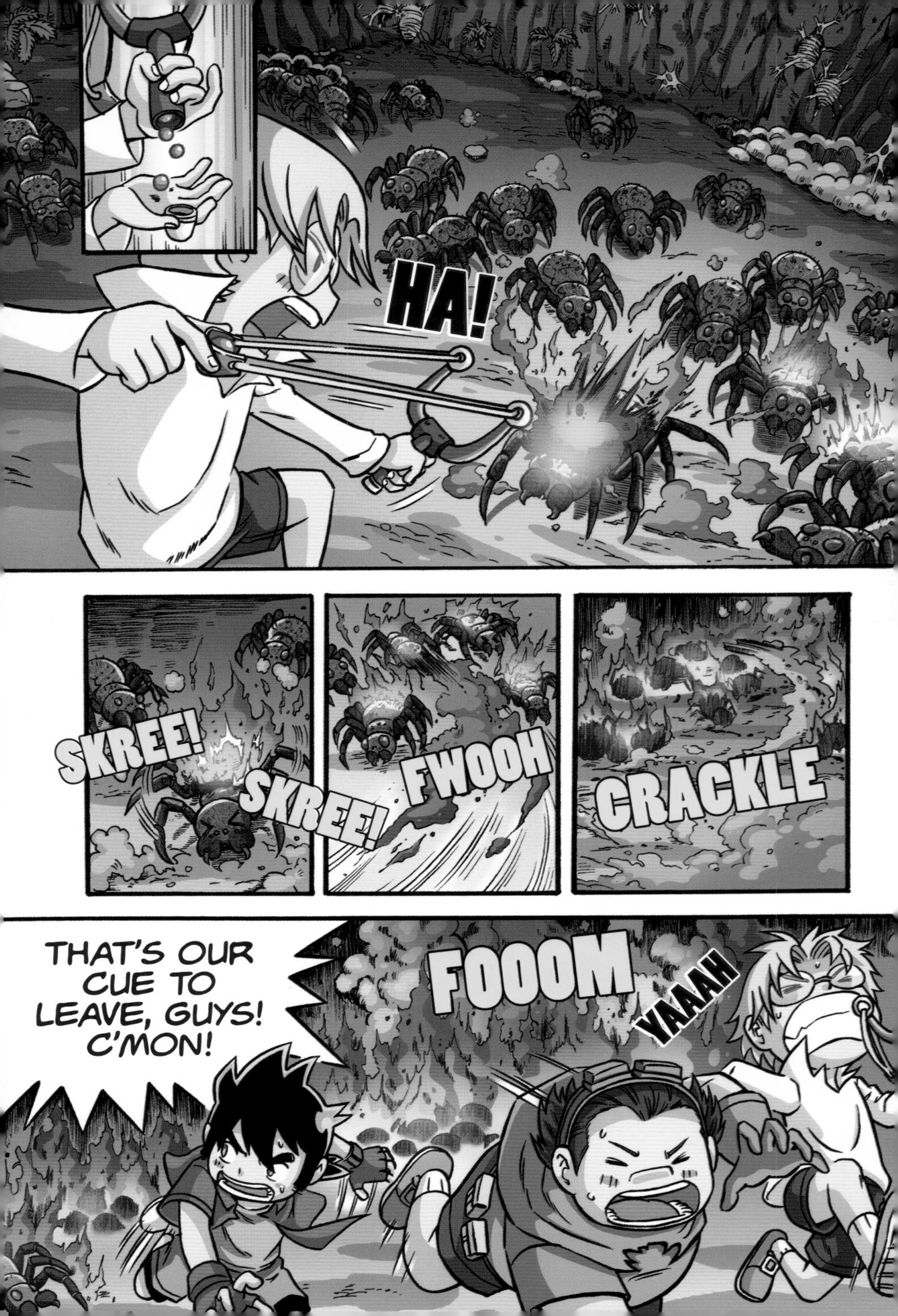
HA!
SKREE!
SKREE!
FWOOH
CRACKLE
THAT'S OUR CUE TO LEAVE, GUYS! C'MON!
FOOOM
YAAAH

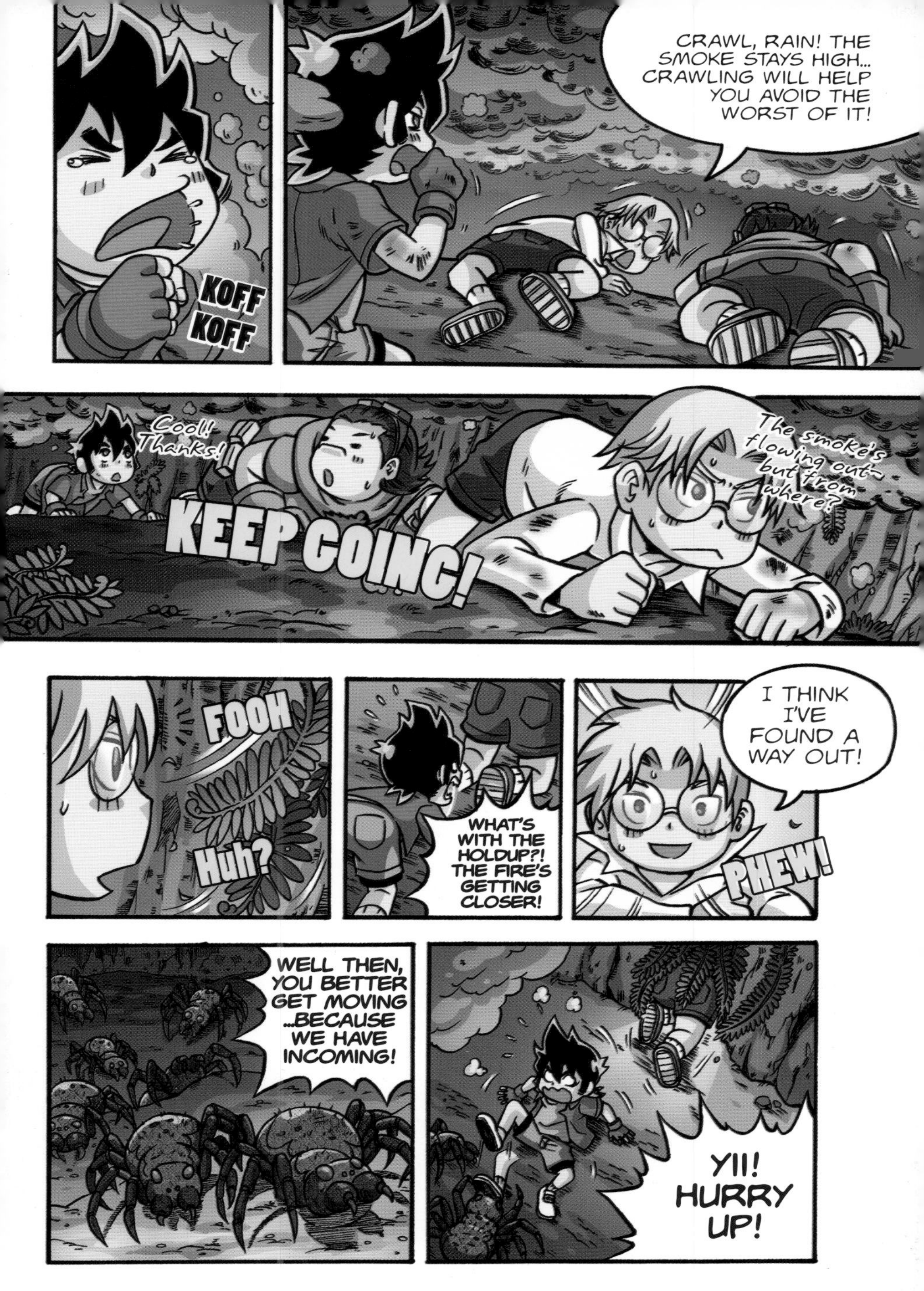
KOFF KOFF
CRAWL, RAIN! THE SMOKE STAYS HIGH... CRAWLING WILL HELP YOU AVOID THE WORST OF IT!
Cool! Thanks!
KEEP GOING!
The smoke's flowing out— but from where?
FOOH
Huh?
WHAT'S WITH THE HOLDUP?! THE FIRE'S GETTING CLOSER!
I THINK I'VE FOUND A WAY OUT!
PHEW!
WELL THEN, YOU BETTER GET MOVING ...BECAUSE WE HAVE INCOMING!
YII! HURRY UP!

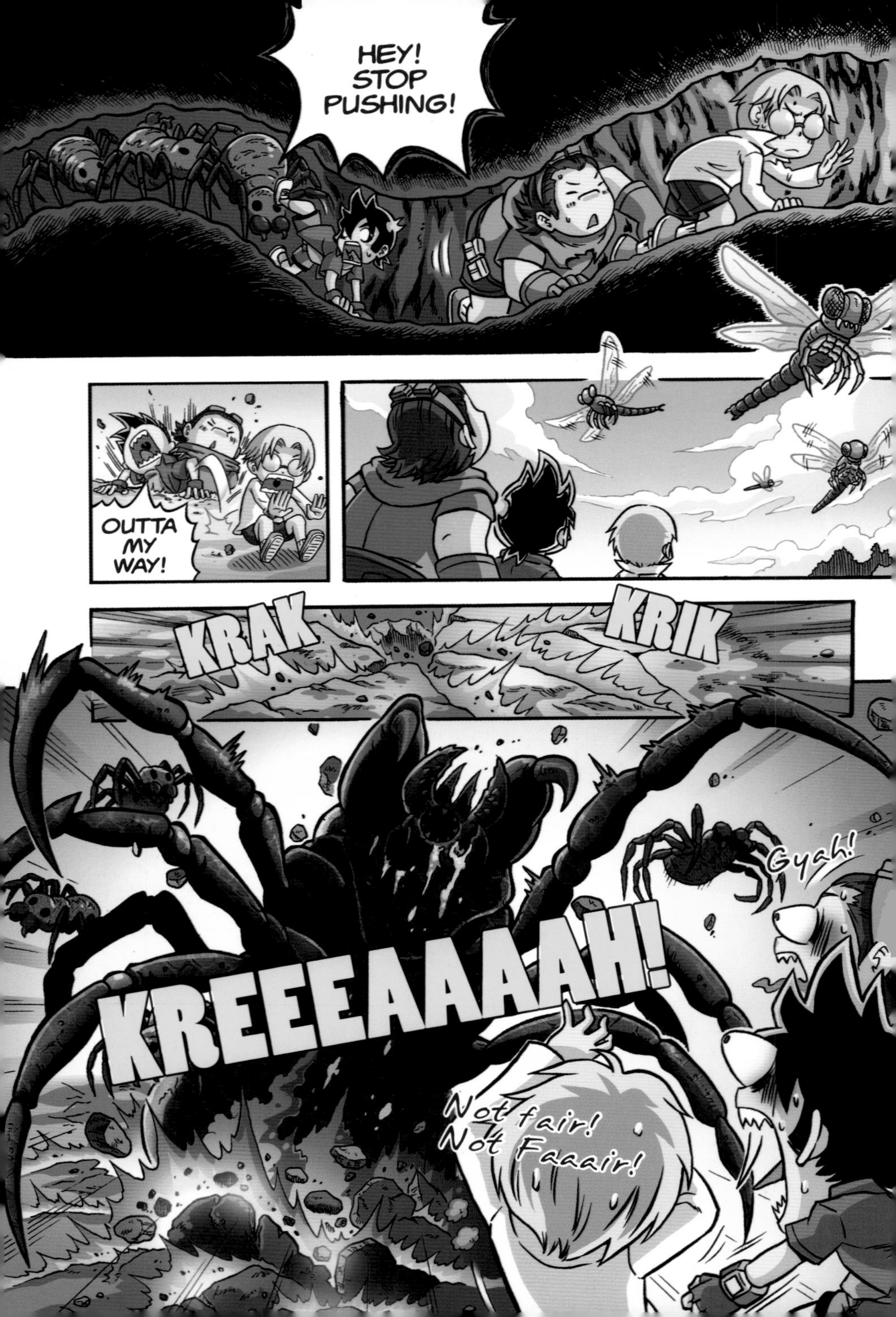
HEY! STOP PUSHING!
OUTTA MY WAY!
KRAK
KRIK
KREEEAAAAAH!
Gyah!
Not fair! Not Faaair!

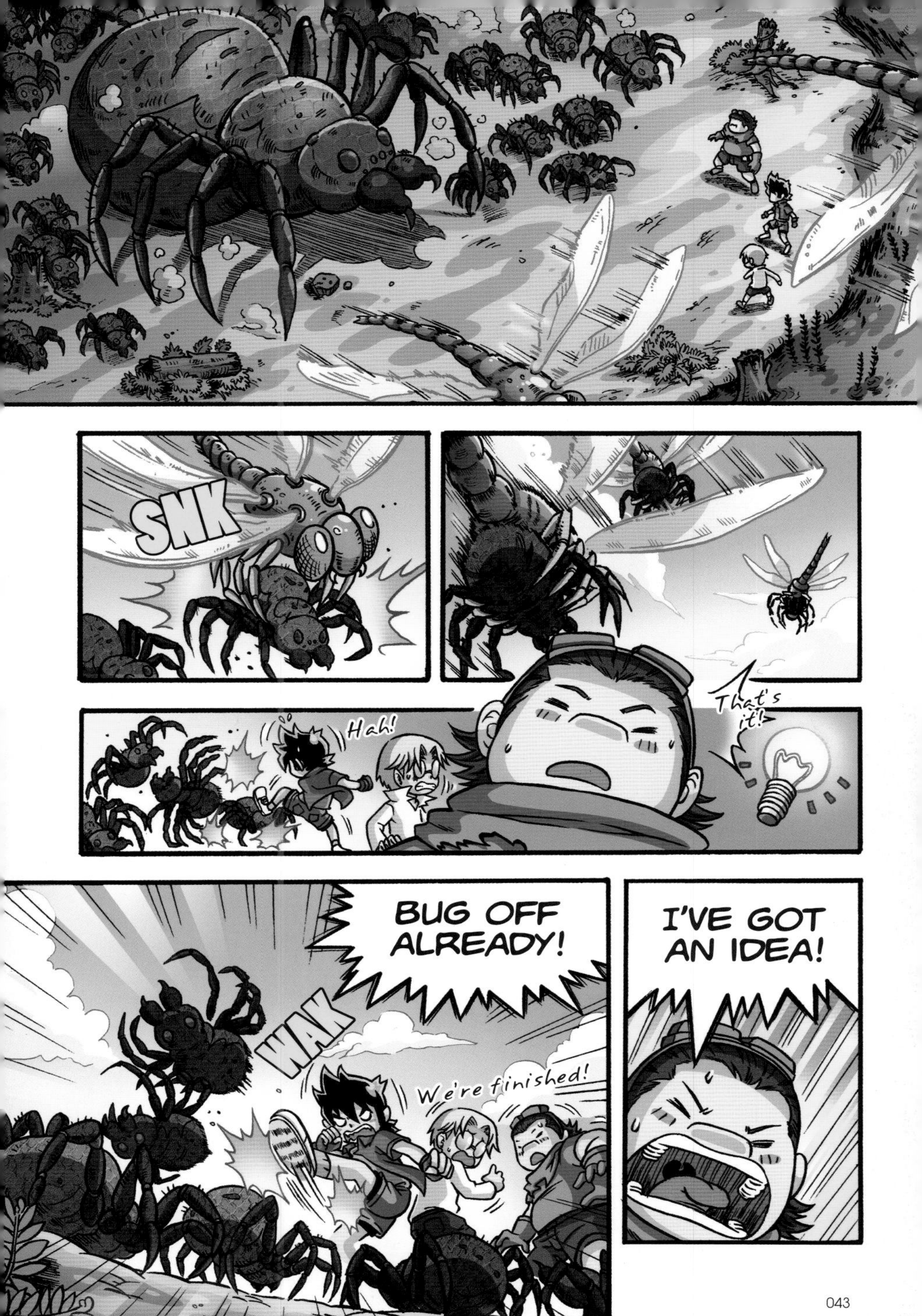
SNK
That's it!
Hah!
BUG OFF ALREADY!
WAK
We're finished!
I'VE GOT AN IDEA!

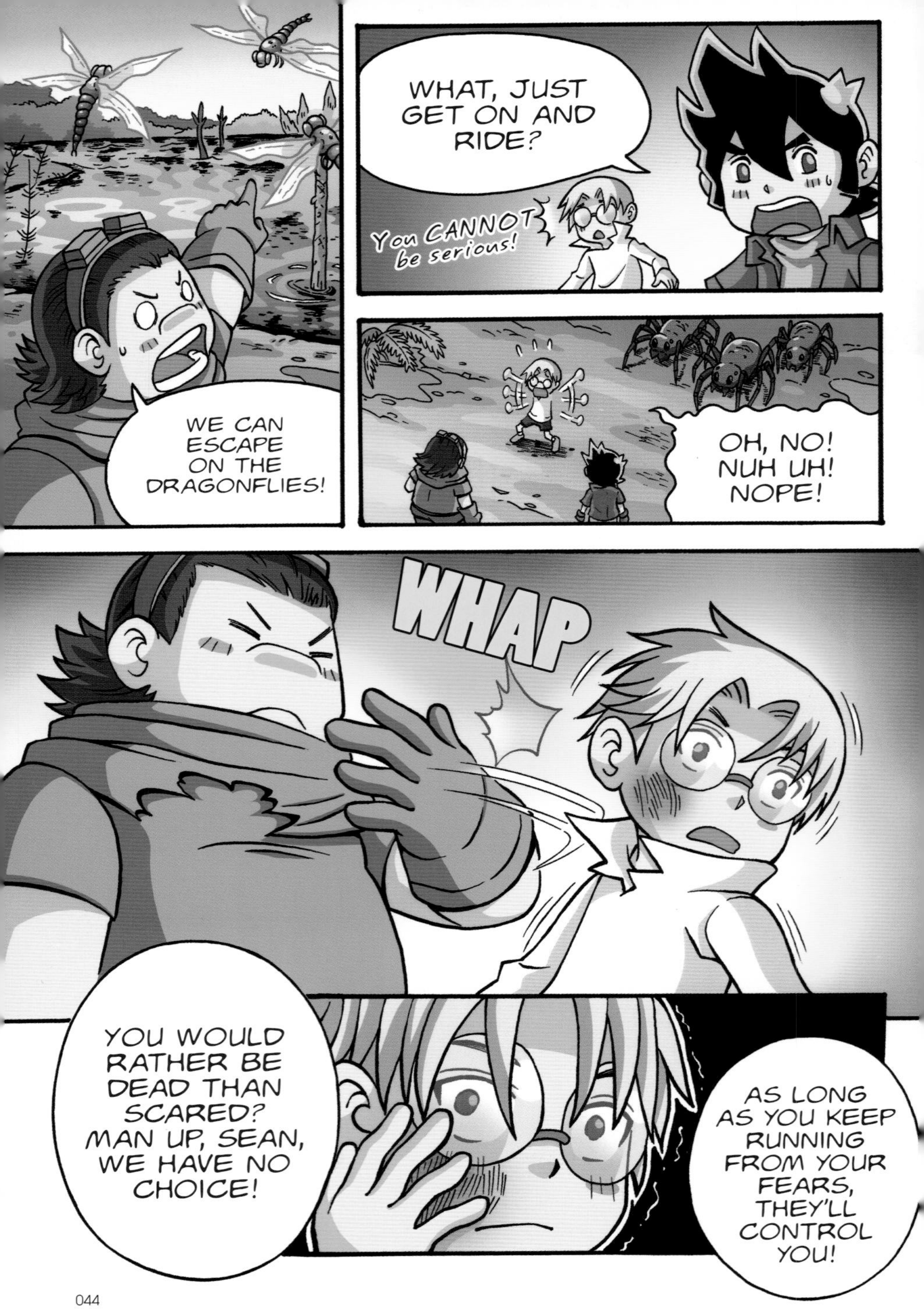
WE CAN ESCAPE ON THE DRAGONFLIES!
WHAT, JUST GET ON AND RIDE?
You CANNOT be serious!
OH, NO! NUH UH! NOPE!
WHAP
YOU WOULD RATHER BE DEAD THAN SCARED? MAN UP, SEAN, WE HAVE NO CHOICE!
AS LONG AS YOU KEEP RUNNING FROM YOUR FEARS, THEY'LL CONTROL YOU!

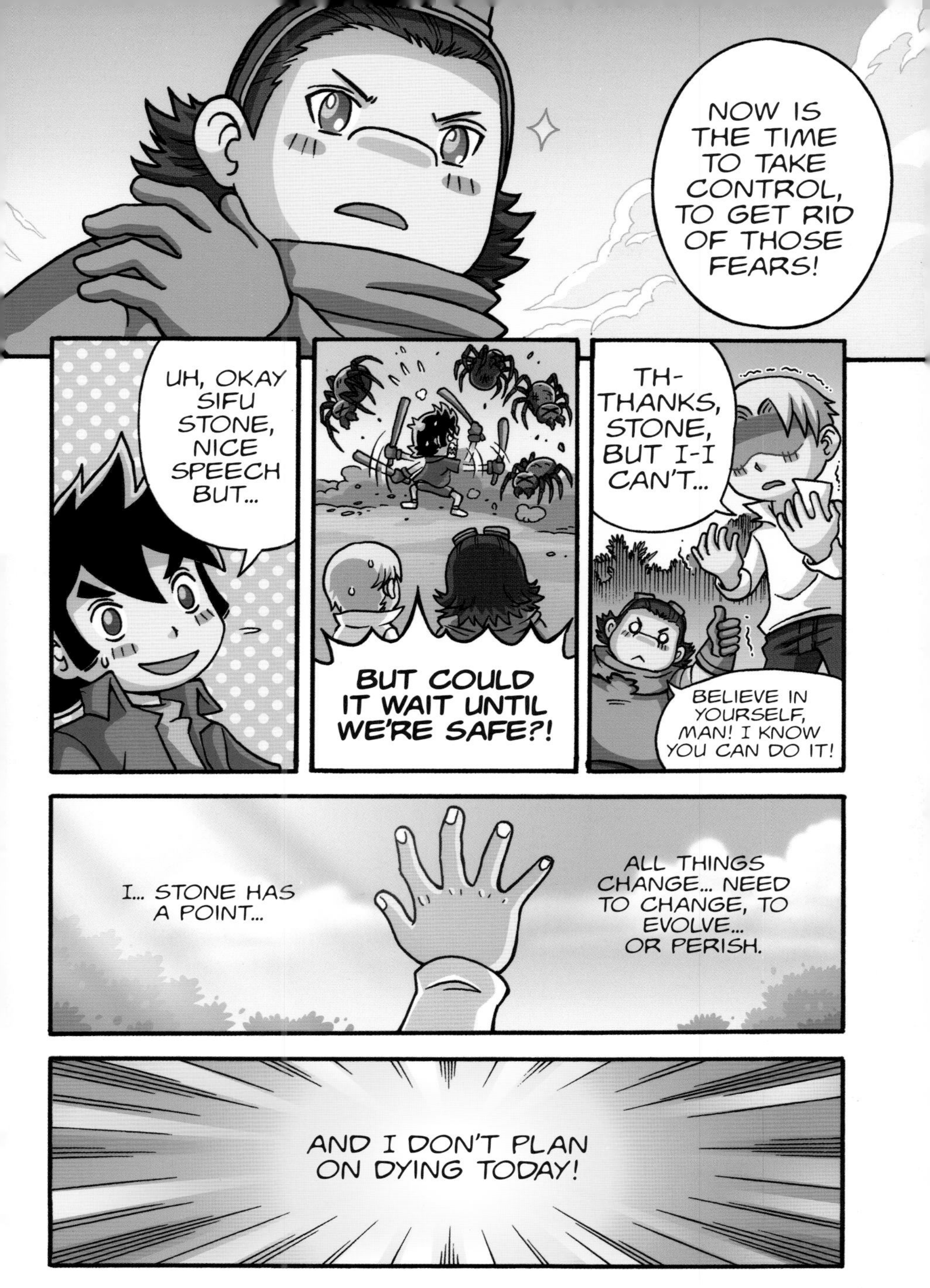
NOW IS THE TIME TO TAKE CONTROL, TO GET RID OF THOSE FEARS!
UH, OKAY SIFU STONE, NICE SPEECH BUT...
BUT COULD IT WAIT UNTIL WE'RE SAFE?!
TH-THANKS, STONE, BUT I-I CAN'T...
BELIEVE IN YOURSELF, MAN! I KNOW YOU CAN DO IT!
I... STONE HAS A POINT...
ALL THINGS CHANGE... NEED TO CHANGE, TO EVOLVE... OR PERISH.
AND I DON'T PLAN ON DYING TODAY!

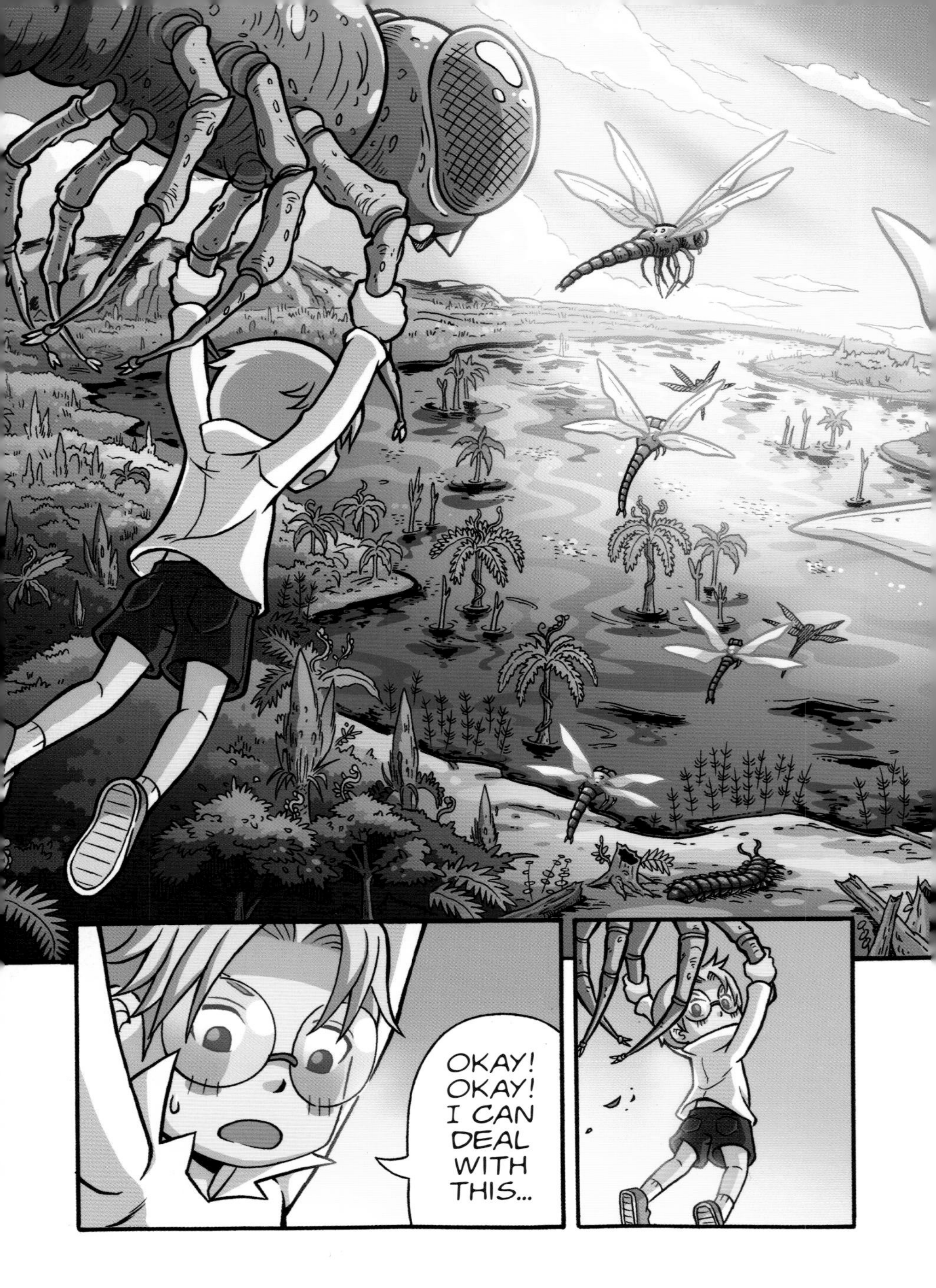
OKAY! OKAY! I CAN DEAL WITH THIS...

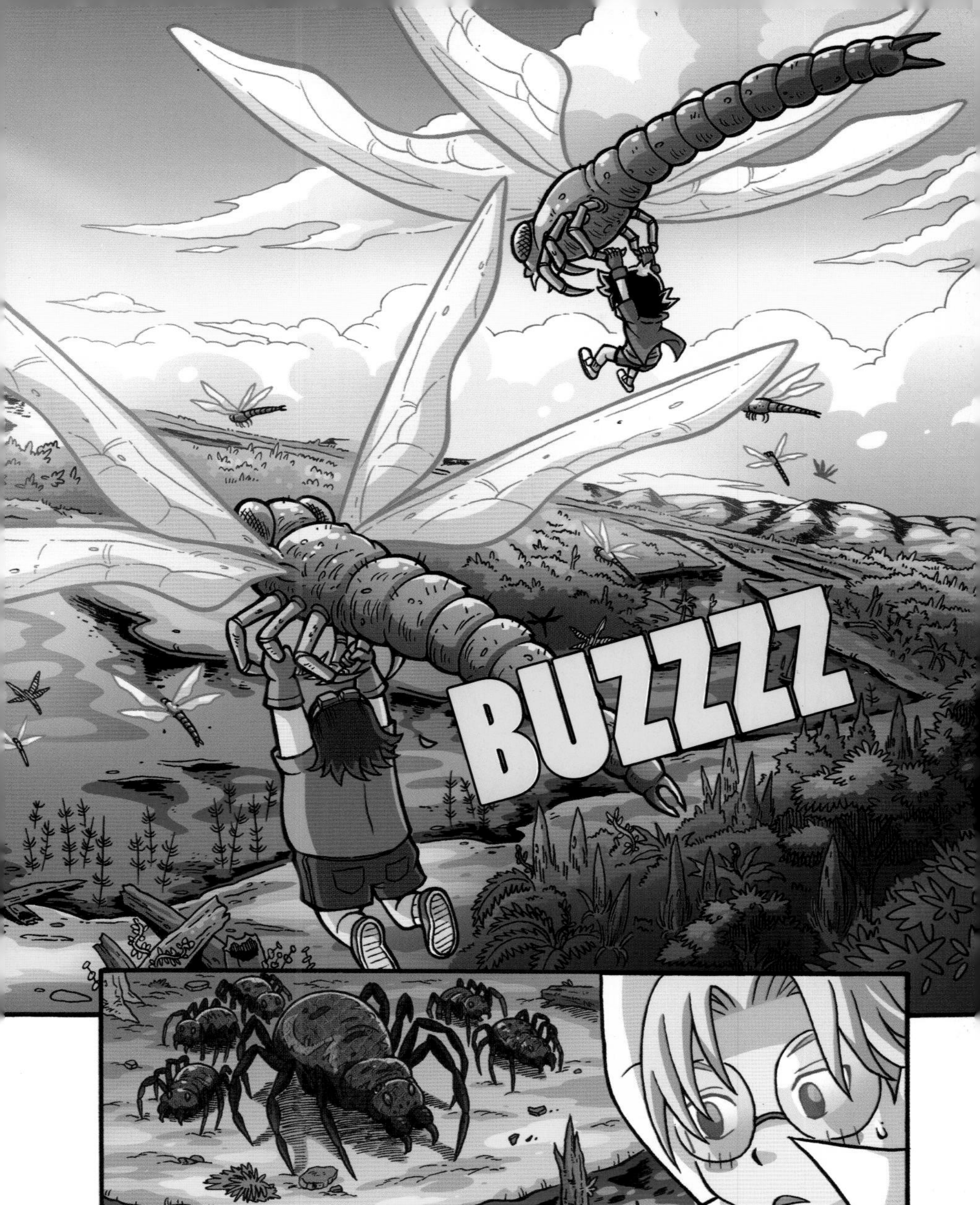
BUZZZZ

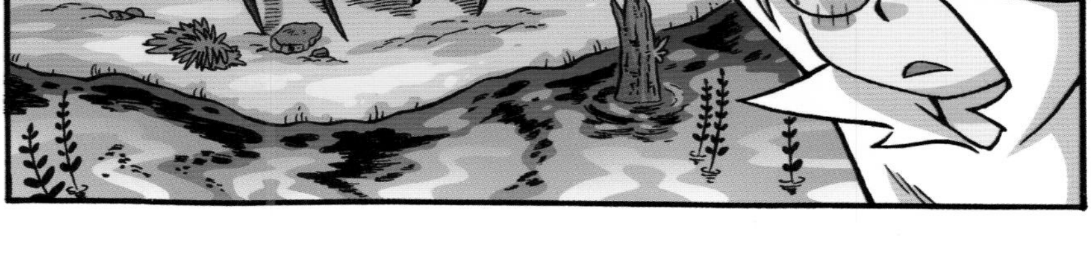

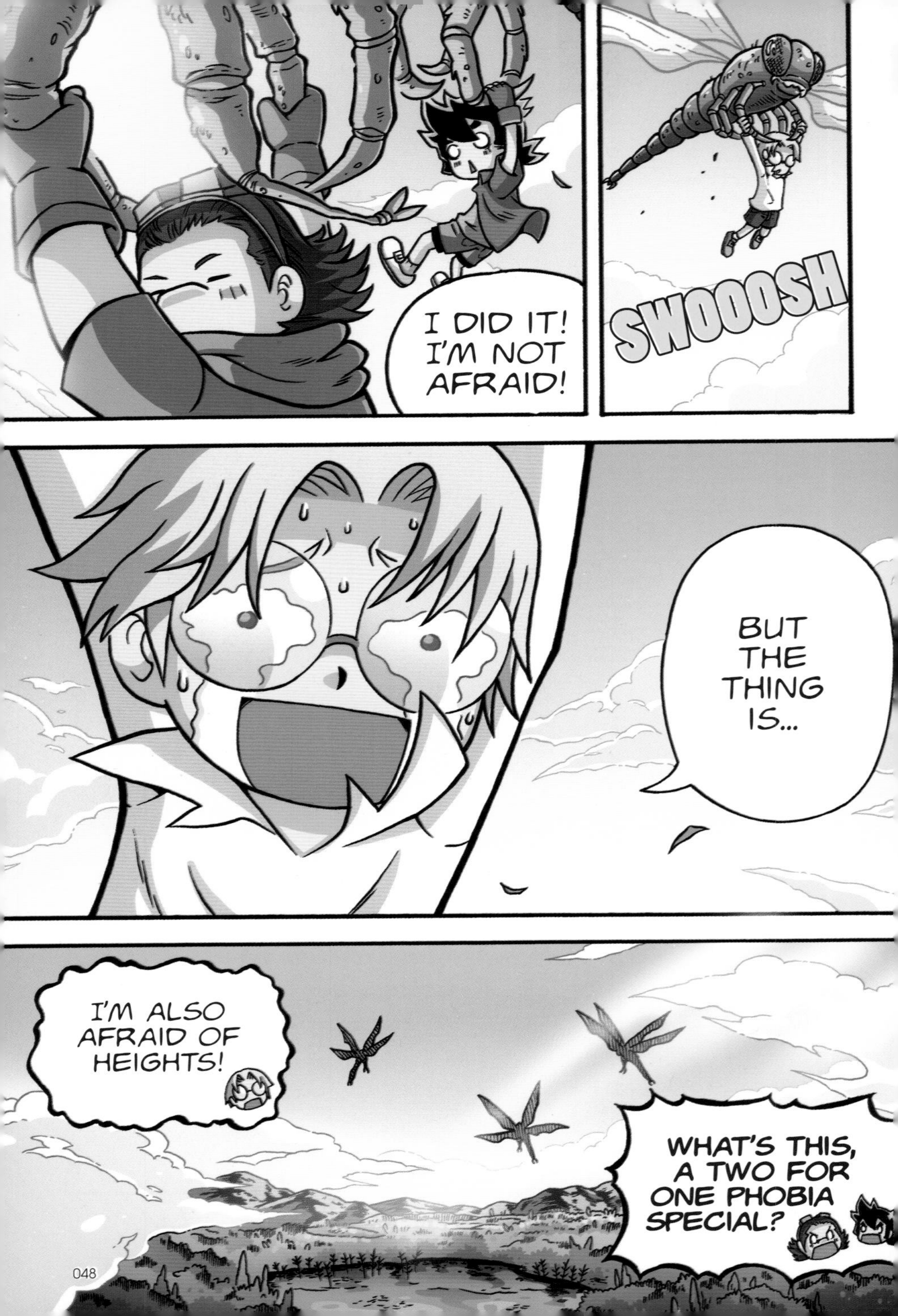
I DID IT! I'M NOT AFRAID!
SWOOOSH
BUT THE THING IS...
I'M ALSO AFRAID OF HEIGHTS!
WHAT'S THIS, A TWO FOR ONE PHOBIA SPECIAL?

How did insects evolve?

In order to avoid predators as well as changing environmental conditions, early arthropods took to land. The vast amounts of oxygen and plant life, along with the lack of any real terrestrial predators, allowed many of them room and resources to evolve into insects!

Are all arthropods insects?

Nope – arthropods are divided into hexapods ("six feet" – basically, insects), crustaceans (e.g. crabs), myriapods ("many legs," such as centipedes and millipedes), and arachnids (spiders and most other eight-legged arthropods). We should not confuse insects with the other arthropods, because all insects have the following in common, while the rest do not:

① A 3 segmented body; head, thorax, and abdomen
② 3 pairs of legs attached to the thorax.

Arthropods commonly mistaken for insects:

Crustaceans

Traits: 1. Body divided only into head and abdomen.
2. 5 pairs of legs (each often divided into up to 7 segments)

Ligiidae

Pillbug

Myriapods

Traits: 1. Many-segmented body.
2. Only one or two pairs of legs on each.

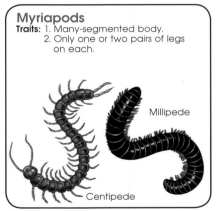

Millipede

Centipede

Arachnids

Traits: 1. Body divided only into head and abdomen.
2. 4 pairs of legs.

Spider

Scorpion

Tick

COMPILING THE CARBONIFEROUS

Blattodea

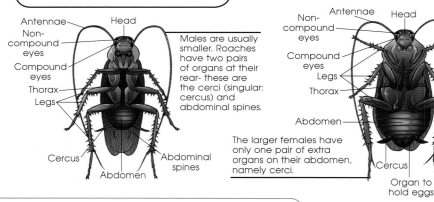

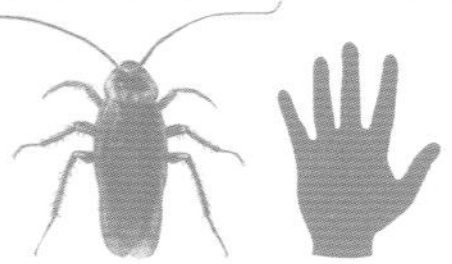

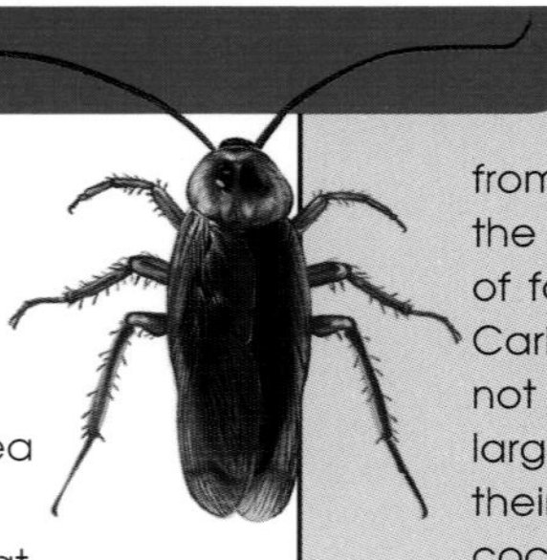

"Cockroach" is simply the common name for insects from the order Blattodea; they are the earliest form of insects capable of folding their wings inward. In the Carboniferous, most insects could not do this, which made them larger targets for predators. With their thin bodies and foldable wings, cockroaches became adept at hiding themselves, a skill they have retained to this day!

Scientific name: Blattodea
Length: 3.5 to 8 inches
Diet: Anything it could eat
Habitat: Tropical swamps
Discovered: Europe
Era: Mid Carboniferous to 21st century

Antennae
Head
Non-compound eyes
Compound eyes
Thorax
Legs
Cercus
Abdomen
Abdominal spines

Males are usually smaller. Roaches have two pairs of organs at their rear- these are the cerci (singular: cercus) and abdominal spines.

Antennae
Head
Non-compound eyes
Compound eyes
Legs
Thorax
Abdomen
Cercus
Organ to hold eggs

The larger females have only one pair of extra organs on their abdomen, namely cerci.

COMPILING THE CARBONIFEROUS

Giant spiders

The giant spiders of our past were from the suborder Mesothelae, and unlike the comic, only grew as large as a human's head or hand. Their abdomens were smaller in comparison to those of modern spiders, and they lacked venom.

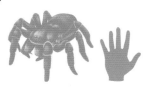

Scientific name: Mesothelae
Length: 12 inches
Diet: Carnivore
Habitat: Tropical swamps
Discovered: Europe
Era: Late Carboniferous

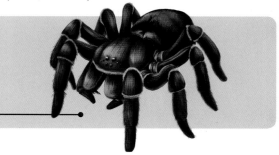

CHAPTER 3

LAKE LANDING

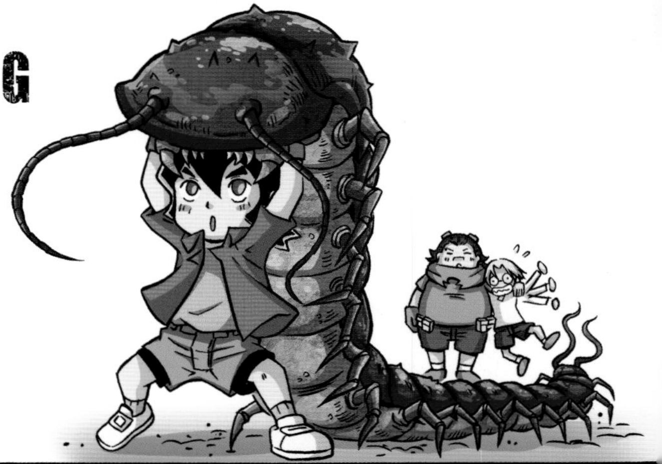

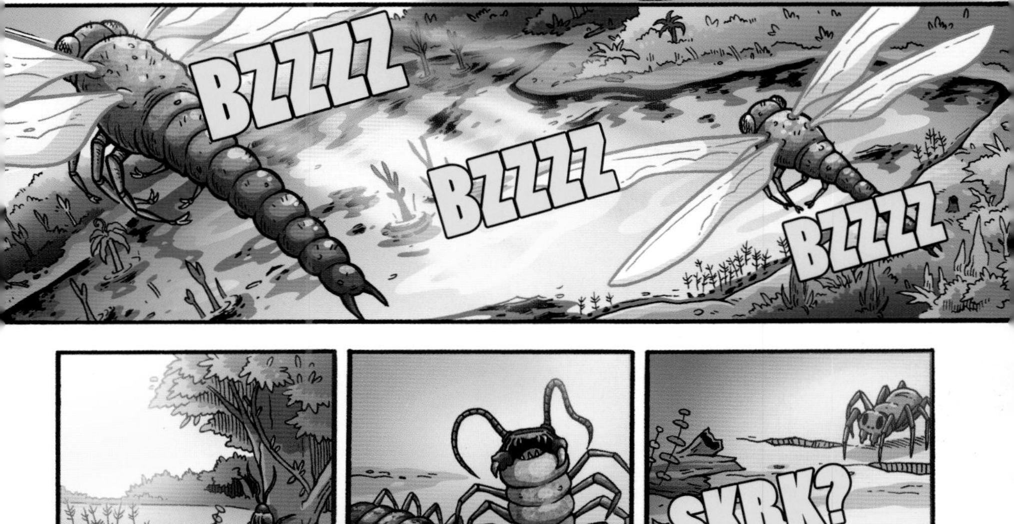
BZZZZ
BZZZZ
BZZZZ

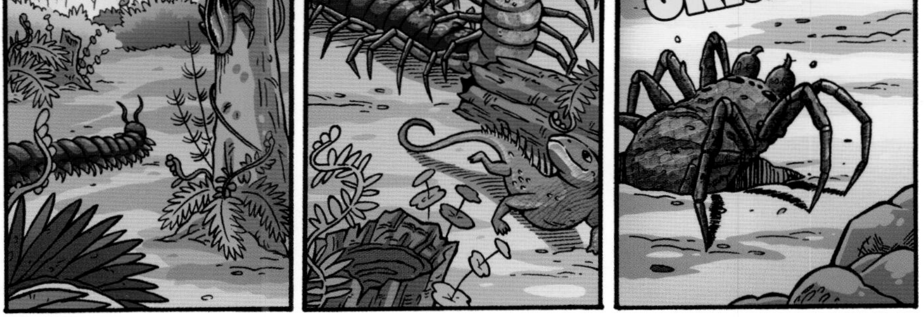
SKRK?

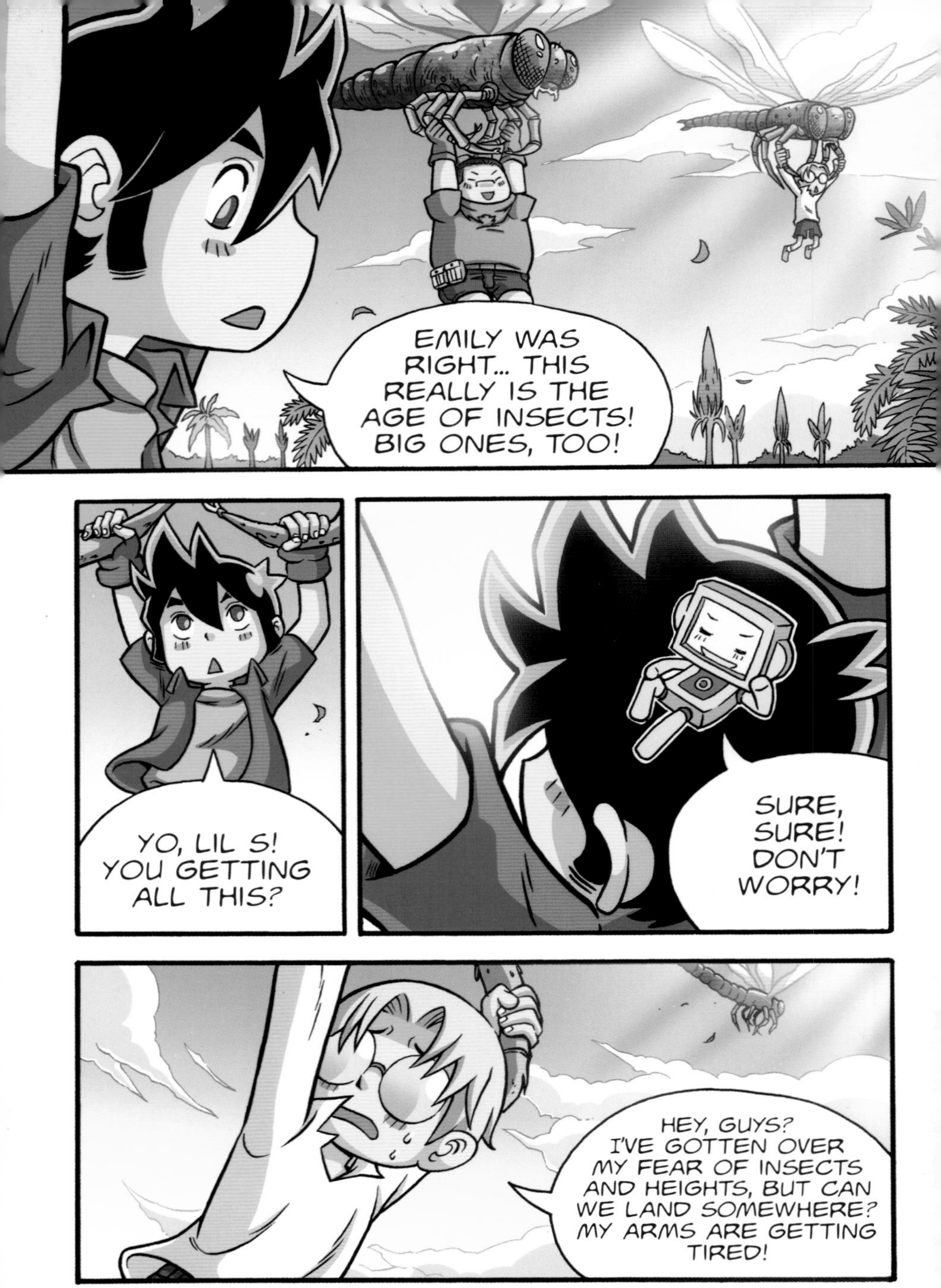
EMILY WAS RIGHT... THIS REALLY IS THE AGE OF INSECTS! BIG ONES, TOO!
YO, LIL S! YOU GETTING ALL THIS?
SURE, SURE! DON'T WORRY!
HEY, GUYS? I'VE GOTTEN OVER MY FEAR OF INSECTS AND HEIGHTS, BUT CAN WE LAND SOMEWHERE? MY ARMS ARE GETTING TIRED!

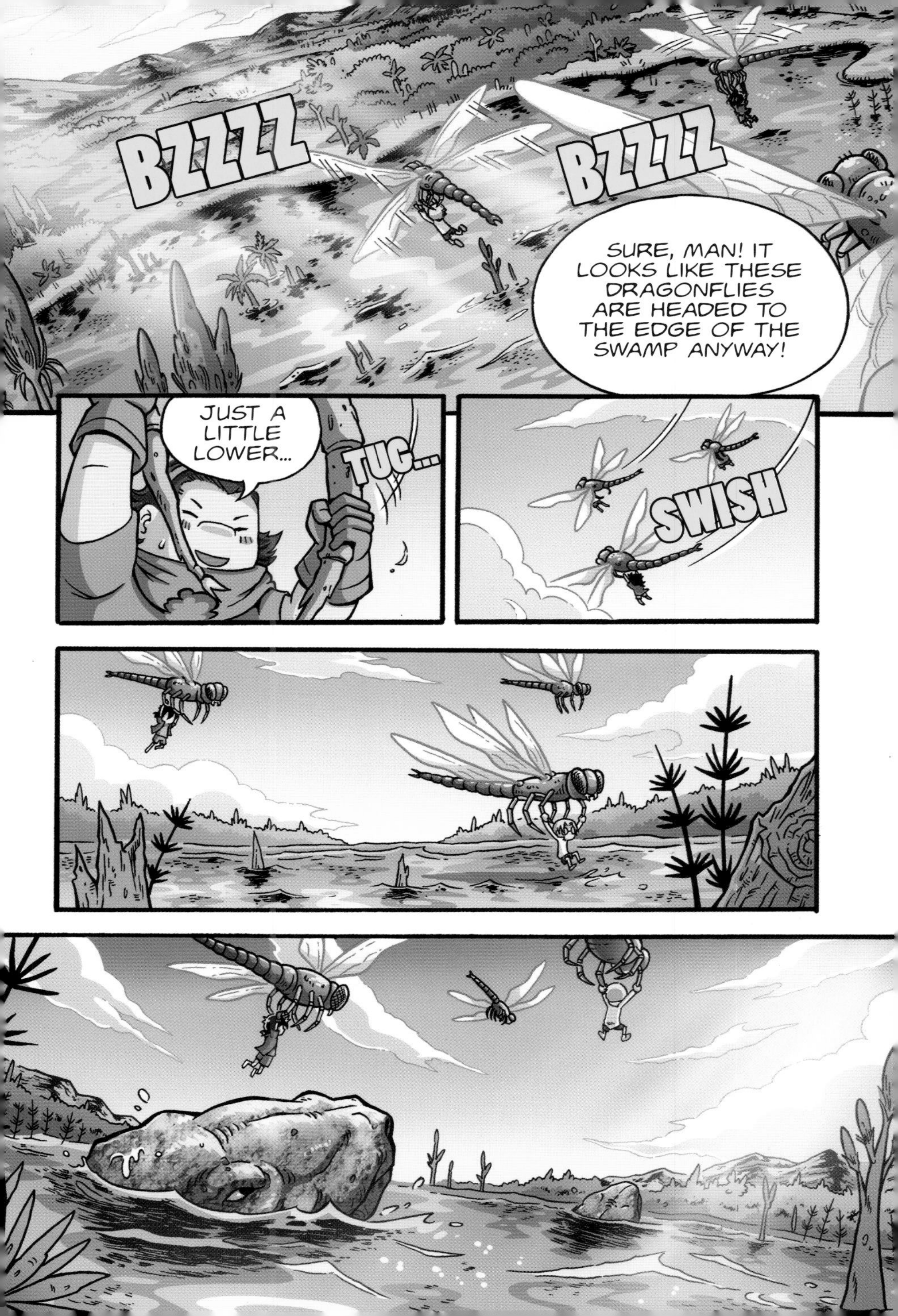
BZZZZ
BZZZZ
SURE, MAN! IT LOOKS LIKE THESE DRAGONFLIES ARE HEADED TO THE EDGE OF THE SWAMP ANYWAY!
JUST A LITTLE LOWER...
TUC...
SWISH

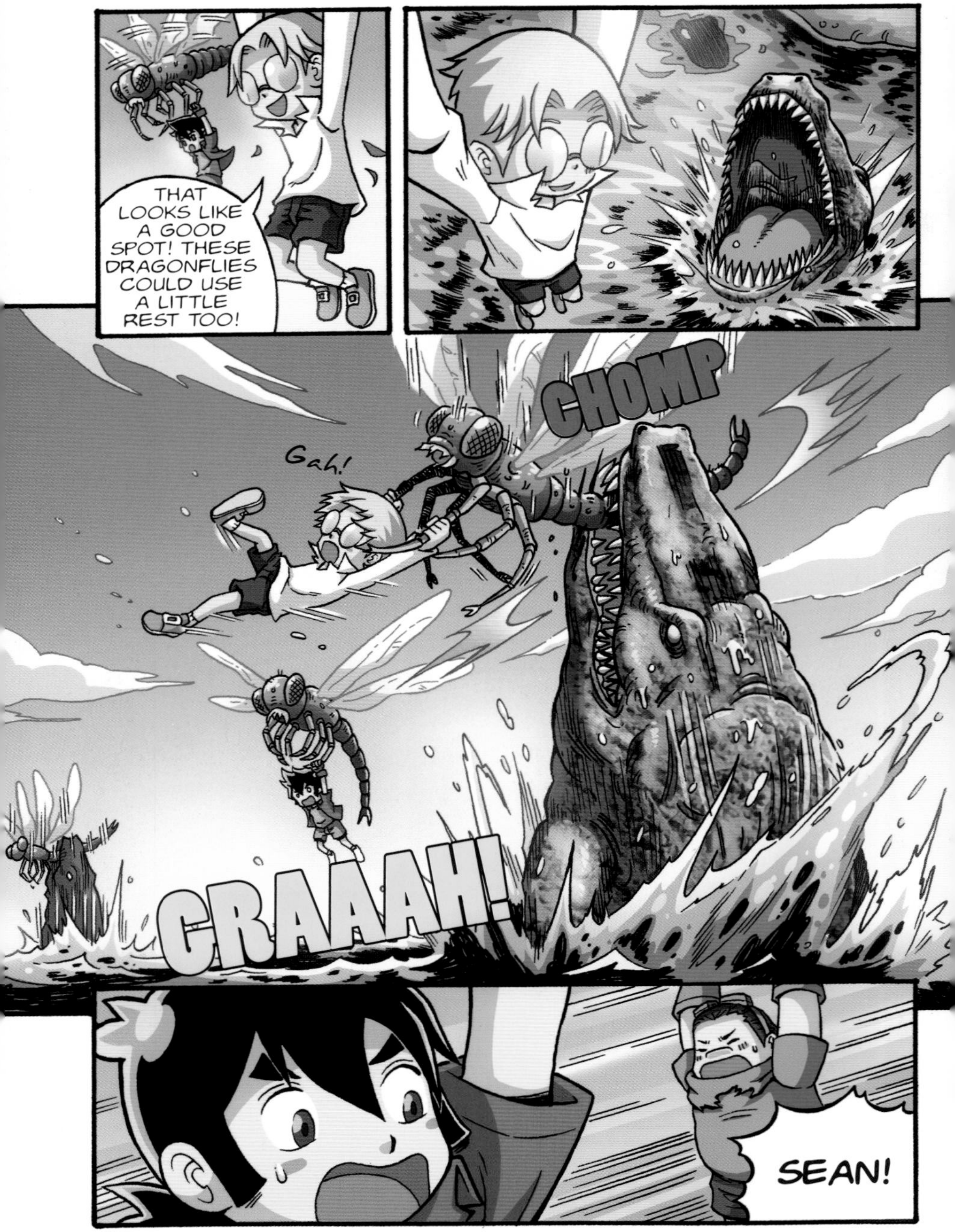
THAT LOOKS LIKE A GOOD SPOT! THESE DRAGONFLIES COULD USE A LITTLE REST TOO!
CHOMP
Gah!
CRAAAH!
SEAN!

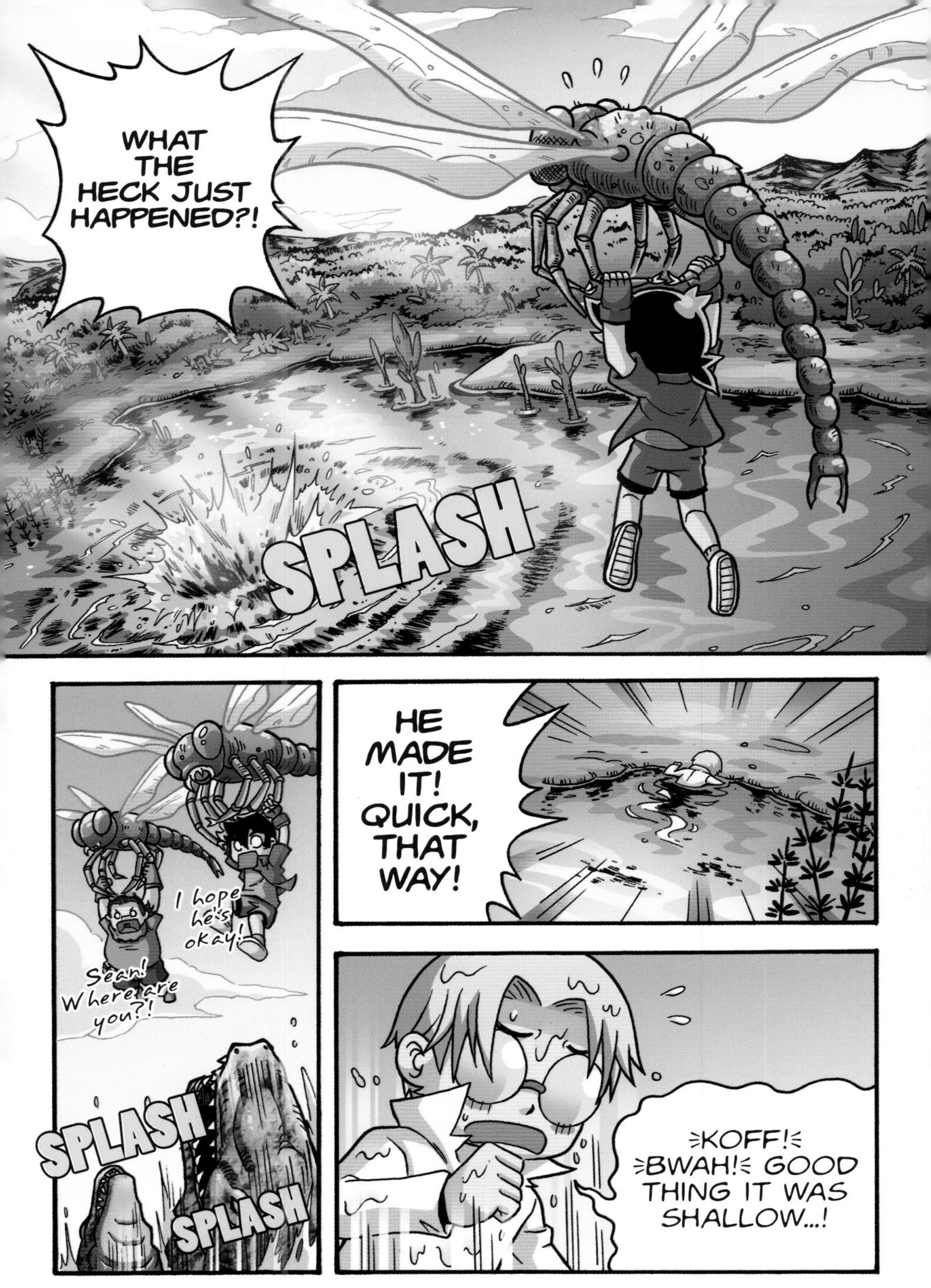
WHAT THE HECK JUST HAPPENED?!
SPLASH
I hope he's okay!
Sean! Where are you?!
SPLASH
SPLASH
HE MADE IT! QUICK, THAT WAY!
KOFF! BWAH! GOOD THING IT WAS SHALLOW...!

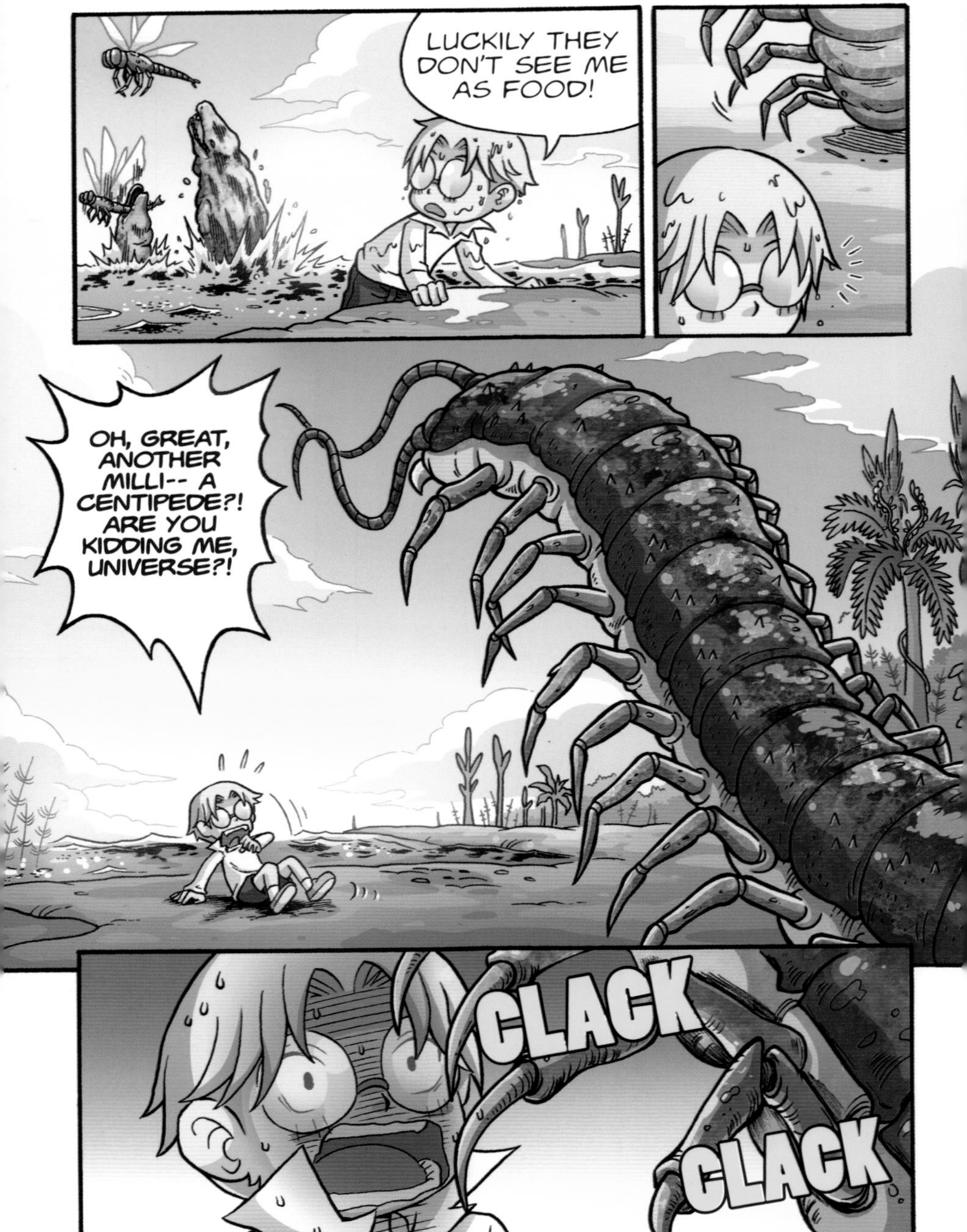
LUCKILY THEY DON'T SEE ME AS FOOD!
OH, GREAT, ANOTHER MILLI-- A CENTIPEDE?! ARE YOU KIDDING ME, UNIVERSE?!
CLACK
CLACK

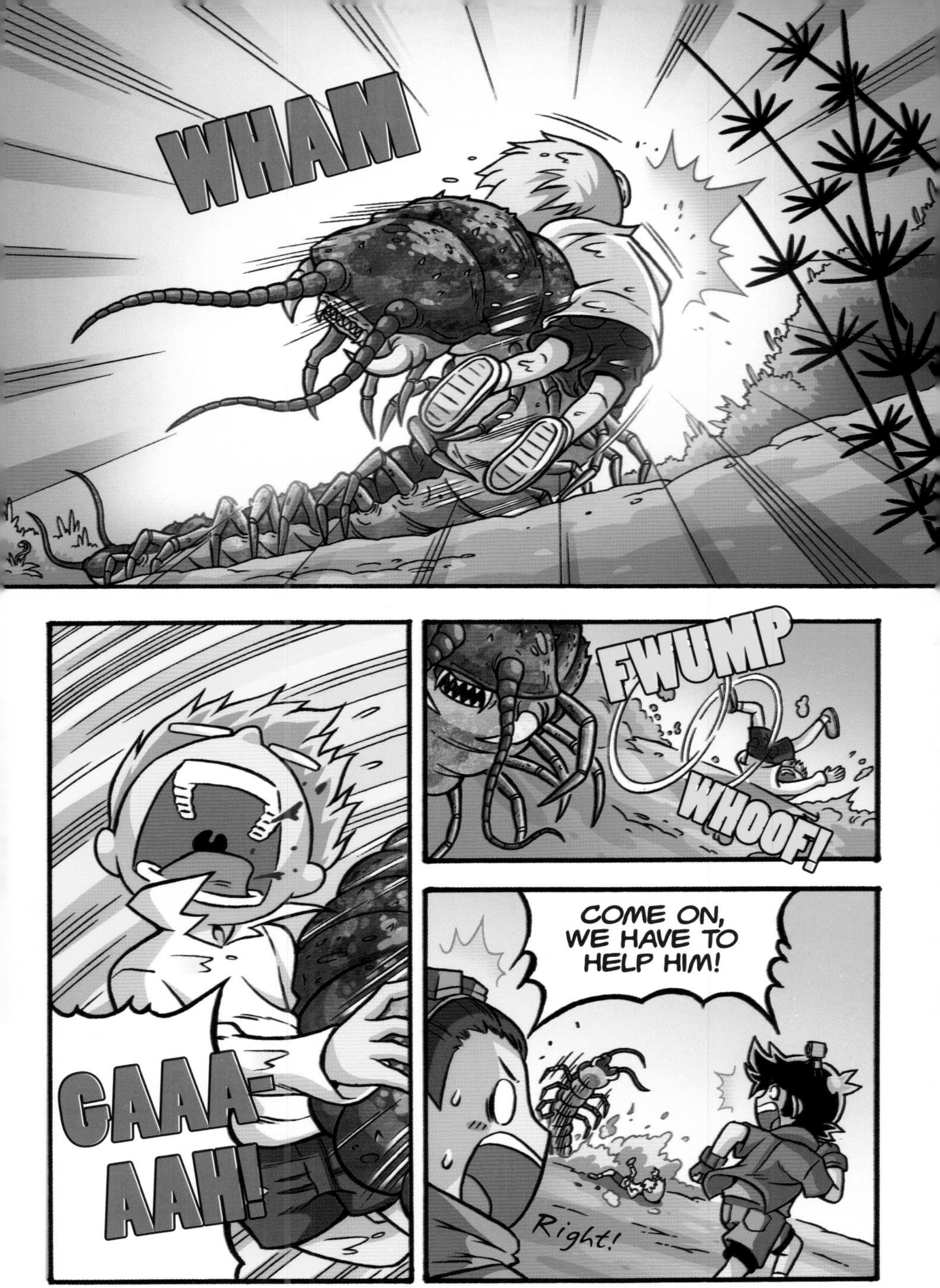
WHAM
GAAA-AAH!
FWUMP
WHOOF!
COME ON, WE HAVE TO HELP HIM!
Right!

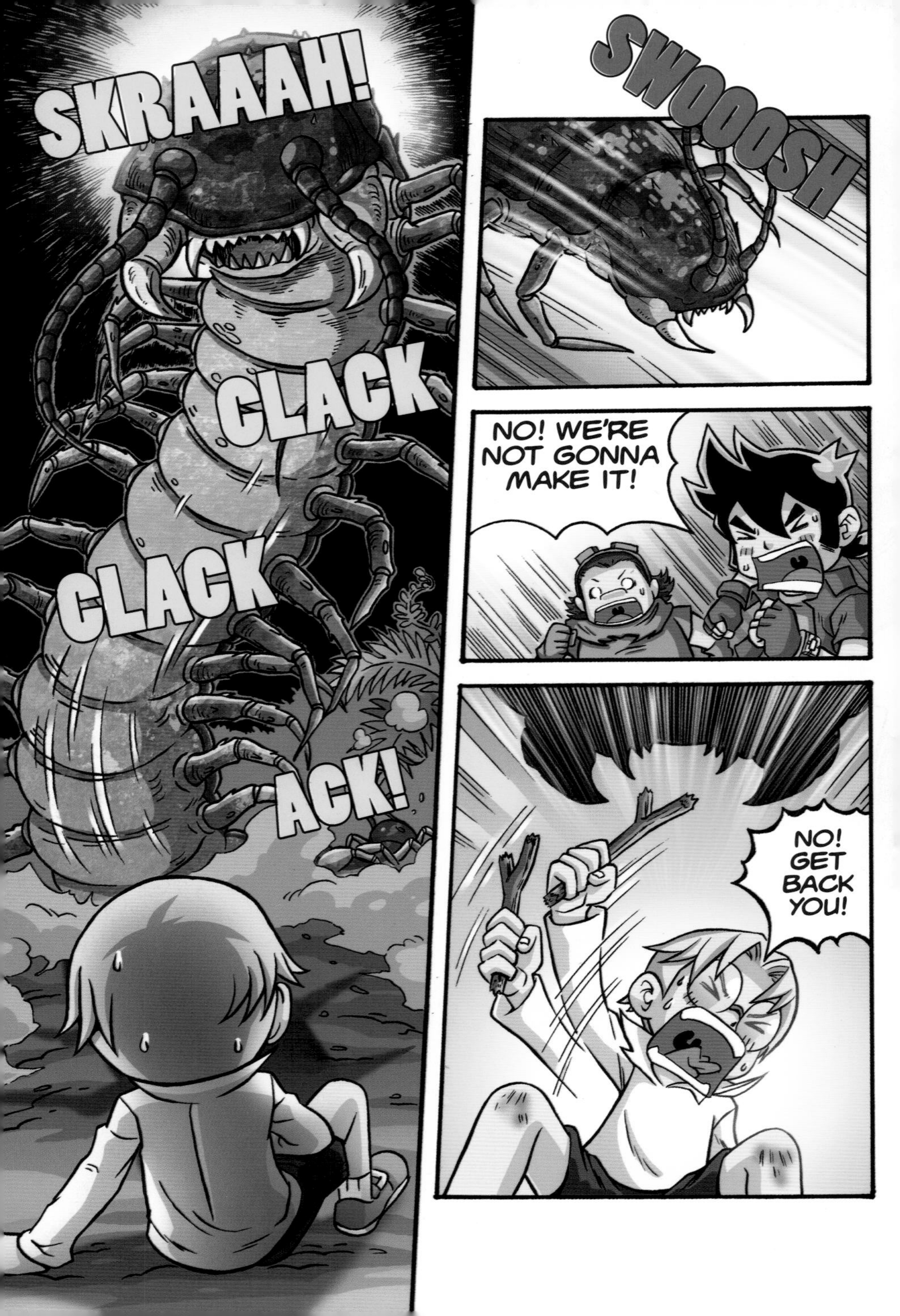
SKRAAAH!
CLACK
CLACK
ACK!
SWOOOSH
NO! WE'RE NOT GONNA MAKE IT!
NO! GET BACK YOU!

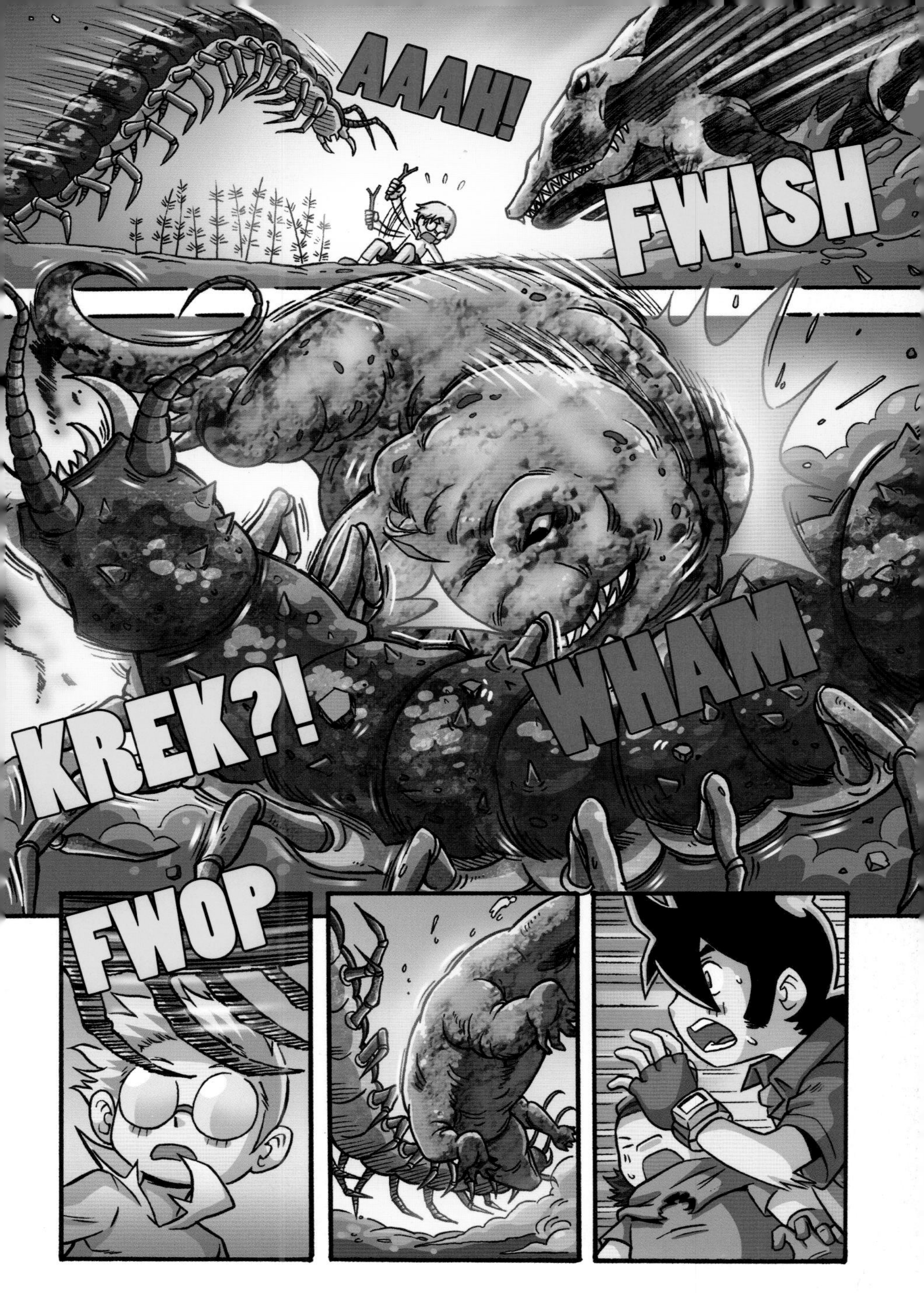
AAAH!
FWISH
KREK?!
WHAM
FWOP

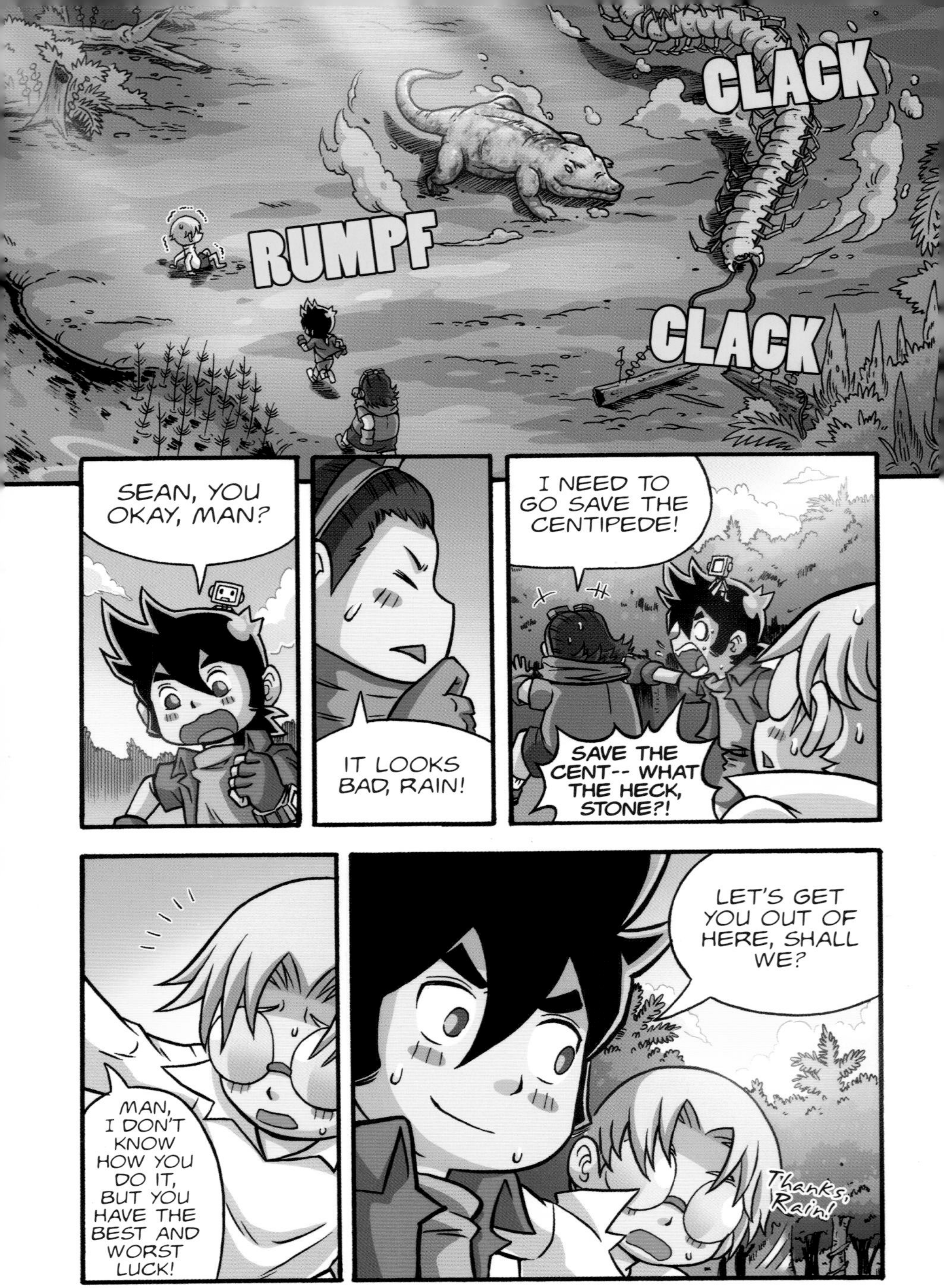

RUMPF
CLACK
CLACK
SEAN, YOU OKAY, MAN?
IT LOOKS BAD, RAIN!
I NEED TO GO SAVE THE CENTIPEDE!
SAVE THE CENT-- WHAT THE HECK, STONE?!
MAN, I DON'T KNOW HOW YOU DO IT, BUT YOU HAVE THE BEST AND WORST LUCK!
LET'S GET YOU OUT OF HERE, SHALL WE?
Thanks, Rain!

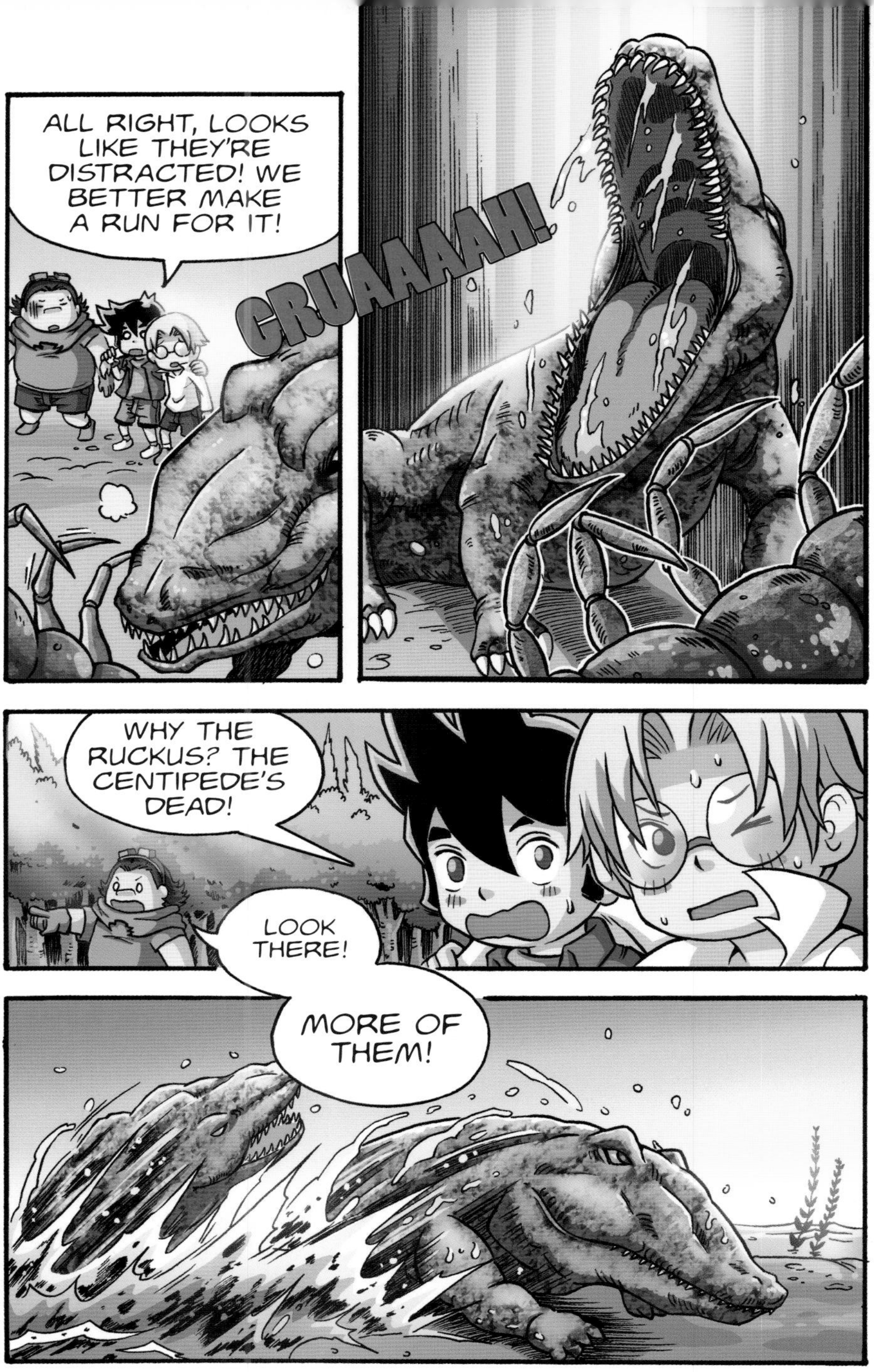
ALL RIGHT, LOOKS LIKE THEY'RE DISTRACTED! WE BETTER MAKE A RUN FOR IT!
CRUAAAAAH!
WHY THE RUCKUS? THE CENTIPEDE'S DEAD!
LOOK THERE!
MORE OF THEM!

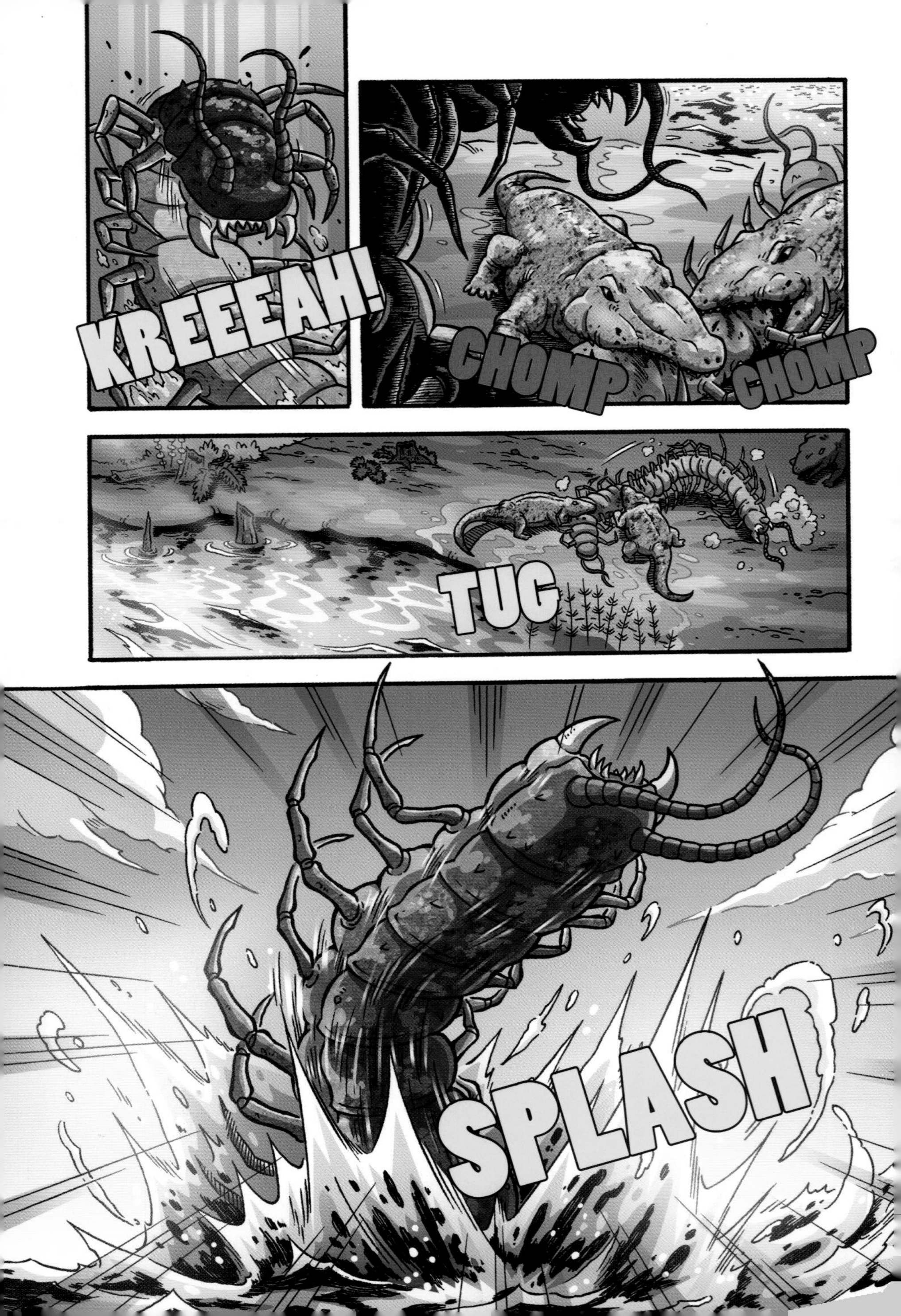
KREEEEAH!
CHOMP
CHOMP
TUG
SPLASH

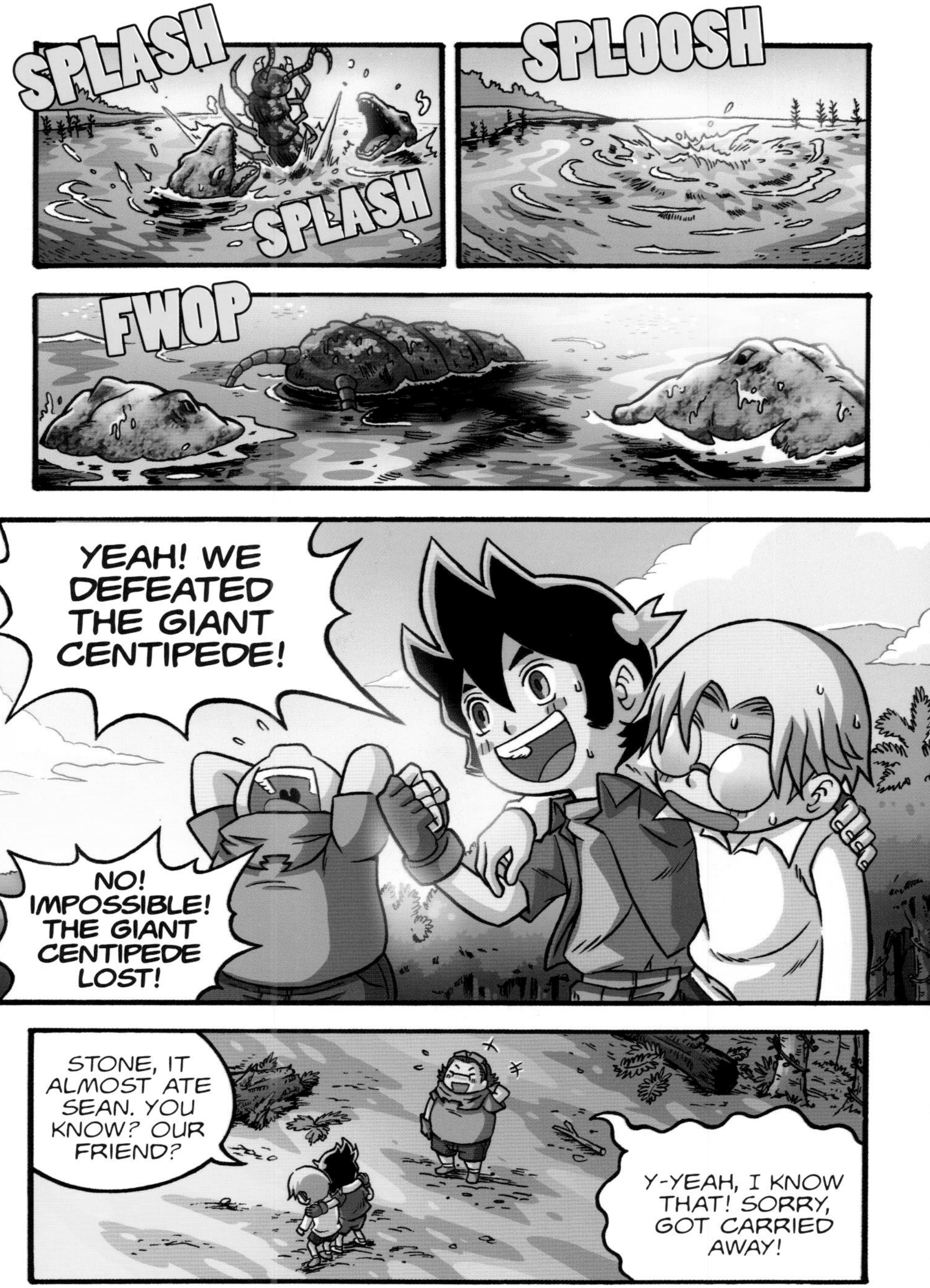
SPLASH
SPLASH
SPLOOSH
FWOP
YEAH! WE DEFEATED THE GIANT CENTIPEDE!
NO! IMPOSSIBLE! THE GIANT CENTIPEDE LOST!
STONE, IT ALMOST ATE SEAN. YOU KNOW? OUR FRIEND?
Y-YEAH, I KNOW THAT! SORRY, GOT CARRIED AWAY!

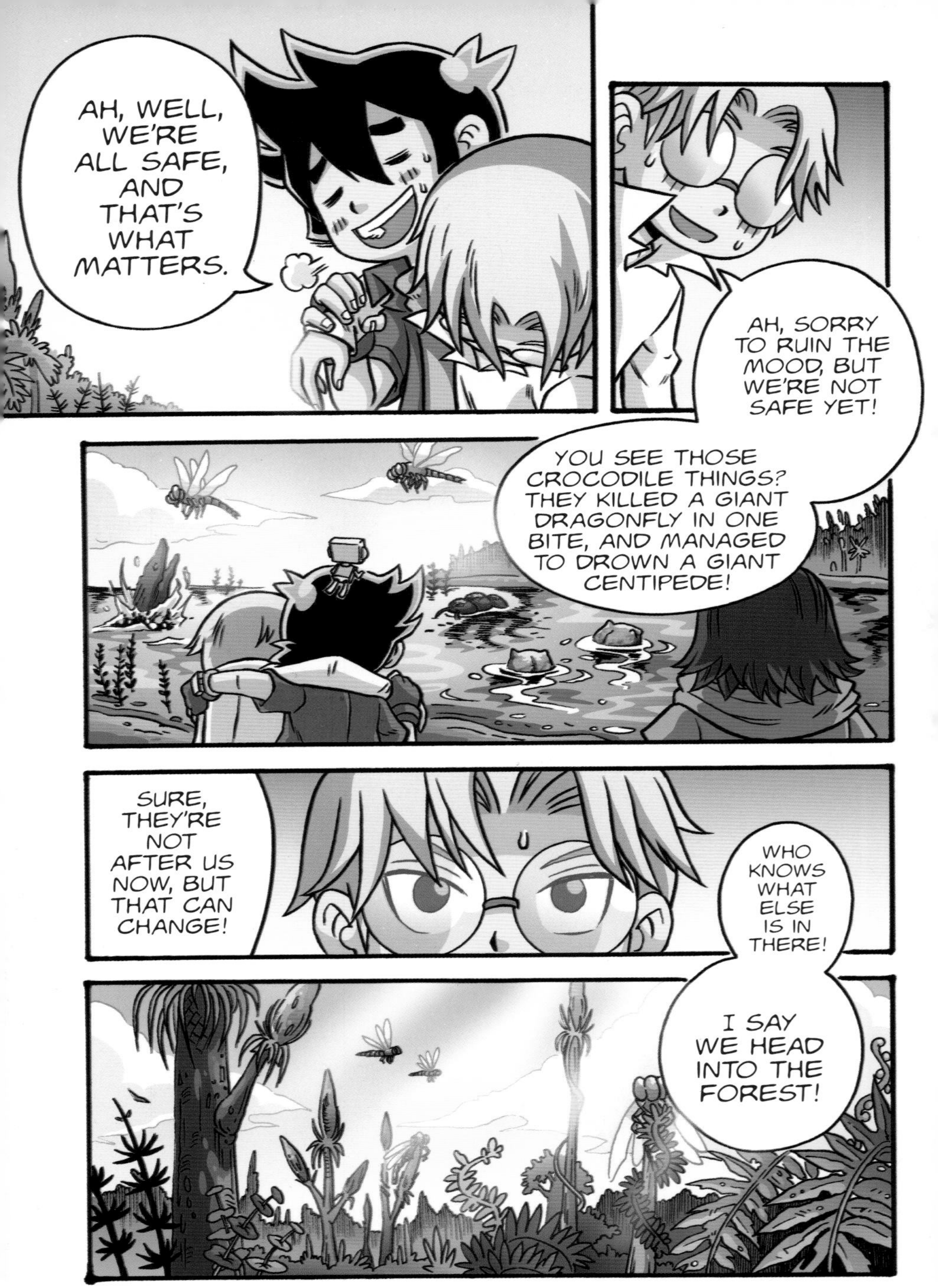
AH, WELL, WE'RE ALL SAFE, AND THAT'S WHAT MATTERS.
AH, SORRY TO RUIN THE MOOD, BUT WE'RE NOT SAFE YET!
YOU SEE THOSE CROCODILE THINGS? THEY KILLED A GIANT DRAGONFLY IN ONE BITE, AND MANAGED TO DROWN A GIANT CENTIPEDE!
SURE, THEY'RE NOT AFTER US NOW, BUT THAT CAN CHANGE!
WHO KNOWS WHAT ELSE IS IN THERE!
I SAY WE HEAD INTO THE FOREST!

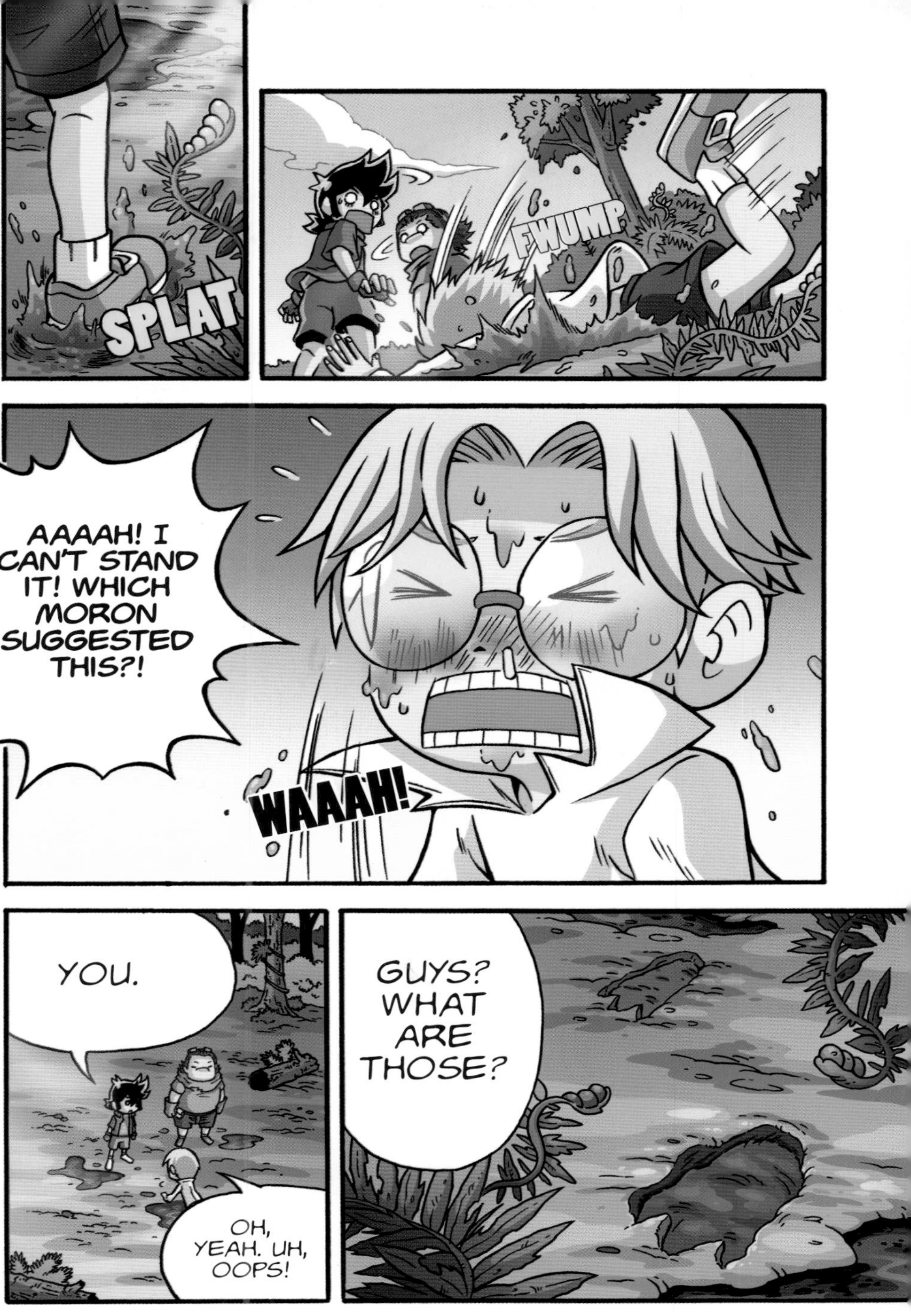

SPLAT
FWUMP
AAAAH! I CAN'T STAND IT! WHICH MORON SUGGESTED THIS?!
WAAAH!
YOU.
OH, YEAH. UH, OOPS!
GUYS? WHAT ARE THOSE?

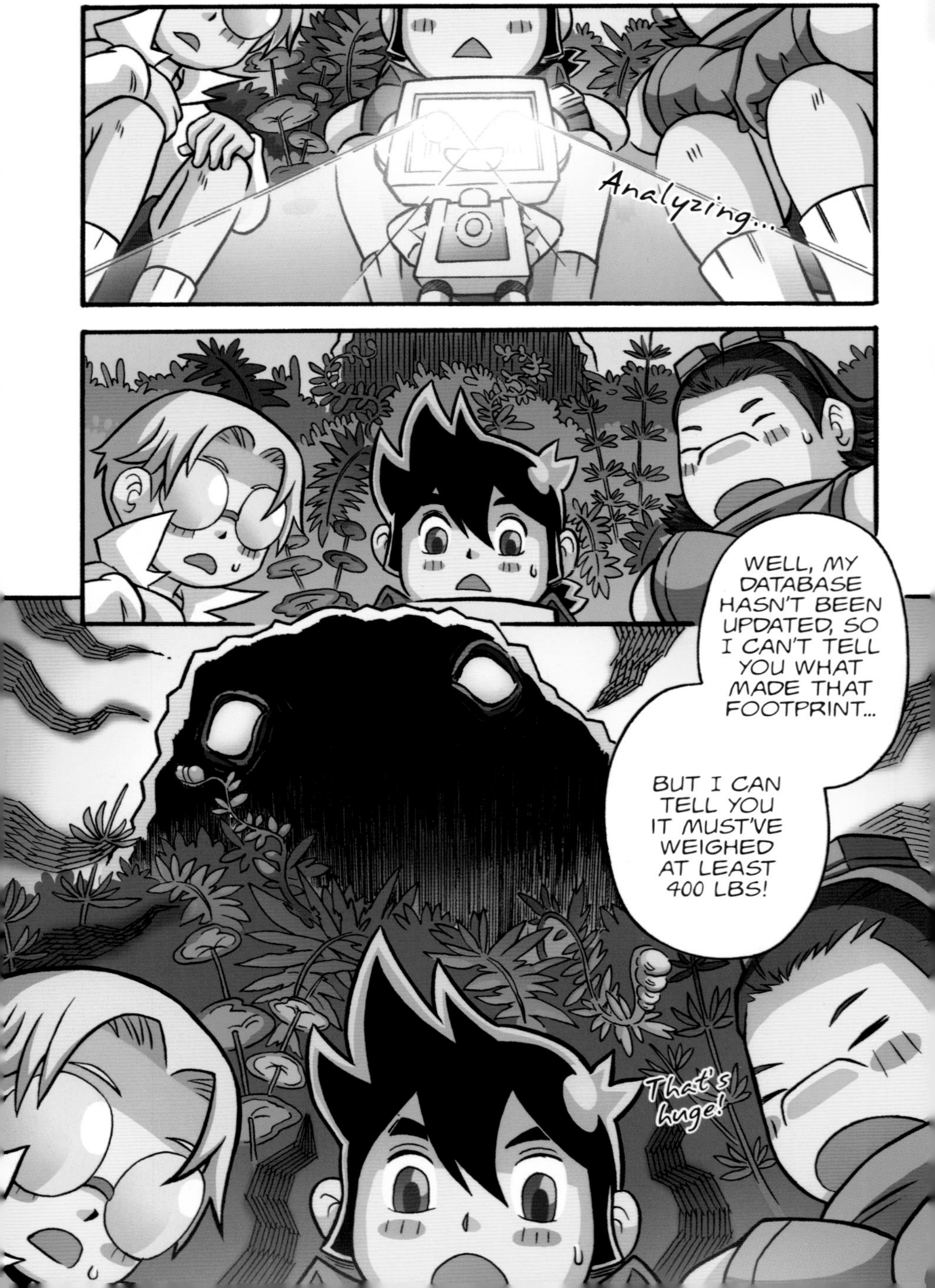
Analyzing...
WELL, MY DATABASE HASN'T BEEN UPDATED, SO I CAN'T TELL YOU WHAT MADE THAT FOOTPRINT...
BUT I CAN TELL YOU IT MUST'VE WEIGHED AT LEAST 400 LBS!
That's huge!

COMPILING THE CARBONIFEROUS
Meganeura

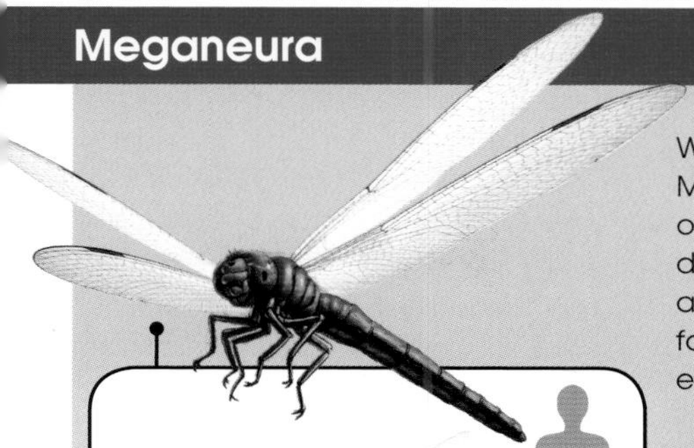

With a wingspan of a yard or more, the Meganeura was truly a majestic ancestor of modern dragonflies, despite being different enough to not be classified as a dragonfly itself. Their inability to fully fold up their wings, however, made them easy targets for predators.

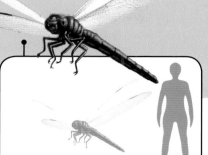

Scientific name: Meganeura monyi
Size: 2.5 to 3.5 feet (with wings fully opened)
Diet: Other animals
Habitat: Swamps
Discovered: Europe
Era: Carboniferous to Permian

Hunting methods:
Flying towards prey at high speeds, catching it with hooked legs.

Compound eyes:
The upper eyes were used to focus on distant objects, while lower eyes helped see what was closer.

COMPILING THE CARBONIFEROUS
Prehistoric centipedes

Classified as a myriapod, the Athropleura was among the first completely land-dwelling animals to make an appearance. At 10 feet, it certainly made an impression, especially considering its near-impenetrable segmented armor and sharp, cleaving jaws.

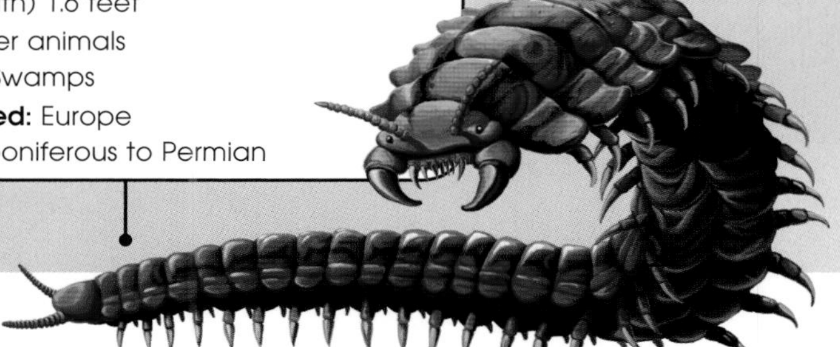

Scientific name: Arthropleura armata
Size: (length) 1 to 10 feet, (width) 1.6 feet
Diet: Other animals
Habitat: Swamps
Discovered: Europe
Era: Carboniferous to Permian

How do paleontologists know about all these prehistoric insects?

From analyzing the fossils they left behind.

How do paleontologists learn about prehistoric insects without fossilized bones to study?

They examine the abundant preserved physical evidence of insect life such as those trapped in amber, or ancient tree resin, an impression or mold of the wing, or mineralized copies and compressed insects in sedimentary rock. In a compression, the fossil may contain chitin, which makes up part of the insect's cuticle, and is a very durable substance. When the rest of the insect decays, the chitinous components often remain.

How many kinds of insect fossils have been discovered?

So far, the insect fossils found can be divided into two large groups;

Paleoptera: They are characterized by having their wings in their resting position, spread out. Examples of the extinct orders are the Paleodictyoptera, Megasecoptera, Meganisoptera, and Diaphanopterodea.

Paleodictyoptera	Megasecoptera	Ephemeroptera (Mayflies)

Neoptera: They have the ability to fold the wings back over their abdomen, using special structures at the base of their wings. Examples are insects from the order of Protorthoptera, Caloneurodea, Zoraptera, Titanoptera, and Orthoptera.

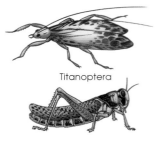

Titanoptera

Protorthoptera

Orthoptera
(Grasshoppers, crickets, and so forth)

Eogyrinus

Eogyrinus was an amphibian descended from Ichthyostega (see DINOSAUR EXPLORERS #2 "Puttering in the Paleozoic"). It had a slim, eel-like body and a crocodilian head.

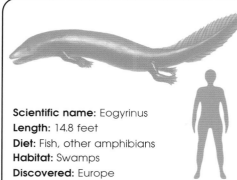

Scientific name: Eogyrinus
Length: 14.8 feet
Diet: Fish, other amphibians
Habitat: Swamps
Discovered: Europe
Era: Carboniferous to Permian

Amphibian evolution

The earliest known amphibians are believed to be the ichthyostegalians. During the Carboniferous, the environment was hospitable to the amphibians. At the end of this period, as the land became dryer, some species evolved into the early reptiles. Lissamphibia, which includes all modern amphibians, could have branched off from Temnospondyli and/or Lepospondyli at some time between the Late Carboniferous and the Early Triassic.

Amphibian classifications

Amphibians can generally be divided into 3 subclasses;

Lepospondyli –
The earliest proto-reptile, emerged during the Carboniferous lasting until the Permian. Eogyrinus was an example.

Temnospondyli –
The earliest amphibians that existed from the Devonian to the Cretaceous. They were ancestors of most reptiles. Eryops was an example.

Lissamphibia –
From the Triassic to the present, they are further subdivided into Apoda, Caudata, and Anura.

Eryops

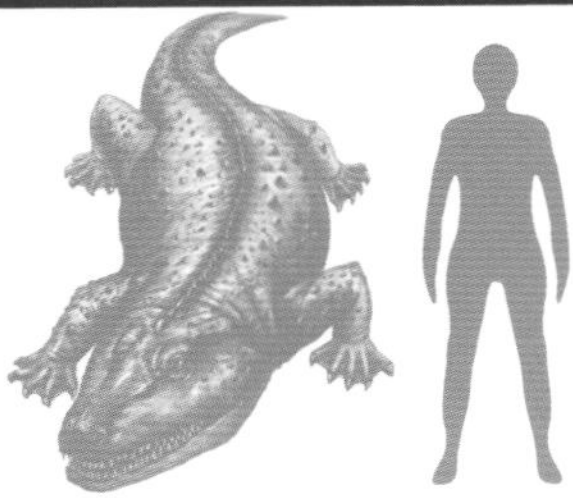

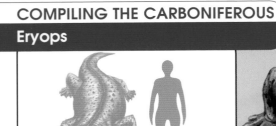

Scientific name: Eryops
Length: 5 to 6.5 feet
Diet: Other animals
Habitat: Sub-desert areas
Discovered: North America and Europe
Era: Carboniferous to Permian

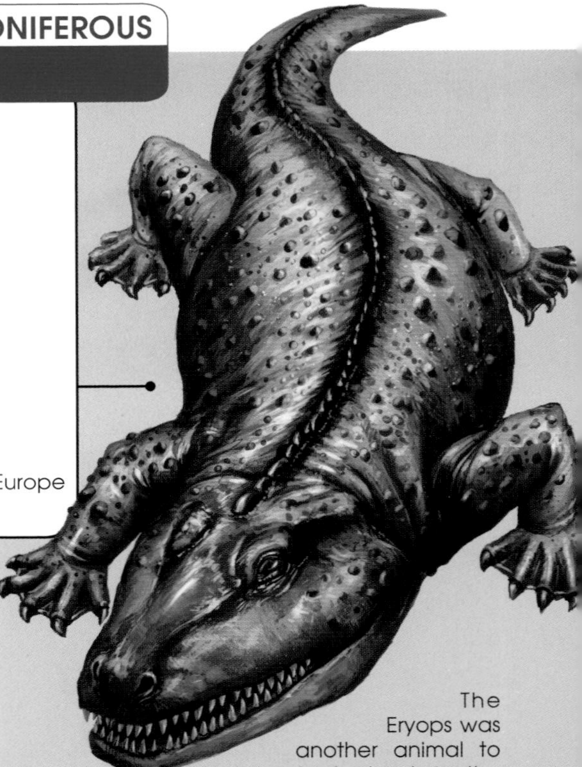

Eryops bone structure

Hard, flat, and studded, its head was meant for tough living.

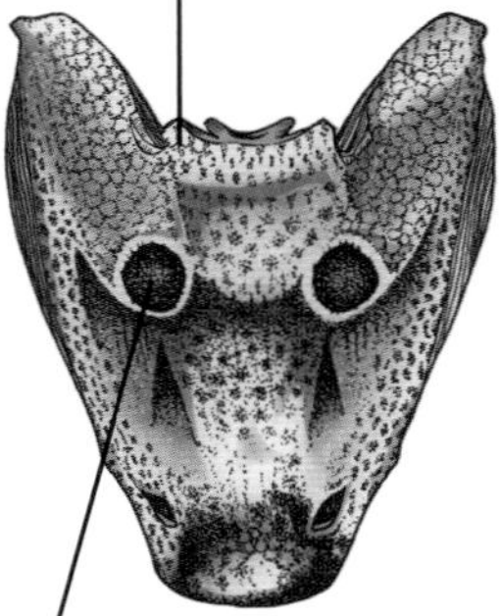
Large, upturned orbit.

The Eryops was another animal to migrate to land, in the manner of the Ichthyostega. It retained some fishlike traits, but adapted powerful legs and bones capable of supporting a heavy body, with gills that evolved into ears.

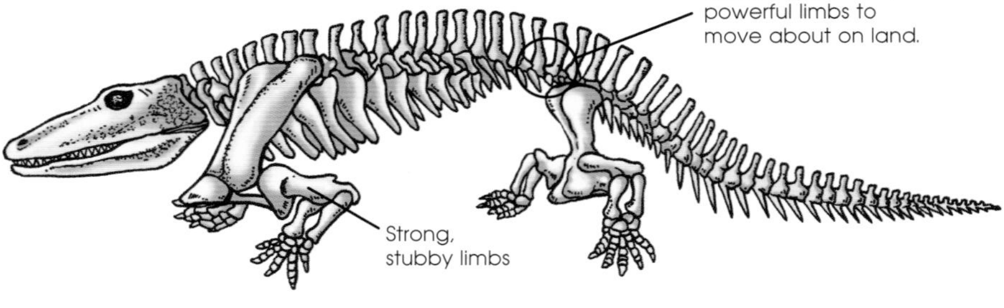
Spinal column and powerful limbs to move about on land.
Strong, stubby limbs

CHAPTER 4
SAYING GOODBYE

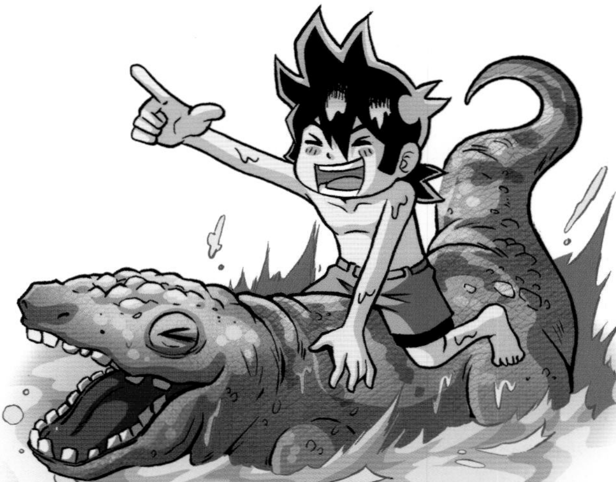

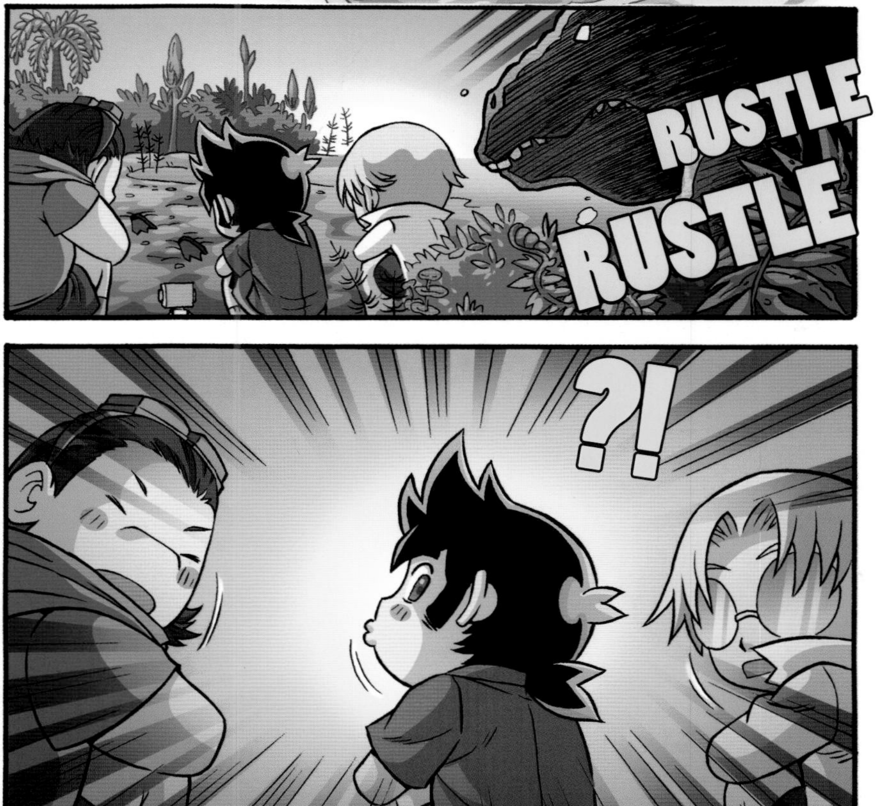
RUSTLE
RUSTLE
?!

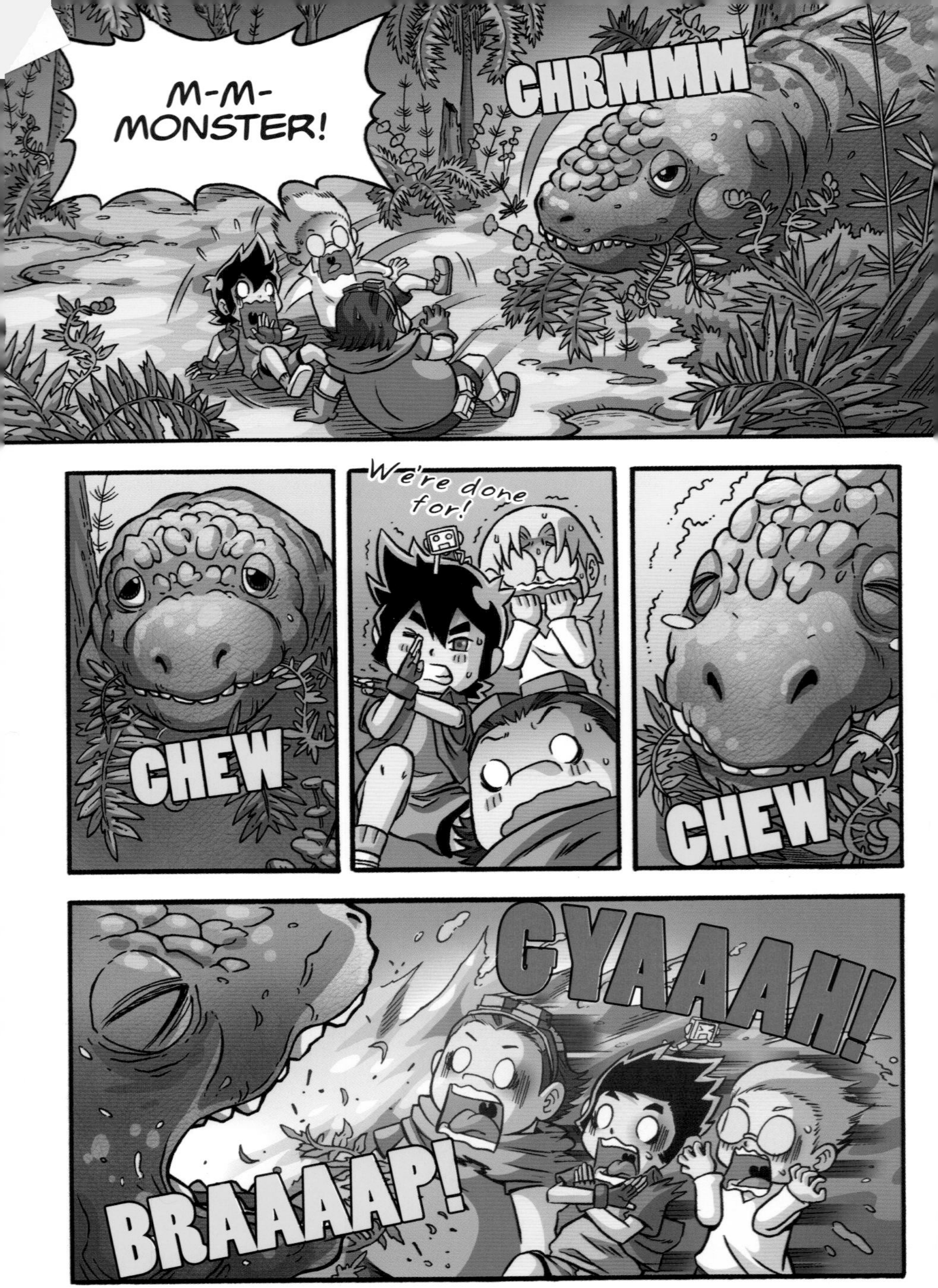
M-M-
MONSTER!
CHRMMM
We're done for!
CHEW
CHEW
CYAAAAH!
BRAAAAP!

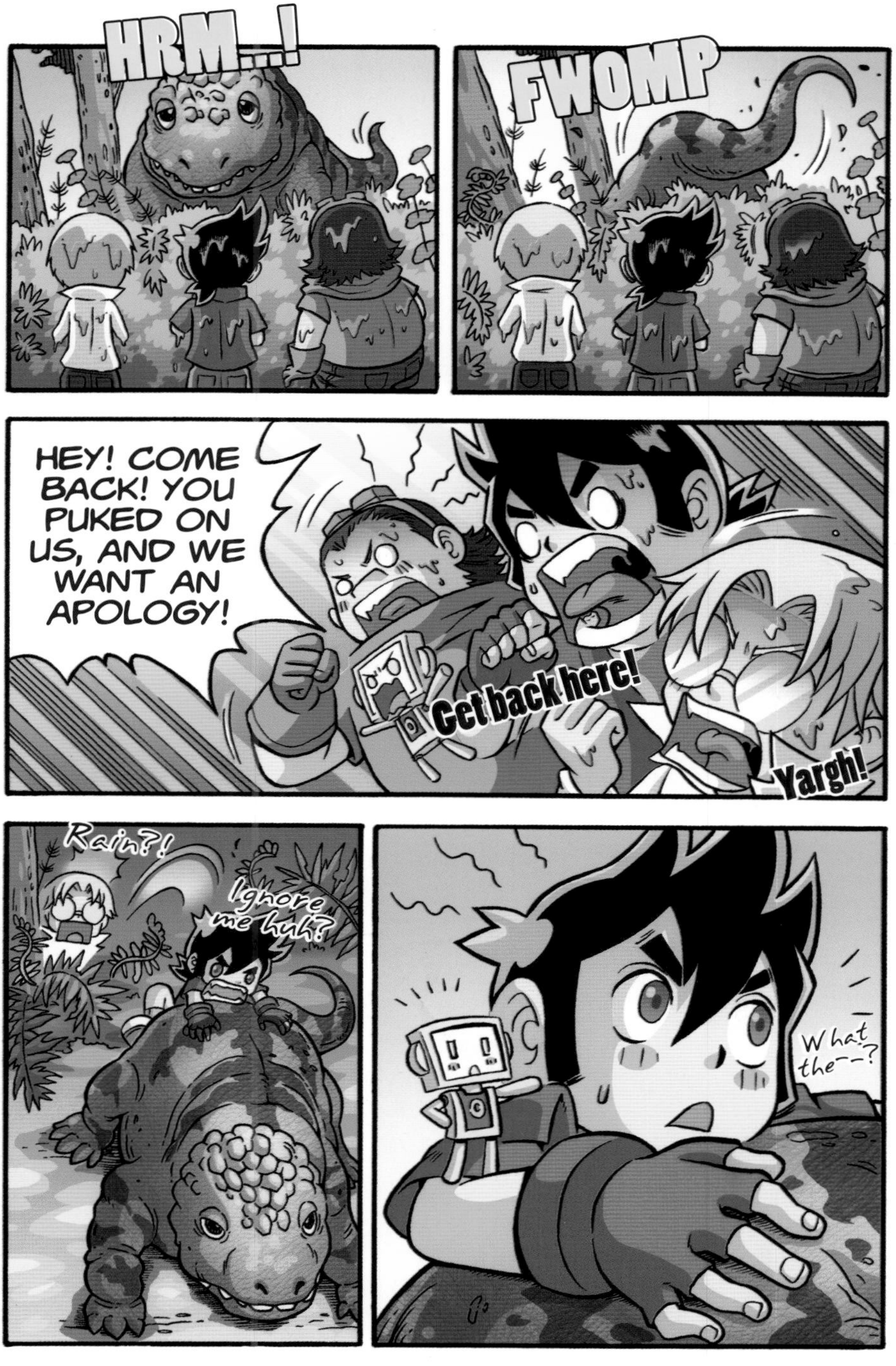
HRM...!
FWOMP
HEY! COME BACK! YOU PUKED ON US, AND WE WANT AN APOLOGY!
Get back here!
Yargh!
Rain?!
Ignore me huh?
What the--?

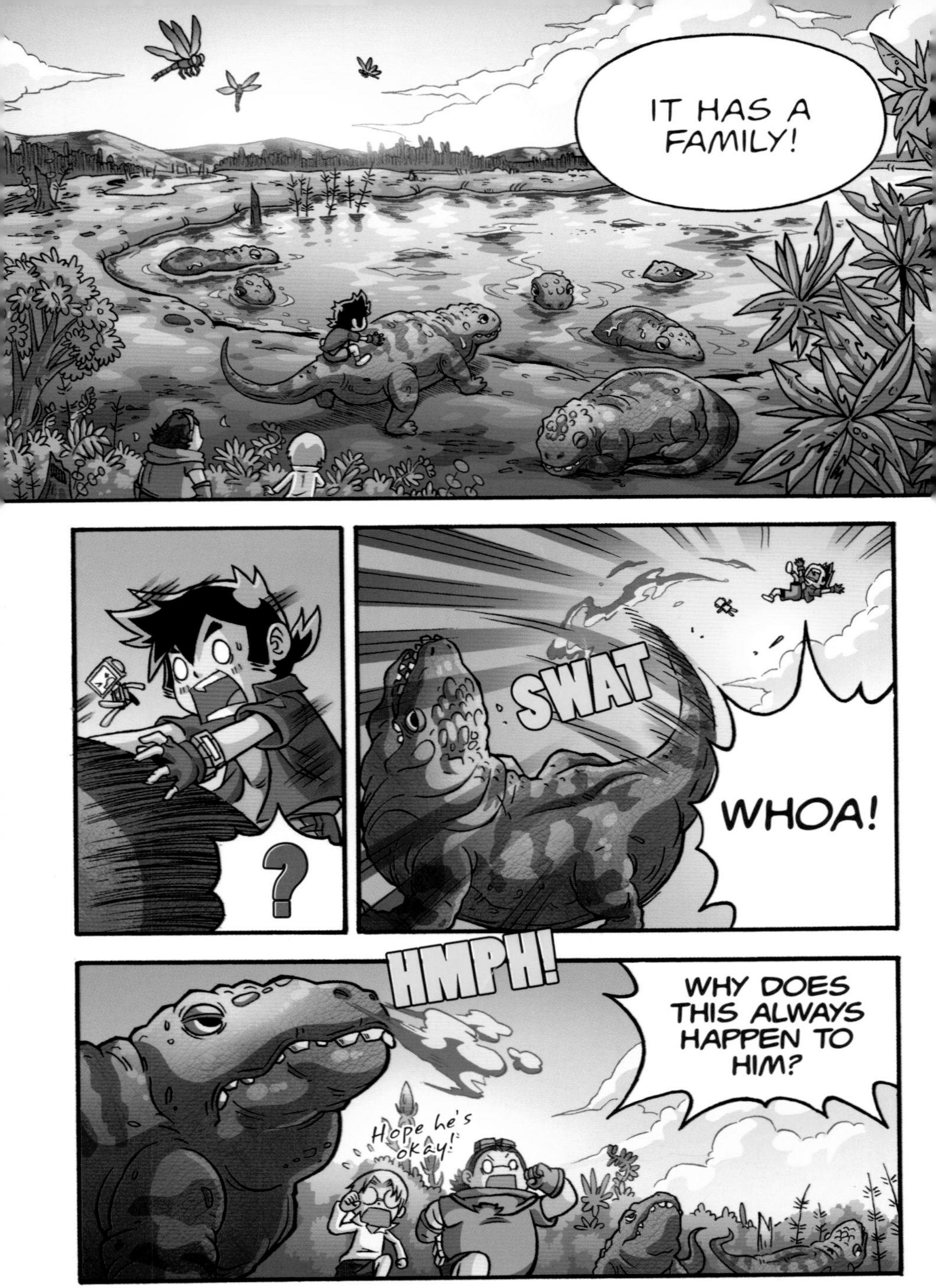
IT HAS A FAMILY!
?
SWAT
WHOA!
HMPH!
WHY DOES THIS ALWAYS HAPPEN TO HIM?
Hope he's okay!

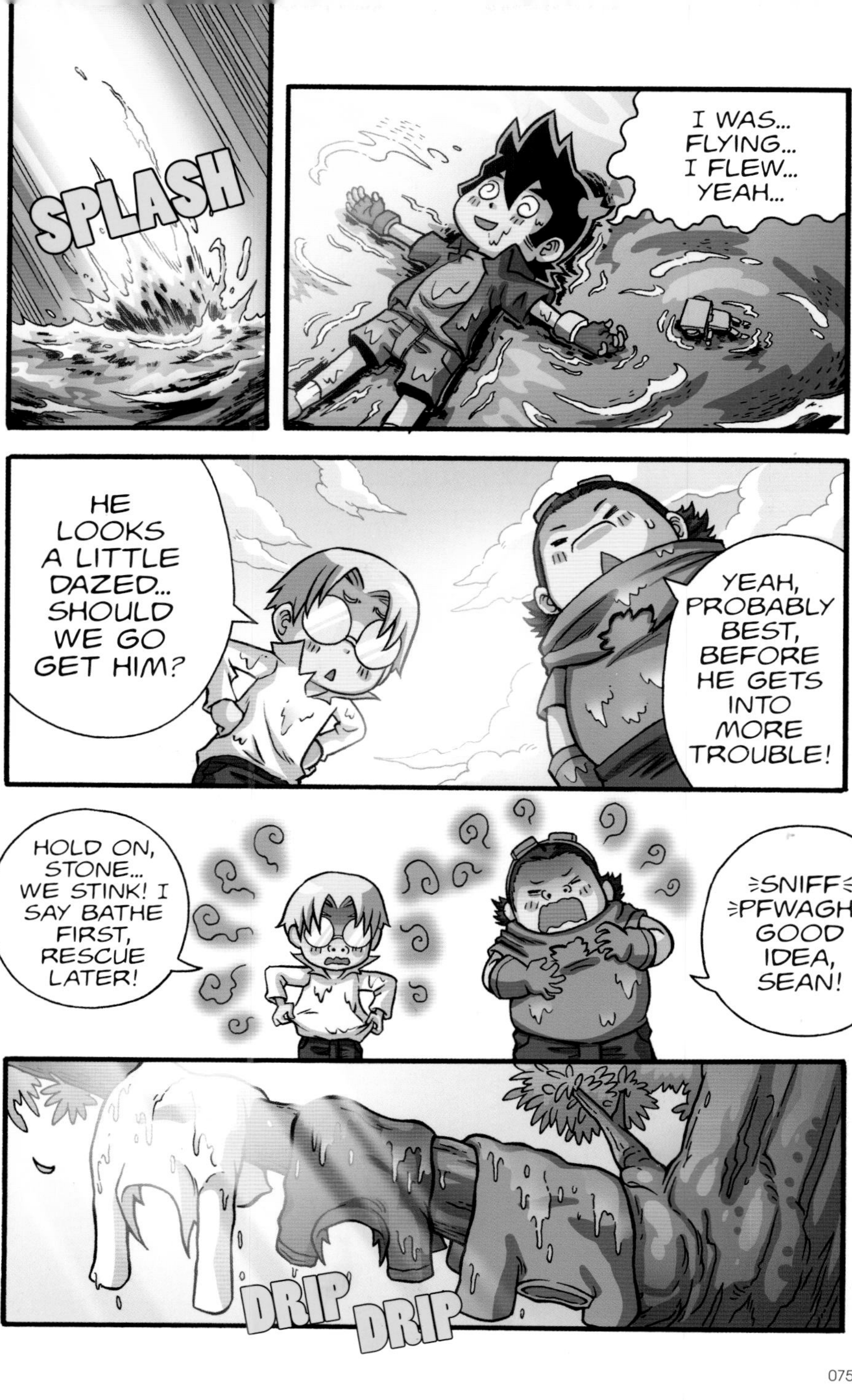
SPLASH
I WAS... FLYING... I FLEW... YEAH...
HE LOOKS A LITTLE DAZED... SHOULD WE GO GET HIM?
YEAH, PROBABLY BEST, BEFORE HE GETS INTO MORE TROUBLE!
HOLD ON, STONE... WE STINK! I SAY BATHE FIRST, RESCUE LATER!
SNIFF PFWAGH! GOOD IDEA, SEAN!
DRIP DRIP

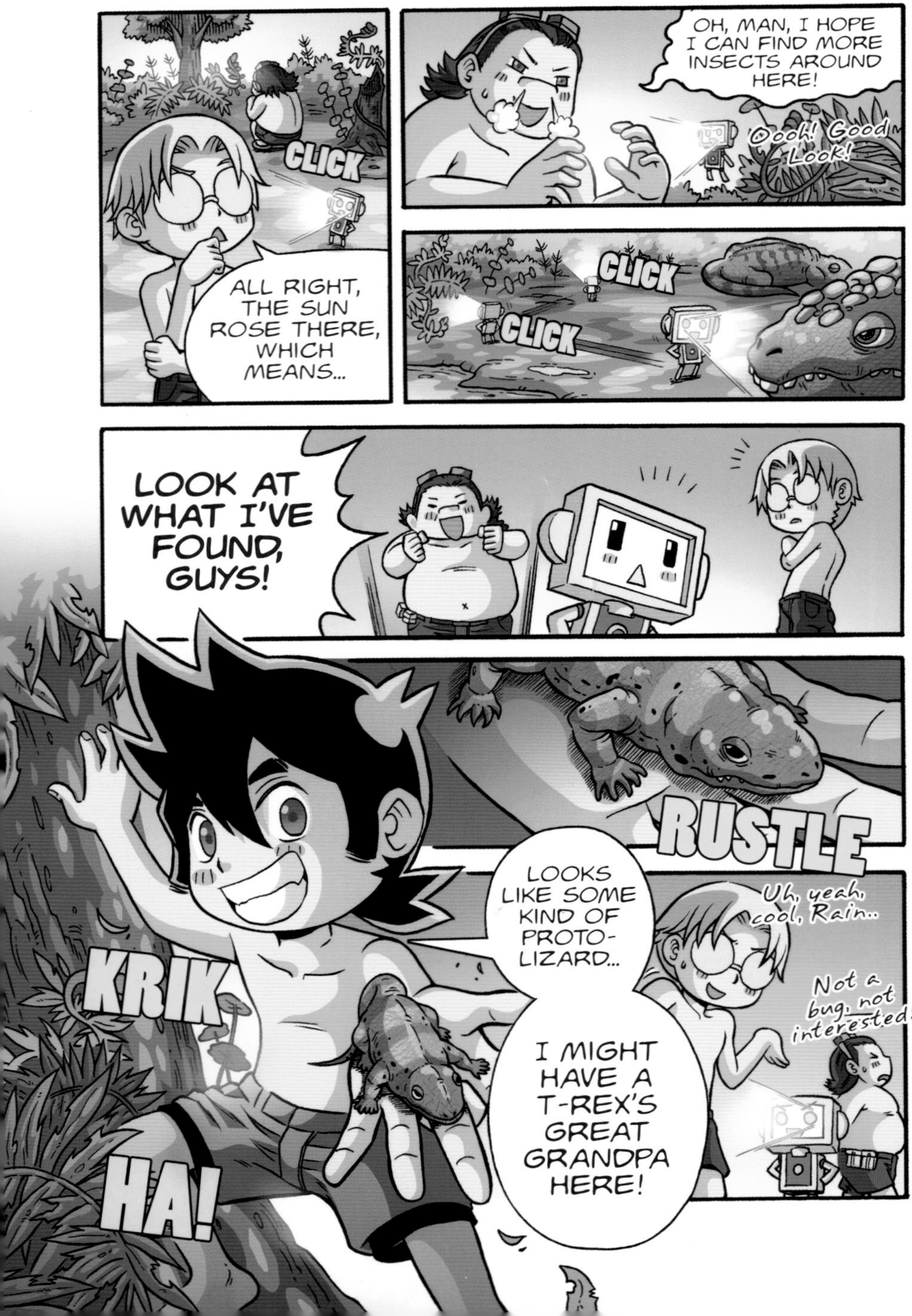
CLICK
ALL RIGHT, THE SUN ROSE THERE, WHICH MEANS...
OH, MAN, I HOPE I CAN FIND MORE INSECTS AROUND HERE!
Oooh! Good Look!
CLICK
CLICK
LOOK AT WHAT I'VE FOUND, GUYS!
RUSTLE
KRIK
HA!
LOOKS LIKE SOME KIND OF PROTO-LIZARD...
I MIGHT HAVE A T-REX'S GREAT GRANDPA HERE!
Uh, yeah, cool, Rain...
Not a bug, not interested!

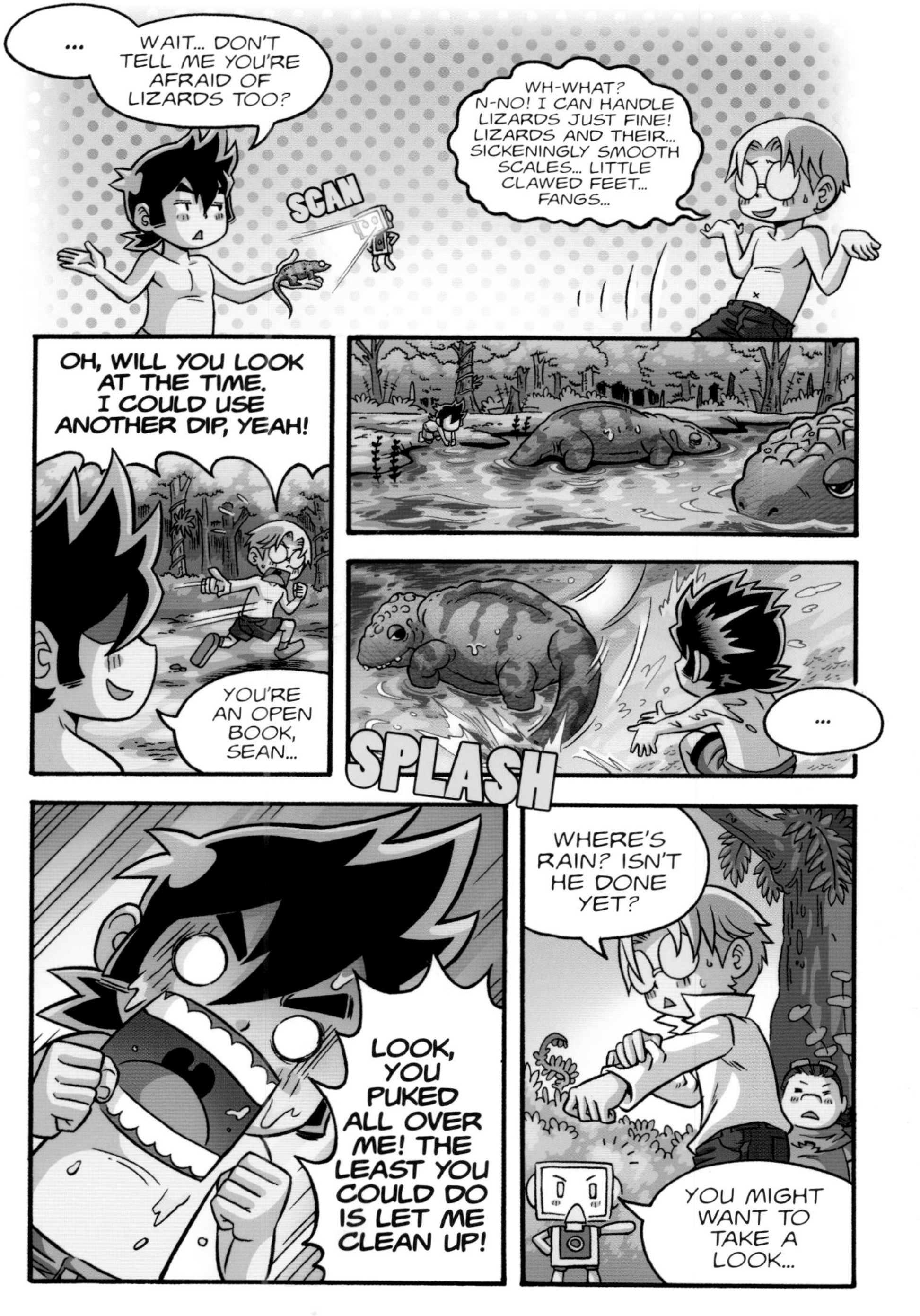
...
WAIT... DON'T TELL ME YOU'RE AFRAID OF LIZARDS TOO?
SCAN
WH-WHAT? N-NO! I CAN HANDLE LIZARDS JUST FINE! LIZARDS AND THEIR... SICKENINGLY SMOOTH SCALES... LITTLE CLAWED FEET... FANGS...
OH, WILL YOU LOOK AT THE TIME. I COULD USE ANOTHER DIP, YEAH!
YOU'RE AN OPEN BOOK, SEAN...
...
SPLASH
LOOK, YOU PUKED ALL OVER ME! THE LEAST YOU COULD DO IS LET ME CLEAN UP!
WHERE'S RAIN? ISN'T HE DONE YET?
YOU MIGHT WANT TO TAKE A LOOK...

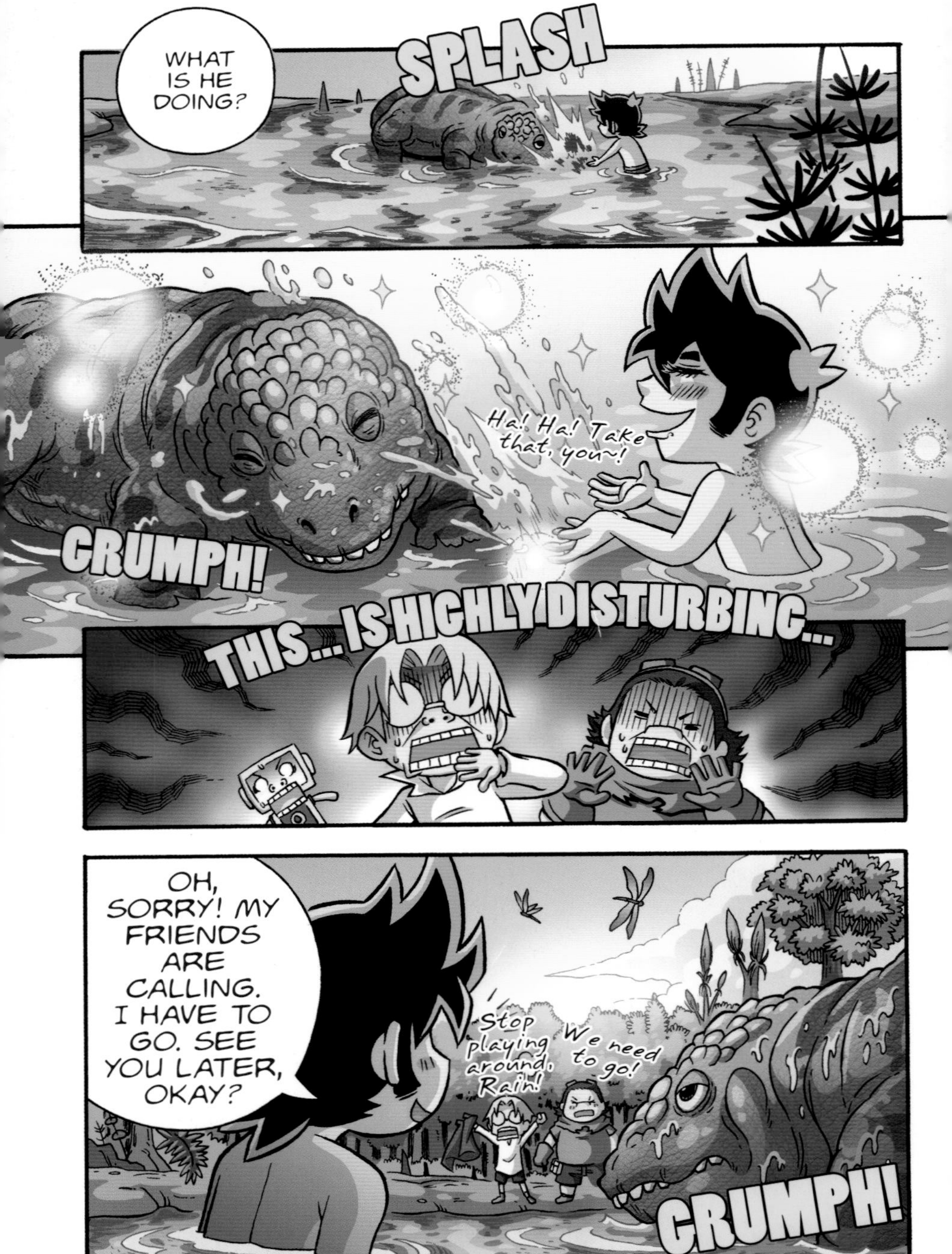
WHAT IS HE DOING?
SPLASH
Ha! Ha! Take that, you~!
CRUMPH!
THIS... IS HIGHLY DISTURBING...
OH, SORRY! MY FRIENDS ARE CALLING. I HAVE TO GO. SEE YOU LATER, OKAY?
Stop playing around, Rain!
We need to go!
CRUMPH!

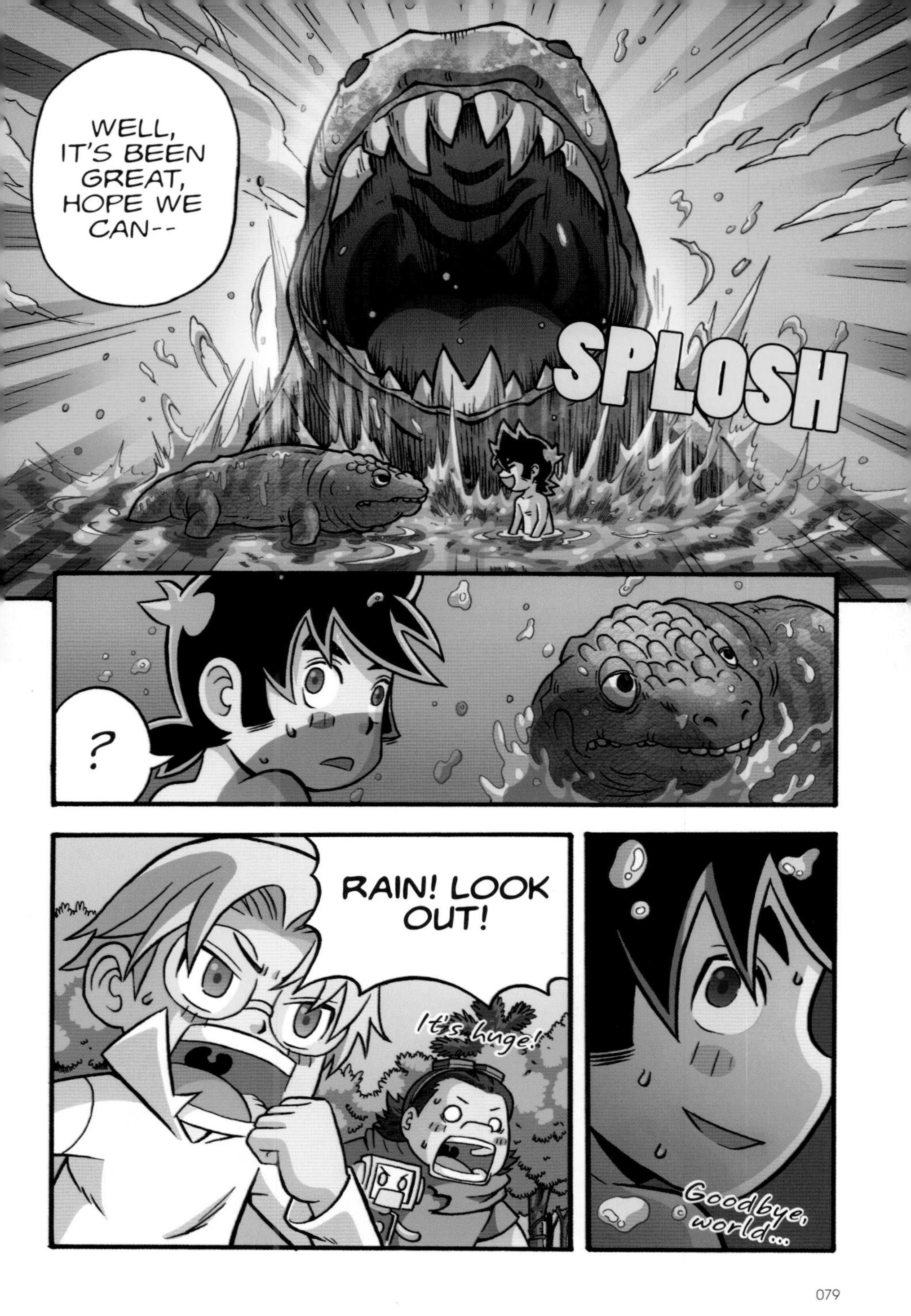
WELL, IT'S BEEN GREAT, HOPE WE CAN--
SPLOSH
?
RAIN! LOOK OUT!
It's huge!
Goodbye, world...

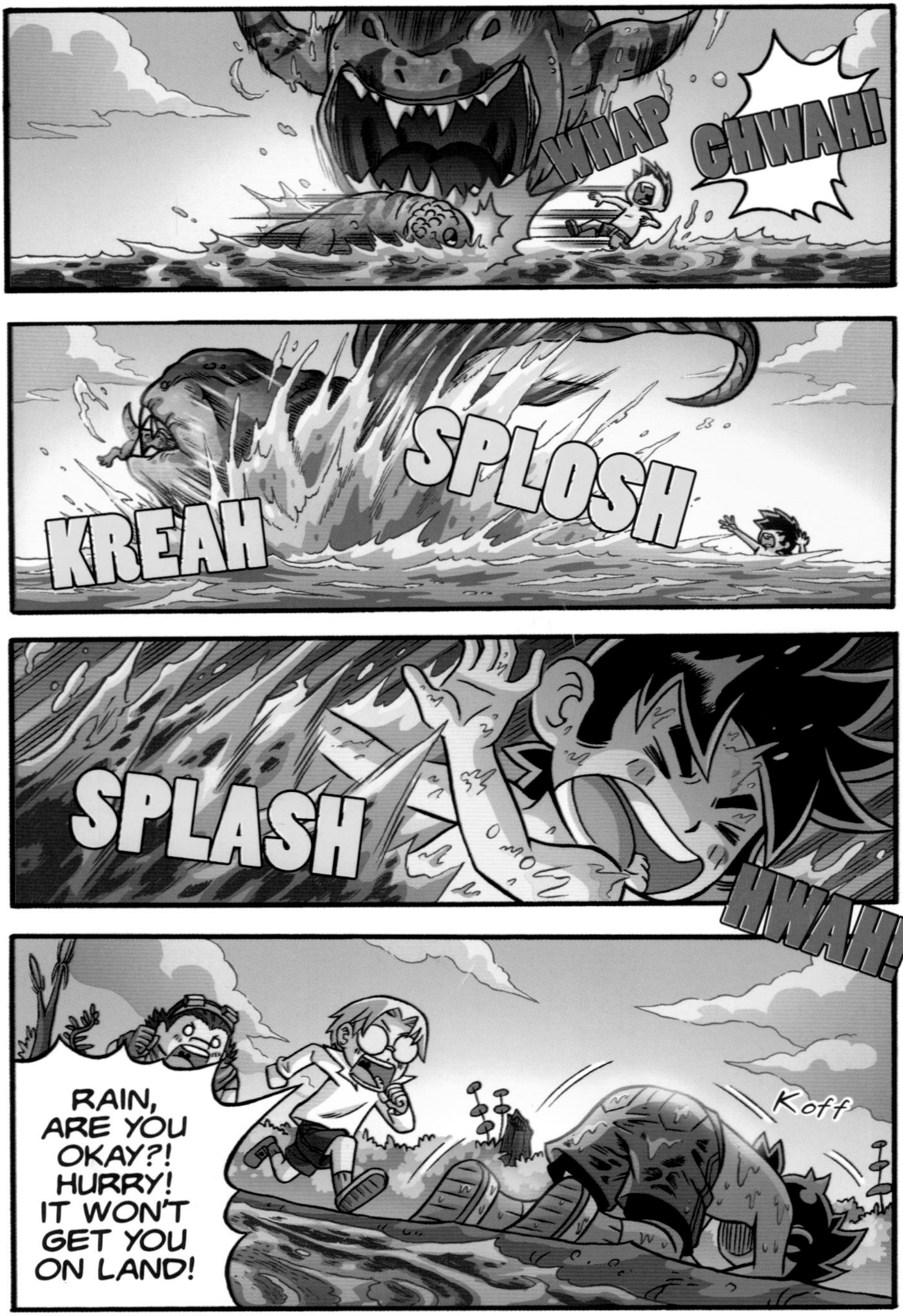
WHAP
CHWAH!
KREAH
SPLOSH
SPLASH
HWAH!
RAIN, ARE YOU OKAY?! HURRY! IT WON'T GET YOU ON LAND!
Koff

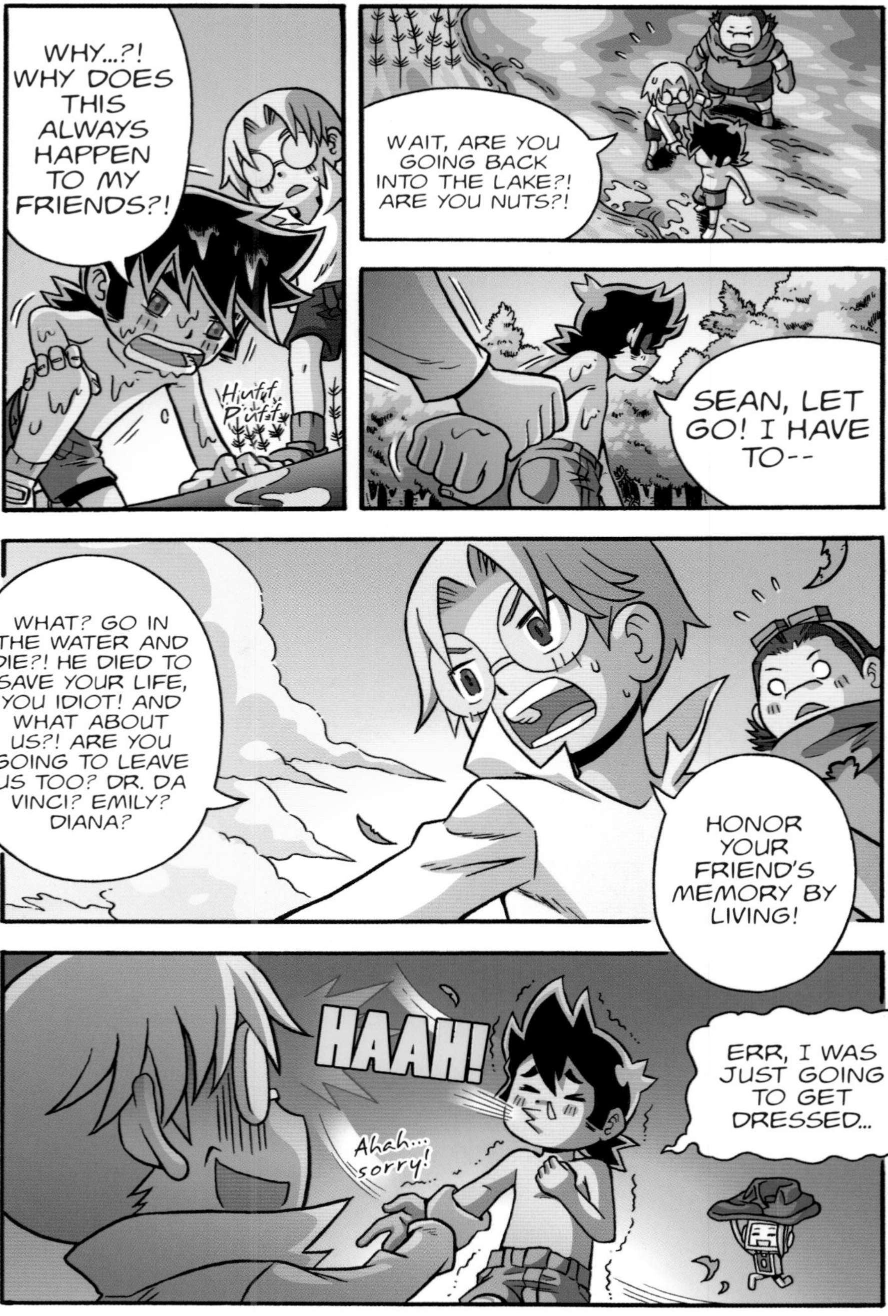
WHY...?! WHY DOES THIS ALWAYS HAPPEN TO MY FRIENDS?!
Huff Puff
WAIT, ARE YOU GOING BACK INTO THE LAKE?! ARE YOU NUTS?!
SEAN, LET GO! I HAVE TO--
WHAT? GO IN THE WATER AND DIE?! HE DIED TO SAVE YOUR LIFE, YOU IDIOT! AND WHAT ABOUT US?! ARE YOU GOING TO LEAVE US TOO? DR. DA VINCI? EMILY? DIANA?
HONOR YOUR FRIEND'S MEMORY BY LIVING!
HAAH!
Ahah... sorry!
ERR, I WAS JUST GOING TO GET DRESSED...

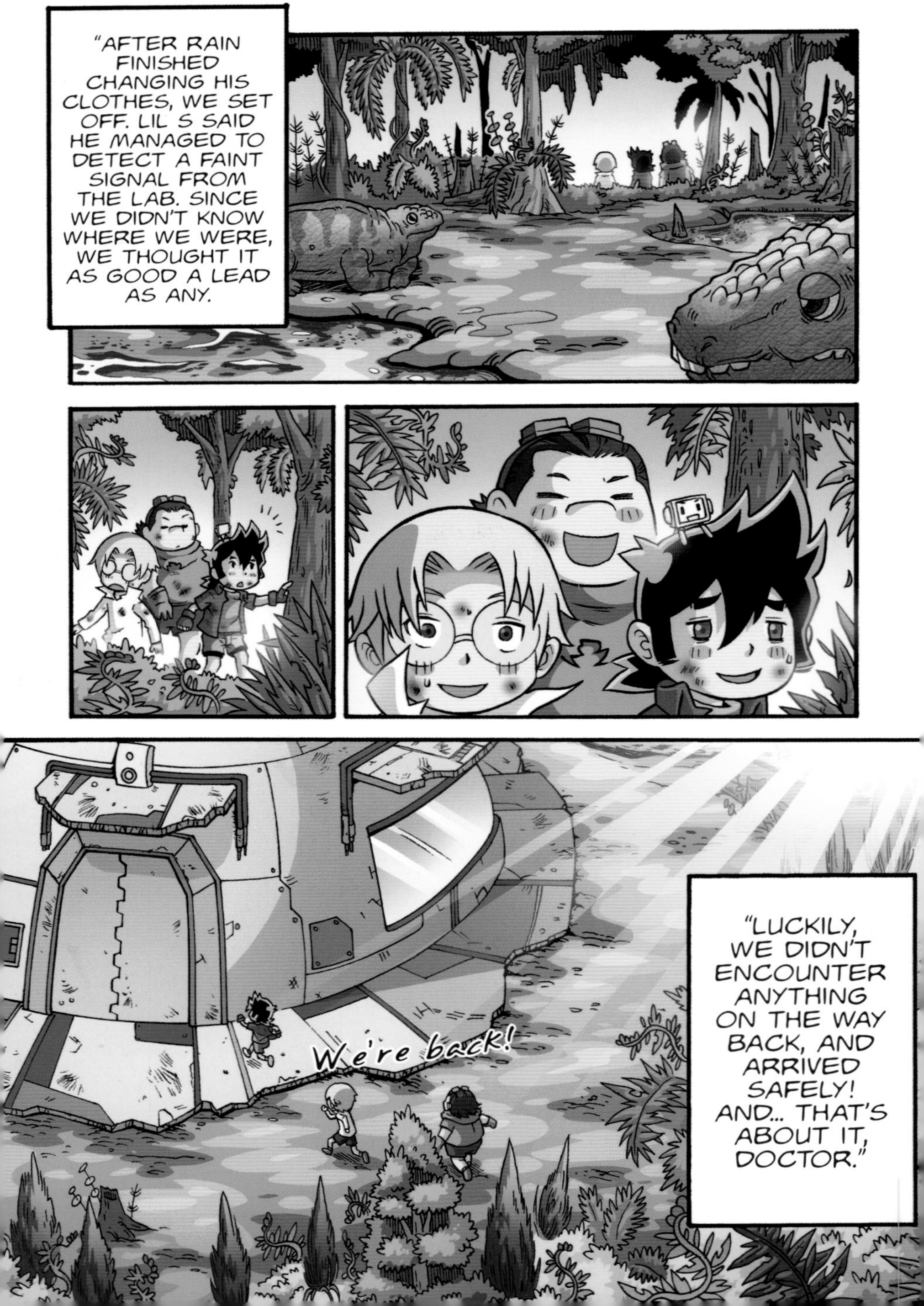
"AFTER RAIN FINISHED CHANGING HIS CLOTHES, WE SET OFF. LIL' S SAID HE MANAGED TO DETECT A FAINT SIGNAL FROM THE LAB. SINCE WE DIDN'T KNOW WHERE WE WERE, WE THOUGHT IT AS GOOD A LEAD AS ANY.
"LUCKILY, WE DIDN'T ENCOUNTER ANYTHING ON THE WAY BACK, AND ARRIVED SAFELY! AND... THAT'S ABOUT IT, DOCTOR."
We're back!

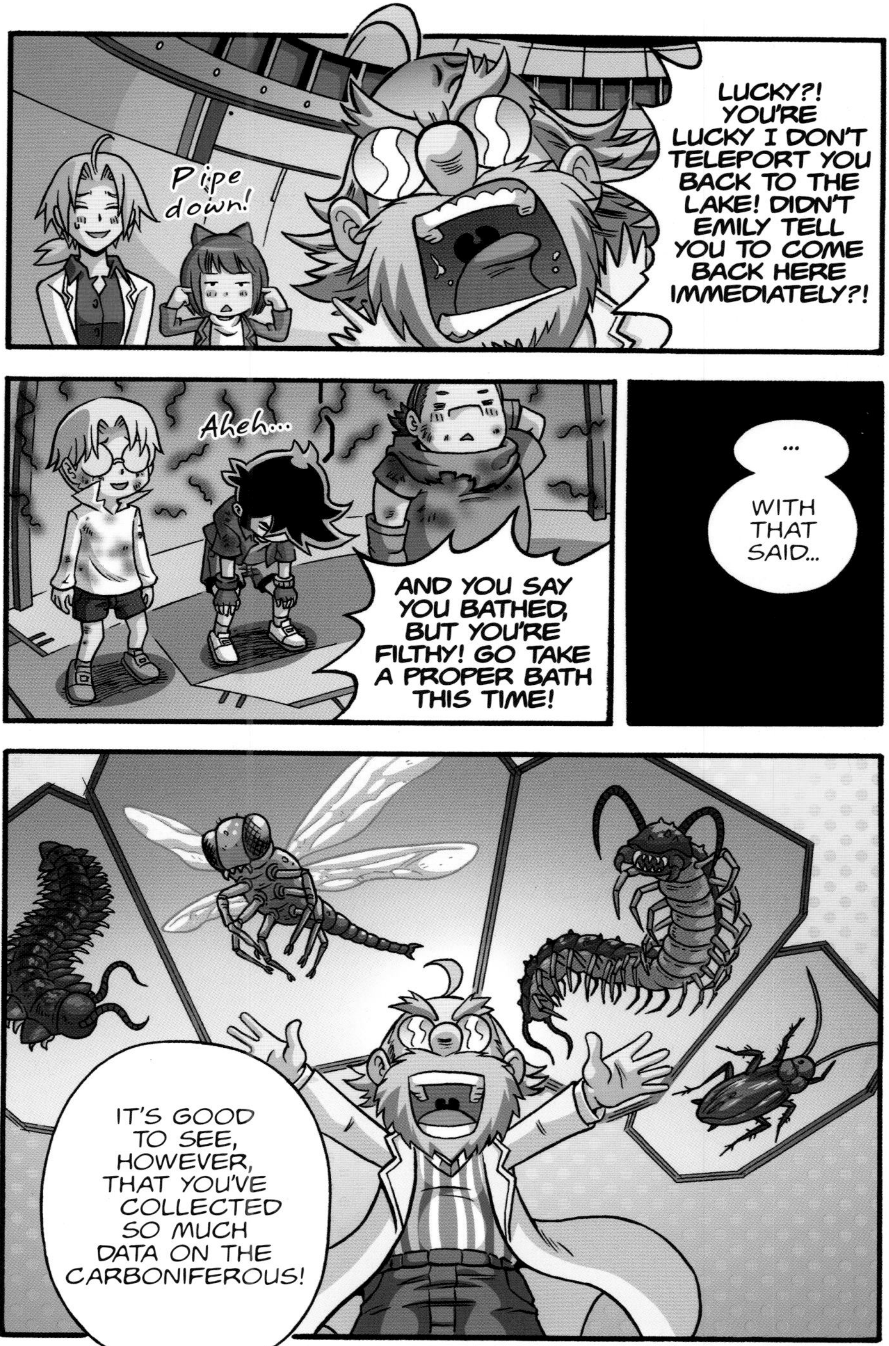
LUCKY?! YOU'RE LUCKY I DON'T TELEPORT YOU BACK TO THE LAKE! DIDN'T EMILY TELL YOU TO COME BACK HERE IMMEDIATELY?!
Pipe down!
Aheh...
AND YOU SAY YOU BATHED, BUT YOU'RE FILTHY! GO TAKE A PROPER BATH THIS TIME!
...
WITH THAT SAID...
IT'S GOOD TO SEE, HOWEVER, THAT YOU'VE COLLECTED SO MUCH DATA ON THE CARBONIFEROUS!

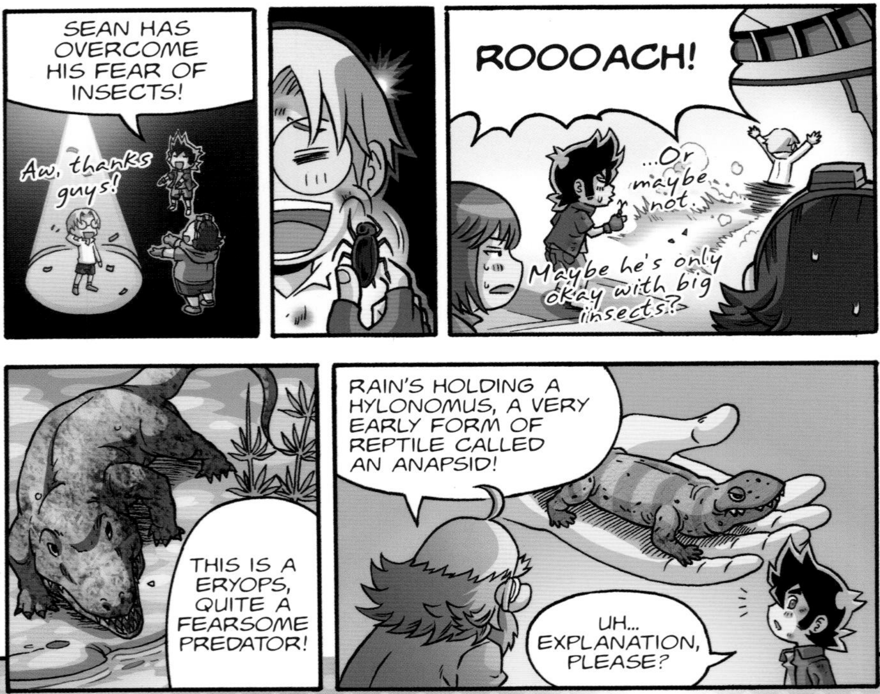

SEAN HAS OVERCOME HIS FEAR OF INSECTS!
Aw, thanks guys!
ROOOACH!
...Or maybe not.
Maybe he's only okay with big insects?
THIS IS A ERYOPS, QUITE A FEARSOME PREDATOR!
RAIN'S HOLDING A HYLONOMUS, A VERY EARLY FORM OF REPTILE CALLED AN ANAPSID!
UH... EXPLANATION, PLEASE?

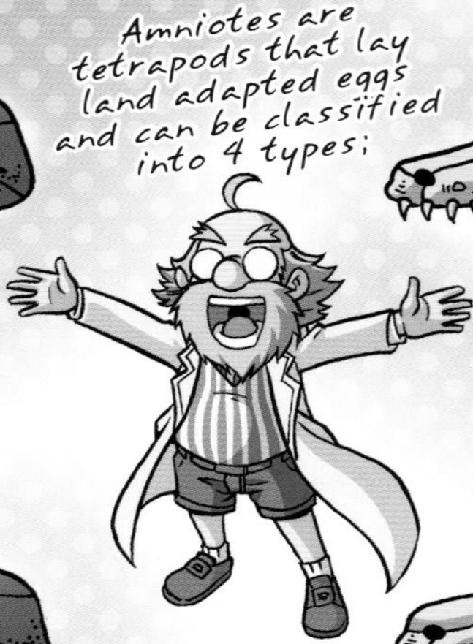

Amniotes are tetrapods that lay land adapted eggs and can be classified into 4 types;

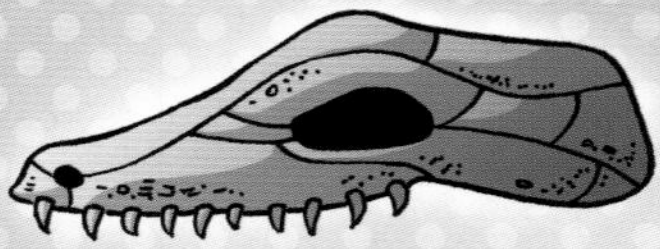

Anapsids
They are amniotes with no temporal openings. The earliest reptiles, the cotylosaurs were anapsids, as are modern turtles.

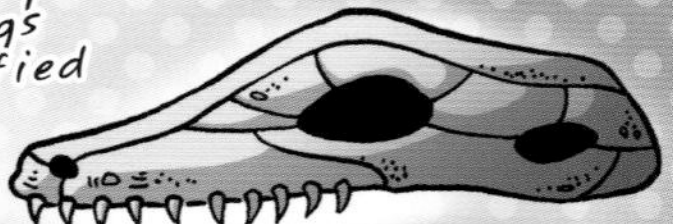

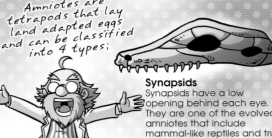

Synapsids
Synapsids have a low opening behind each eye. They are one of the evolved amniotes that include mammal-like reptiles and true mammals. The Dimetrodon was an example of the pre-mammalian synapsids.

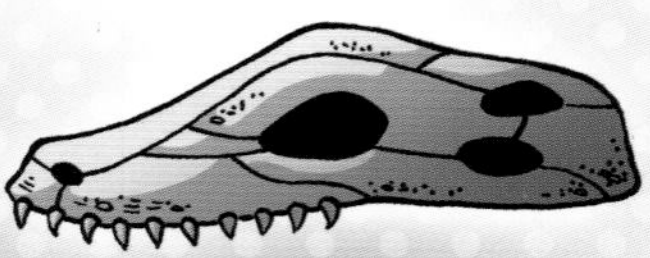

Diapsids
They are reptiles that had 2 holes in each side of their skulls. Living diapsids include all crocodiles, lizards and snakes.

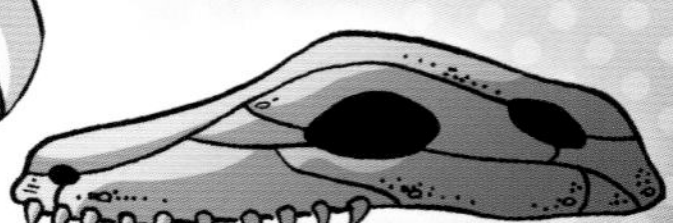

Euryapsids
Euryapsids were reptiles that had one opening behind their eye sockets. There are no surviving descendants of the euryapsids. Prehistoric examples were Ichthyosaurs, Plesiosaurs, and Placodonts.

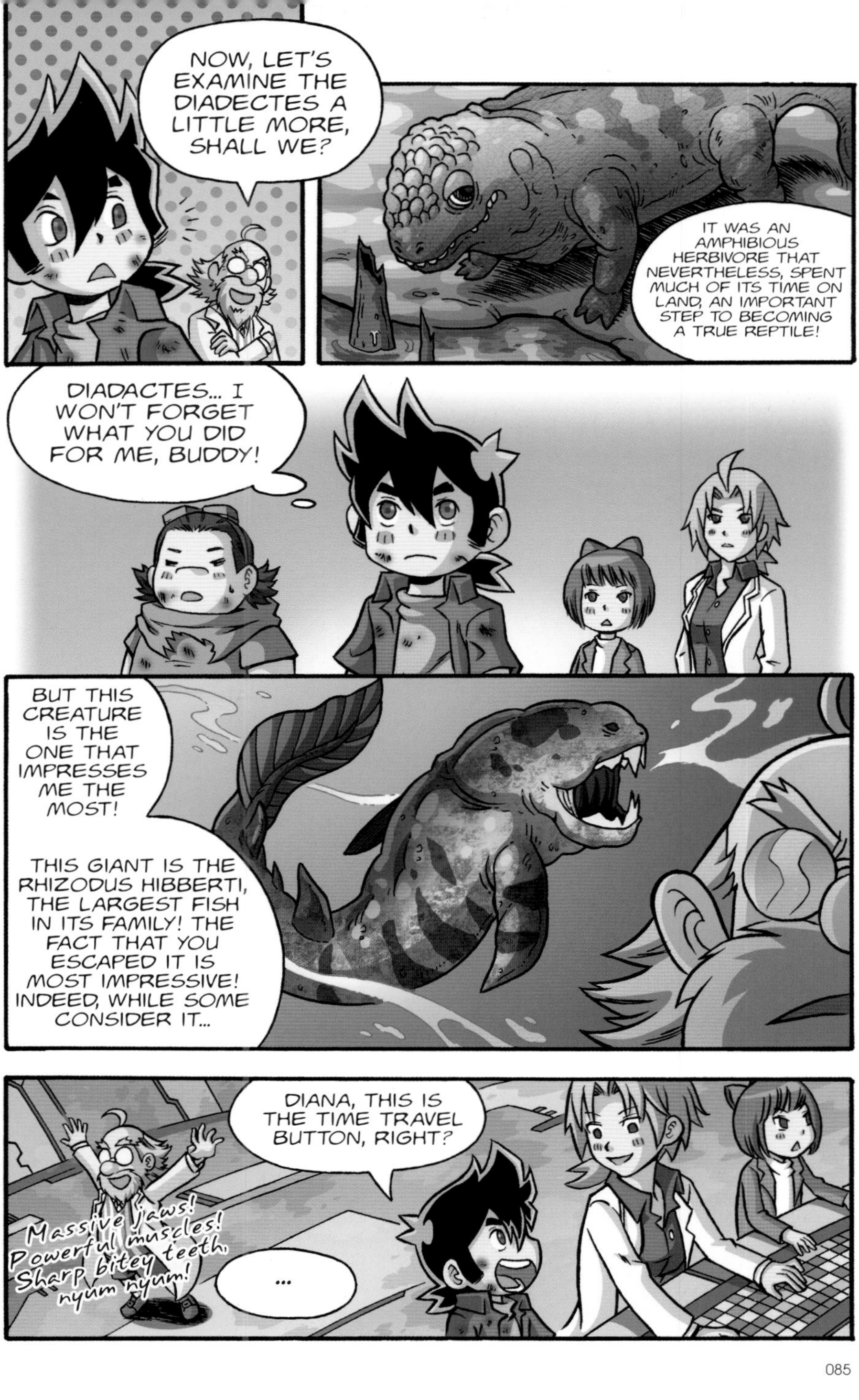
NOW, LET'S EXAMINE THE DIADECTES A LITTLE MORE, SHALL WE?
IT WAS AN AMPHIBIOUS HERBIVORE THAT NEVERTHELESS, SPENT MUCH OF ITS TIME ON LAND, AN IMPORTANT STEP TO BECOMING A TRUE REPTILE!
DIADACTES... I WON'T FORGET WHAT YOU DID FOR ME, BUDDY!
BUT THIS CREATURE IS THE ONE THAT IMPRESSES ME THE MOST!
THIS GIANT IS THE RHIZODUS HIBBERTI, THE LARGEST FISH IN ITS FAMILY! THE FACT THAT YOU ESCAPED IT IS MOST IMPRESSIVE! INDEED, WHILE SOME CONSIDER IT...
DIANA, THIS IS THE TIME TRAVEL BUTTON, RIGHT?
Massive jaws! Powerful muscles! Sharp bitey teeth, nyum nyum!
...

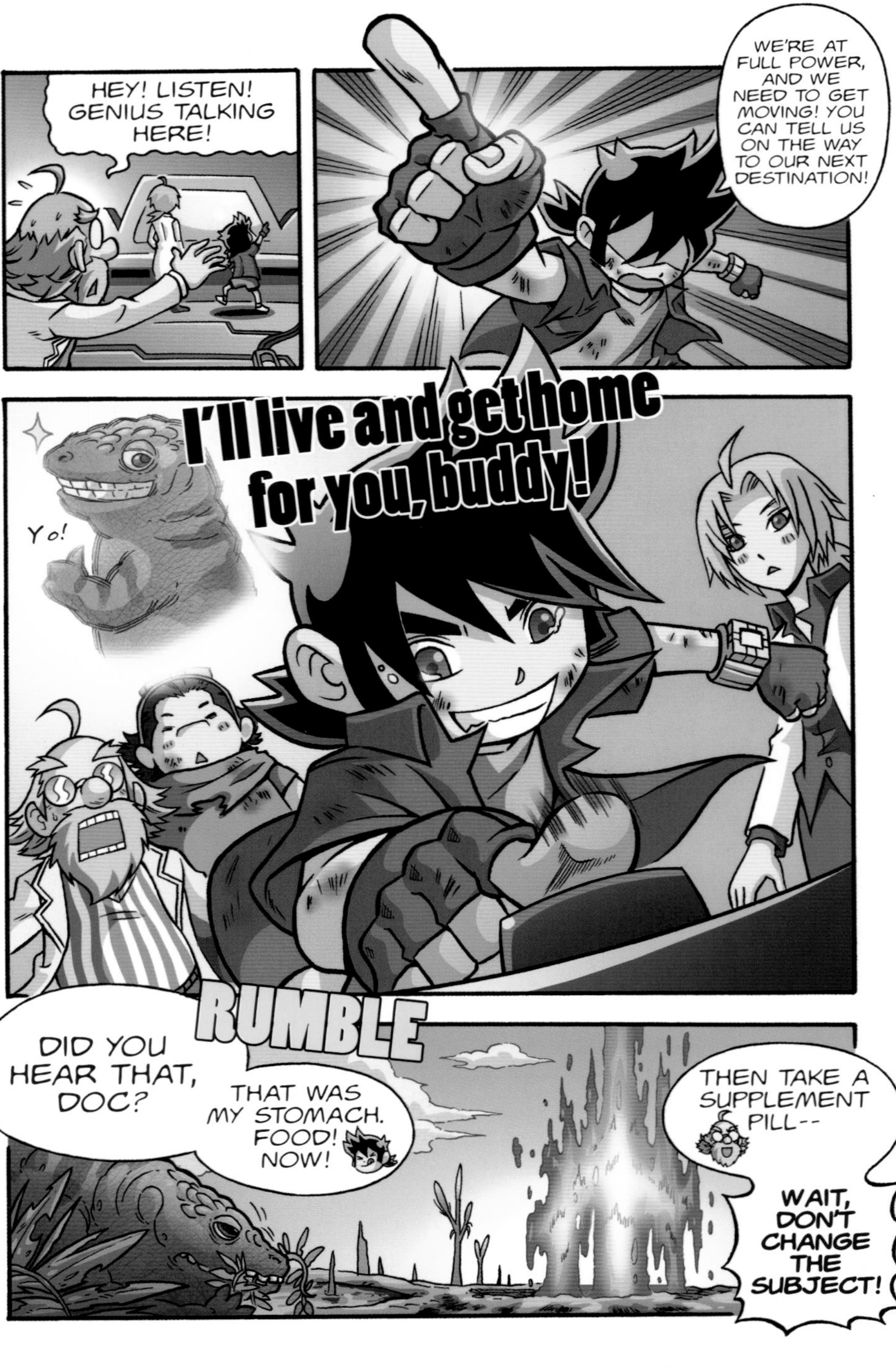
HEY! LISTEN! GENIUS TALKING HERE!
WE'RE AT FULL POWER, AND WE NEED TO GET MOVING! YOU CAN TELL US ON THE WAY TO OUR NEXT DESTINATION!
I'll live and get home for you, buddy!
Yo!
RUMBLE
DID YOU HEAR THAT, DOC?
THAT WAS MY STOMACH. FOOD! NOW!
THEN TAKE A SUPPLEMENT PILL--
WAIT, DON'T CHANGE THE SUBJECT!

COMPILING THE CARBONIFEROUS

Hylonomus

Hylonomus is the earliest known anapsid, and perhaps the earliest classified reptile as well. Like most modern lizards, it had a flat, triangular head, and long, tooth-lined jaws.

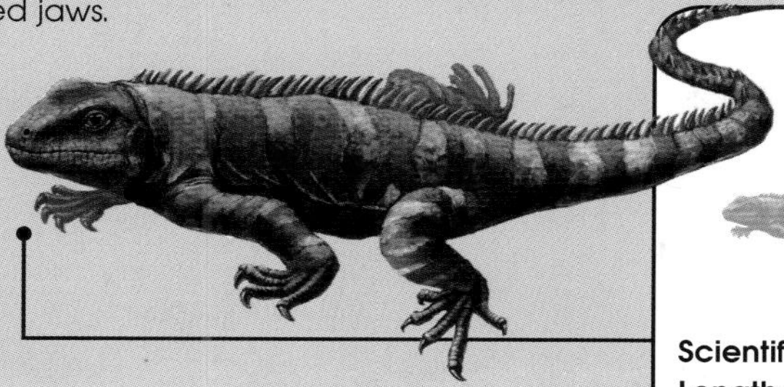

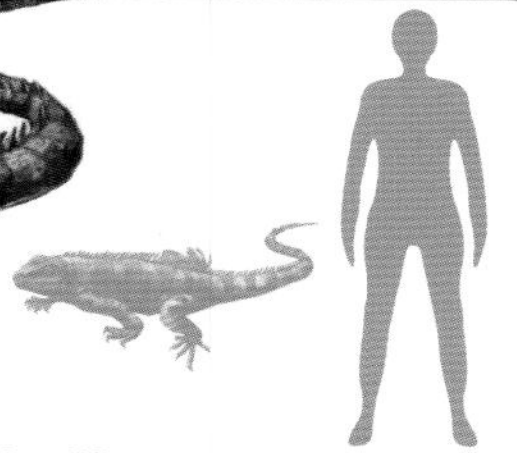

Scientific name: Hylonomus
Length: 7.9 to 27.6 inches
Diet: Insects
Habitat: Tropical swamps
Discovered: Canada
Era: Late Carboniferous

Differences between reptile and amphibian skulls

Reptile skuls
Early reptiles retained an anapsid skull inherited from their amphibian ancestors. The base of the skull is level.

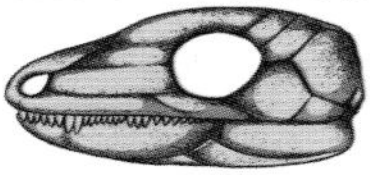

Reptiles have hinged jaws, capable of biting off and chewing large pieces of food, whether plant or animal.

Amphibian skull
Early amphibians had membrane-covered holes in their skulls.

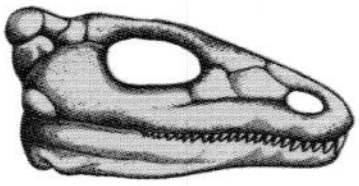

Amphibians have simplified jaws called mandibles, capable only of opening and closing.

COMPILING THE CARBONIFEROUS

Rhizodus hibberti

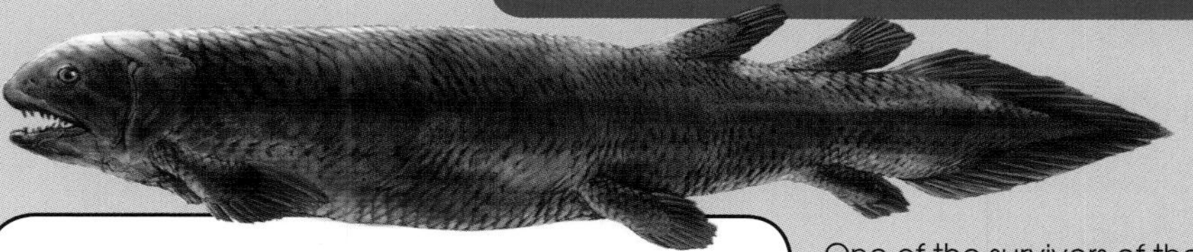

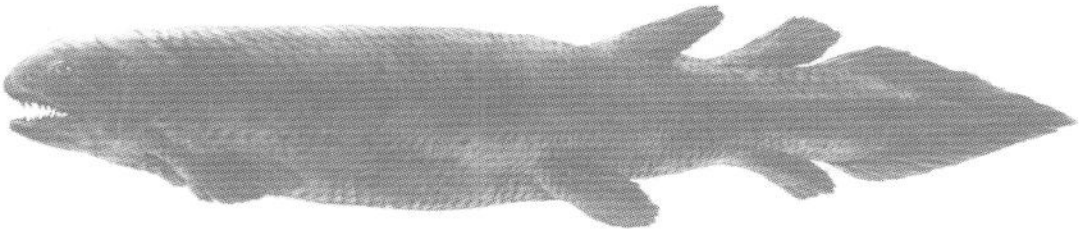

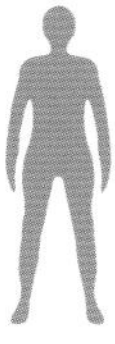

Scientific name: Rhizodus hibberti
Length: 23 to 26 feet
Diet: Fish
Habitat: Estuaries, rivers, and lakes
Discovered: Europe and North America
Era: Late Carboniferous

One of the survivors of the Devonian extinction, the massive Rhizodus hibberti was an ambush predator. Its arsenal consisted of a mouthful of sharp fangs and tusks, some of which grew up to 2 inches in length!

CLADOGRAM OF TETRAPODS AND EARLY AMPHIBIANS

The early tetrapods were the first vertebrates with four limbs, having evolved from sarcopterygian (lobe-finned fishes) in the Devonian. Early tetrapods spent a great deal of time in the water, and only came on land for short periods. As their limbs and vertebrae evolved, however, they became much more capable of moving about on land.

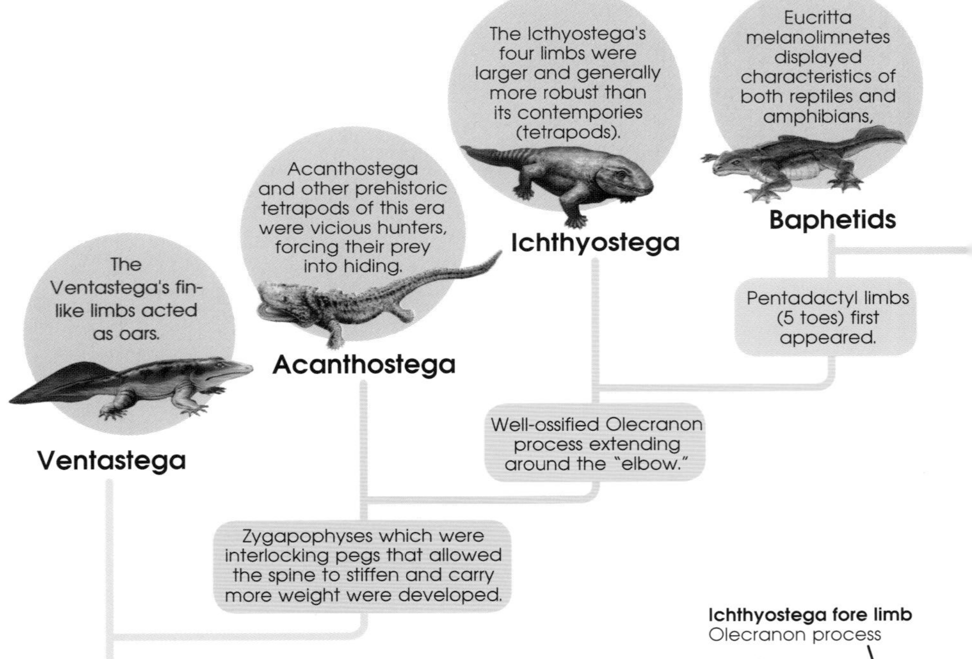

The Icthyostega's four limbs were larger and generally more robust than its contempories (tetrapods).

Eucritta melanolimnetes displayed characteristics of both reptiles and amphibians,

Baphetids

Acanthostega and other prehistoric tetrapods of this era were vicious hunters, forcing their prey into hiding.

Ichthyostega

The Ventastega's fin-like limbs acted as oars.

Pentadactyl limbs (5 toes) first appeared.

Acanthostega

Well-ossified Olecranon process extending around the "elbow."

Ventastega

Zygapophyses which were interlocking pegs that allowed the spine to stiffen and carry more weight were developed.

Ichthyostega fore limb
Olecranon process

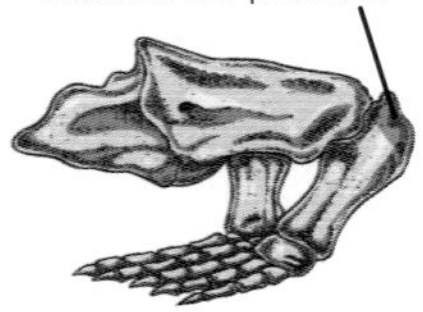

Tetrapods

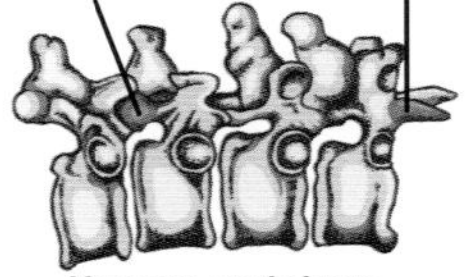

Prezygapophyses   Postzygapophyses

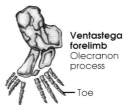

Ventastega forelimb
Olecranon process

Human vertebrae

— Toe

Olecranon process
Tetrapods after the Acanthostega had Olecranon processes which were the structures that curved around the bottom of the humerus bone in the upper arm and encapsulated the elbow joint allowing muscles to swing better and exert more energy.

Distinct toes on each foot
We classify tetrapods through their most basic features, like their feet and whether or not they have toes on them.

Zygapophyses are two pairs of unique vertebral protrusions that serve to link vertebrae making the backbone more stable. This structure gave tetrapods enough strength to support themselves on land.

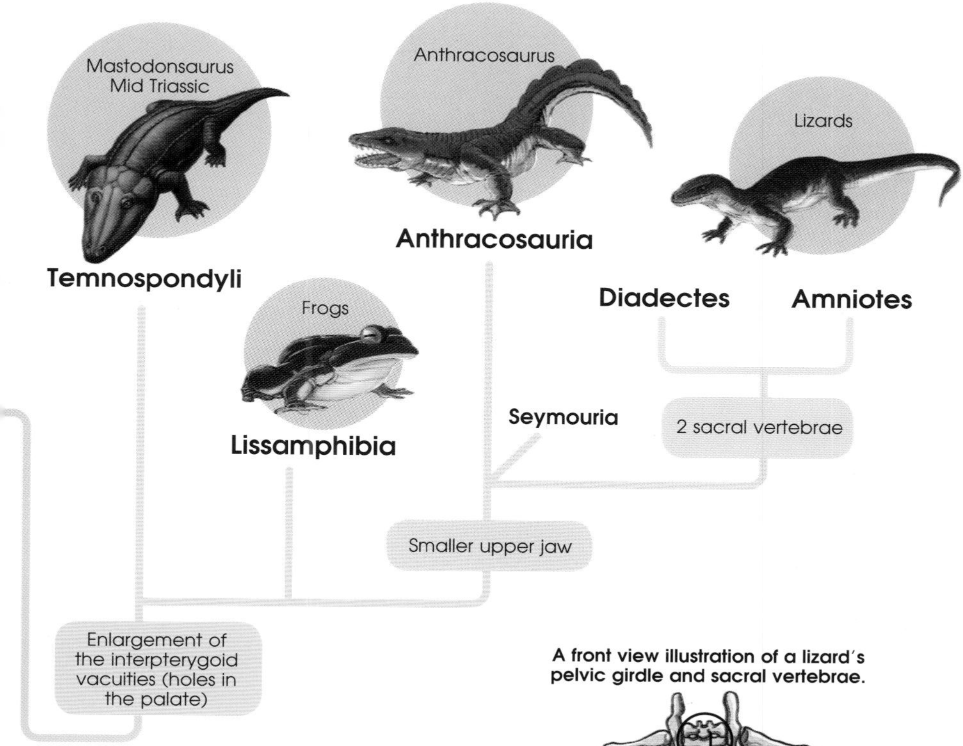
Mastodonsaurus
Mid Triassic
Temnospondyli
Anthracosaurus
Anthracosauria
Lizards
Diadectes
Amniotes
Frogs
Lissamphibia
Seymouria
2 sacral vertebrae
Smaller upper jaw
Enlargement of the interpterygoid vacuities (holes in the palate)

Pentadactyl limbs

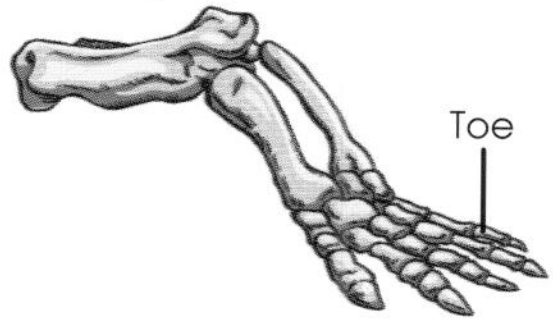
Toe

A front view illustration of a lizard's pelvic girdle and sacral vertebrae.

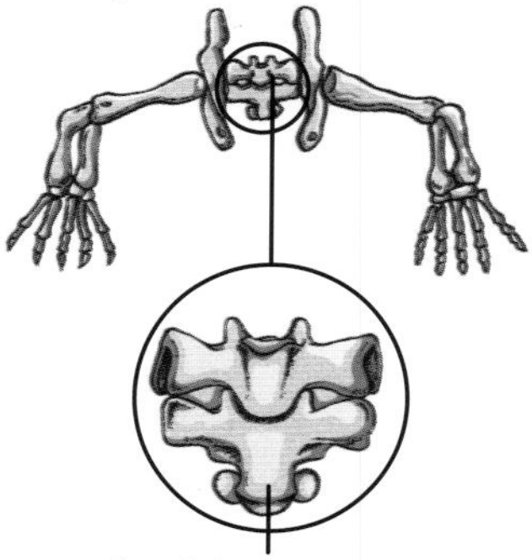
2 vertebral segments

Five-toed limbs
Advanced tetrapods had five toes on their forelimbs, perfect for walking.

Sacrum with 2 vertebral segments
The sacrum of Diadectes and Amniotes evolved from one segment into two, which strengthened them and allowed for larger body sizes.

VIEW OF THE CARBONIFEROUS

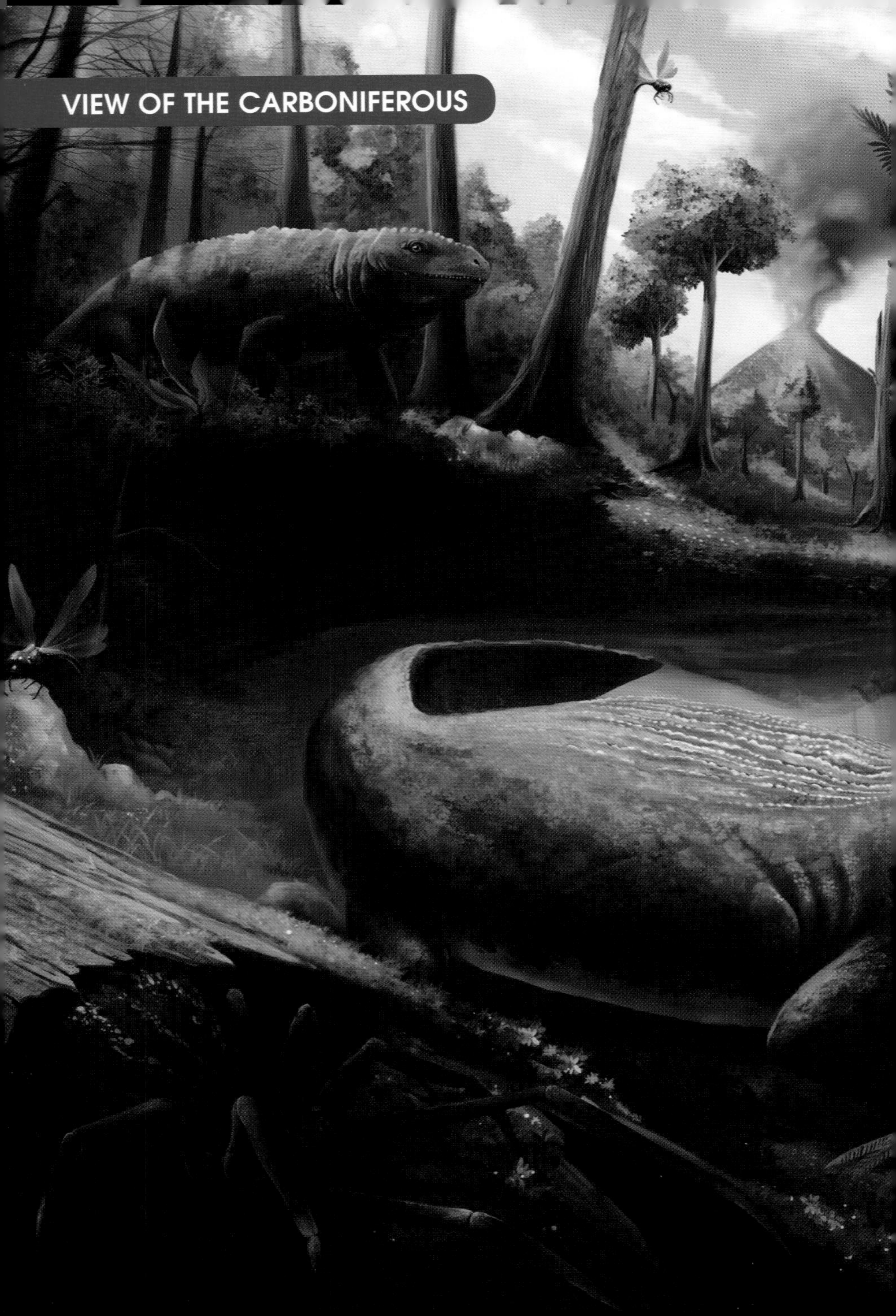

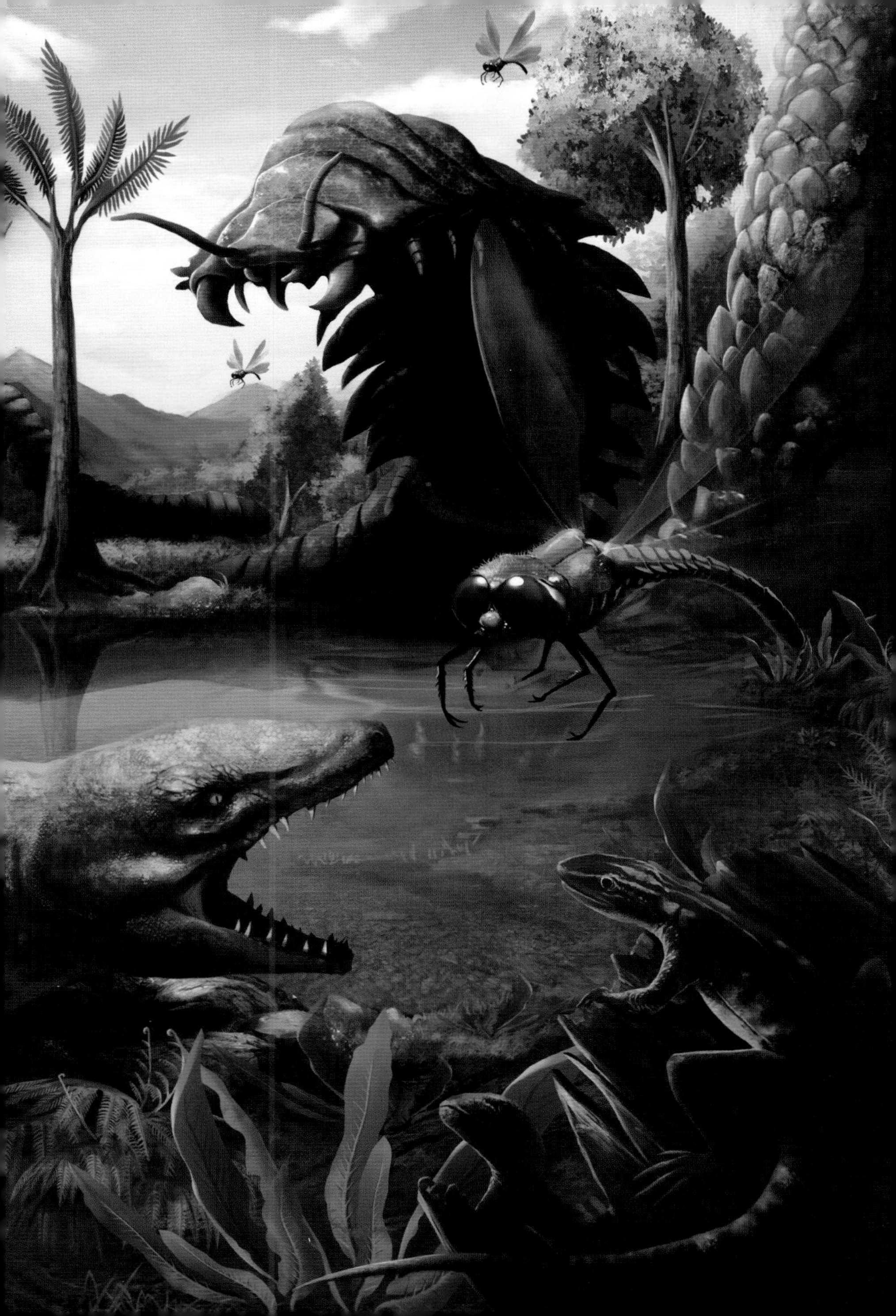

Diadectes

Diadectes had short, strong limbs to support its heavy body. It was a gentle herbivore, quite possibly the first in existence. The Diadectes' upper jaw was such that it was able to eat while breathing.

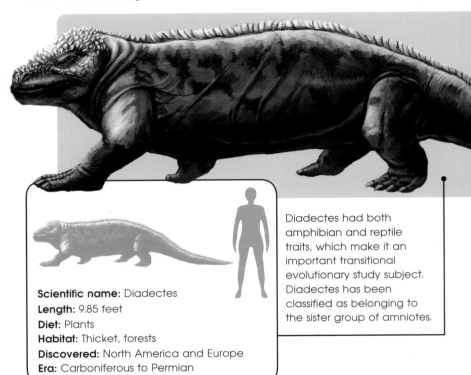

Scientific name: Diadectes
Length: 9.85 feet
Diet: Plants
Habitat: Thicket, forests
Discovered: North America and Europe
Era: Carboniferous to Permian

Diadectes had both amphibian and reptile traits, which make it an important transitional evolutionary study subject. Diadectes has been classified as belonging to the sister group of amniotes.

Diadectes bone structure

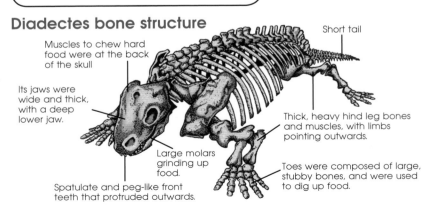

Short tail

Muscles to chew hard food were at the back of the skull

Its jaws were wide and thick, with a deep lower jaw.

Thick, heavy hind leg bones and muscles, with limbs pointing outwards.

Large molars grinding up food.

Toes were composed of large, stubby bones, and were used to dig up food.

Spatulate and peg-like front teeth that protruded outwards.

CHAPTER 5

THE PERNICIOUS PERMIAN

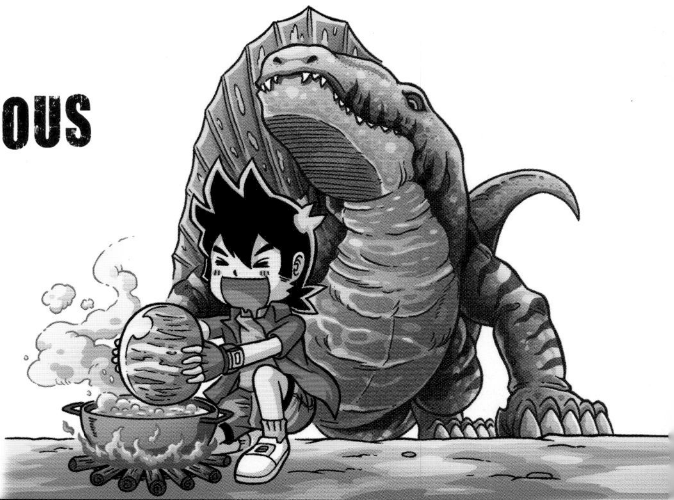

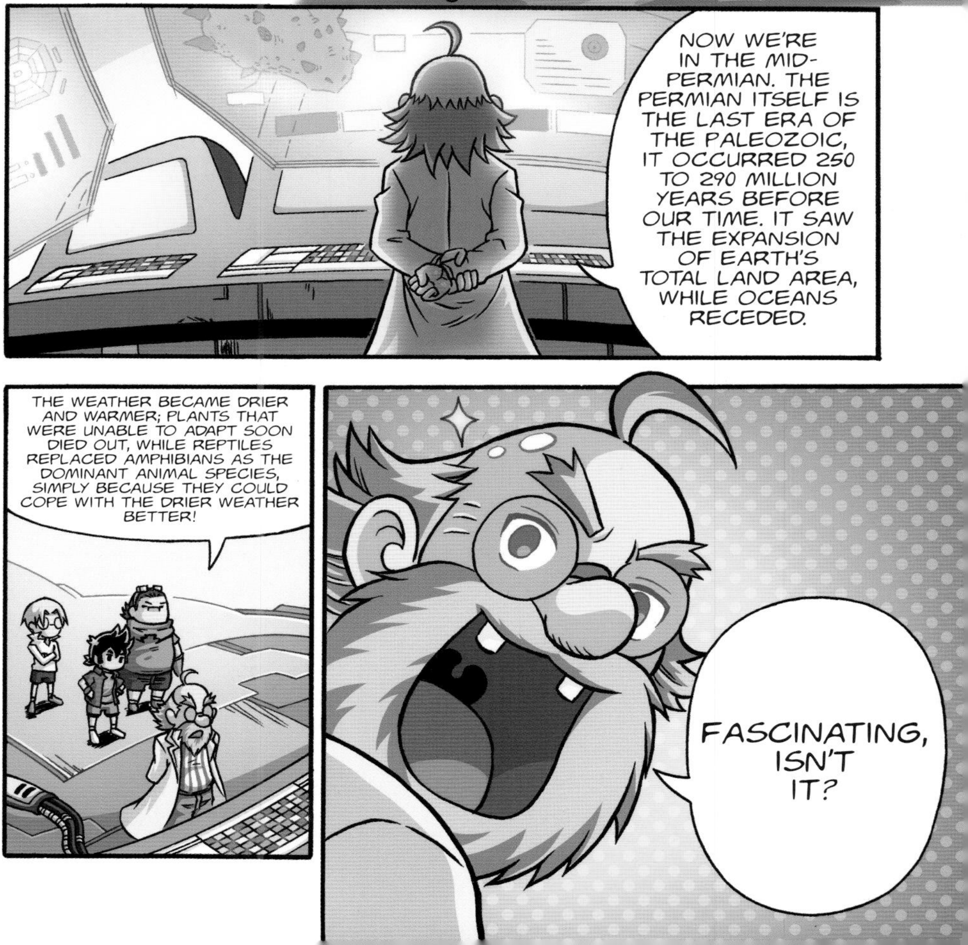
NOW WE'RE IN THE MID-PERMIAN. THE PERMIAN ITSELF IS THE LAST ERA OF THE PALEOZOIC, IT OCCURRED 250 TO 290 MILLION YEARS BEFORE OUR TIME. IT SAW THE EXPANSION OF EARTH'S TOTAL LAND AREA, WHILE OCEANS RECEDED.
THE WEATHER BECAME DRIER AND WARMER; PLANTS THAT WERE UNABLE TO ADAPT SOON DIED OUT, WHILE REPTILES REPLACED AMPHIBIANS AS THE DOMINANT ANIMAL SPECIES, SIMPLY BECAUSE THEY COULD COPE WITH THE DRIER WEATHER BETTER!
FASCINATING, ISN'T IT?

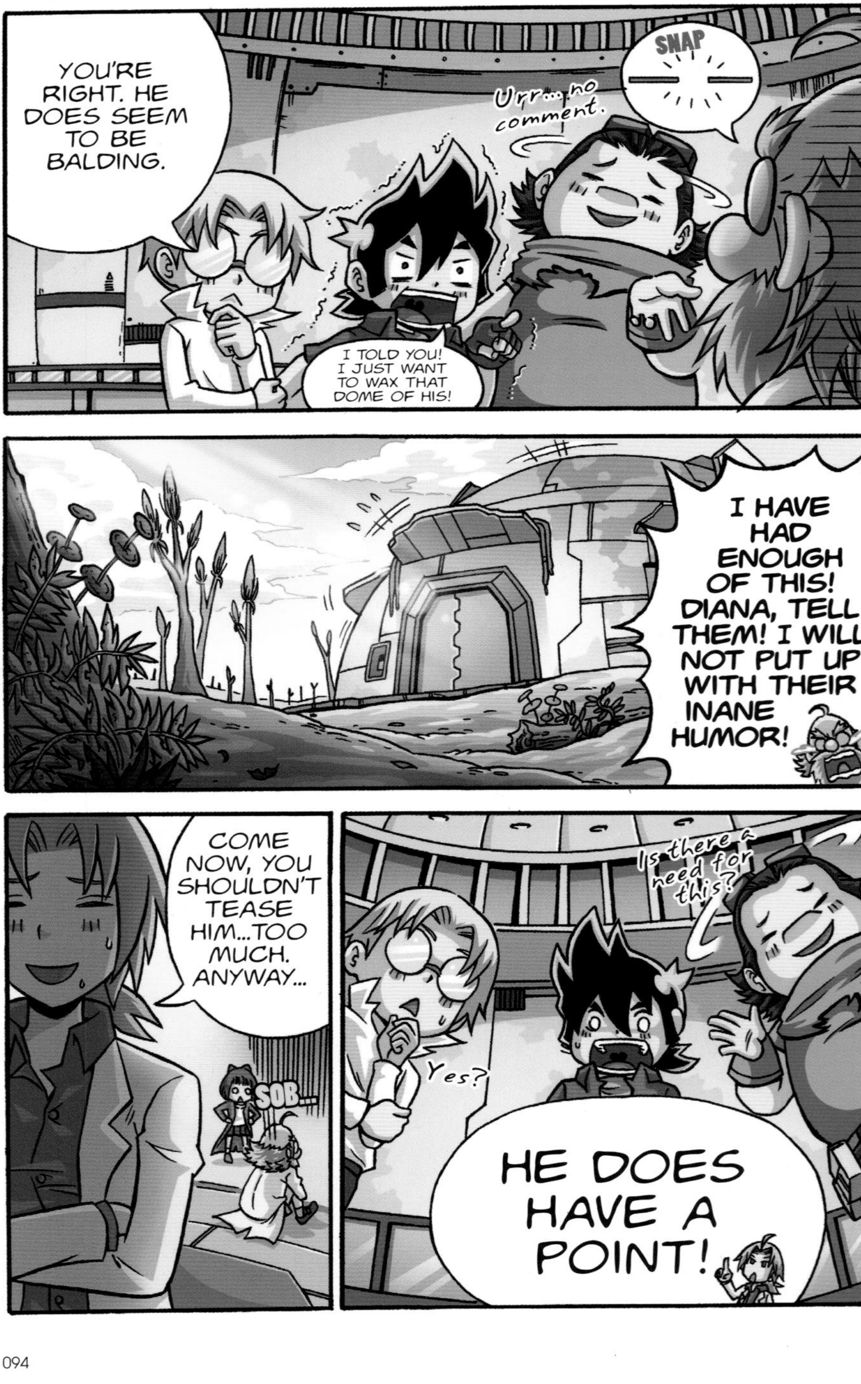
YOU'RE RIGHT. HE DOES SEEM TO BE BALDING.
SNAP
Urr... no comment.
I TOLD YOU! I JUST WANT TO WAX THAT DOME OF HIS!
I HAVE HAD ENOUGH OF THIS! DIANA, TELL THEM! I WILL NOT PUT UP WITH THEIR INANE HUMOR!
COME NOW, YOU SHOULDN'T TEASE HIM...TOO MUCH. ANYWAY...
SOB...
Is there a need for this?
Yes?
HE DOES HAVE A POINT!

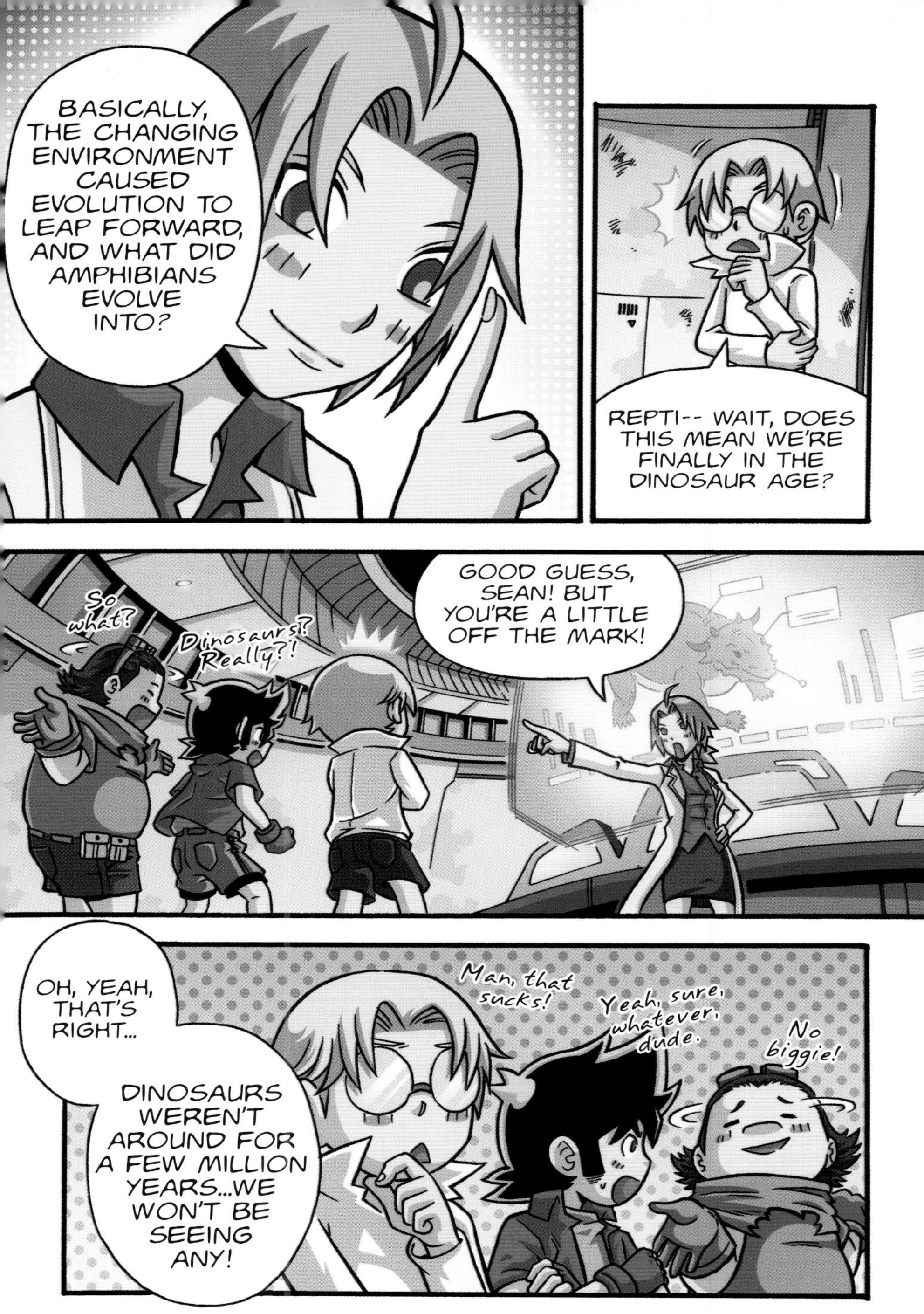
BASICALLY, THE CHANGING ENVIRONMENT CAUSED EVOLUTION TO LEAP FORWARD, AND WHAT DID AMPHIBIANS EVOLVE INTO?
REPTI-- WAIT, DOES THIS MEAN WE'RE FINALLY IN THE DINOSAUR AGE?
So what?
Dinosaurs? Really?!
GOOD GUESS, SEAN! BUT YOU'RE A LITTLE OFF THE MARK!
OH, YEAH, THAT'S RIGHT...
DINOSAURS WEREN'T AROUND FOR A FEW MILLION YEARS...WE WON'T BE SEEING ANY!
Man, that sucks!
Yeah, sure, whatever, dude.
No biggie!

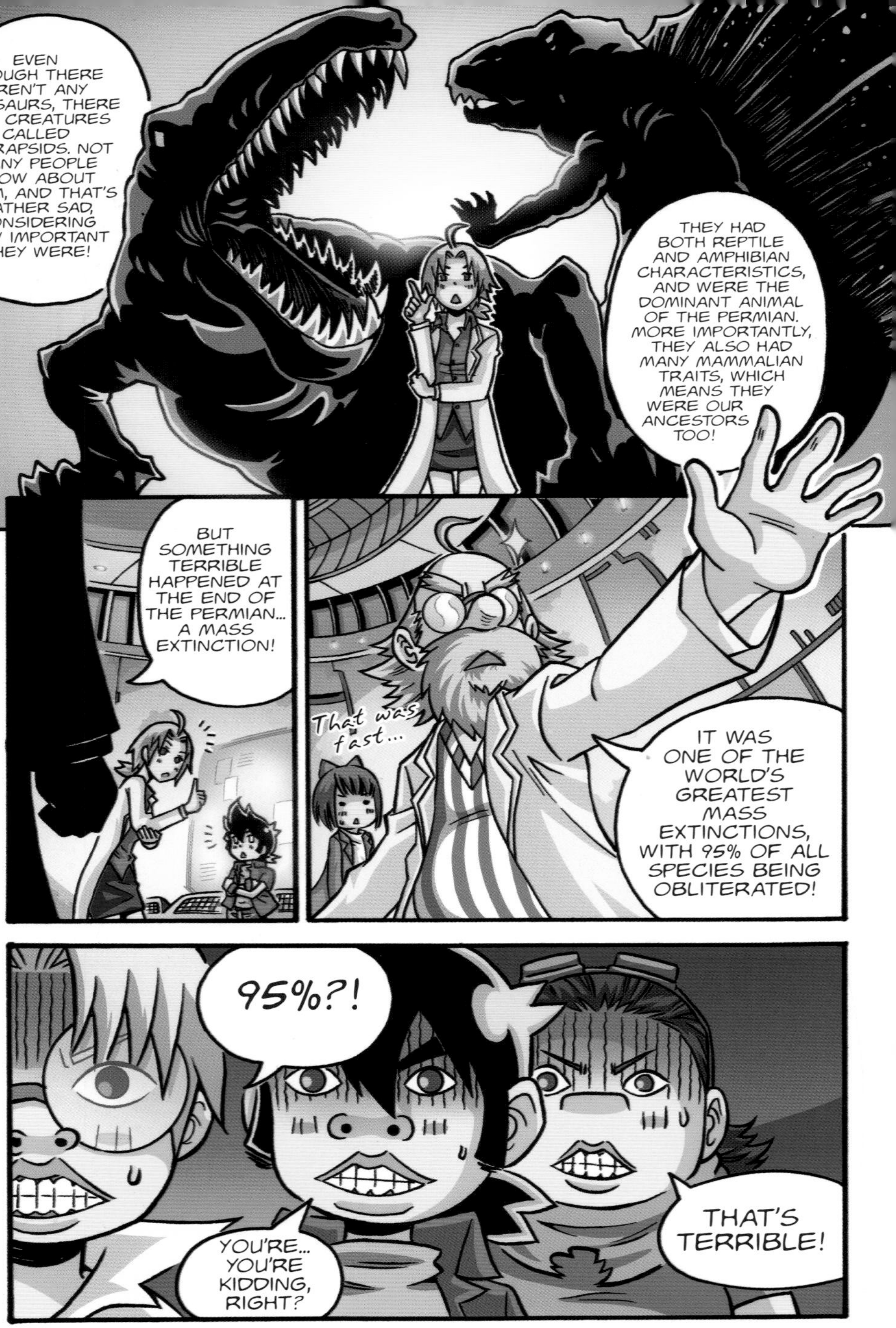
EVEN THOUGH THERE AREN'T ANY DINOSAURS, THERE ARE CREATURES CALLED THERAPSIDS. NOT MANY PEOPLE KNOW ABOUT THEM, AND THAT'S RATHER SAD, CONSIDERING HOW IMPORTANT THEY WERE!
THEY HAD BOTH REPTILE AND AMPHIBIAN CHARACTERISTICS, AND WERE THE DOMINANT ANIMAL OF THE PERMIAN. MORE IMPORTANTLY, THEY ALSO HAD MANY MAMMALIAN TRAITS, WHICH MEANS THEY WERE OUR ANCESTORS TOO!
BUT SOMETHING TERRIBLE HAPPENED AT THE END OF THE PERMIAN... A MASS EXTINCTION!
That was fast...
IT WAS ONE OF THE WORLD'S GREATEST MASS EXTINCTIONS, WITH 95% OF ALL SPECIES BEING OBLITERATED!
95%?!
YOU'RE... YOU'RE KIDDING, RIGHT?
THAT'S TERRIBLE!

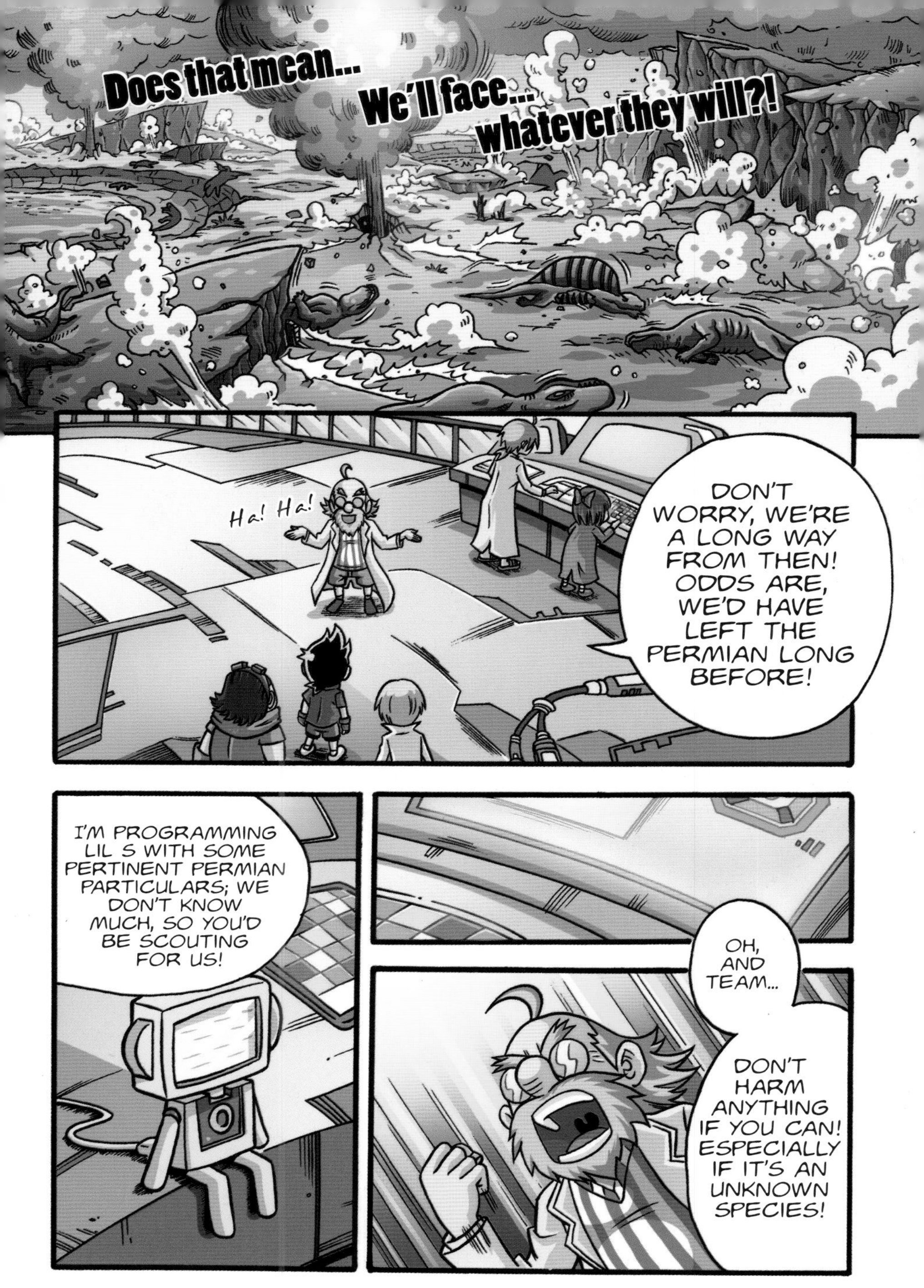
Does that mean...
We'll face...
whatever they will?!
Ha! Ha!
DON'T WORRY, WE'RE A LONG WAY FROM THEN! ODDS ARE, WE'D HAVE LEFT THE PERMIAN LONG BEFORE!
I'M PROGRAMMING LIL S WITH SOME PERTINENT PERMIAN PARTICULARS; WE DON'T KNOW MUCH, SO YOU'D BE SCOUTING FOR US!
OH, AND TEAM...
DON'T HARM ANYTHING IF YOU CAN! ESPECIALLY IF IT'S AN UNKNOWN SPECIES!

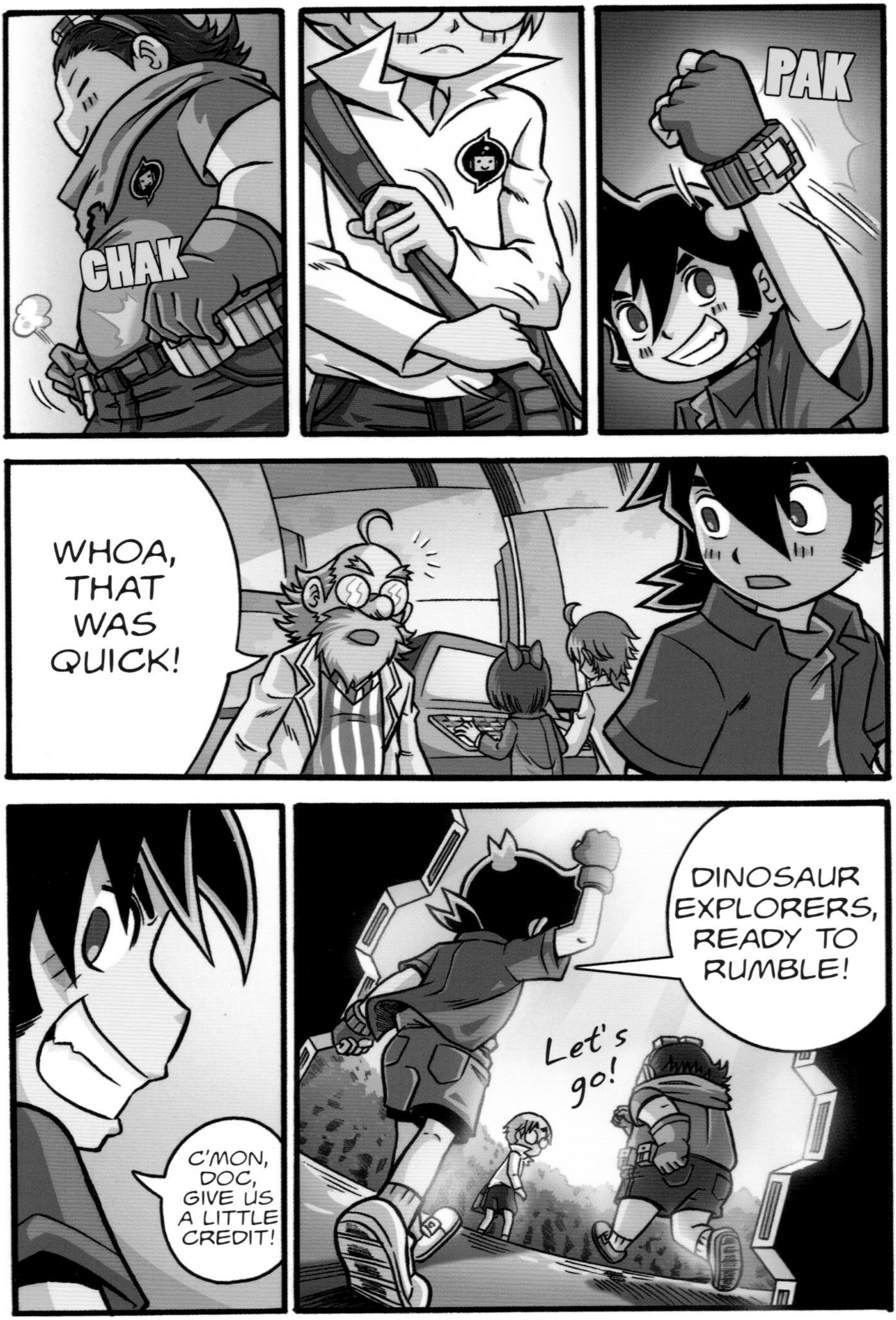
CHAK
PAK
WHOA, THAT WAS QUICK!
C'MON, DOC, GIVE US A LITTLE CREDIT!
DINOSAUR EXPLORERS, READY TO RUMBLE!
Let's go!

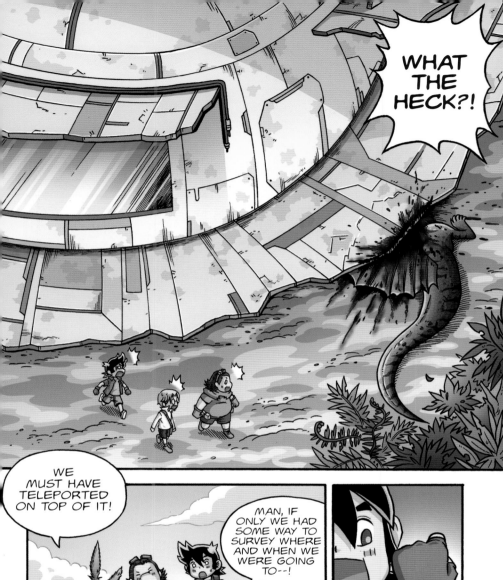

WHAT THE HECK?!

WE MUST HAVE TELEPORTED ON TOP OF IT!

MAN, IF ONLY WE HAD SOME WAY TO SURVEY WHERE AND WHEN WE WERE GOING TO--!

LET'S NOT WASTE THIS OPPORTUNITY... LIL S, YOU HAVE ANY INFO ON THIS?

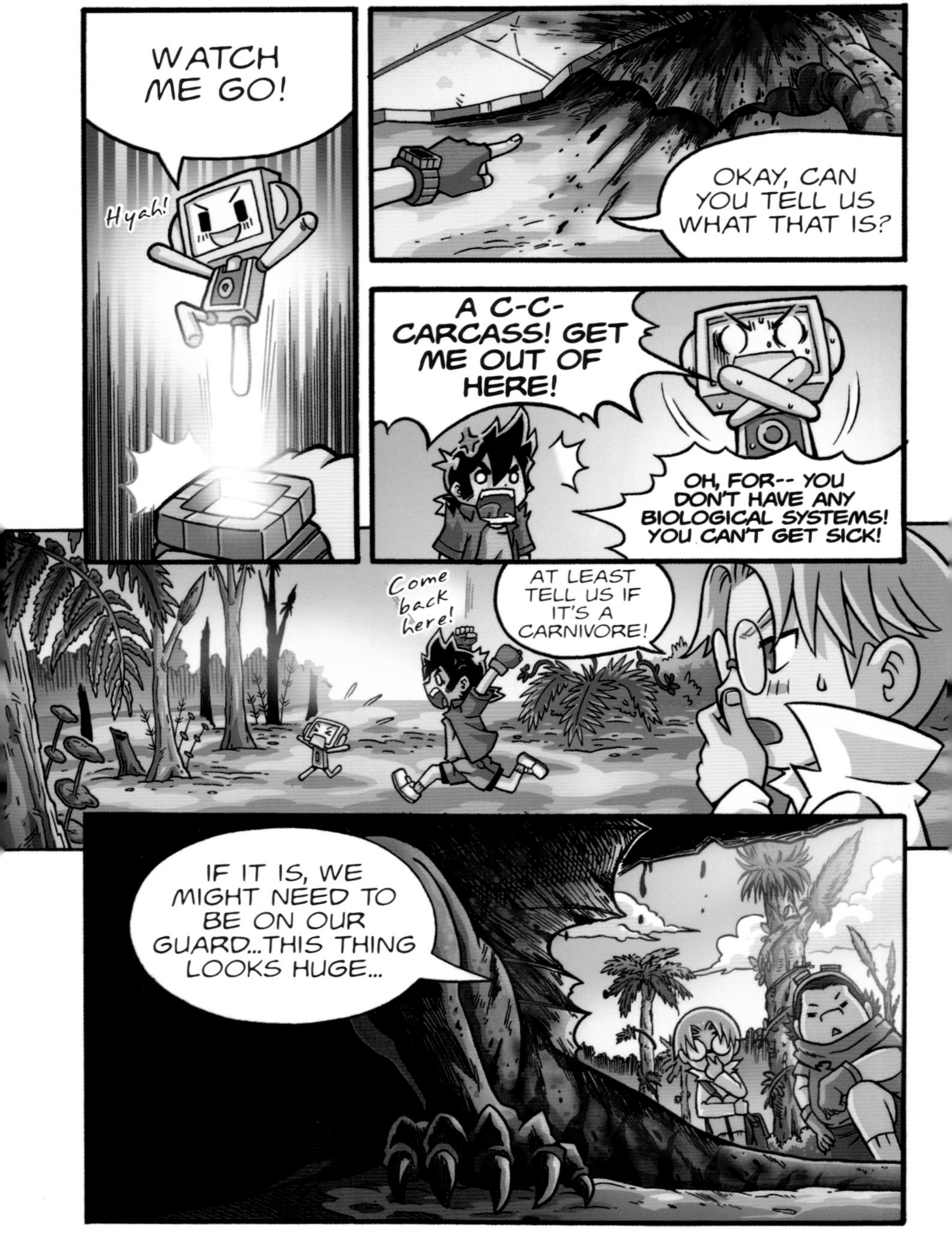
WATCH ME GO!
Hyah!
OKAY, CAN YOU TELL US WHAT THAT IS?
A C-C-CARCASS! GET ME OUT OF HERE!
OH, FOR-- YOU DON'T HAVE ANY BIOLOGICAL SYSTEMS! YOU CAN'T GET SICK!
Come back here!
AT LEAST TELL US IF IT'S A CARNIVORE!
IF IT IS, WE MIGHT NEED TO BE ON OUR GUARD...THIS THING LOOKS HUGE...

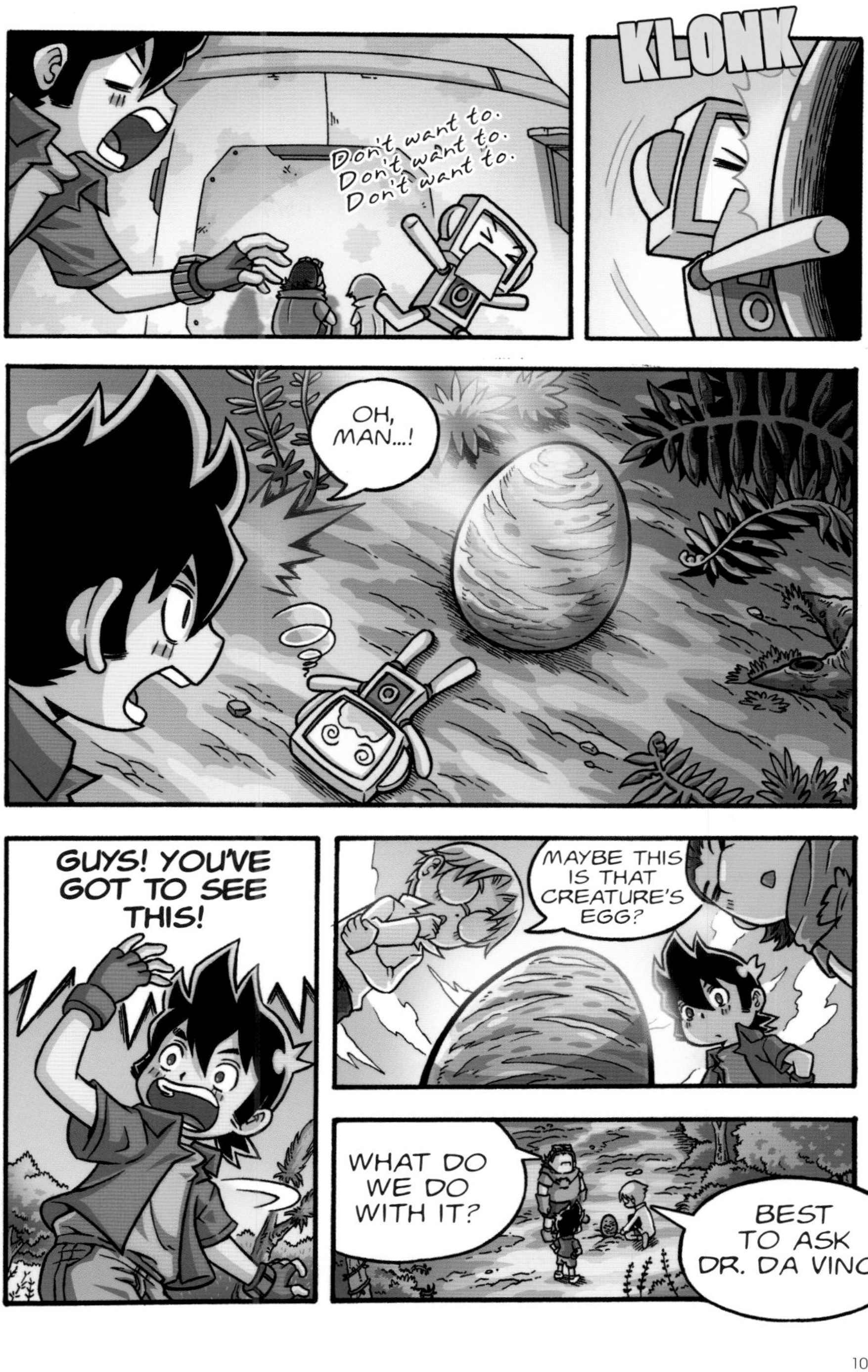

Don't want to.
Don't want to.
Don't want to.
KLONK
OH, MAN...!
GUYS! YOU'VE GOT TO SEE THIS!
MAYBE THIS IS THAT CREATURE'S EGG?
WHAT DO WE DO WITH IT?
BEST TO ASK DR. DA VINCI.

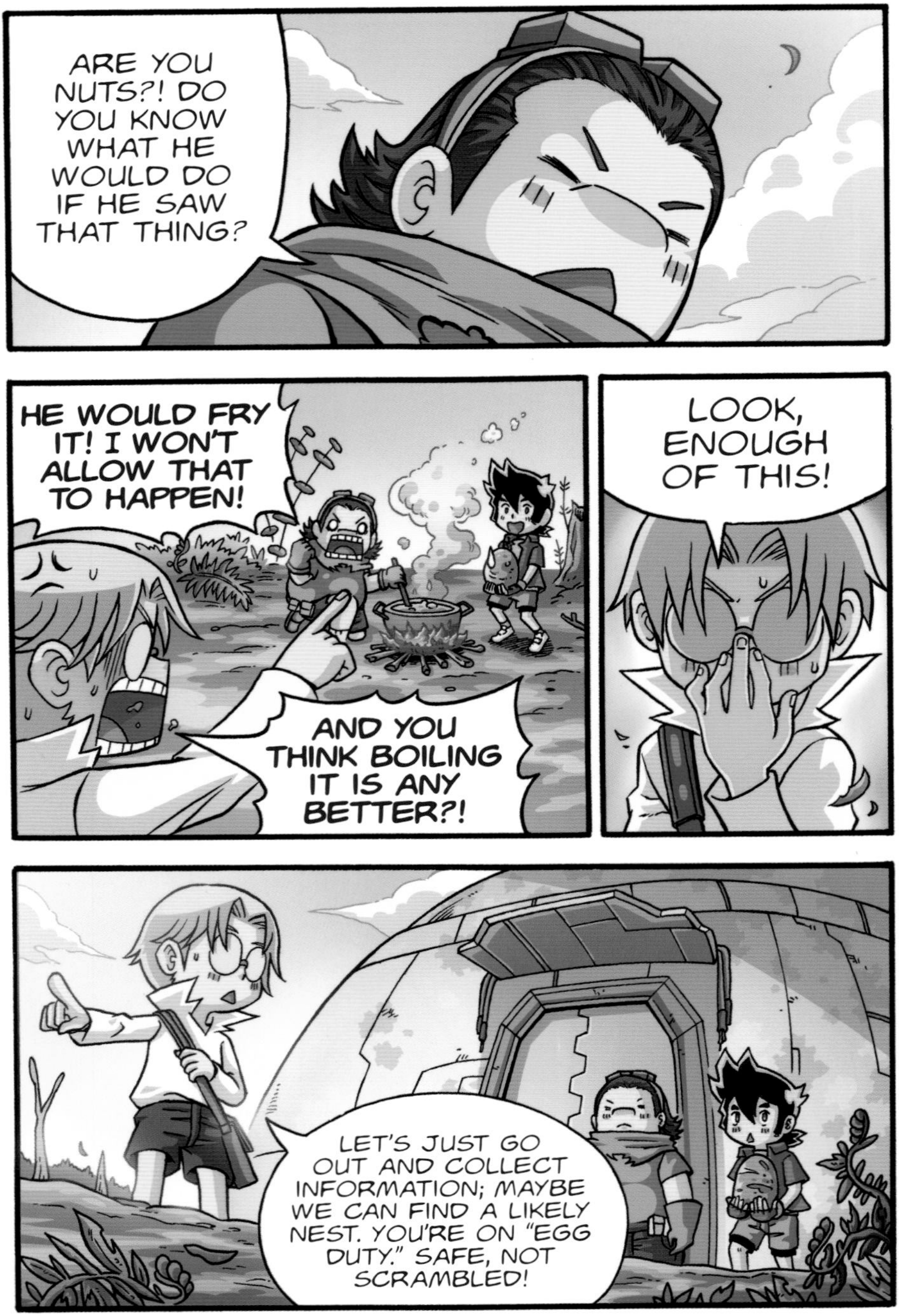
ARE YOU NUTS?! DO YOU KNOW WHAT HE WOULD DO IF HE SAW THAT THING?
HE WOULD FRY IT! I WON'T ALLOW THAT TO HAPPEN!
AND YOU THINK BOILING IT IS ANY BETTER?!
LOOK, ENOUGH OF THIS!
LET'S JUST GO OUT AND COLLECT INFORMATION; MAYBE WE CAN FIND A LIKELY NEST. YOU'RE ON "EGG DUTY." SAFE, NOT SCRAMBLED!

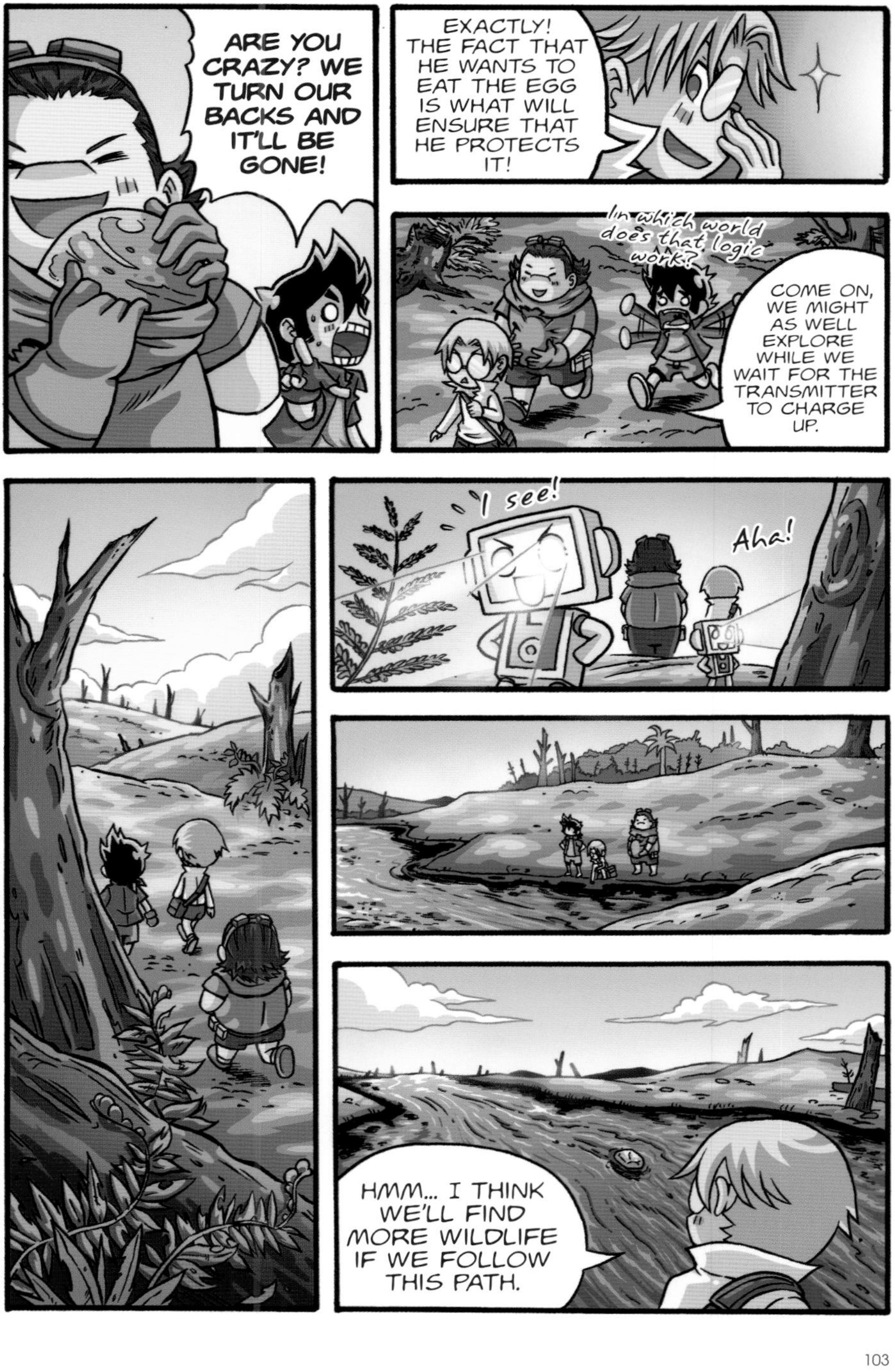
ARE YOU CRAZY? WE TURN OUR BACKS AND IT'LL BE GONE!
EXACTLY! THE FACT THAT HE WANTS TO EAT THE EGG IS WHAT WILL ENSURE THAT HE PROTECTS IT!
In which world does that logic work?
COME ON, WE MIGHT AS WELL EXPLORE WHILE WE WAIT FOR THE TRANSMITTER TO CHARGE UP.
I see!
Aha!
HMM... I THINK WE'LL FIND MORE WILDLIFE IF WE FOLLOW THIS PATH.

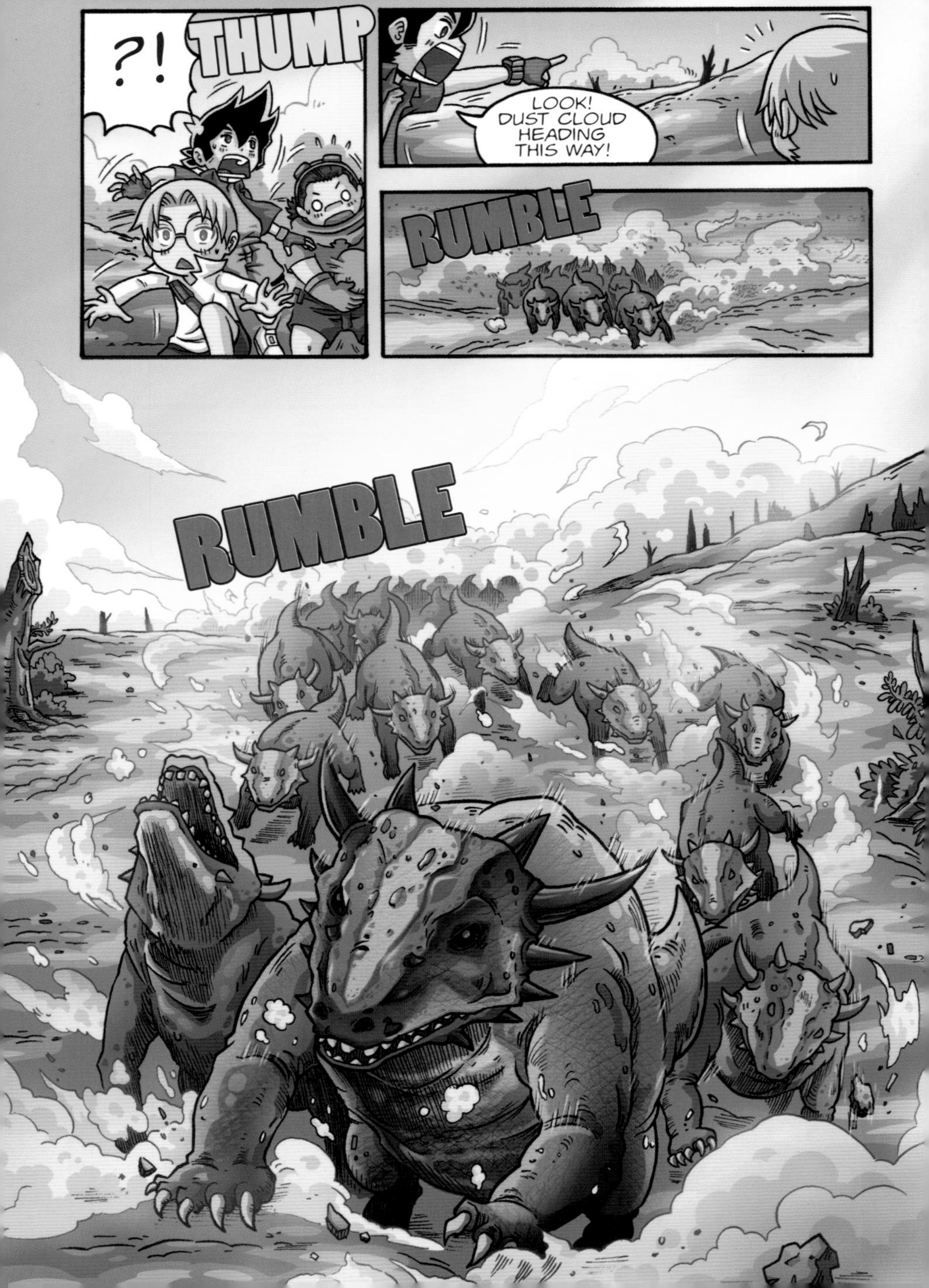
?!
THUMP
LOOK! DUST CLOUD HEADING THIS WAY!
RUMBLE
RUMBLE

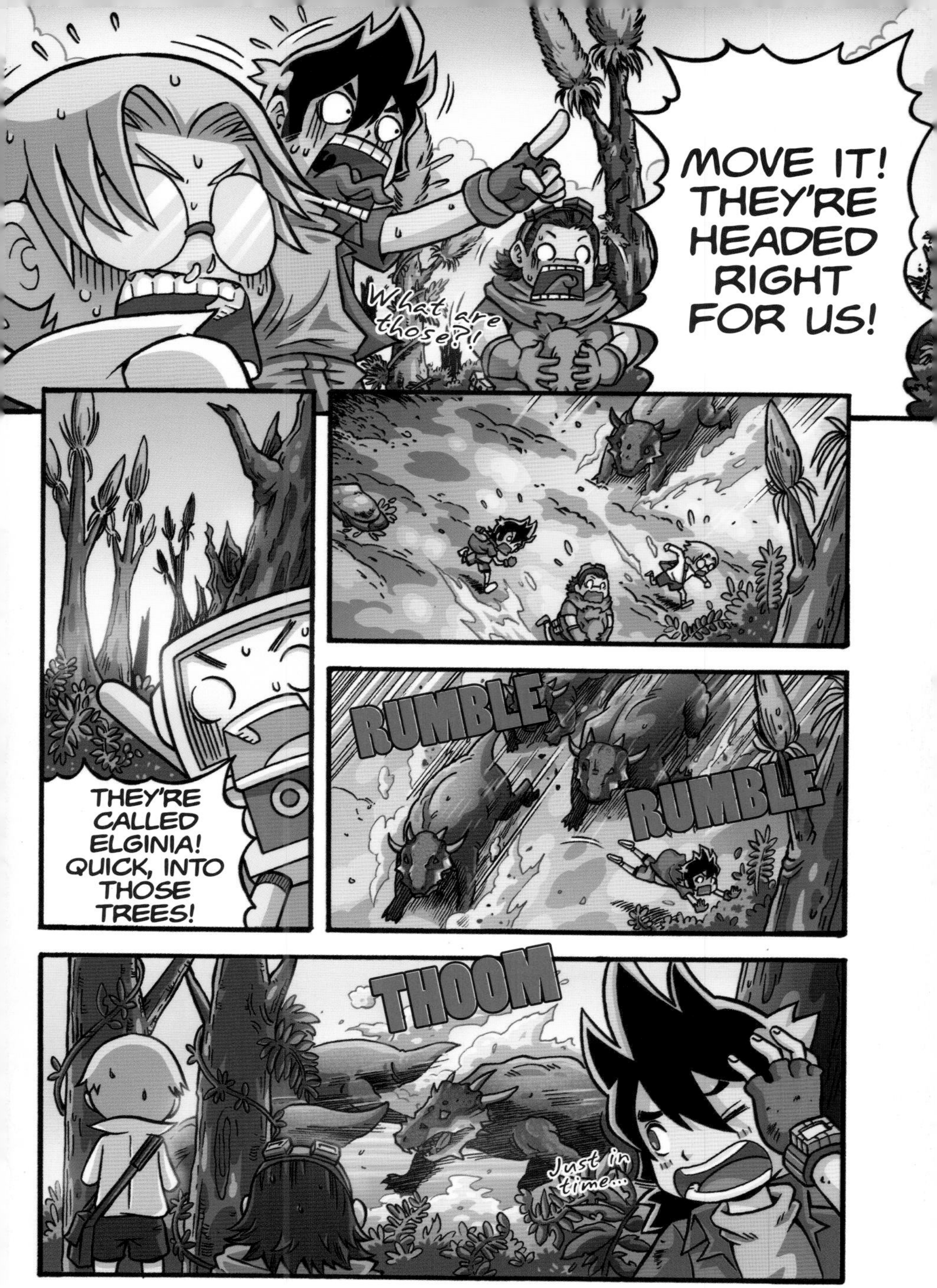

MOVE IT! THEY'RE HEADED RIGHT FOR US!
What are those?!
THEY'RE CALLED ELGINIA! QUICK, INTO THOSE TREES!
RUMBLE
RUMBLE
THOOM
Just in time...

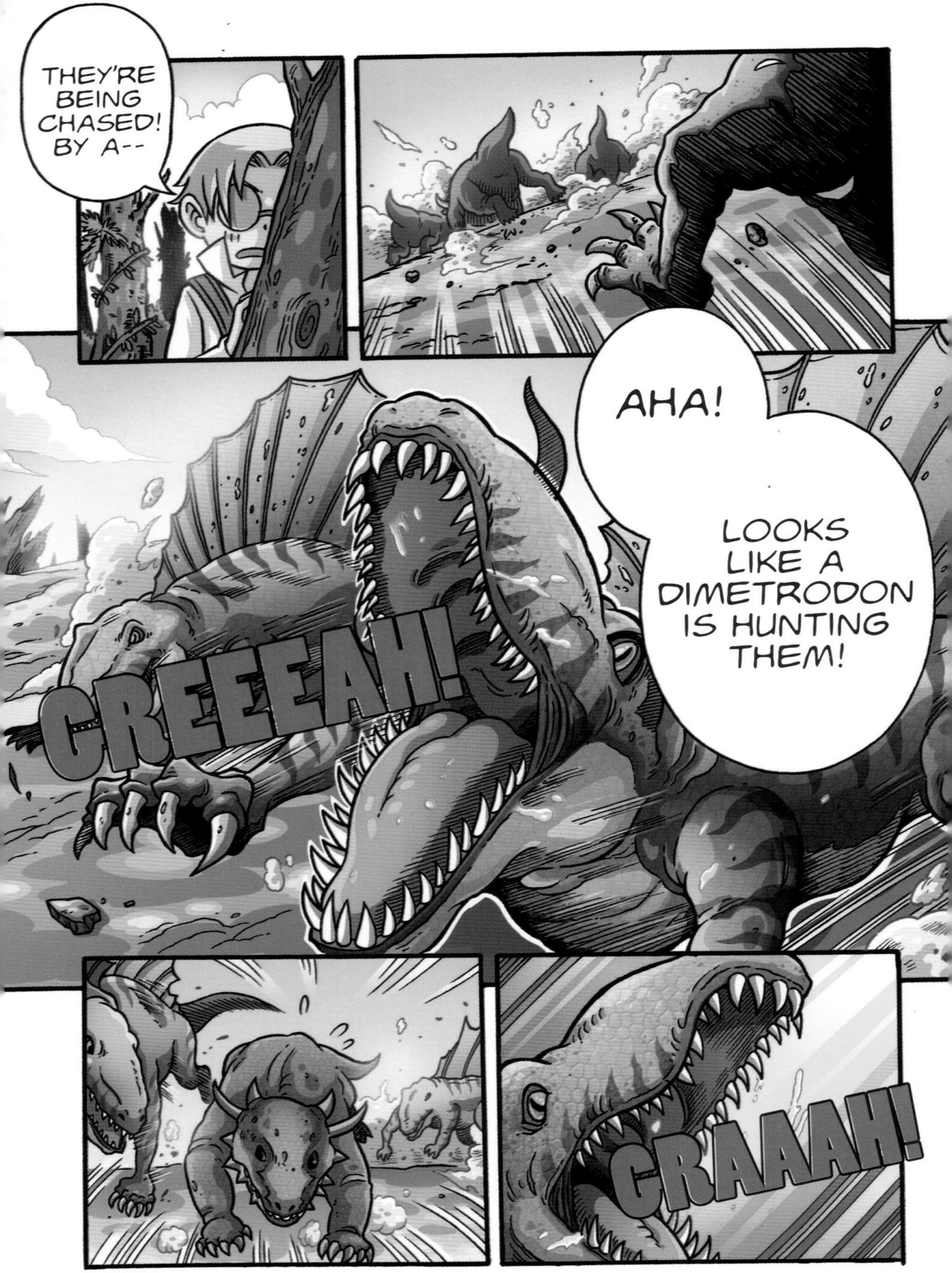
THEY'RE BEING CHASED! BY A--
AHA!
LOOKS LIKE A DIMETRODON IS HUNTING THEM!
CREEEAH!
GRAAAH!

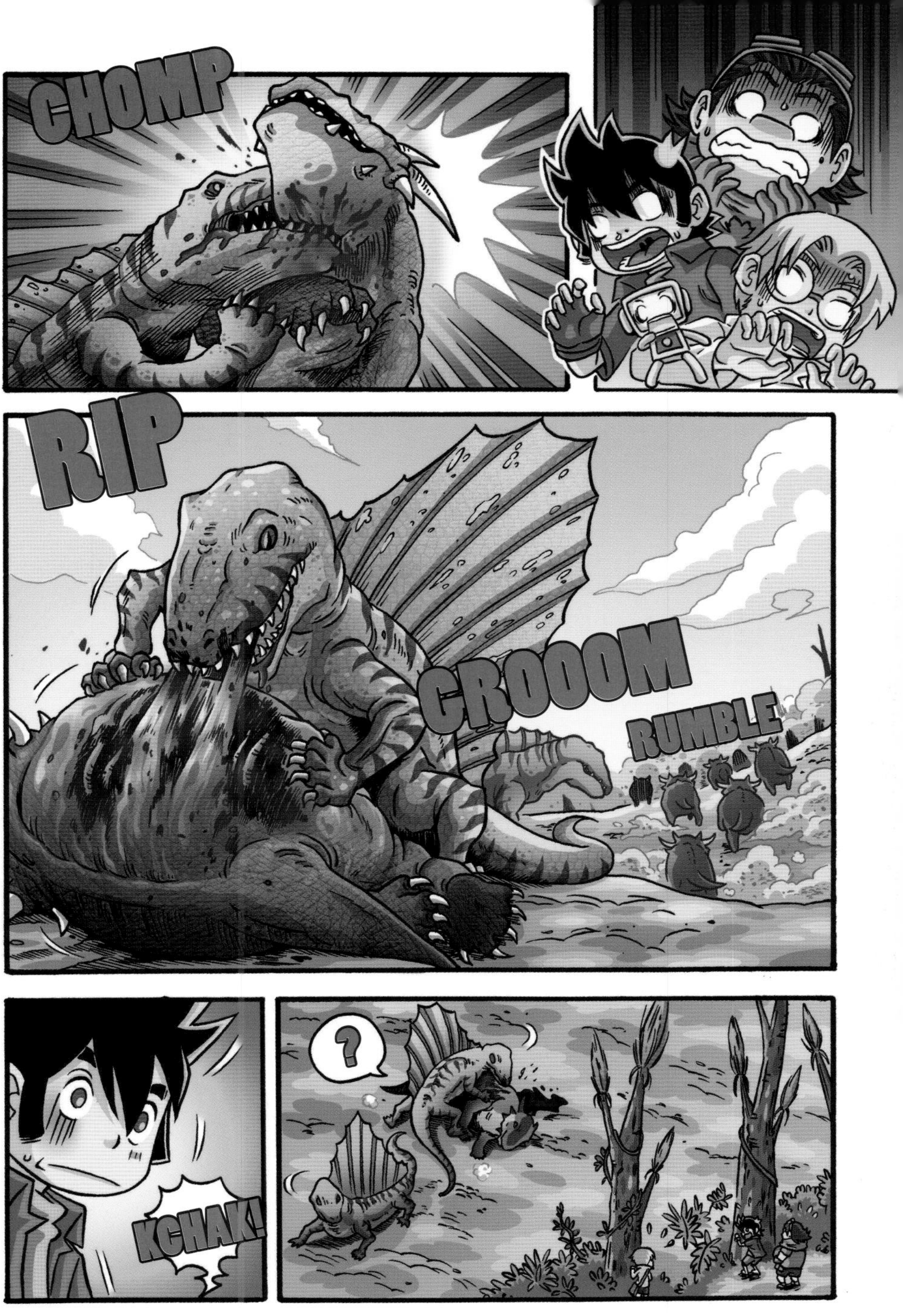
CHOMP
RIP
GROOOM
RUMBLE
KCHAK!
?

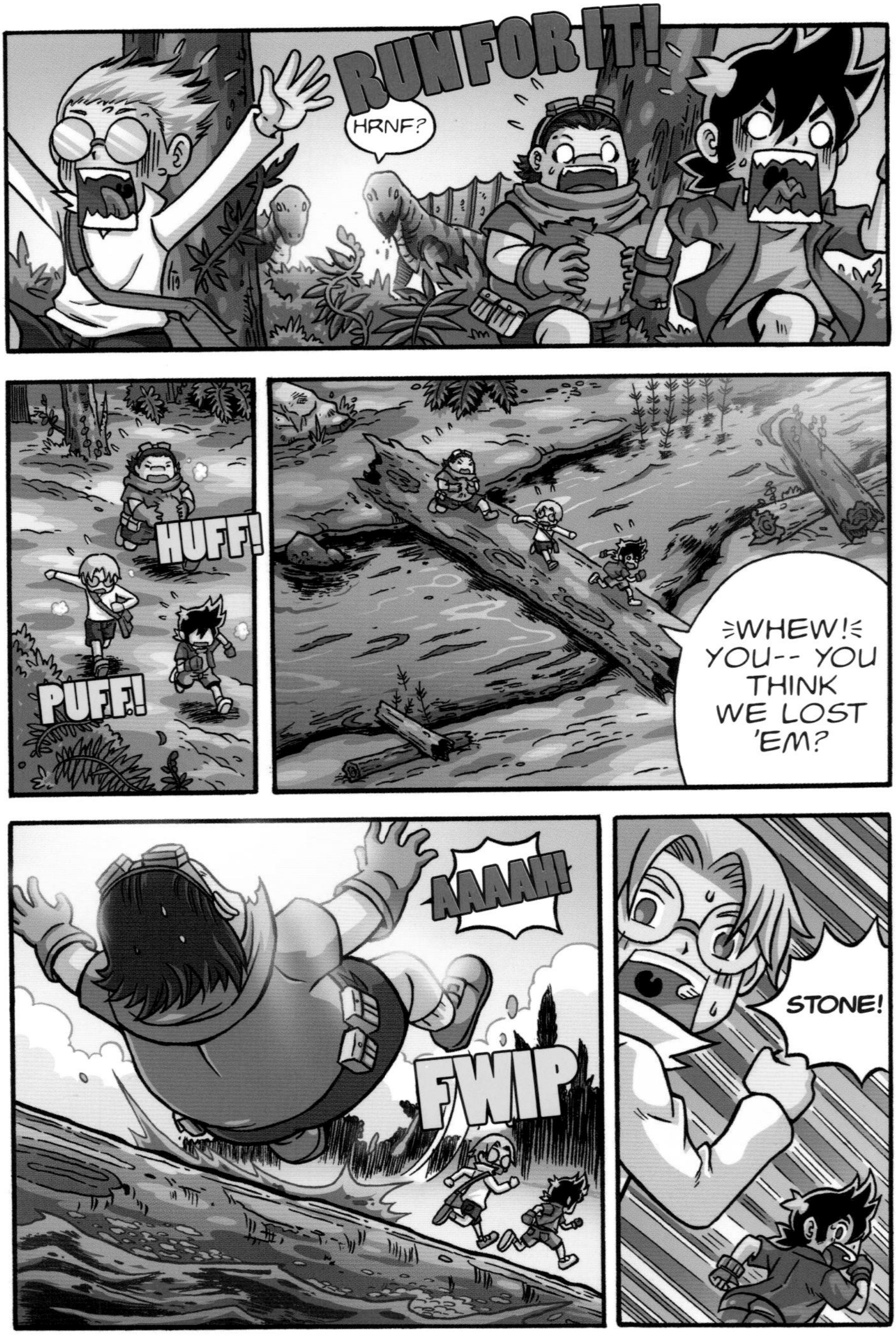
RUN FOR IT!
HRNF?
HUFF!
PUFF!
WHEW! YOU-- YOU THINK WE LOST 'EM?
AAAAH!
FWIP
STONE!

CONTINENTS OF THE PERMIAN

The Permian saw Laurentia in the north and Gondwana in the south still somewhat close by; indeed, by the end of the Late Permian they would have forcefully merged, creating the massive supercontinent Pangaea. This would have caused a large loss of shallow seas as well as enlarged deserts. Sea levels all over the world dropped.

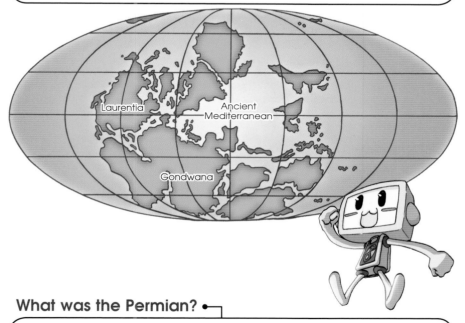

Laurentia

Ancient Mediterranean

Gondwana

What was the Permian?

The Permian was the sixth and last period of the Paleozoic era. It (the Permian) began around 290 million years ago, and lasted until 250 million years ago. In the millennia heading into the Mesozoic, the Earth underwent several great changes, as mentioned above. These radical changes were said to be factors in the massive extinction that followed it, erasing over 90% of all known species. This mass extinction, however, gave those species that remained room to evolve anew!

How did Pangaea form?

It was all due to something called "continental drift." This was first discovered by German geologist Alfred Wegener in 1912, however, his theory was only proved correct in the 1980s. Continents move because they are actually mounted on "plates" of crust floating about on the magma layer below. As they move about, they can, and do, collide, and Pangaea was formed out of one of these collisions.

Traits of Permian life:

Under the ocean, brachiopods and corals started spreading everywhere, with molluscs being the dominant ocean life. Amphibians still predominated on land, but reptile numbers were steadily increasing. Insect population and variation were also on the rise. Cordaites (gymnosperms) and glossopteris (seed ferns) plants were winding down, while lycophytes were gearing up.

How bad was the extinction at the end of the Permian?

The Late Permian Extinction is the third mass extinction in Earth's history, and the most devastating of all time. 70% of vertebrates, 90% of sea life, and a large portion of insect life died off. The primary marine and terrestrial victims included the trilobites, rugose corals, acanthodians, placoderms, opabinia, eurypterids, and pelycosaurs. This had a "knock-on" effect, affecting creatures that might have relied on them but had not gone extinct yet. Because so much biodiversity was lost, the recovery of life on Earth took significantly longer than any other extinction ever.

Ocean life was the most badly affected!

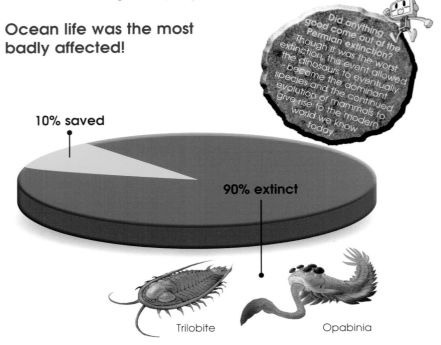

Did anything good come out of the Permian extinction? Though it was the worst extinction, this event allowed the dinosaurs to eventually become the dominant species and the continued evolution of mammals to give rise to the modern world we know today.

10% saved

90% extinct

Trilobite

Opabinia

What caused the extinction?

To this day, no one is certain why so many species and entire ecosystems disappeared. Proposed theories include severe volcanism, a nearby supernova, environmental changes wrought by the formation of a super-continent, the devastating impact of a large asteroid – or some combination.

What were gymnosperms and angiosperms?

Basically, gymnosperms are plants with exposed seeds such as pines and their cones, while angiosperms have seeds in ovaries or within the fruit.

Schematic of a pine tree

A pine tree has both male and female cones hanging from its branches.

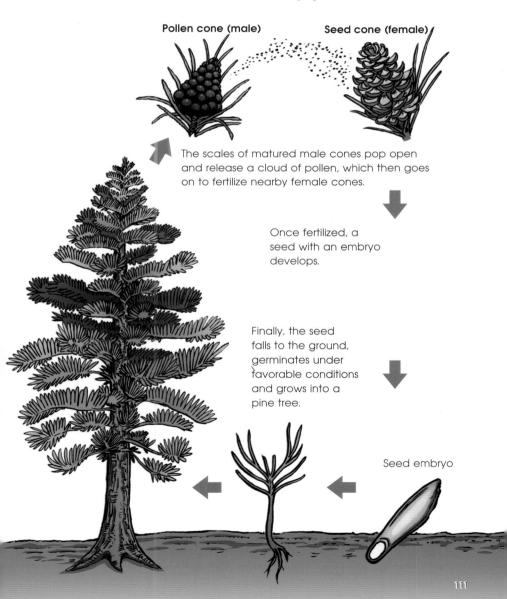

Pollen cone (male)

Seed cone (female)

The scales of matured male cones pop open and release a cloud of pollen, which then goes on to fertilize nearby female cones.

Once fertilized, a seed with an embryo develops.

Finally, the seed falls to the ground, germinates under favorable conditions and grows into a pine tree.

Seed embryo

Reptiles are amniotes; that is, they lay eggs protected by hard shells. They were the dominant life form in the Paleozoic and Mesozoic. Along with amphibians and birds, reptiles are the most successful amniotes today. Most reptiles were (and still are) skilled hunters, with fangs and specialized holes in their skulls for sensory purposes giving them superb hunting capabilities.

Archelon
(Late Cretaceous)

The largest extinct sea turtle ever documented.

Hylonomus
(Carboniferous)

Hylonomus was one of the earliest known reptiles and the first to have fully adapted to life on land.

Parareptilia
(Anapsids)

Eureptilia and Parareptilia

Fangs on the upper jaw

Stem Reptiles
(Amniotes with suborbital fenestra but lack holes near the temples)

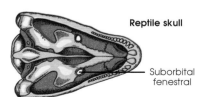

Reptile skull

Suborbital fenestral

Eureptilia skull

Fangs

Suborbital fenestra
Many ancient and modern reptiles have suborbital fenestra which are holes on each side of the skull between the eye sockets and the nostrils. What these holes do is still being studied, but it serves as a handy guide to species.

Fangs
Eureptilia and other extant reptiles have fangs on their upper jaw. The fangs are multipurpose, and can be used to clamp down on prey, or cut up plant matter.

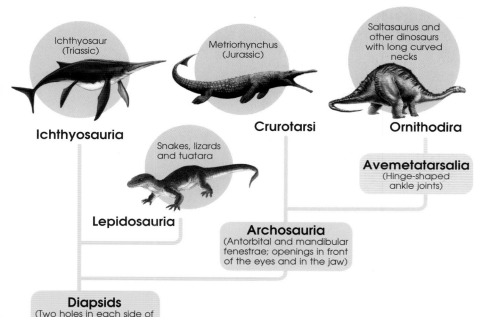

Ichthyosauria

Ichthyosaur (Triassic)

Metriorhynchus (Jurassic)

Crurotarsi

Saltasaurus and other dinosaurs with long curved necks

Ornithodira

Avemetatarsalia
(Hinge-shaped ankle joints)

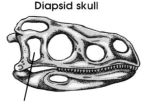

Snakes, lizards and tuatara

Lepidosauria

Archosauria
(Antorbital and mandibular fenestrae; openings in front of the eyes and in the jaw)

Diapsids
(Two holes in each side of their skulls and suborbital fenestra in palates)

Tyrannosaurus leg bones

Diapsid skull

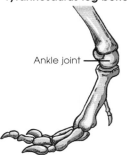

Ankle joint

Temporal fenestra; holes theorised to reduce pressure at the back of the head when chewing food.

Diapsid holes
Diapsids are a group of reptiles that developed two holes in each side of their skulls. It allows for the attachment of larger, stronger jaw muscles, and enables the jaw to open more widely.

Hinge-shaped joint
Avemetatarsalia (includes dinosaurs and pterosaurs) had hinge-shaped ankle joints.

Elginia

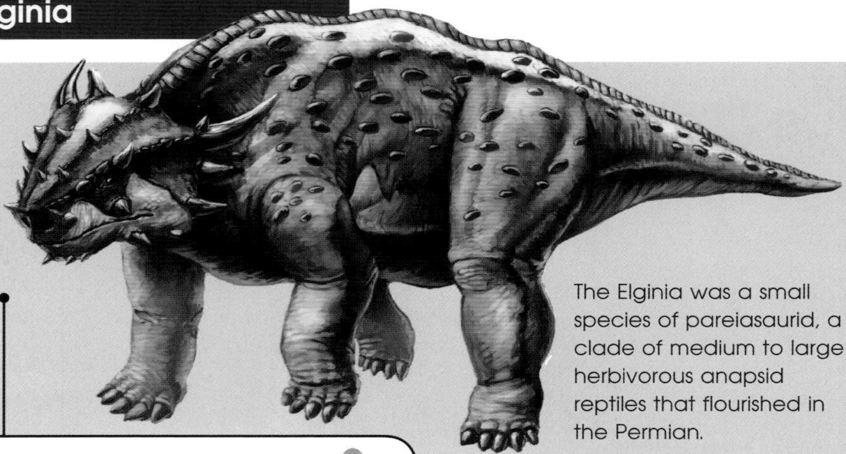

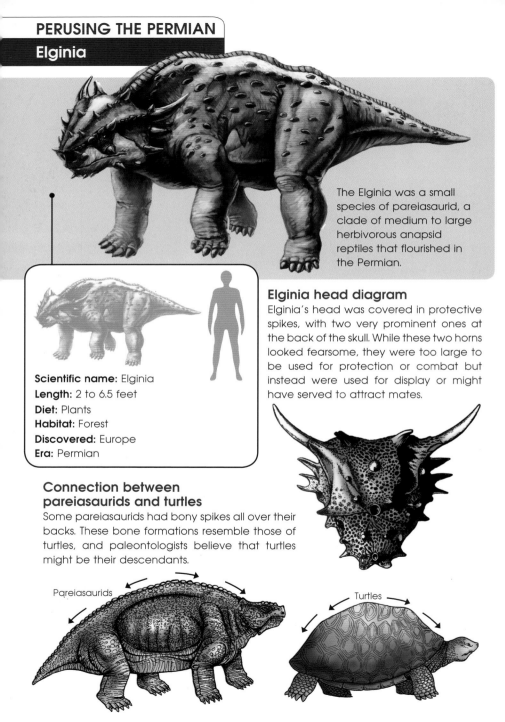

The Elginia was a small species of pareiasaurid, a clade of medium to large herbivorous anapsid reptiles that flourished in the Permian.

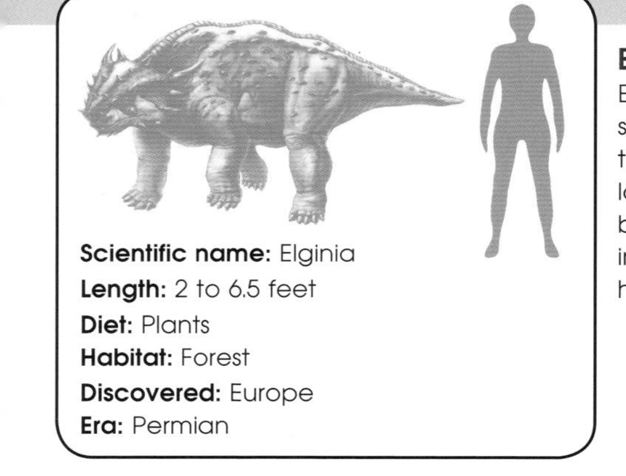

Scientific name: Elginia
Length: 2 to 6.5 feet
Diet: Plants
Habitat: Forest
Discovered: Europe
Era: Permian

Elginia head diagram

Elginia's head was covered in protective spikes, with two very prominent ones at the back of the skull. While these two horns looked fearsome, they were too large to be used for protection or combat but instead were used for display or might have served to attract mates.

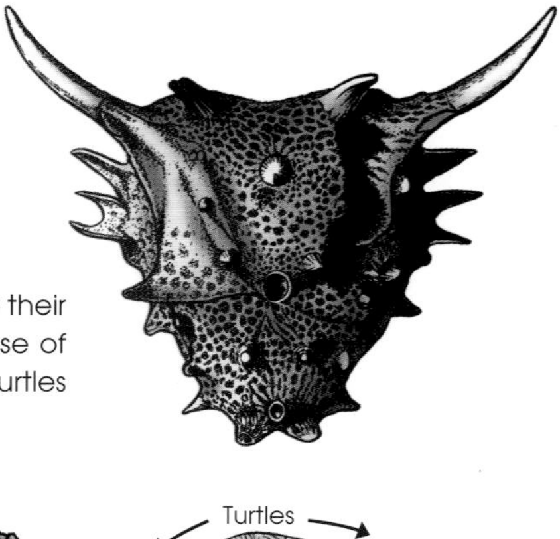

Connection between pareiasaurids and turtles

Some pareiasaurids had bony spikes all over their backs. These bone formations resemble those of turtles, and paleontologists believe that turtles might be their descendants.

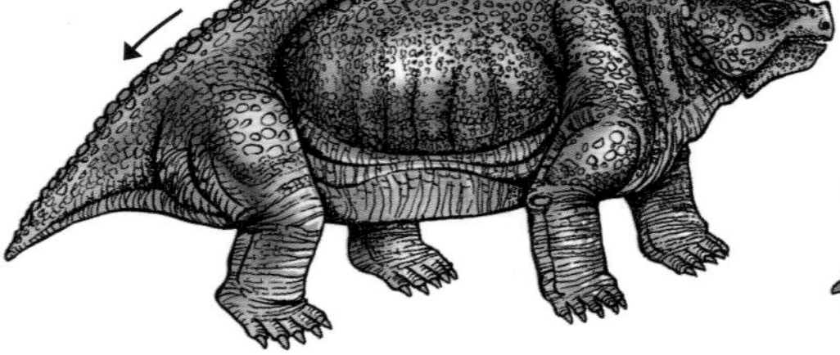
Pareiasaurids

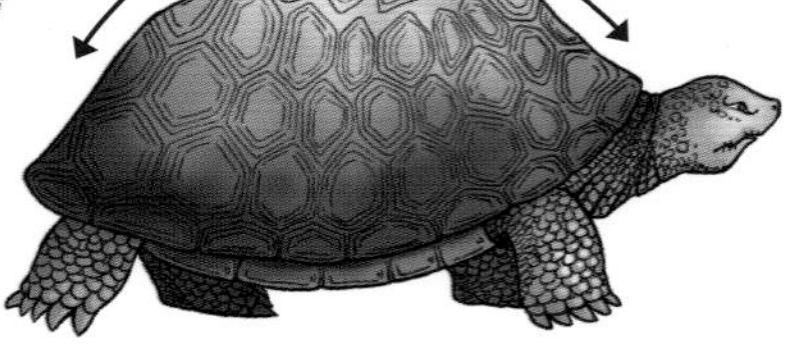
Turtles

CHAPTER 6
PREPARE FOR TROUBLE

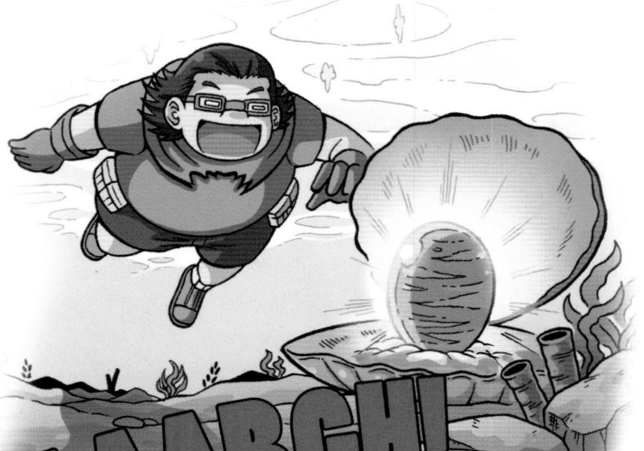

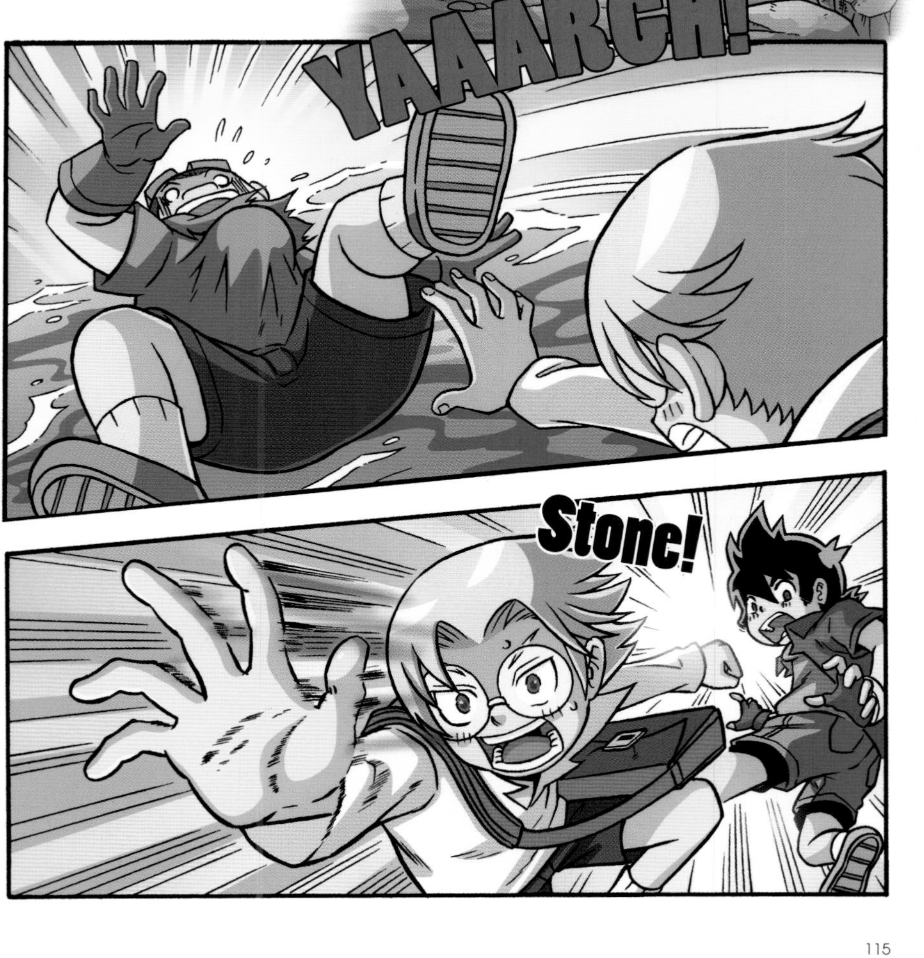
YAAARCH!
Stone!

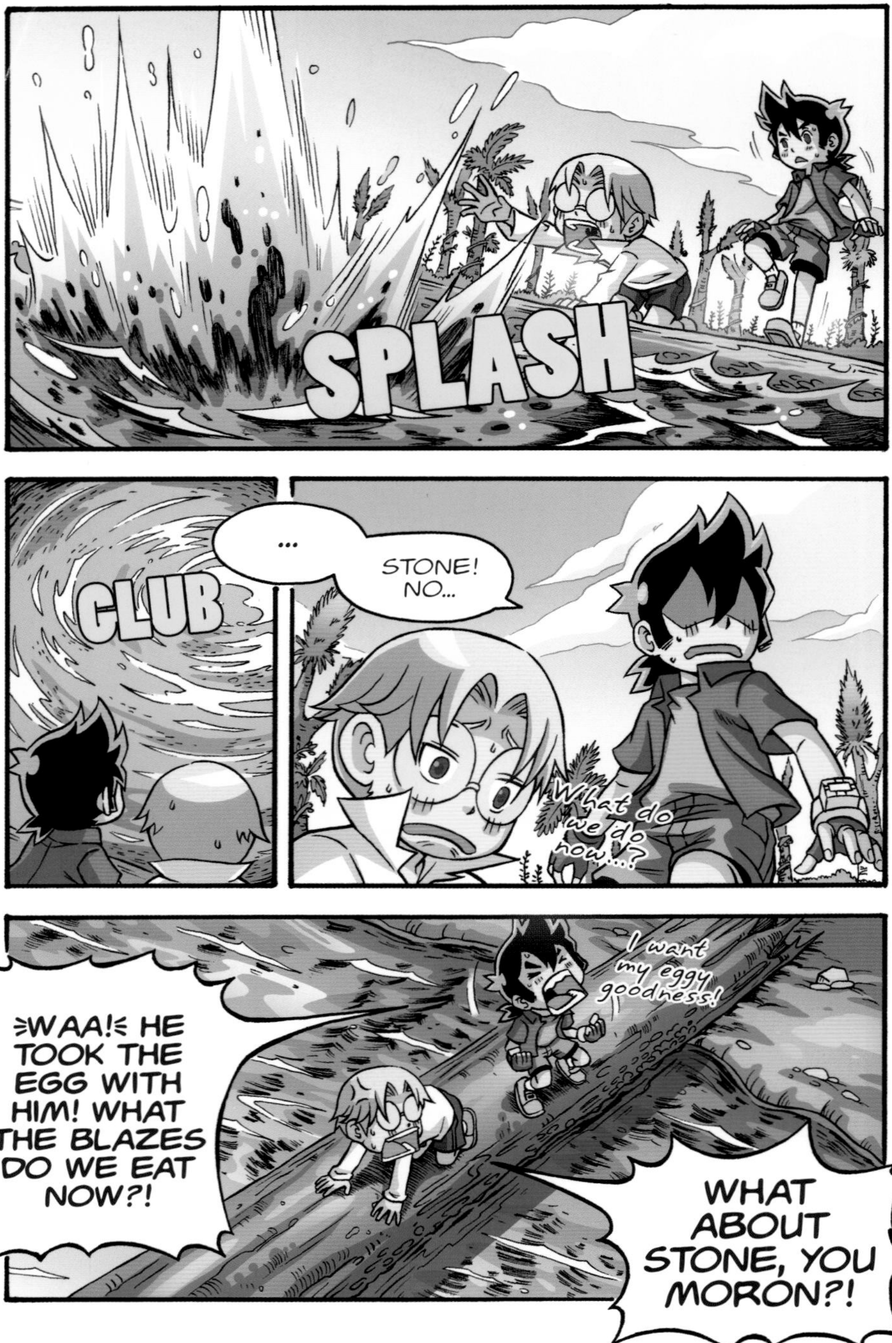
SPLASH
CLUB
...
STONE! NO...
What do we do now...?
I want my eggy goodness!
≋WAA!≋ HE TOOK THE EGG WITH HIM! WHAT THE BLAZES DO WE EAT NOW?!
WHAT ABOUT STONE, YOU MORON?!

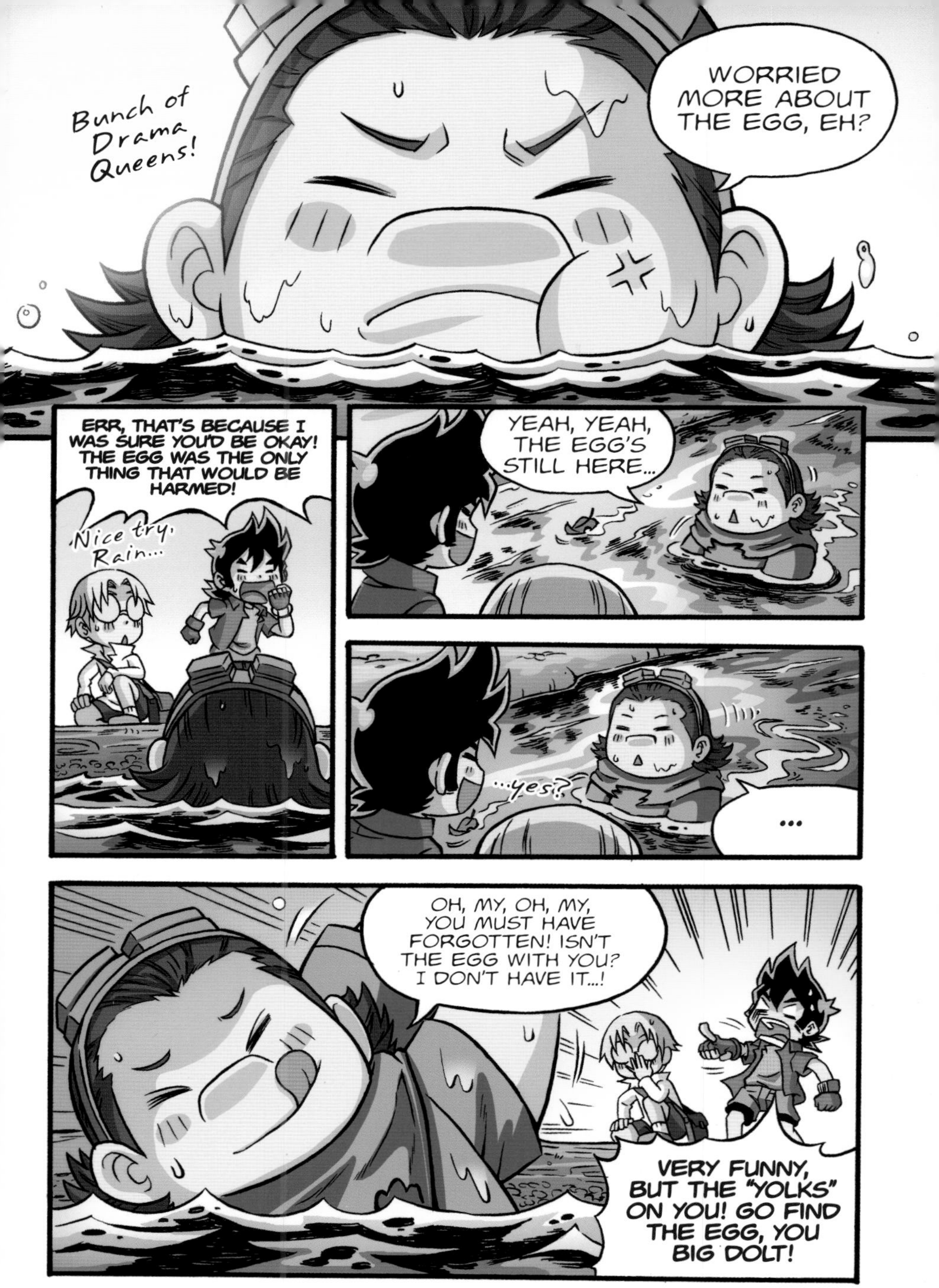
Bunch of Drama Queens!
WORRIED MORE ABOUT THE EGG, EH?
ERR, THAT'S BECAUSE I WAS SURE YOU'D BE OKAY! THE EGG WAS THE ONLY THING THAT WOULD BE HARMED!
Nice try, Rain...
YEAH, YEAH, THE EGG'S STILL HERE...
...yes?
...
OH, MY, OH, MY, YOU MUST HAVE FORGOTTEN! ISN'T THE EGG WITH YOU? I DON'T HAVE IT...!
VERY FUNNY, BUT THE "YOLKS" ON YOU! GO FIND THE EGG, YOU BIG DOLT!

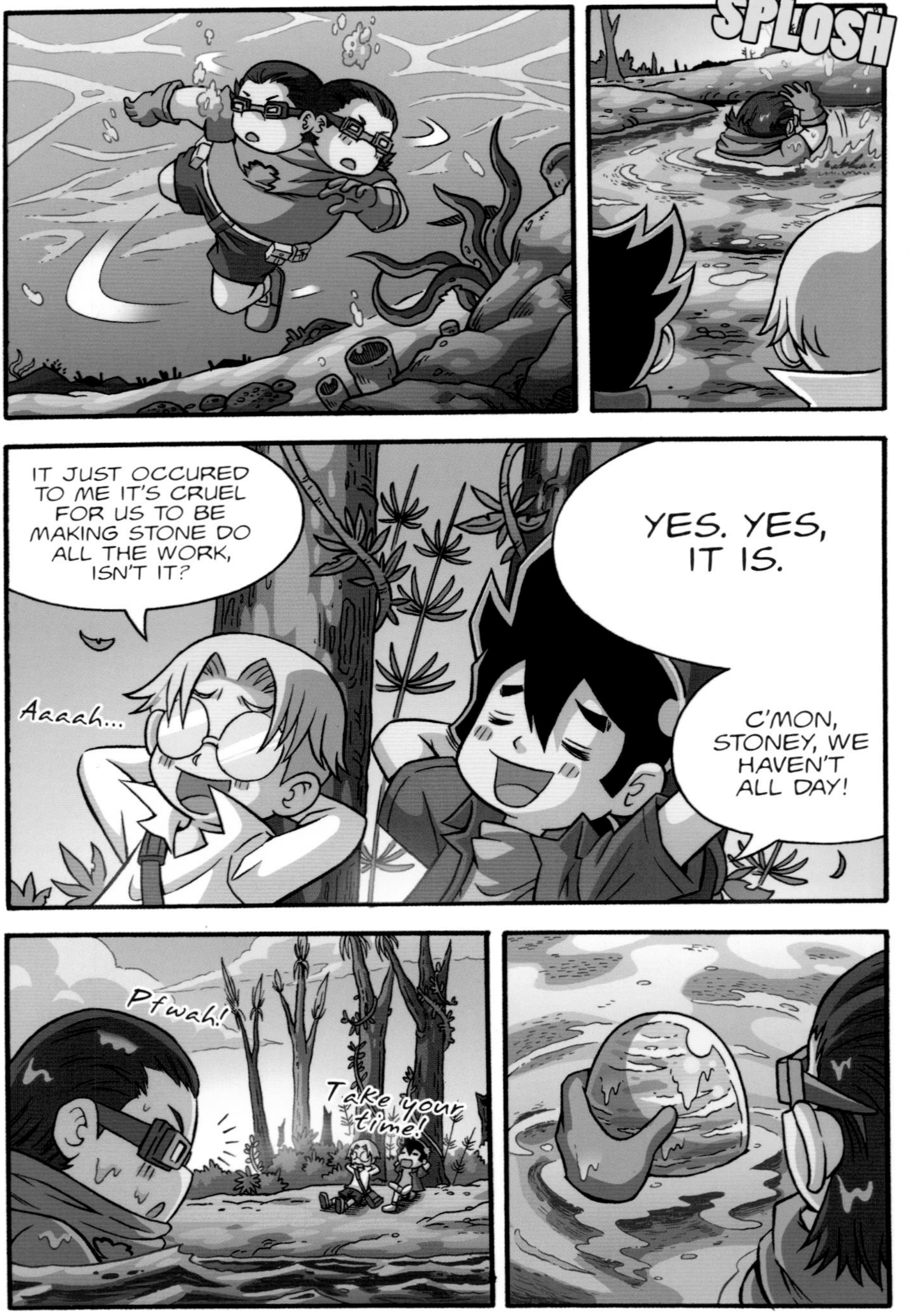
SPLOSH
IT JUST OCCURED TO ME IT'S CRUEL FOR US TO BE MAKING STONE DO ALL THE WORK, ISN'T IT?
YES. YES, IT IS.
Aaaah...
C'MON, STONEY, WE HAVEN'T ALL DAY!
Pfwah!
Take your time!

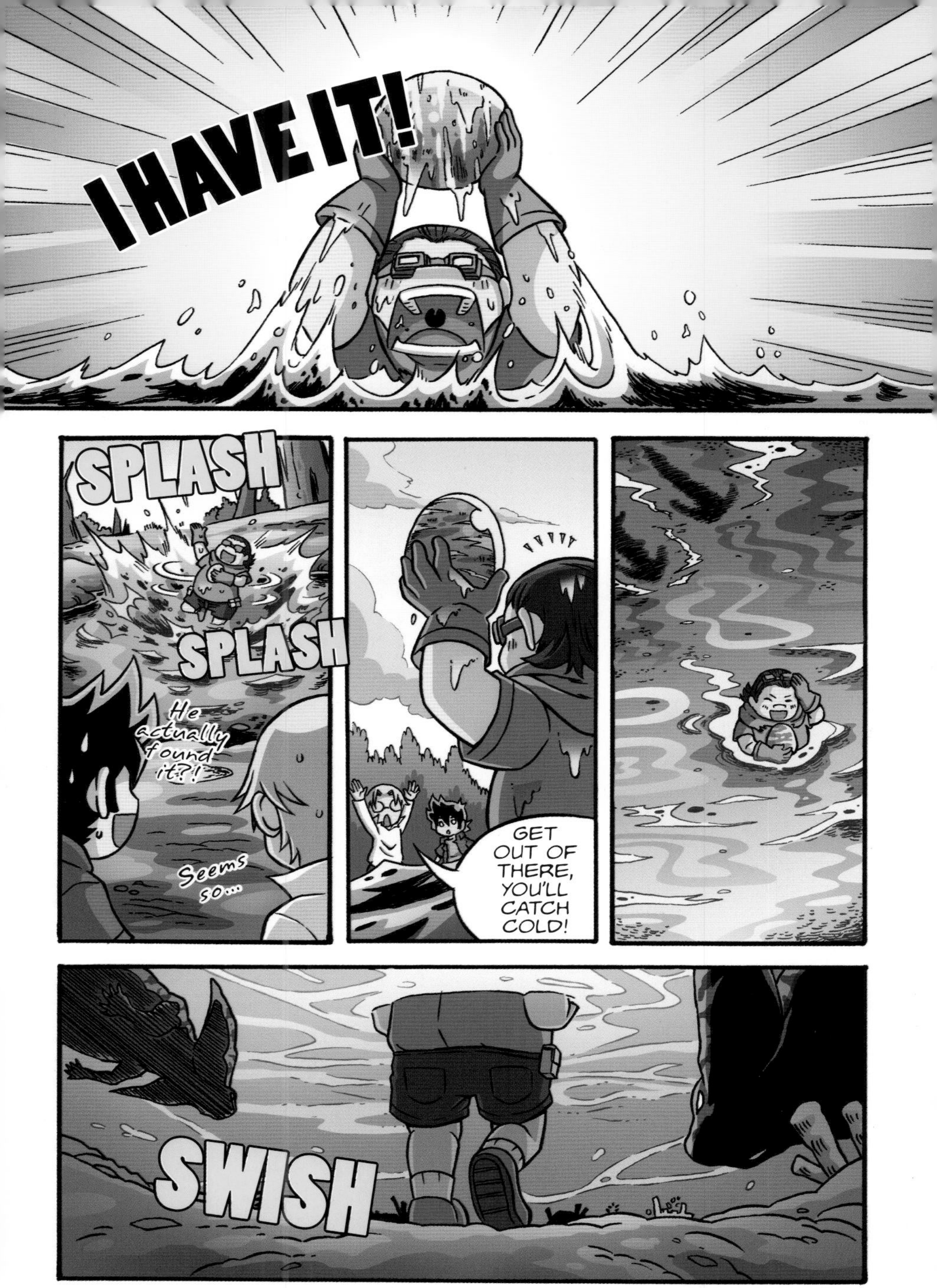
I HAVE IT!
SPLASH
SPLASH
He actually found it?!
Seems so...
GET OUT OF THERE, YOU'LL CATCH COLD!
SWISH

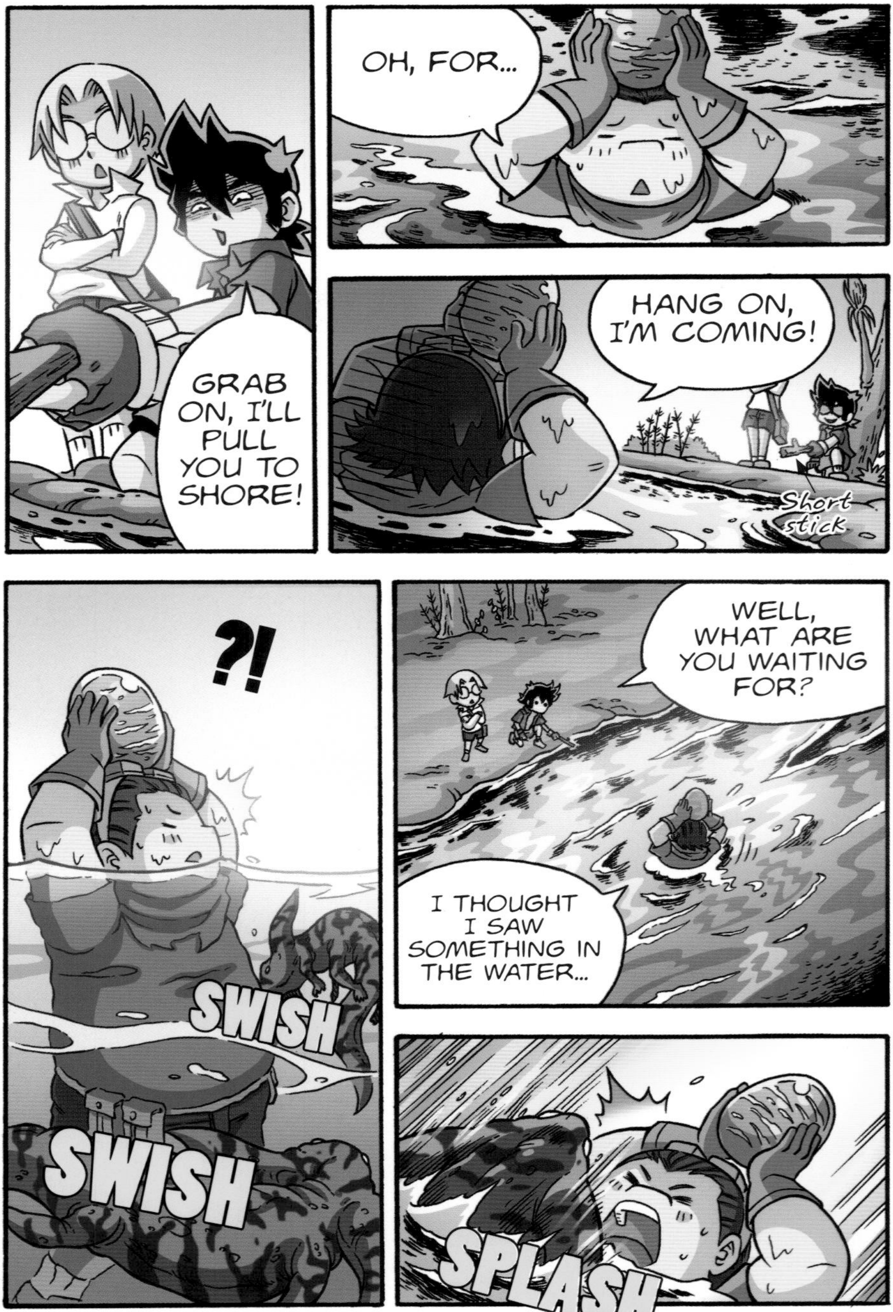
GRAB ON, I'LL PULL YOU TO SHORE!
OH, FOR...
HANG ON, I'M COMING!
Short stick
?!
SWISH
SWISH
WELL, WHAT ARE YOU WAITING FOR?
I THOUGHT I SAW SOMETHING IN THE WATER...
SPLASH

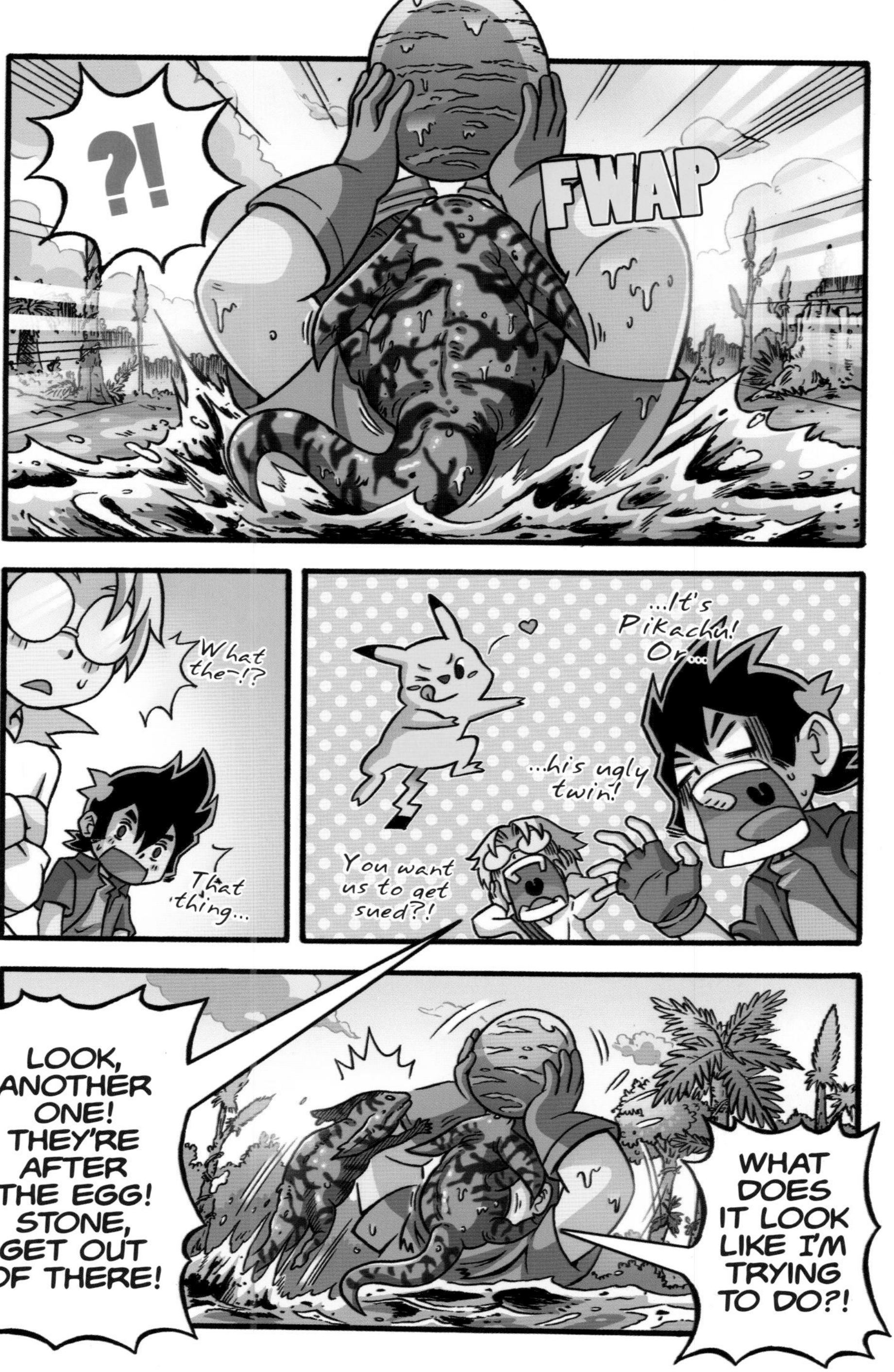

?!
FWAP
What the~!?
That thing...
...It's Pikachu! Or...
...his ugly twin!
You want us to get sued?!
LOOK, ANOTHER ONE! THEY'RE AFTER THE EGG! STONE, GET OUT OF THERE!
WHAT DOES IT LOOK LIKE I'M TRYING TO DO?!

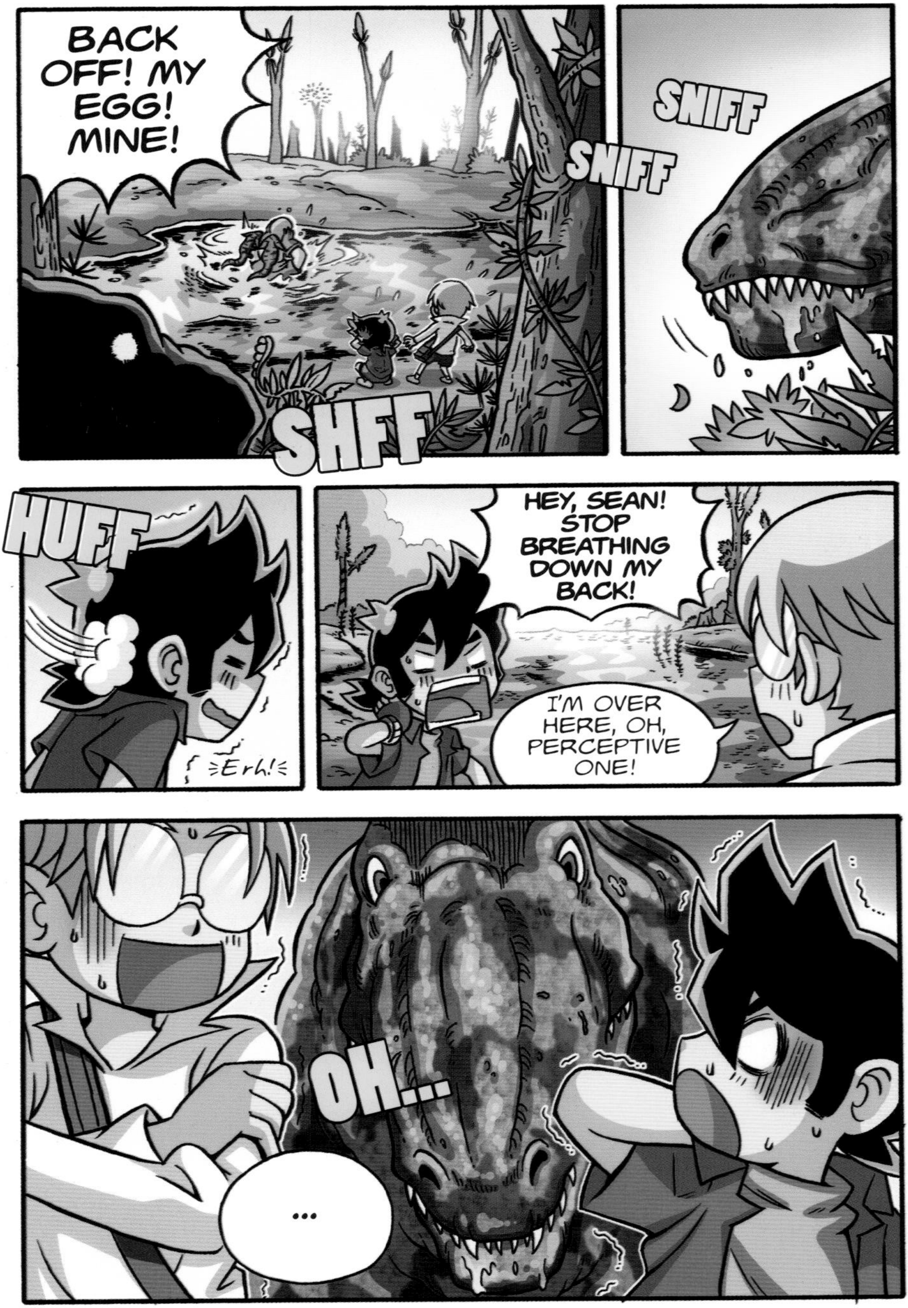
BACK OFF! MY EGG! MINE!
SHFF
SNIFF
SNIFF
HUFF
Erh!
HEY, SEAN! STOP BREATHING DOWN MY BACK!
I'M OVER HERE, OH, PERCEPTIVE ONE!
OH...
...

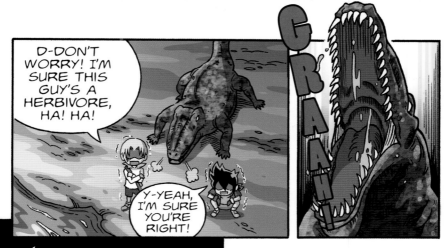

D-DON'T WORRY! I'M SURE THIS GUY'S A HERBIVORE, HA! HA!

Y-YEAH, I'M SURE YOU'RE RIGHT!

GRAAH

I SAID BACK OFF, YOU OVERGROWN SALAMANDER!

TEETH! SHARP POINTY MEAT MINCING TEETH!

I WARNED YOU!

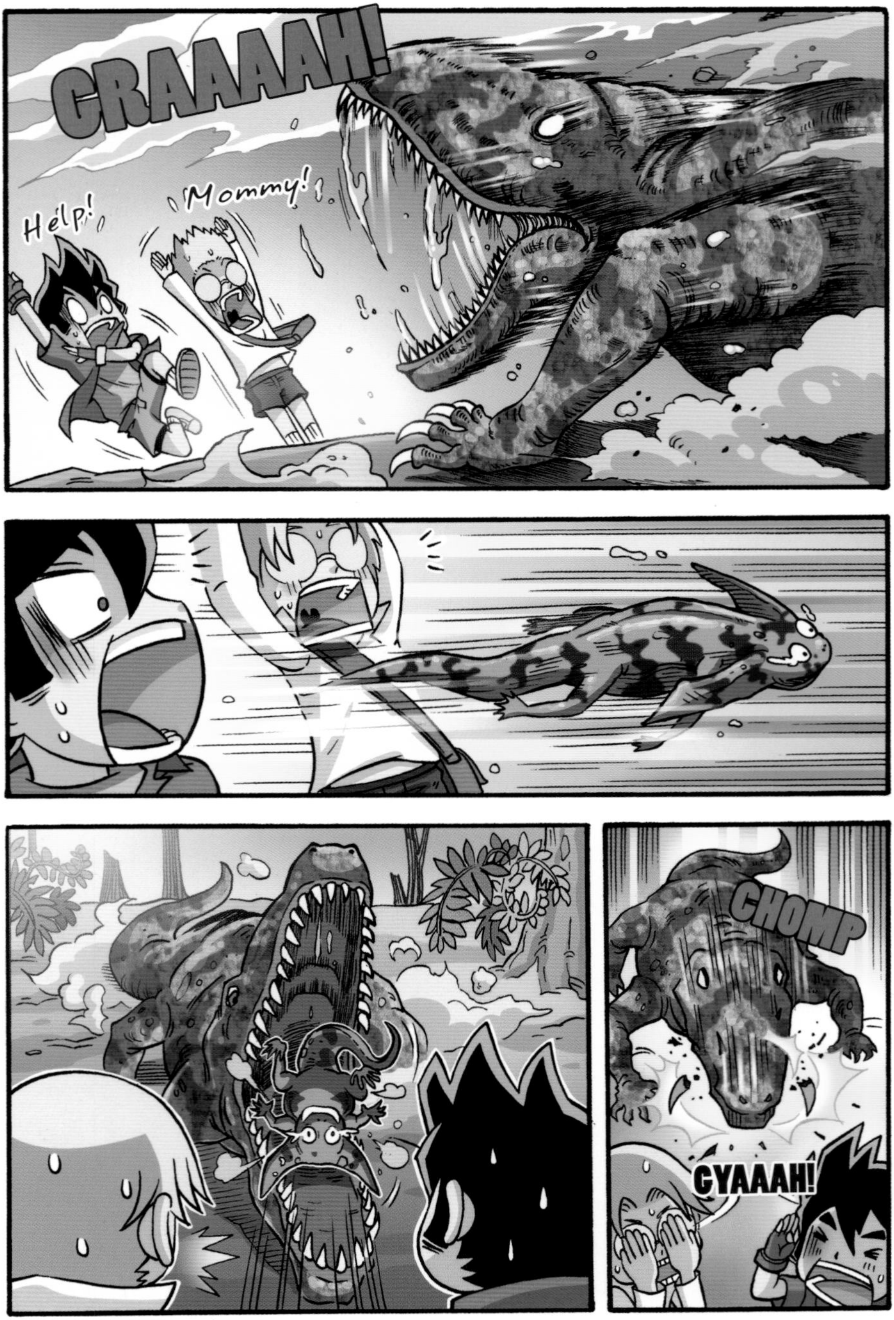
CRAAAAH!
Help!
Mommy!
CHOMP
GYAAAH!

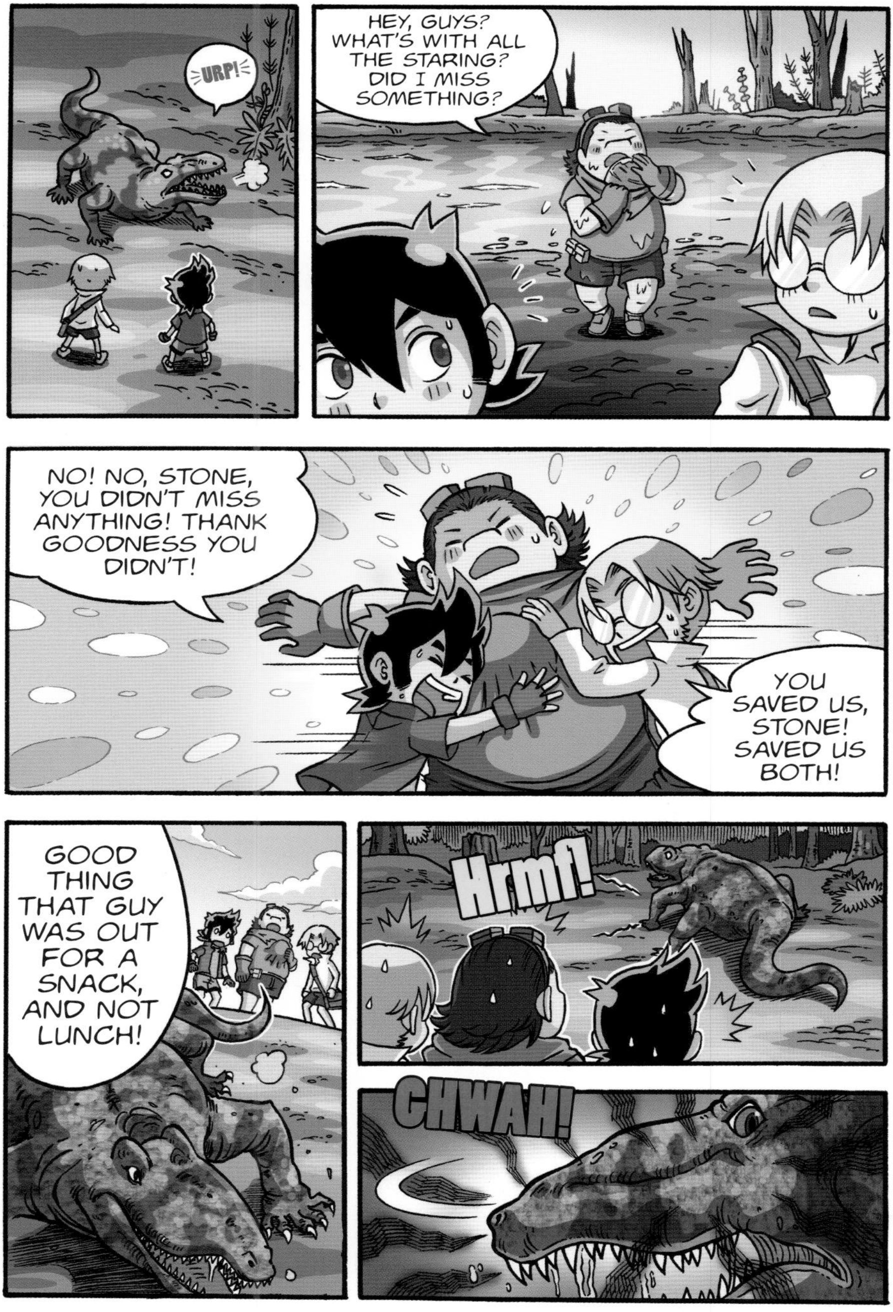
URP!
HEY, GUYS? WHAT'S WITH ALL THE STARING? DID I MISS SOMETHING?
NO! NO, STONE, YOU DIDN'T MISS ANYTHING! THANK GOODNESS YOU DIDN'T!
YOU SAVED US, STONE! SAVED US BOTH!
GOOD THING THAT GUY WAS OUT FOR A SNACK, AND NOT LUNCH!
Hrmf!
CHWAH!

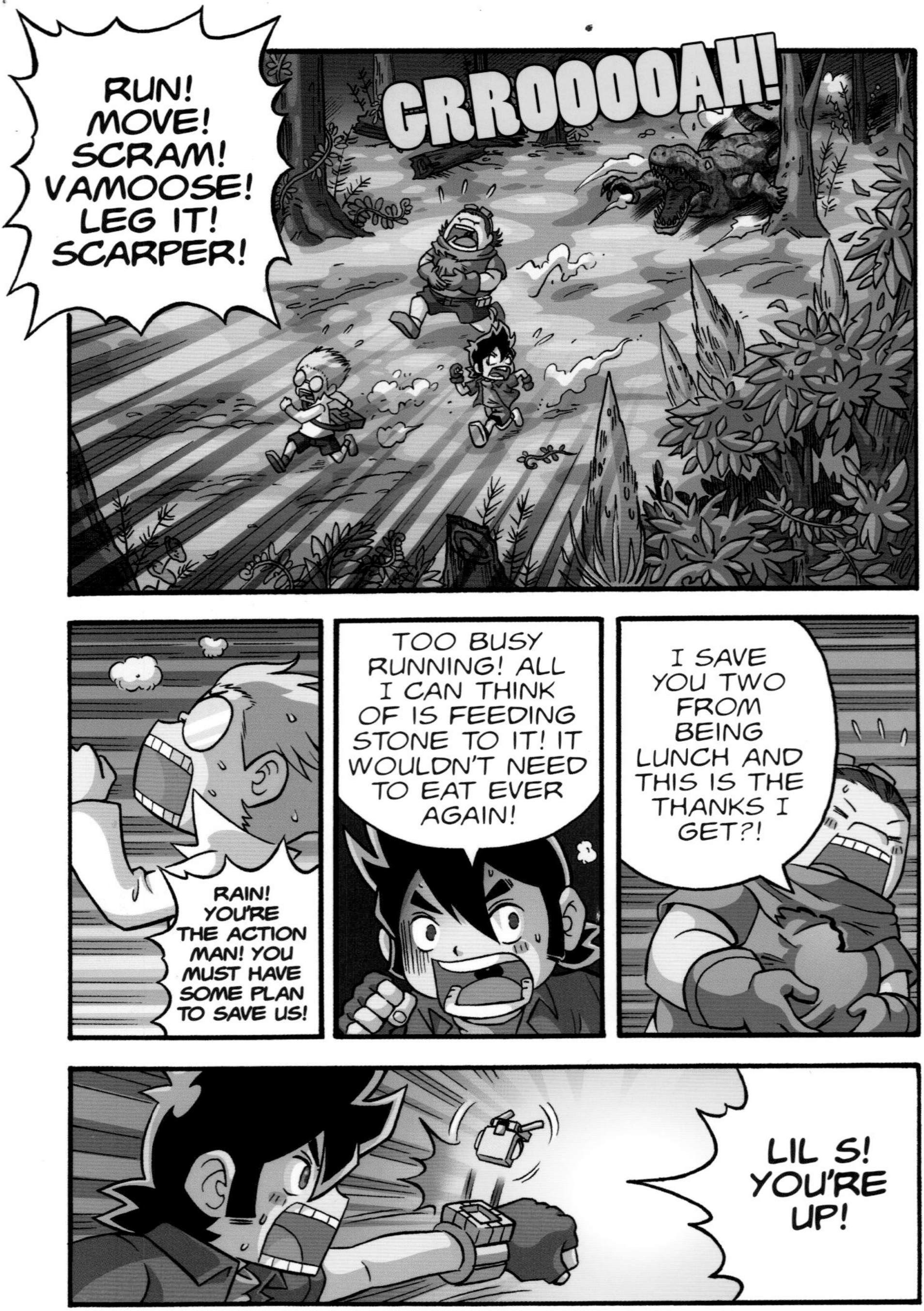

RUN! MOVE! SCRAM! VAMOOSE! LEG IT! SCARPER!
CRROOOOOAH!
RAIN! YOU'RE THE ACTION MAN! YOU MUST HAVE SOME PLAN TO SAVE US!
TOO BUSY RUNNING! ALL I CAN THINK OF IS FEEDING STONE TO IT! IT WOULDN'T NEED TO EAT EVER AGAIN!
I SAVE YOU TWO FROM BEING LUNCH AND THIS IS THE THANKS I GET?!
LIL S! YOU'RE UP!

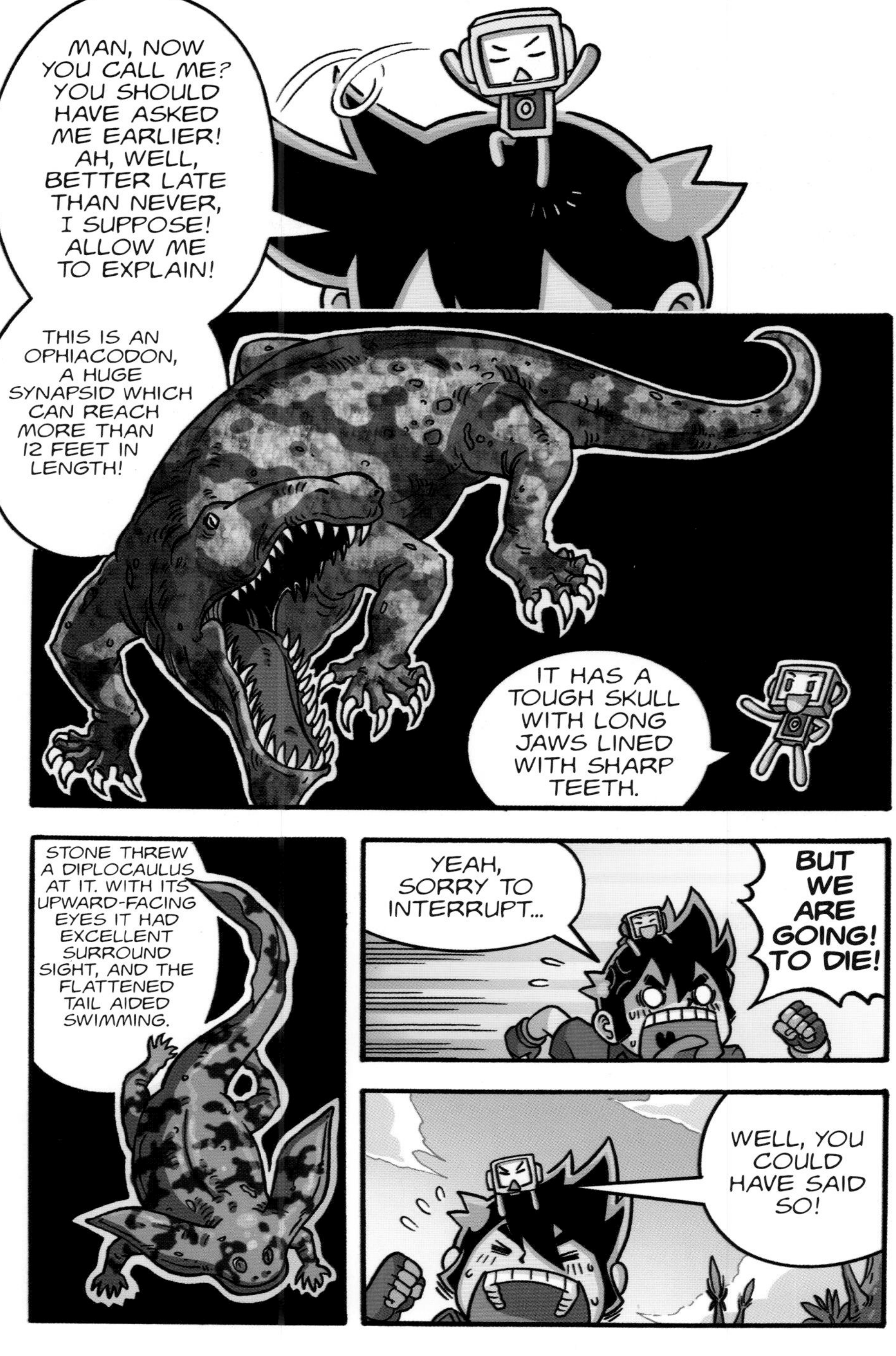
MAN, NOW YOU CALL ME? YOU SHOULD HAVE ASKED ME EARLIER! AH, WELL, BETTER LATE THAN NEVER, I SUPPOSE! ALLOW ME TO EXPLAIN!
THIS IS AN OPHIACODON, A HUGE SYNAPSID WHICH CAN REACH MORE THAN 12 FEET IN LENGTH!
IT HAS A TOUGH SKULL WITH LONG JAWS LINED WITH SHARP TEETH.
STONE THREW A DIPLOCAULUS AT IT. WITH ITS UPWARD-FACING EYES IT HAD EXCELLENT SURROUND SIGHT, AND THE FLATTENED TAIL AIDED SWIMMING.
YEAH, SORRY TO INTERRUPT...
BUT WE ARE GOING! TO DIE!
WELL, YOU COULD HAVE SAID SO!

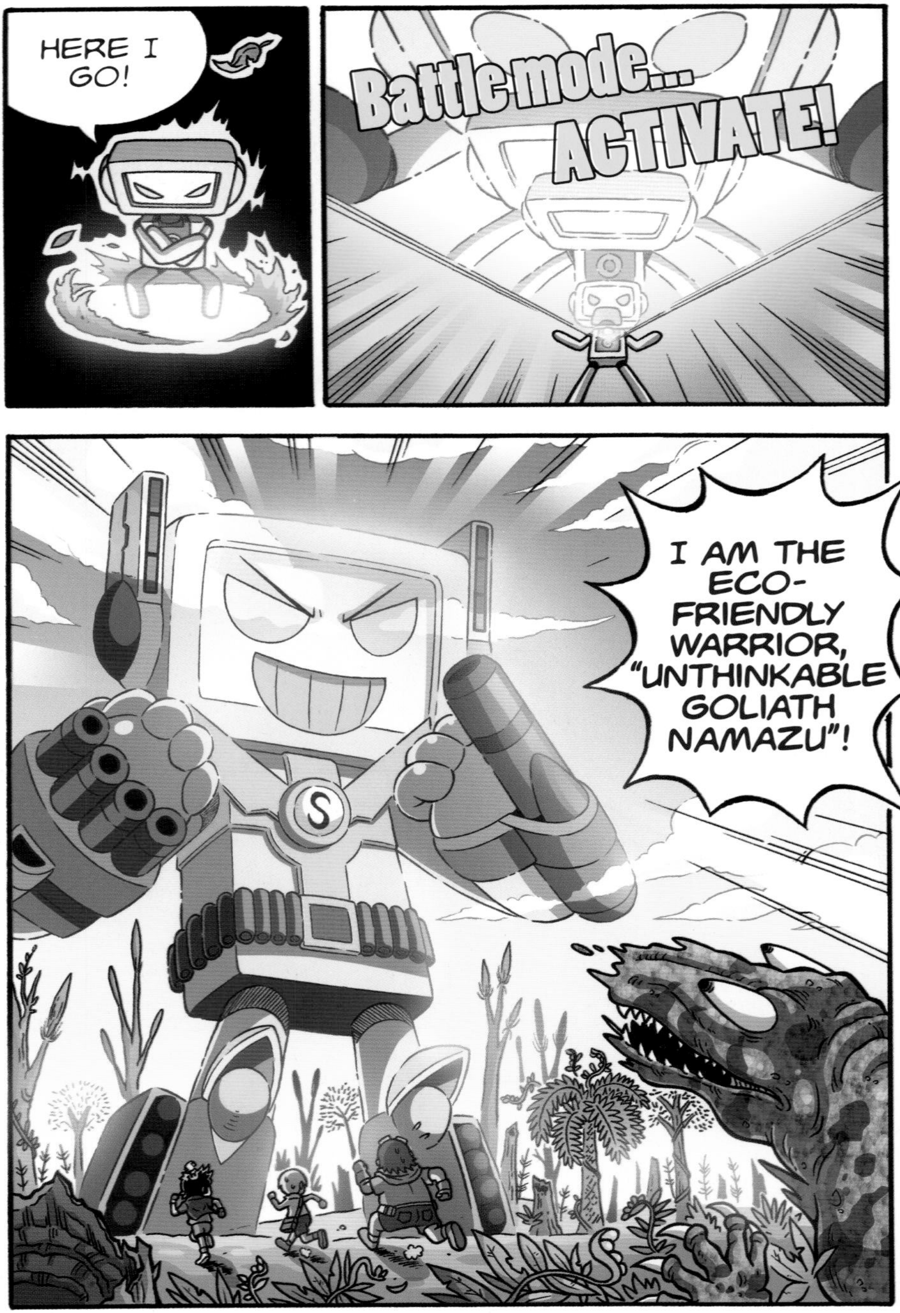
HERE I GO!
Battle mode... ACTIVATE!
I AM THE ECO-FRIENDLY WARRIOR, "UNTHINKABLE GOLIATH NAMAZU"!

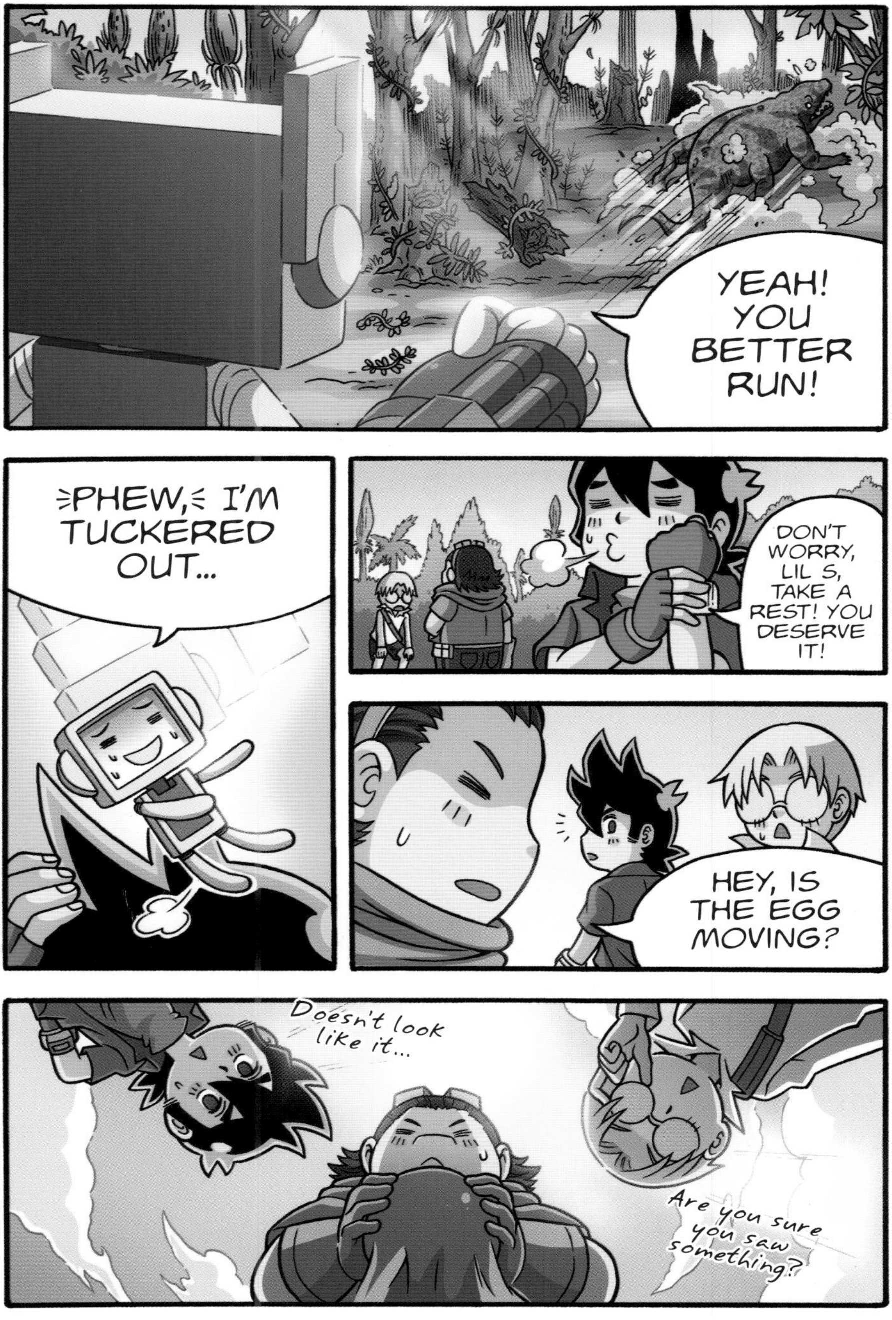
YEAH! YOU BETTER RUN!
PHEW, I'M TUCKERED OUT...
DON'T WORRY, LIL S, TAKE A REST! YOU DESERVE IT!
HEY, IS THE EGG MOVING?
Doesn't look like it...
Are you sure you saw something?

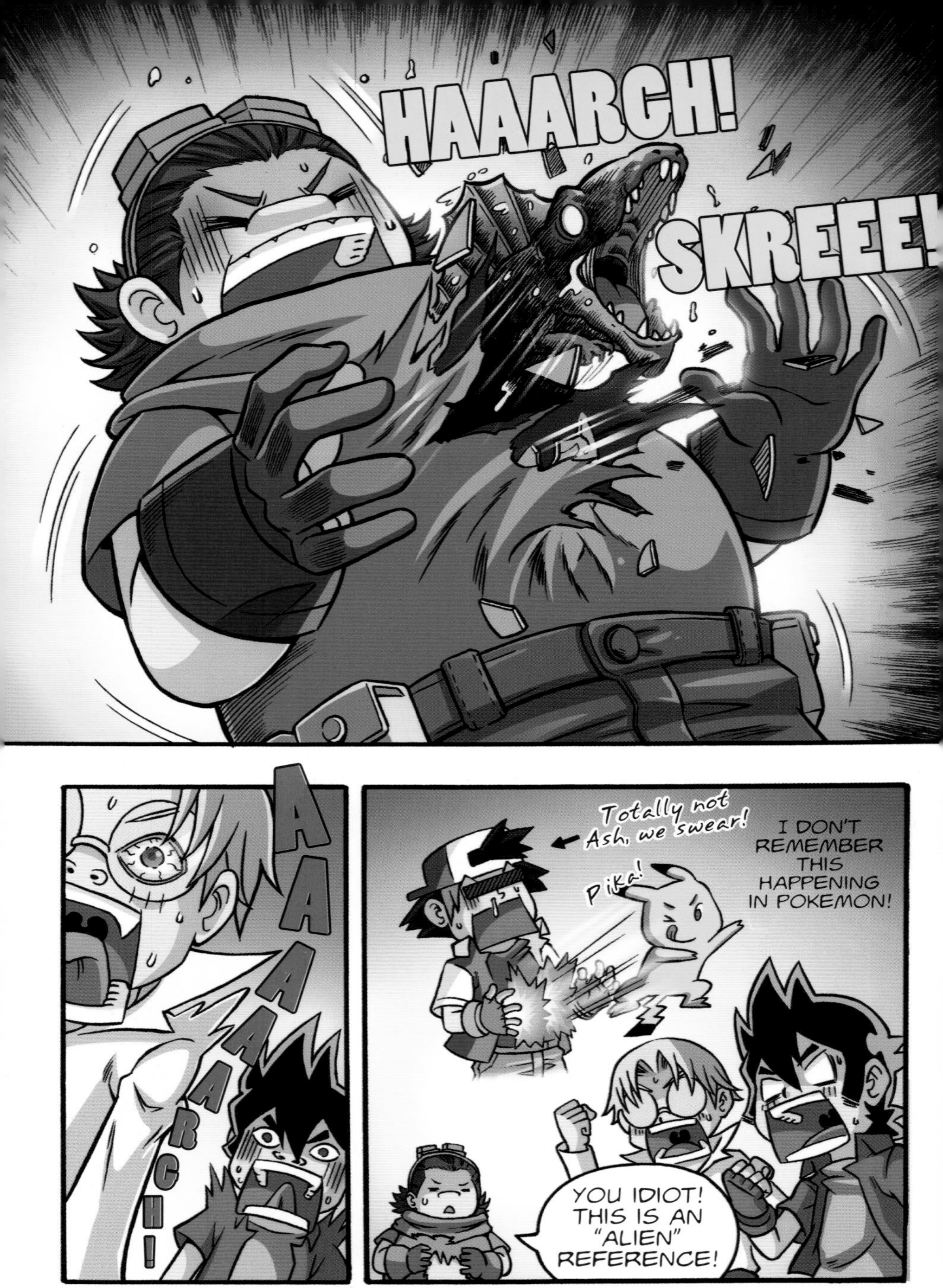
HAAARGH!
SKREEE!
AAAAAAARGH!
Totally not Ash, we swear!
Pika!
I DON'T REMEMBER THIS HAPPENING IN POKEMON!
YOU IDIOT! THIS IS AN "ALIEN" REFERENCE!

PERUSING THE PERMIAN
Ophiacodon

Ophiacodon was an early example of a pelycosaurian, a primitive synapsid. Synapsids had been steadily growing in size; the Ophiacodon itself reached up to 10 feet in length! It was also a key species in mammalian evolution.

Scientific name: Ophiacodon
Length: 6 to 10 feet
Diet: Fish, amphibians
Habitat: Rivers, ponds, and swamps
Discovered: North America
Era: Permian

Cladogram of ancient reptile evolution

Reptiles began emerging 300 million years ago during the Carboniferous, and were divided into 4 groups: Anapsids, Diapsids, Synapsids, and Euryapsids. The Euryapsids, however, are now extinct.

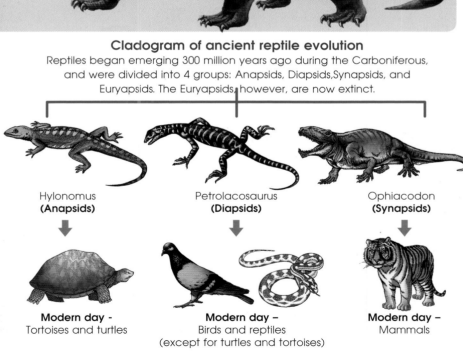

Hylonomus
(Anapsids)

Petrolacosaurus
(Diapsids)

Ophiacodon
(Synapsids)

Modern day -
Tortoises and turtles

Modern day –
Birds and reptiles
(except for turtles and tortoises)

Modern day –
Mammals

Diplocaulus

Diplocaulus is famous because of its boomerang-shaped head, which it used to aid swimming. Given its peculiar head shape, and judging by how short its body and tail were, scientists believe it swam not by waving its body from side to side like fish, but up and down, like dolphins.

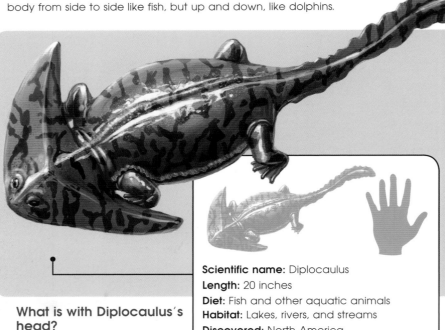

Scientific name: Diplocaulus
Length: 20 inches
Diet: Fish and other aquatic animals
Habitat: Lakes, rivers, and streams
Discovered: North America
Era: Permian

What is with Diplocaulus's head?

The diagram below shows a Diplocaulus's skull; its head was composed of several bony segments, instead of one piece.

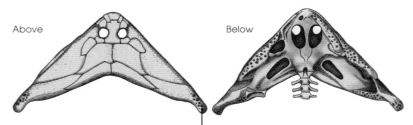

Above

Below

Many scientists still debate what all the strange structures in the Diplocaulus's skull did. One theory is that, apart from helping it swim normally, its streamlined shape allowed Diplocaulus to easily swim against the current. If it needed to surface, it could turn its head up and easily swim upwards, just like how an airplane's wings work.

CHAPTER 7
A LITTLE PROBLEM

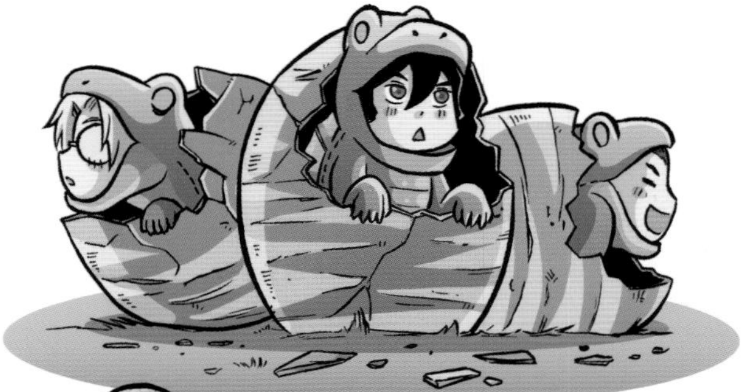

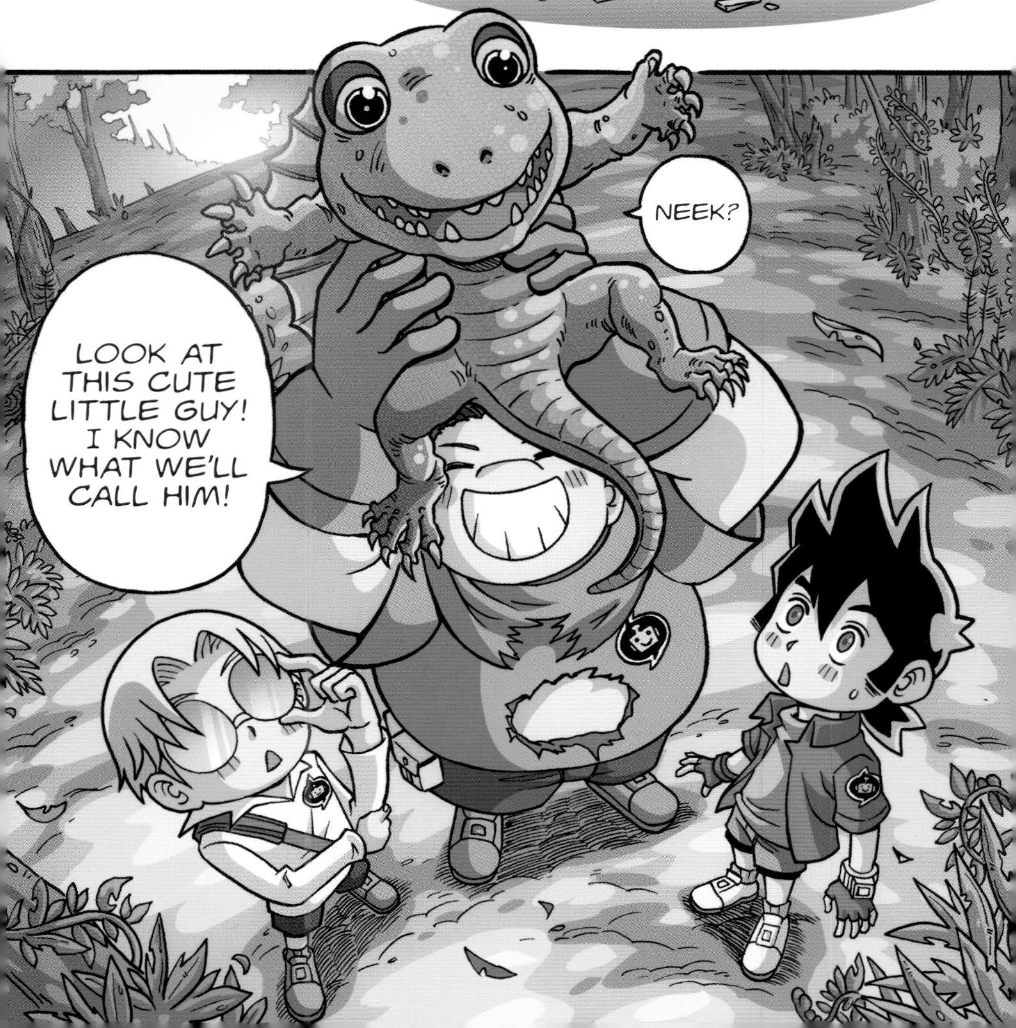
NEEK?
LOOK AT THIS CUTE LITTLE GUY! I KNOW WHAT WE'LL CALL HIM!

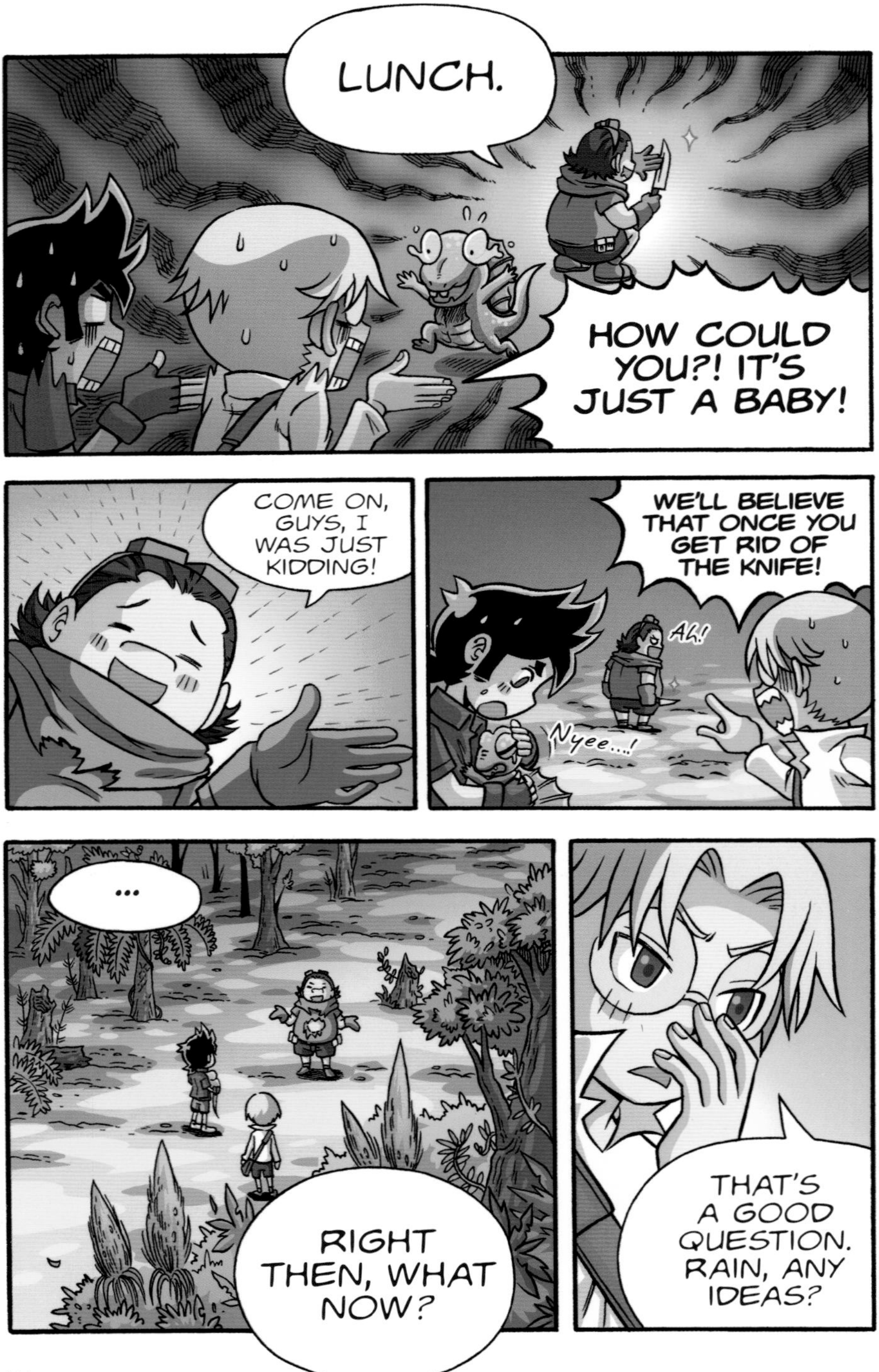
LUNCH.
HOW COULD YOU?! IT'S JUST A BABY!
COME ON, GUYS, I WAS JUST KIDDING!
WE'LL BELIEVE THAT ONCE YOU GET RID OF THE KNIFE!
AH!
Nyee...!
...
RIGHT THEN, WHAT NOW?
THAT'S A GOOD QUESTION. RAIN, ANY IDEAS?

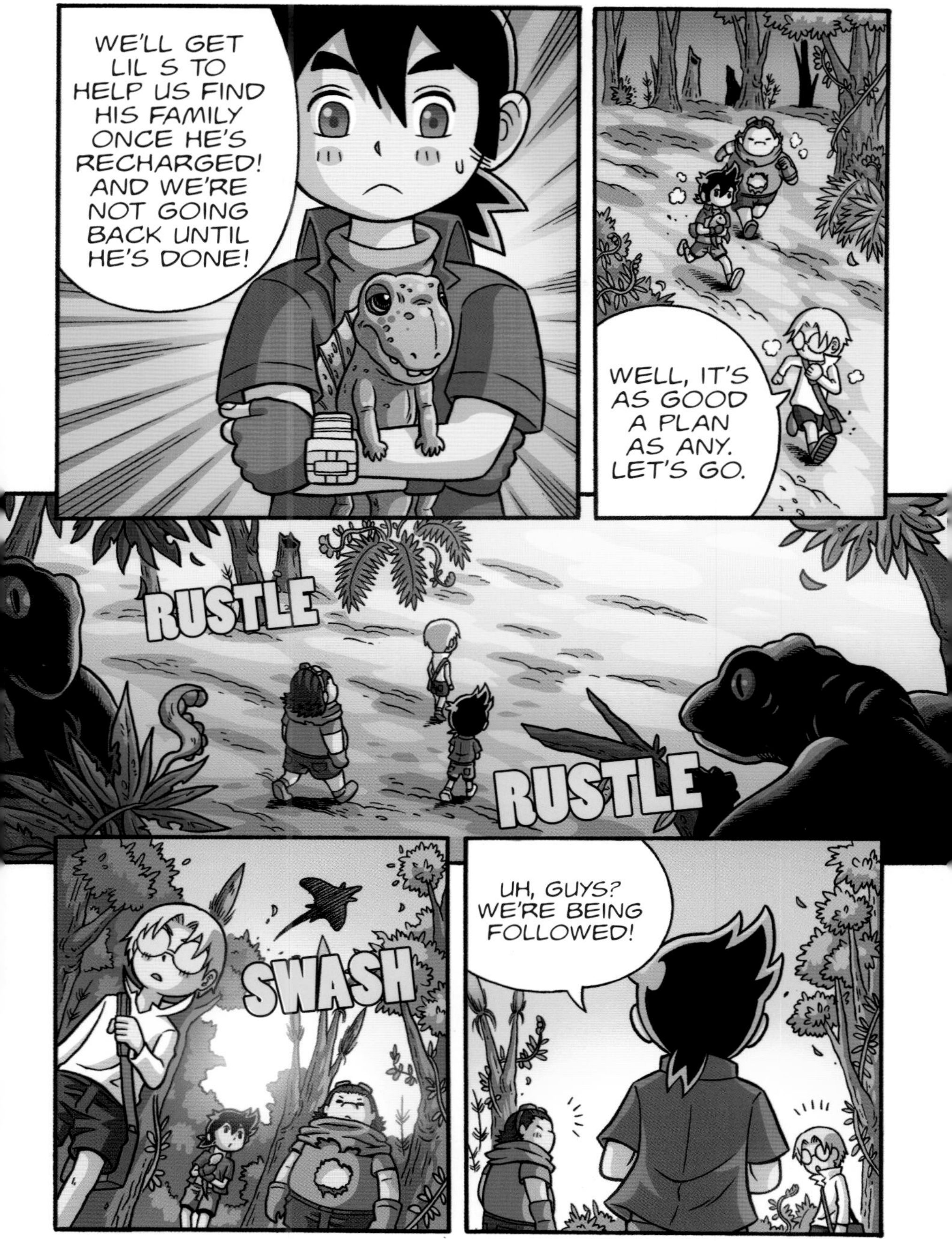

WE'LL GET LIL S TO HELP US FIND HIS FAMILY ONCE HE'S RECHARGED! AND WE'RE NOT GOING BACK UNTIL HE'S DONE!
WELL, IT'S AS GOOD A PLAN AS ANY. LET'S GO.
RUSTLE
RUSTLE
SWASH
UH, GUYS? WE'RE BEING FOLLOWED!

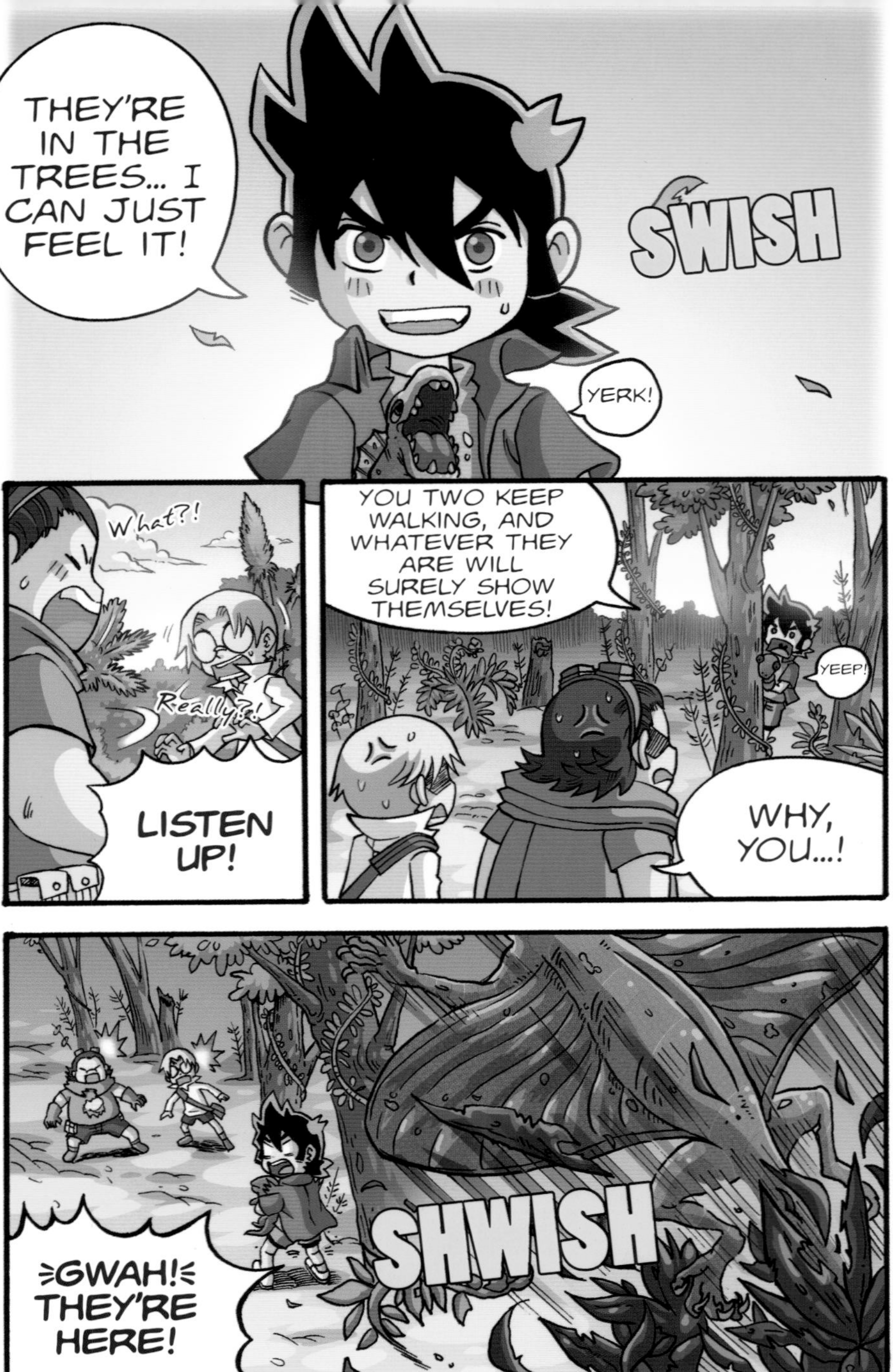

THEY'RE IN THE TREES... I CAN JUST FEEL IT!
SWISH
YERK!
What?!
Really?!
LISTEN UP!
YOU TWO KEEP WALKING, AND WHATEVER THEY ARE WILL SURELY SHOW THEMSELVES!
YEEP!
WHY, YOU...!
SHWISH
GWAH! THEY'RE HERE!

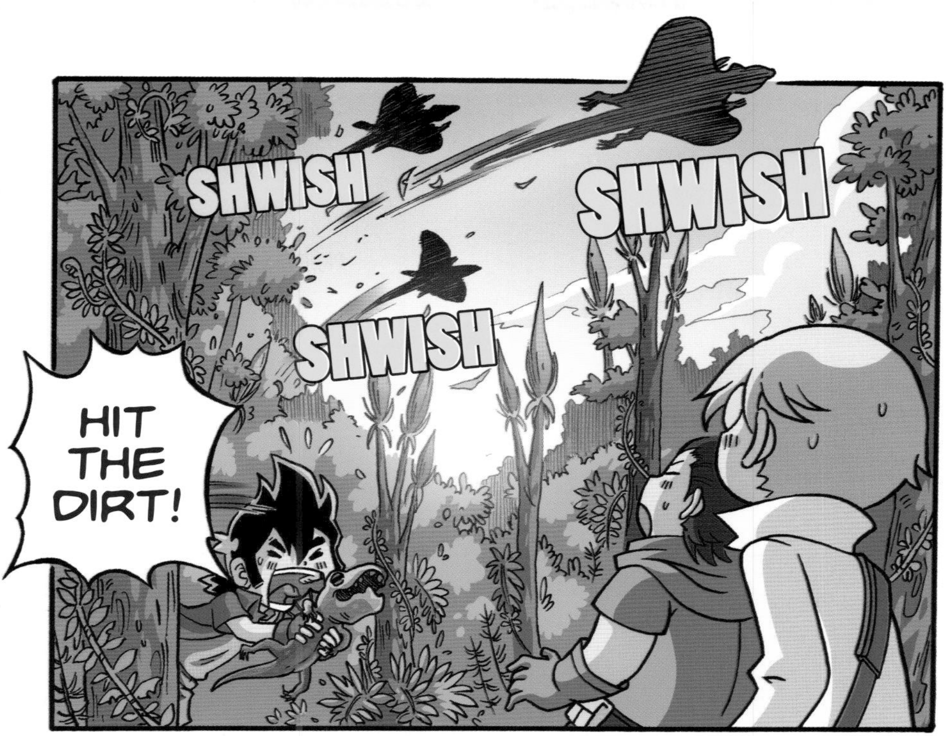
SHWISH
SHWISH
SHWISH
HIT THE DIRT!

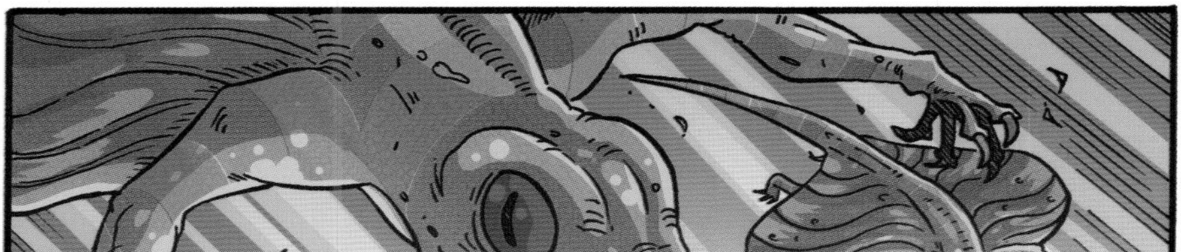

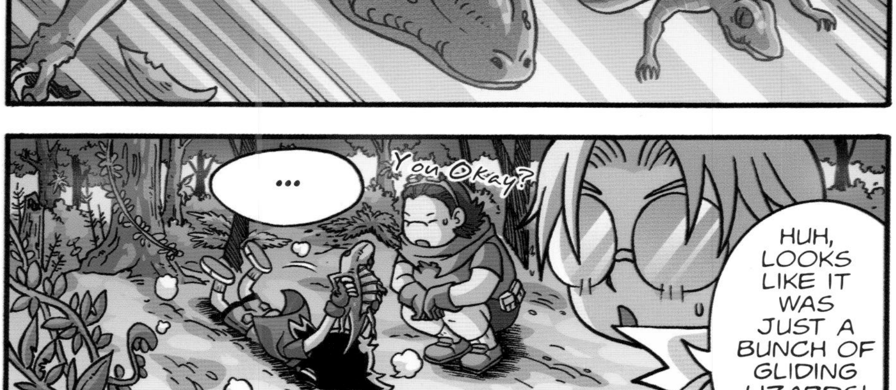
...
You Okay?
HUH, LOOKS LIKE IT WAS JUST A BUNCH OF GLIDING LIZARDS!

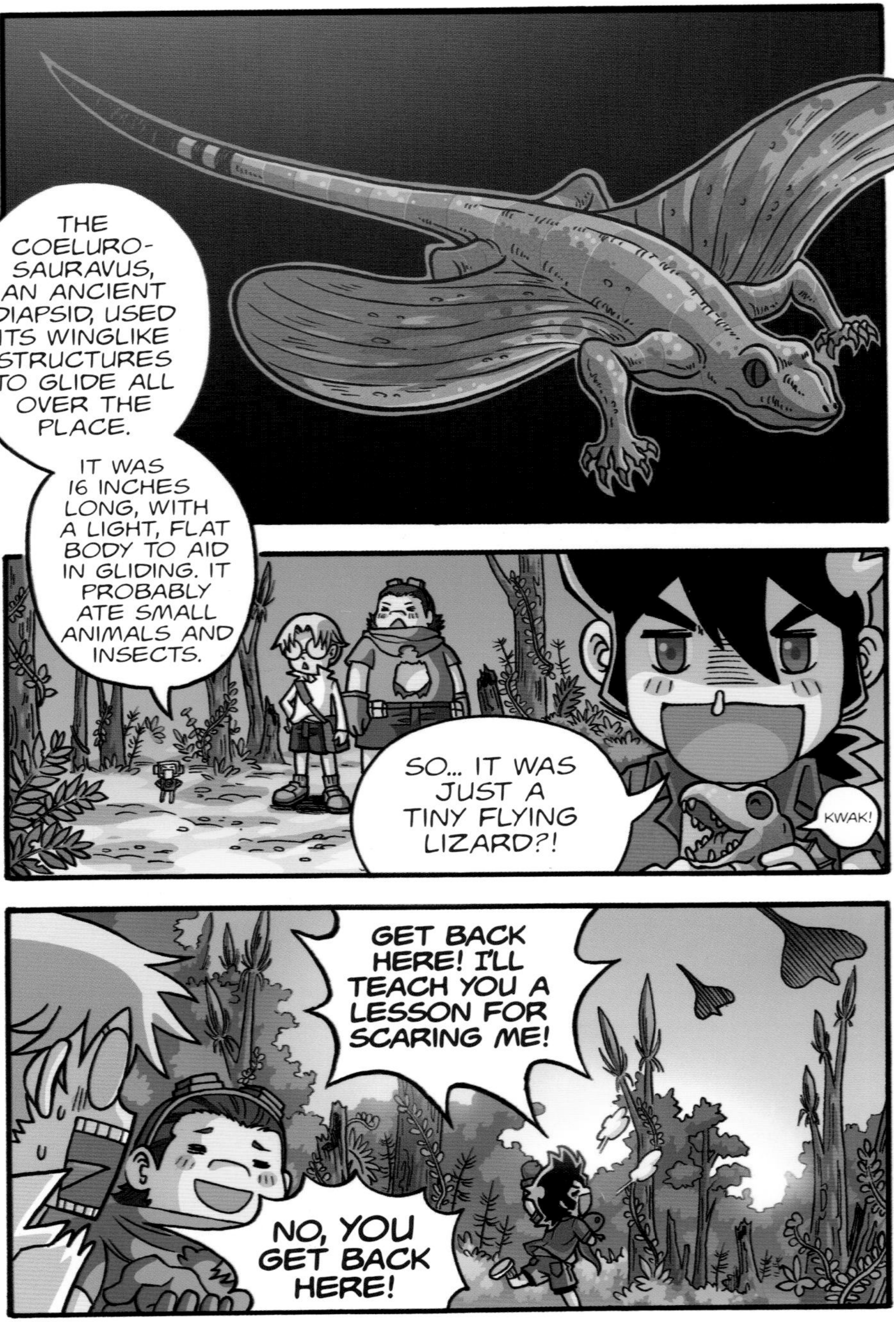
THE COELURO-SAURAVUS, AN ANCIENT DIAPSID, USED ITS WINGLIKE STRUCTURES TO GLIDE ALL OVER THE PLACE.
IT WAS 16 INCHES LONG, WITH A LIGHT, FLAT BODY TO AID IN GLIDING. IT PROBABLY ATE SMALL ANIMALS AND INSECTS.
SO... IT WAS JUST A TINY FLYING LIZARD?!
KWAK!
GET BACK HERE! I'LL TEACH YOU A LESSON FOR SCARING ME!
NO, YOU GET BACK HERE!

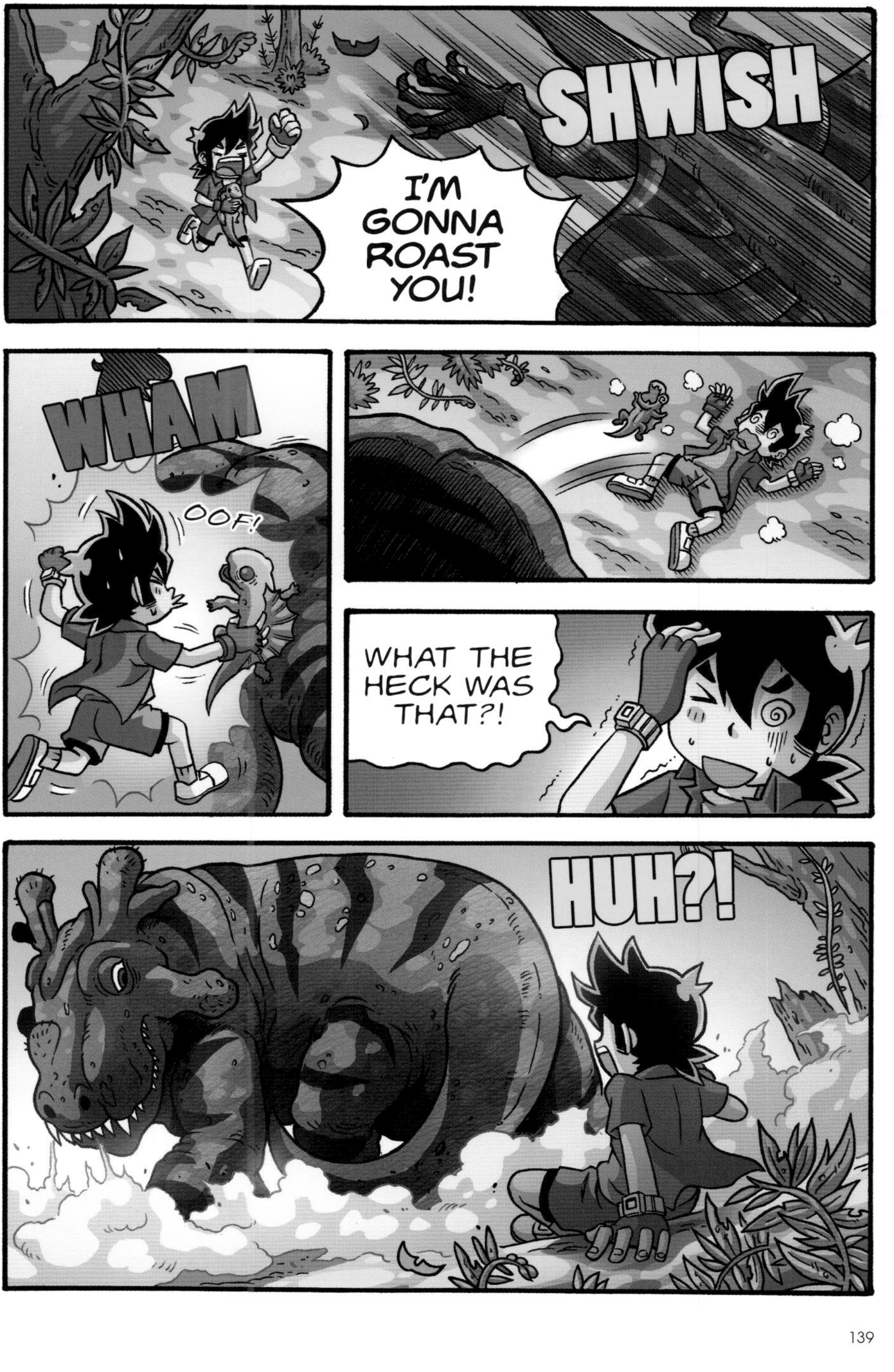
SHWISH
I'M GONNA ROAST YOU!
WHAM
OOF!
WHAT THE HECK WAS THAT?!
HUH?!

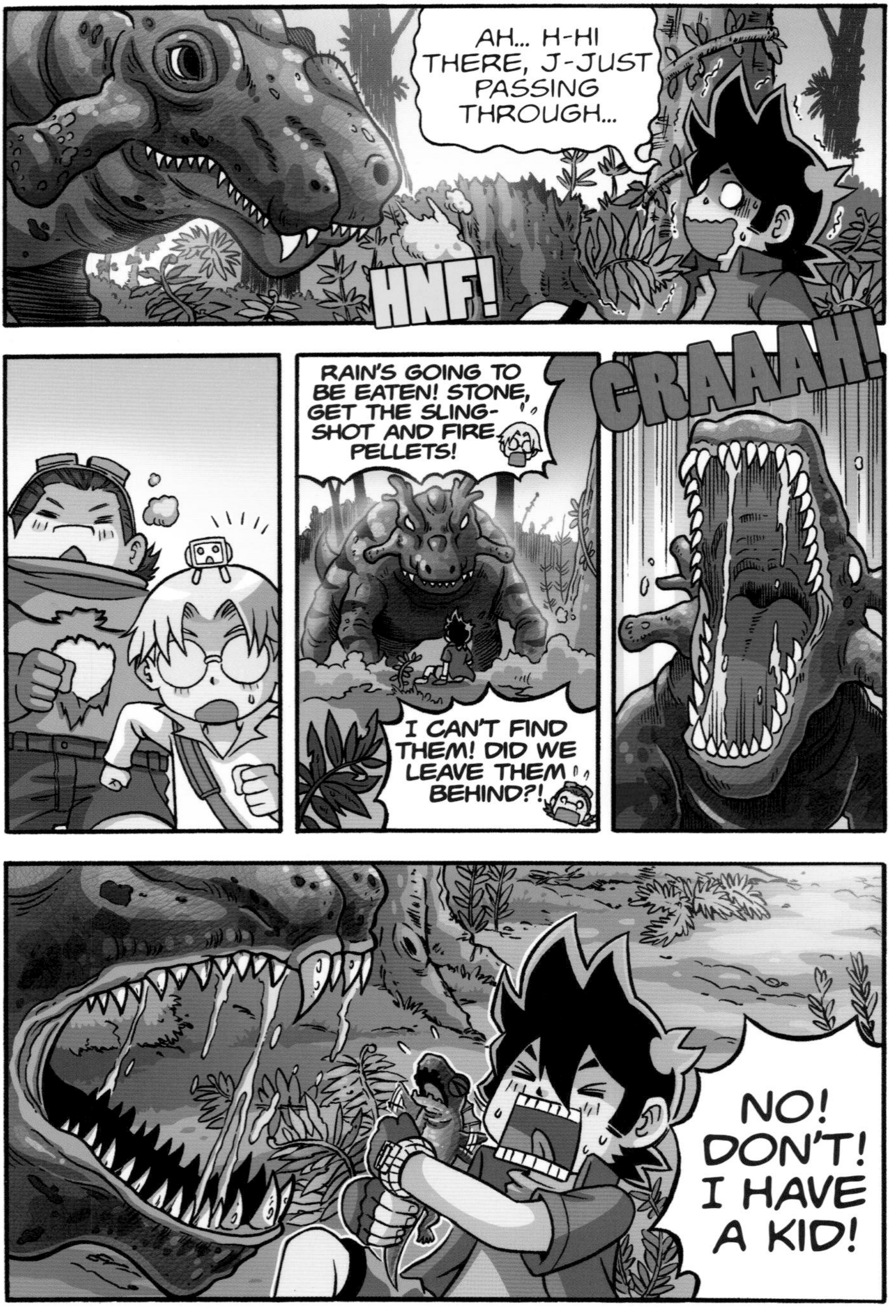
AH... H-HI THERE, J-JUST PASSING THROUGH...
HNF!
RAIN'S GOING TO BE EATEN! STONE, GET THE SLING-SHOT AND FIRE PELLETS!
I CAN'T FIND THEM! DID WE LEAVE THEM BEHIND?!
CRAAAAH!
NO! DON'T! I HAVE A KID!

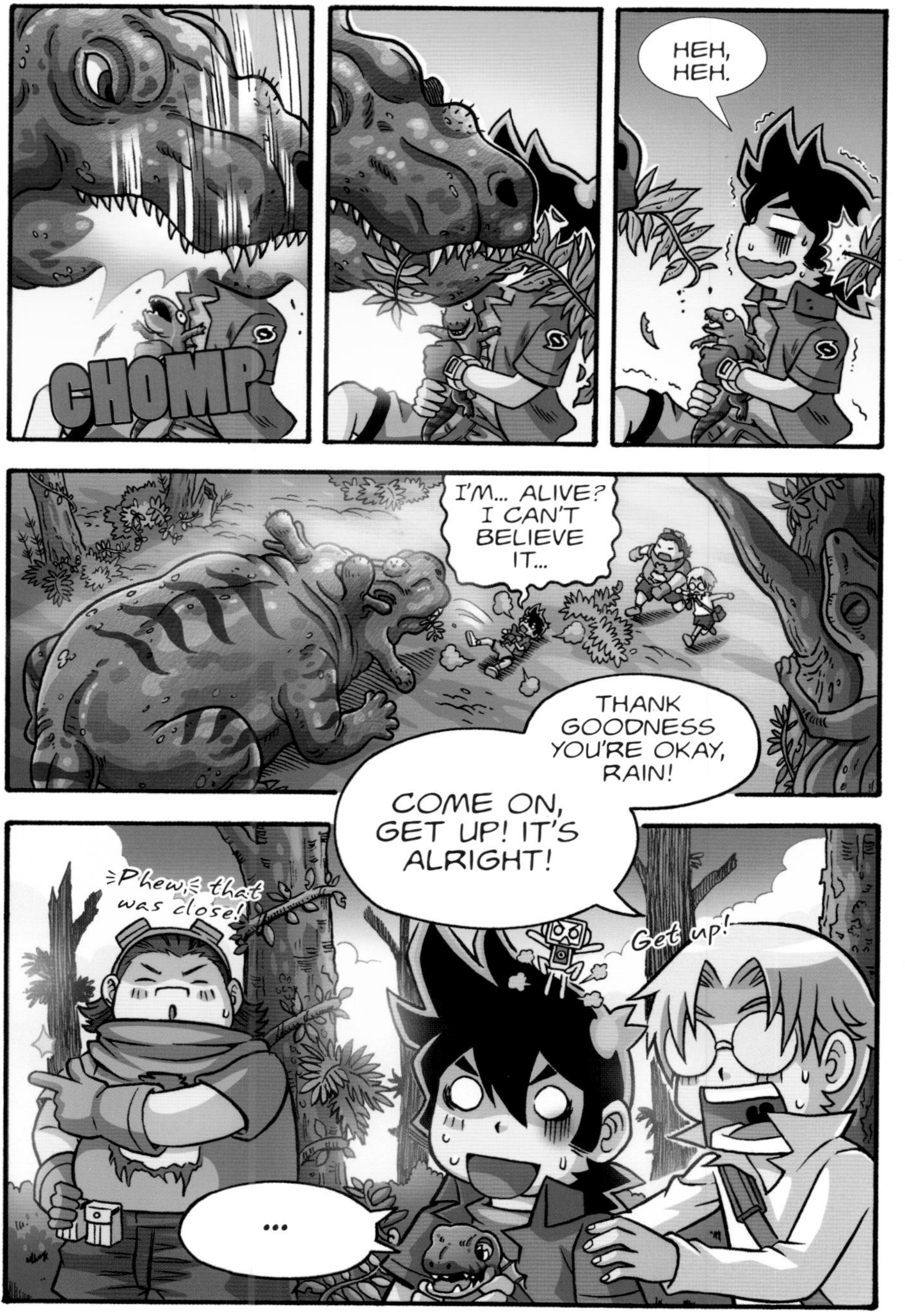

CHOMP
HEH, HEH.
I'M... ALIVE? I CAN'T BELIEVE IT...
THANK GOODNESS YOU'RE OKAY, RAIN!
COME ON, GET UP! IT'S ALRIGHT!
Phew, that was close!
Get up!
...

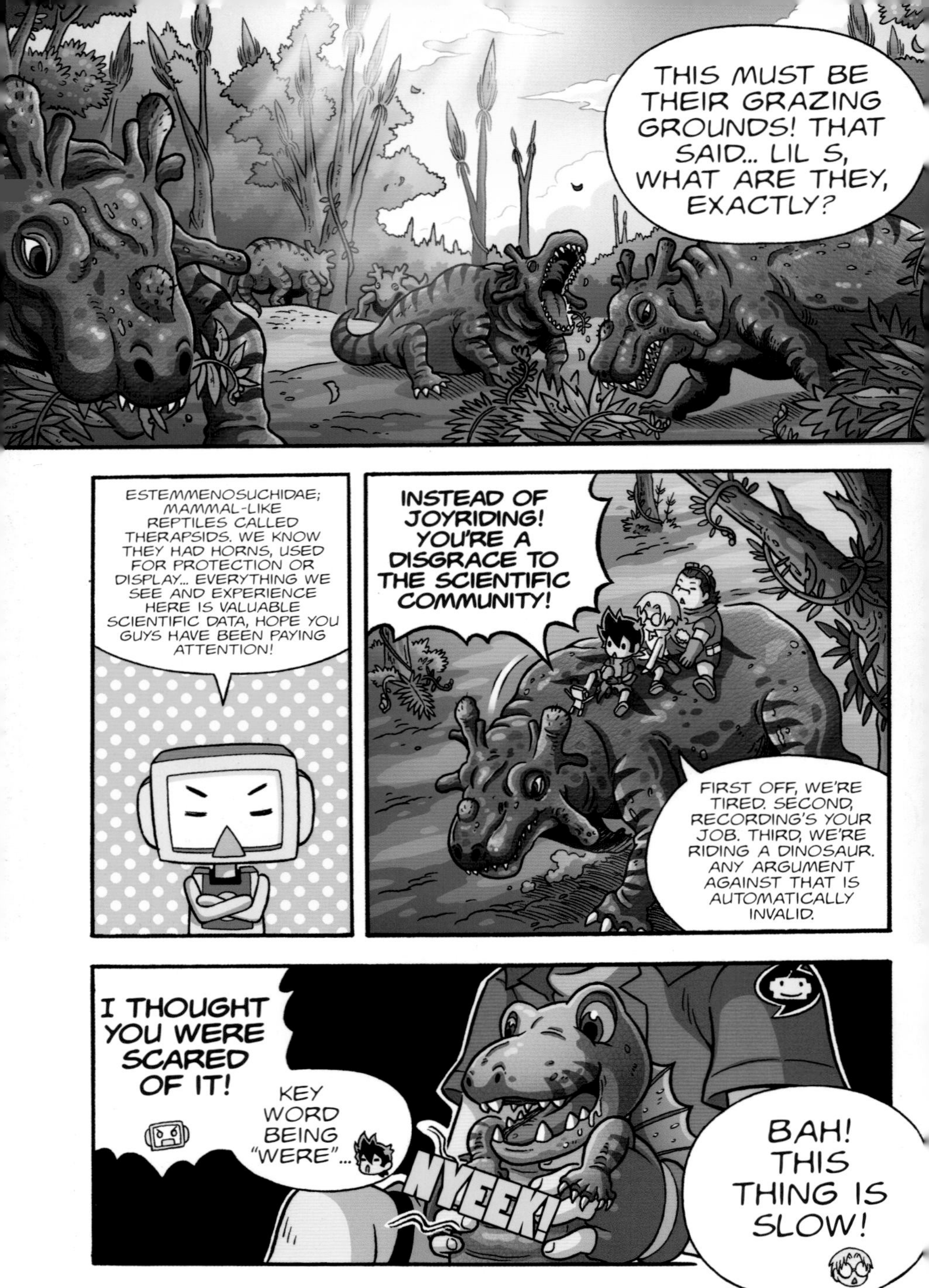
THIS MUST BE THEIR GRAZING GROUNDS! THAT SAID... LIL S, WHAT ARE THEY, EXACTLY?
ESTEMMENOSUCHIDAE; MAMMAL-LIKE REPTILES CALLED THERAPSIDS. WE KNOW THEY HAD HORNS, USED FOR PROTECTION OR DISPLAY... EVERYTHING WE SEE AND EXPERIENCE HERE IS VALUABLE SCIENTIFIC DATA, HOPE YOU GUYS HAVE BEEN PAYING ATTENTION!
INSTEAD OF JOYRIDING! YOU'RE A DISGRACE TO THE SCIENTIFIC COMMUNITY!
FIRST OFF, WE'RE TIRED. SECOND, RECORDING'S YOUR JOB. THIRD, WE'RE RIDING A DINOSAUR. ANY ARGUMENT AGAINST THAT IS AUTOMATICALLY INVALID.
I THOUGHT YOU WERE SCARED OF IT!
KEY WORD BEING "WERE"...
NYEEK!
BAH! THIS THING IS SLOW!

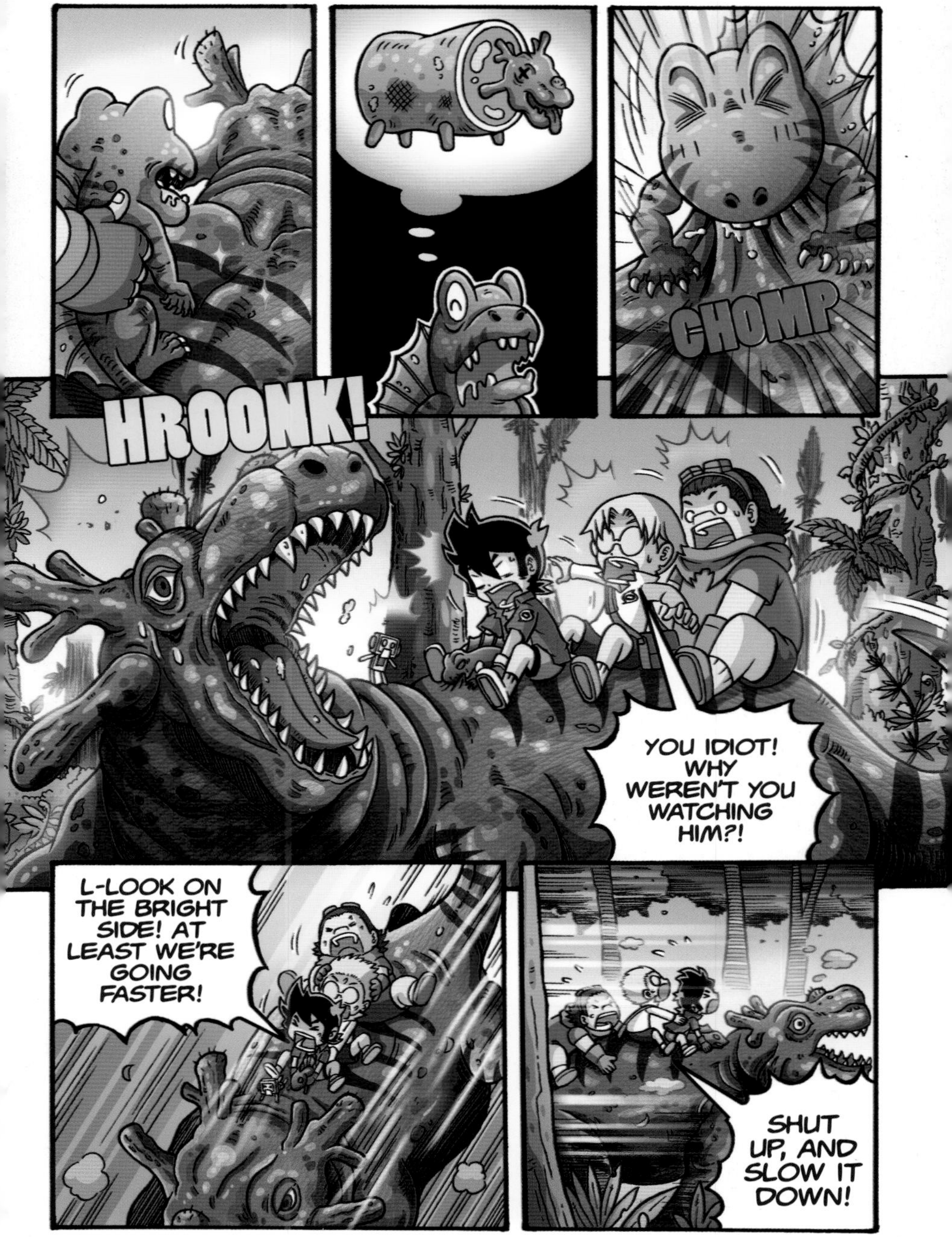
CHOMP
HROONK!
YOU IDIOT! WHY WEREN'T YOU WATCHING HIM?!
L-LOOK ON THE BRIGHT SIDE! AT LEAST WE'RE GOING FASTER!
SHUT UP, AND SLOW IT DOWN!

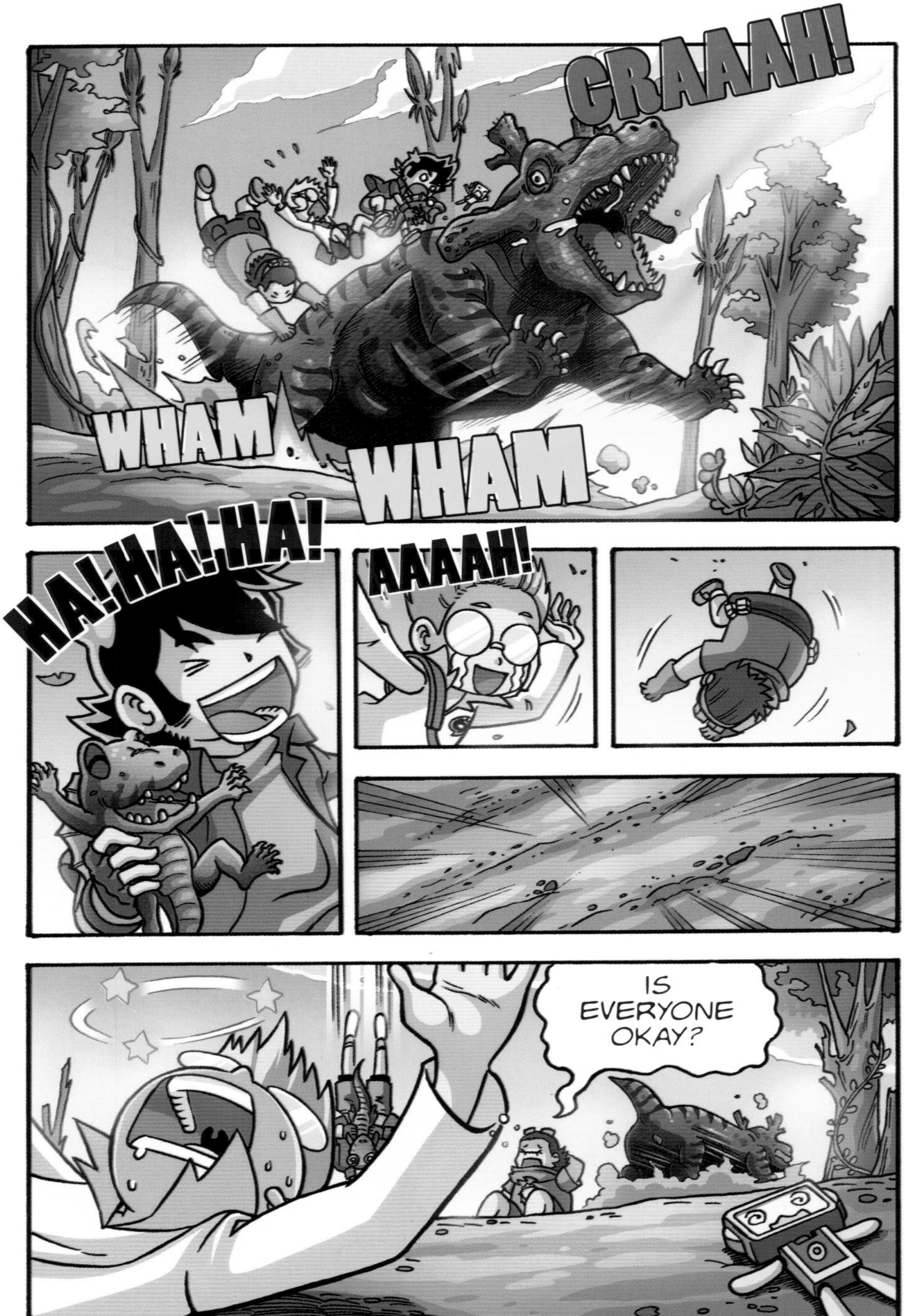
GRAAAH!
WHAM
WHAM
HA! HA! HA!
AAAAH!
IS EVERYONE OKAY?

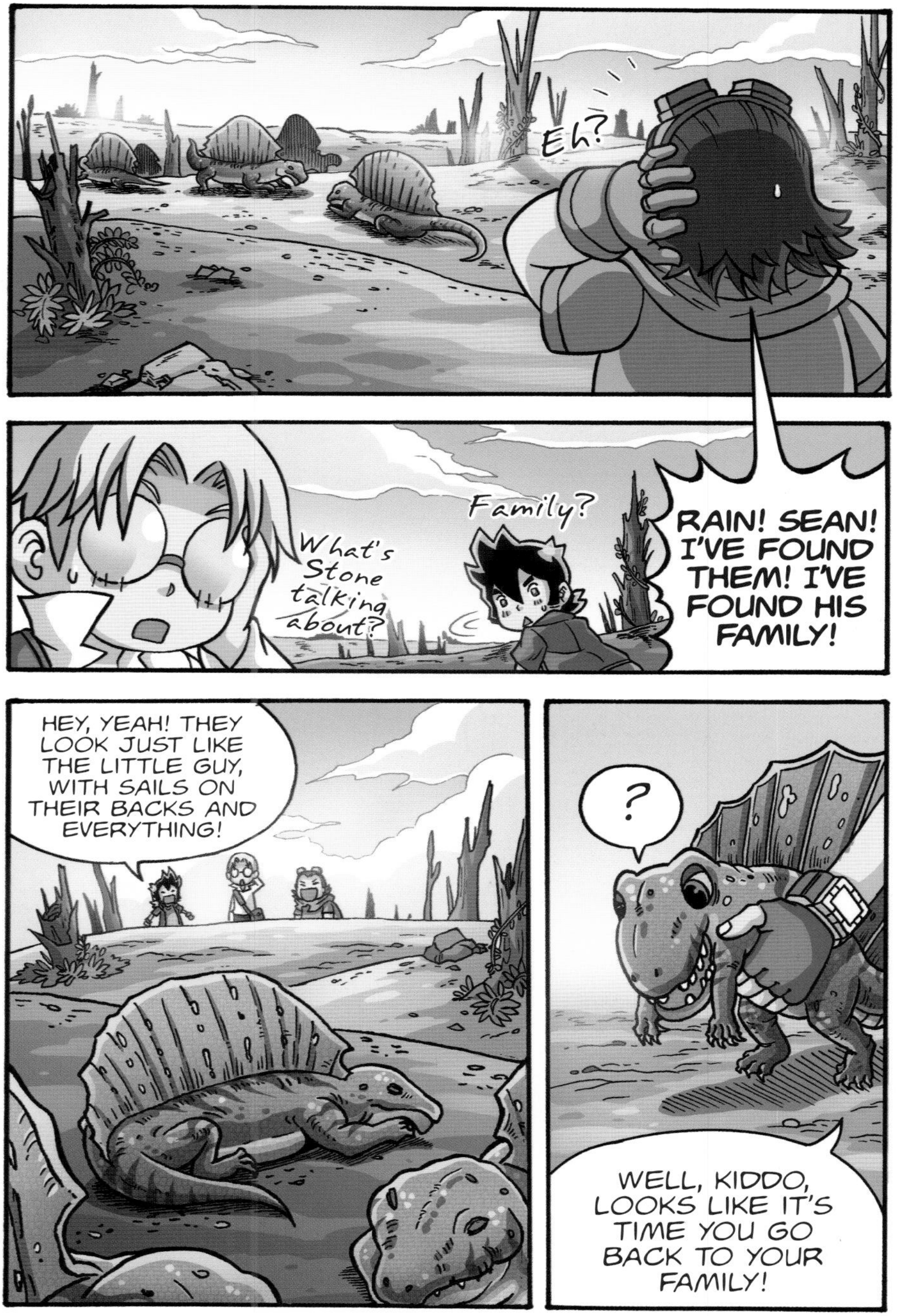
Eh?
RAIN! SEAN! I'VE FOUND THEM! I'VE FOUND HIS FAMILY!
Family?
What's Stone talking about?
HEY, YEAH! THEY LOOK JUST LIKE THE LITTLE GUY, WITH SAILS ON THEIR BACKS AND EVERYTHING!
?
WELL, KIDDO, LOOKS LIKE IT'S TIME YOU GO BACK TO YOUR FAMILY!

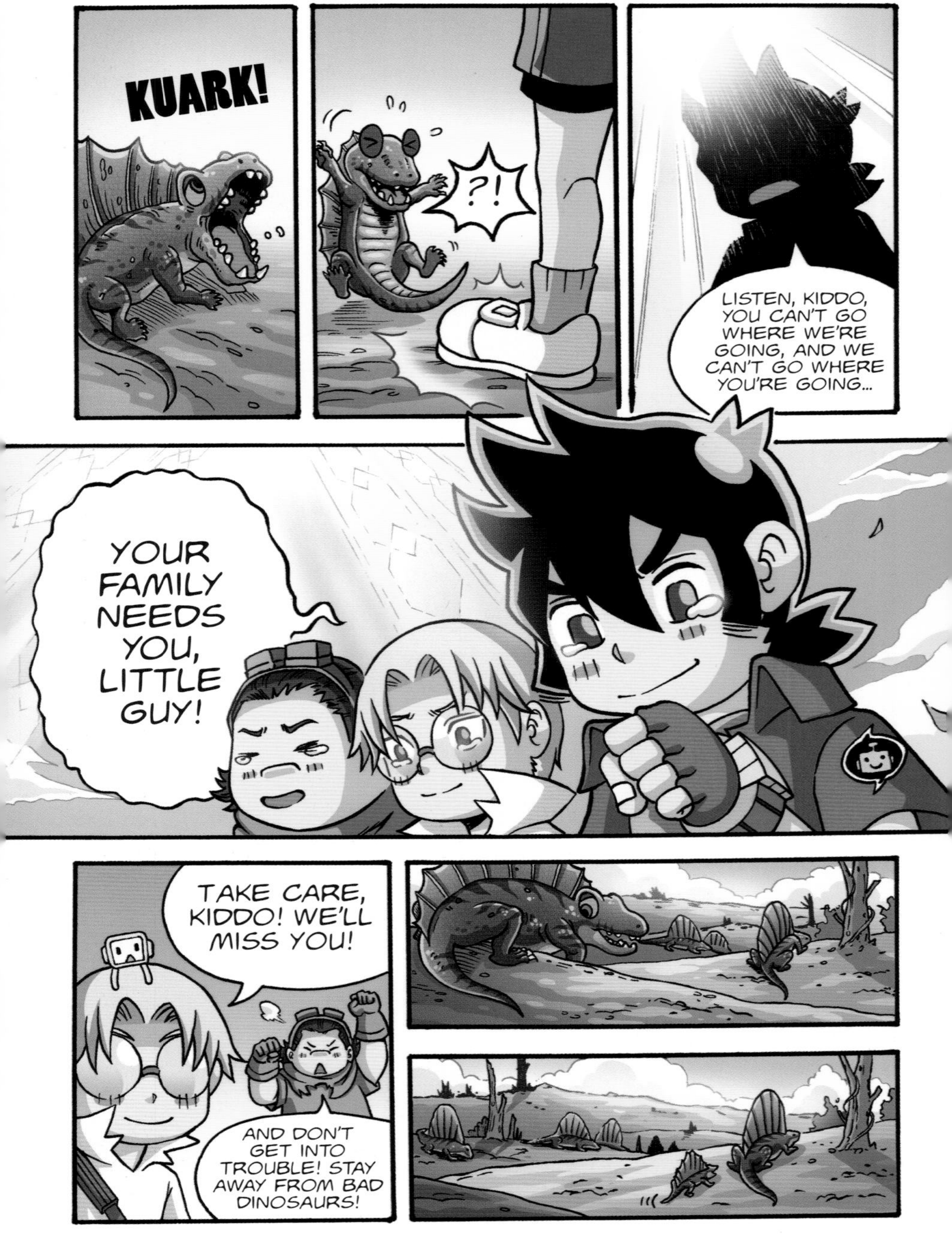
KUARK!
?!
LISTEN, KIDDO, YOU CAN'T GO WHERE WE'RE GOING, AND WE CAN'T GO WHERE YOU'RE GOING...
YOUR FAMILY NEEDS YOU, LITTLE GUY!
TAKE CARE, KIDDO! WE'LL MISS YOU!
AND DON'T GET INTO TROUBLE! STAY AWAY FROM BAD DINOSAURS!

RIGHT! DONE AND DONE. LET'S HEAD ON BACK, TEAM!

CRRROO-OOAAH!

WHAT THE HECK'S GOING ON?!

NYEK!

RAAAGH!

WHAT THE-- WHAT'S THE MATTER?

HOLD ON A SEC...

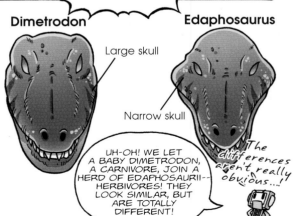

Dimetrodon

Large skull

Edaphosaurus

Narrow skull

UH-OH! WE LET A BABY DIMETRODON, A CARNIVORE, JOIN A HERD OF EDAPHOSAURII-- HERBIVORES! THEY LOOK SIMILAR, BUT ARE TOTALLY DIFFERENT!

The differences aren't really obvious...!

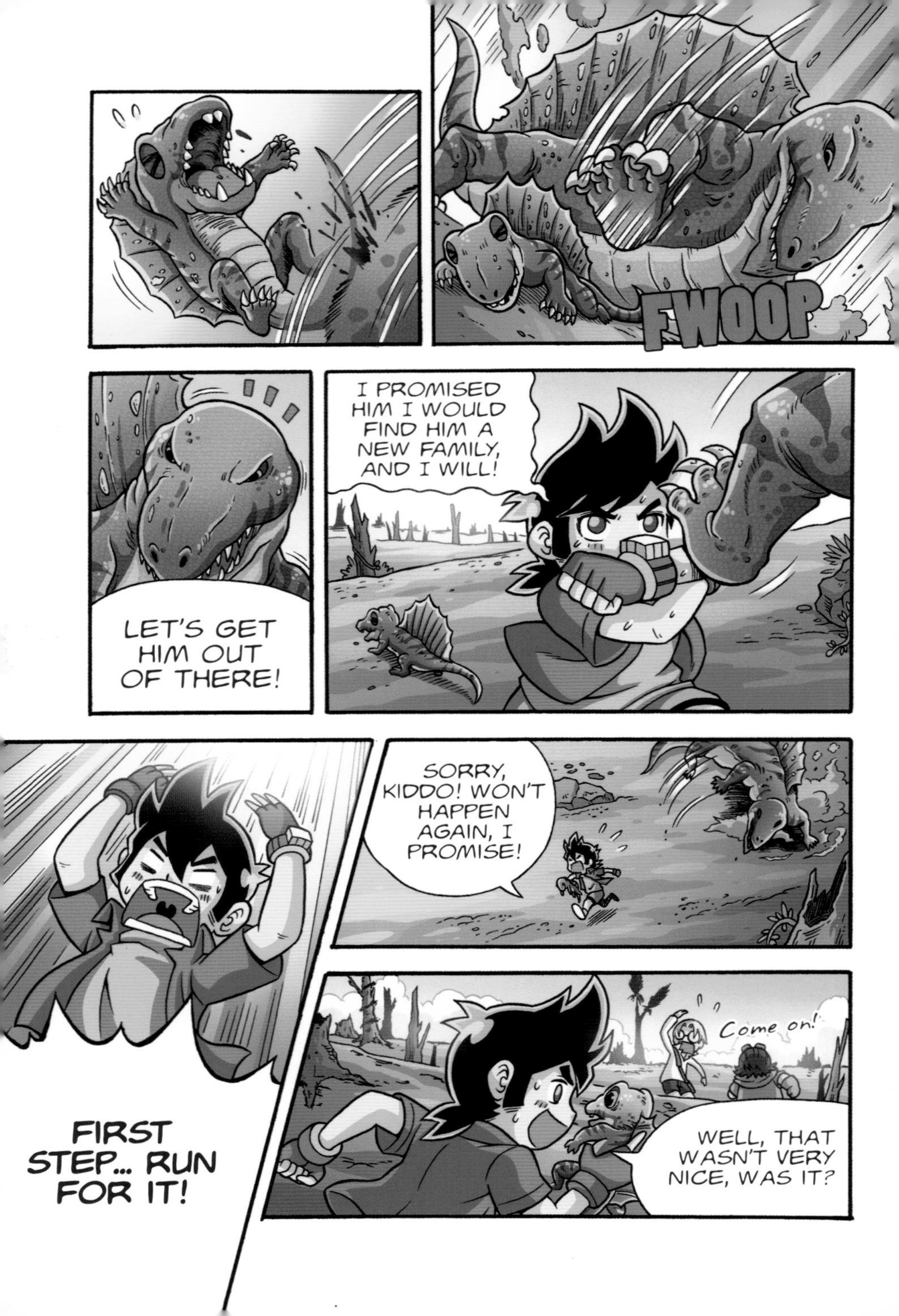
FWOOP
I PROMISED HIM I WOULD FIND HIM A NEW FAMILY, AND I WILL!
LET'S GET HIM OUT OF THERE!
FIRST STEP... RUN FOR IT!
SORRY, KIDDO! WON'T HAPPEN AGAIN, I PROMISE!
Come on!
WELL, THAT WASN'T VERY NICE, WAS IT?

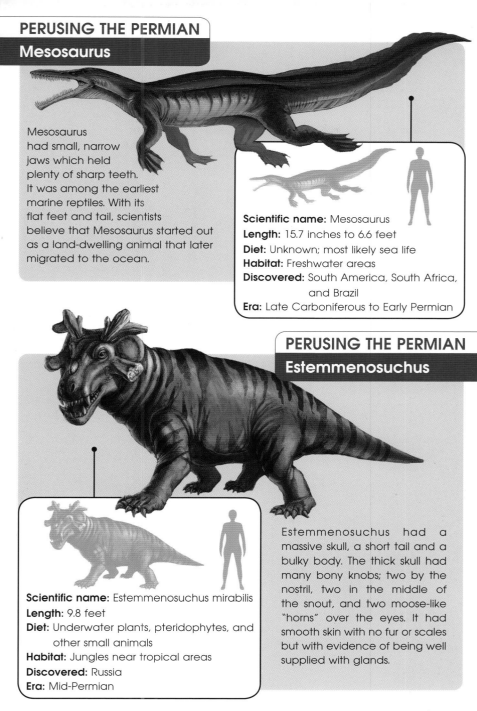

Mesosaurus

Mesosaurus had small, narrow jaws which held plenty of sharp teeth. It was among the earliest marine reptiles. With its flat feet and tail, scientists believe that Mesosaurus started out as a land-dwelling animal that later migrated to the ocean.

Scientific name: Mesosaurus
Length: 15.7 inches to 6.6 feet
Diet: Unknown; most likely sea life
Habitat: Freshwater areas
Discovered: South America, South Africa, and Brazil
Era: Late Carboniferous to Early Permian

PERUSING THE PERMIAN
Estemmenosuchus

Scientific name: Estemmenosuchus mirabilis
Length: 9.8 feet
Diet: Underwater plants, pteridophytes, and other small animals
Habitat: Jungles near tropical areas
Discovered: Russia
Era: Mid-Permian

Estemmenosuchus had a massive skull, a short tail and a bulky body. The thick skull had many bony knobs; two by the nostril, two in the middle of the snout, and two moose-like "horns" over the eyes. It had smooth skin with no fur or scales but with evidence of being well supplied with glands.

Edaphosaurus

Edaphosaurus was one of the earliest known herbivorous tetrapods. Its head was short and shallow, remarkably small compared to its body size. The sail along its back was supported by hugely elongated neural spines which helped to maintain its body temperature. The deep lower jaw had powerful muscles and the front teeth were barbed at the cutting edges, helping it cut bite-sized pieces from tough terrestrial plants. The palate and the inside of the lower jaw were covered with small teeth forming a large biting surface.

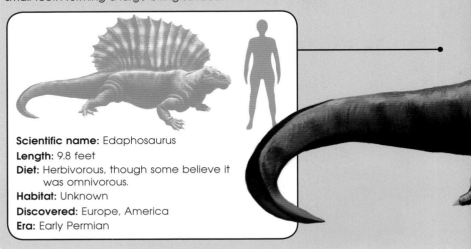

Scientific name: Edaphosaurus
Length: 9.8 feet
Diet: Herbivorous, though some believe it was omnivorous.
Habitat: Unknown
Discovered: Europe, America
Era: Early Permian

External differences between an Edaphosaurus and a Dimetrodon

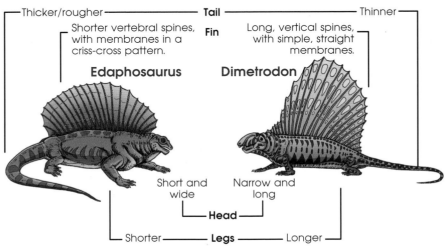

Thicker/rougher —————— **Tail** —————— Thinner

Shorter vertebral spines, with membranes in a criss-cross pattern. — **Fin** — Long, vertical spines, with simple, straight membranes.

Edaphosaurus   **Dimetrodon**

Short and wide   Narrow and long
—— **Head** ——

—— Shorter —————— **Legs** —————— Longer ——

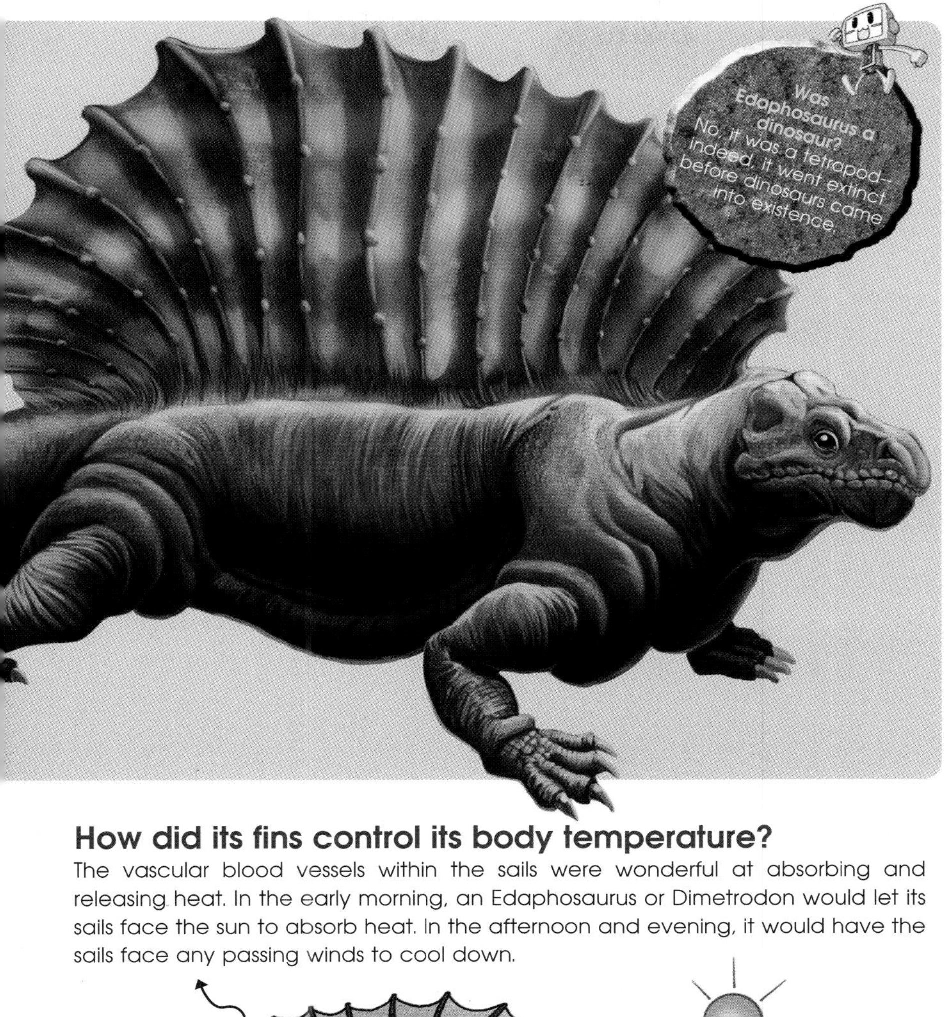
Was Edaphosaurus a dinosaur?
No, it was a tetrapod--indeed, it went extinct before dinosaurs came into existence.

How did its fins control its body temperature?

The vascular blood vessels within the sails were wonderful at absorbing and releasing heat. In the early morning, an Edaphosaurus or Dimetrodon would let its sails face the sun to absorb heat. In the afternoon and evening, it would have the sails face any passing winds to cool down.

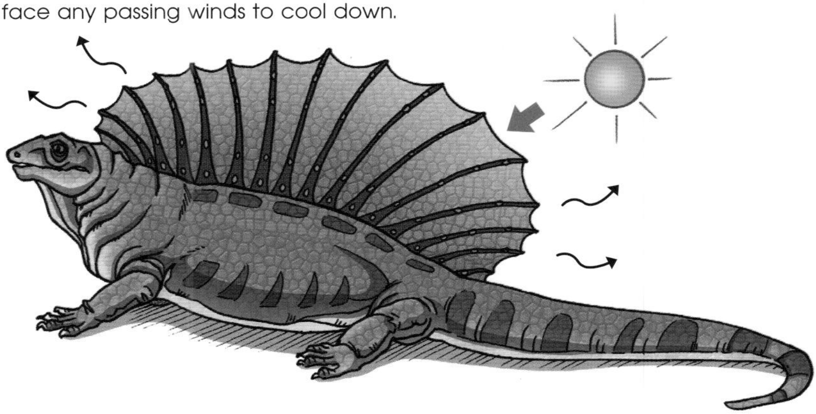

Coelurosauravus

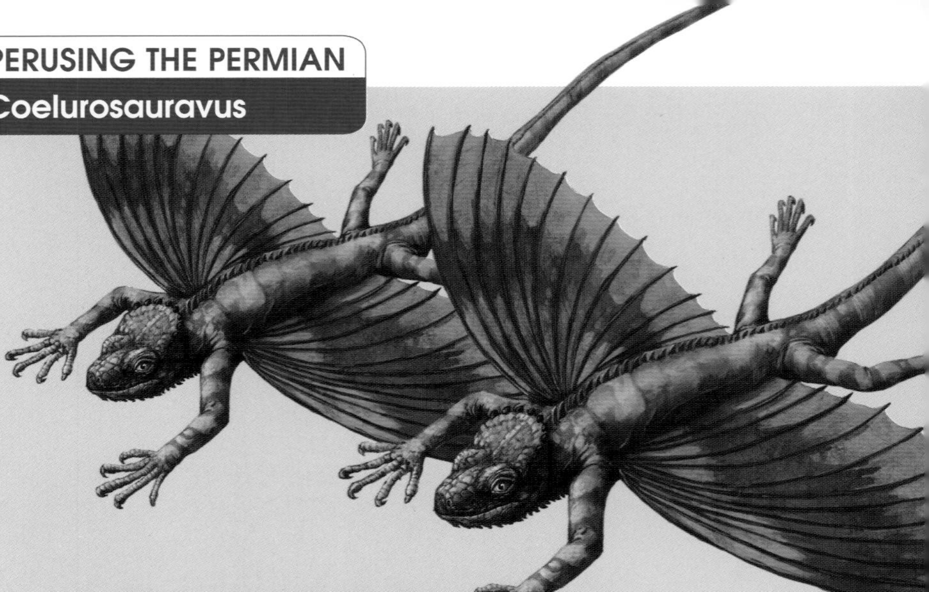

Coelurosauravus was a unique diapsid, with two skin-covered flaps on its flanks which allowed it to glide.

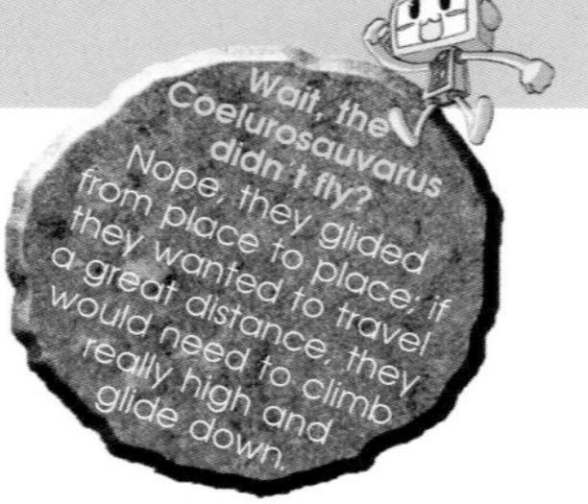
Wait, the Coelurosauravus didn't fly?
Nope, they glided from place to place; if they wanted to travel a great distance, they would need to climb really high and glide down.

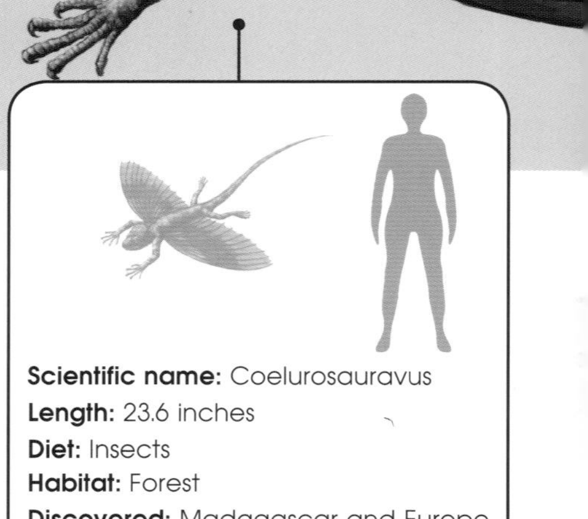

Scientific name: Coelurosauravus
Length: 23.6 inches
Diet: Insects
Habitat: Forest
Discovered: Madagascar and Europe
Era: Late Permian

Coelurosauravus bone structure

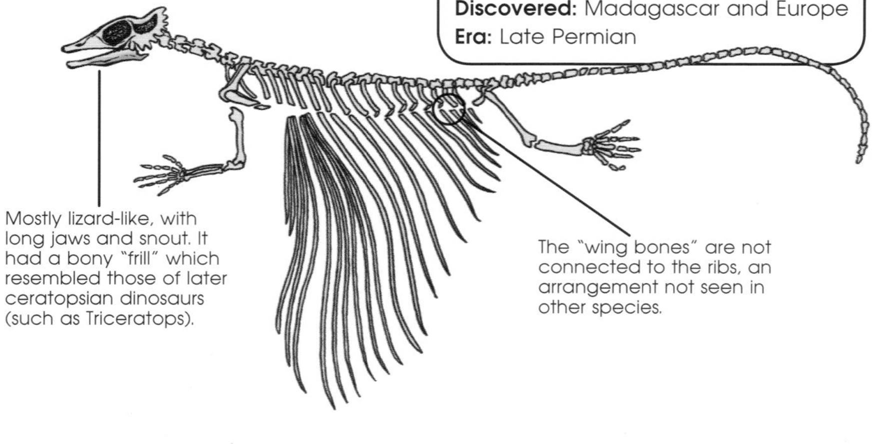
Mostly lizard-like, with long jaws and snout. It had a bony "frill" which resembled those of later ceratopsian dinosaurs (such as Triceratops).
The "wing bones" are not connected to the ribs, an arrangement not seen in other species.

CHAPTER 8

ESCAPE

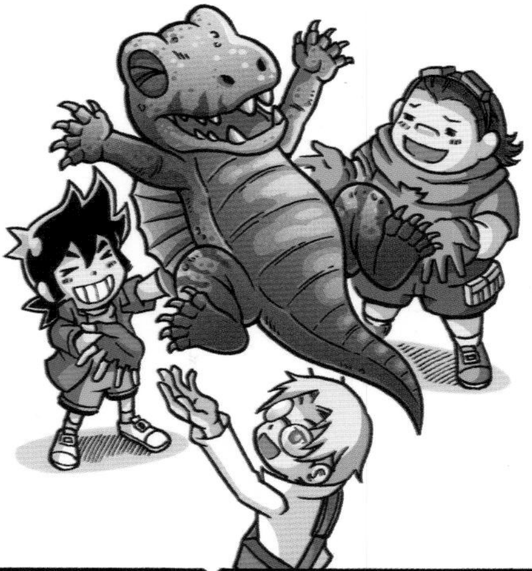

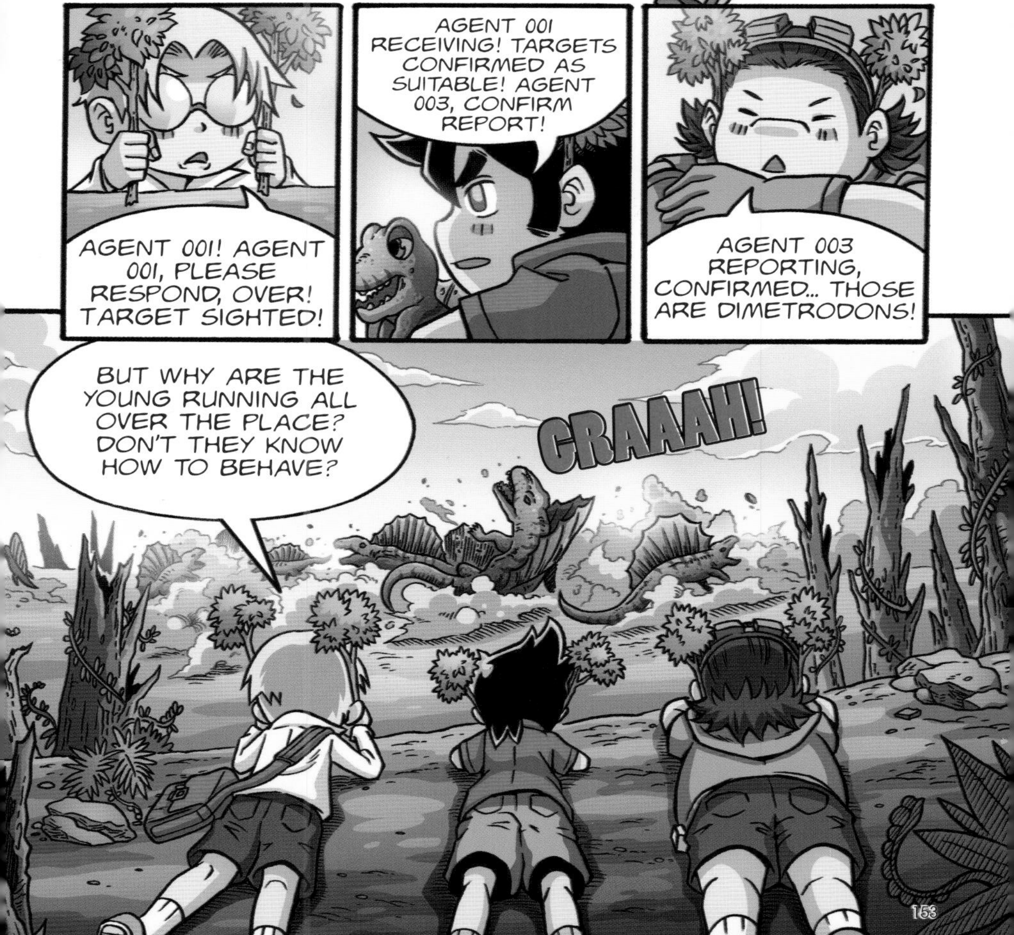
AGENT 001! AGENT 001, PLEASE RESPOND, OVER! TARGET SIGHTED!
AGENT 001 RECEIVING! TARGETS CONFIRMED AS SUITABLE! AGENT 003, CONFIRM REPORT!
AGENT 003 REPORTING, CONFIRMED... THOSE ARE DIMETRODONS!
BUT WHY ARE THE YOUNG RUNNING ALL OVER THE PLACE? DON'T THEY KNOW HOW TO BEHAVE?
CRAAAH!

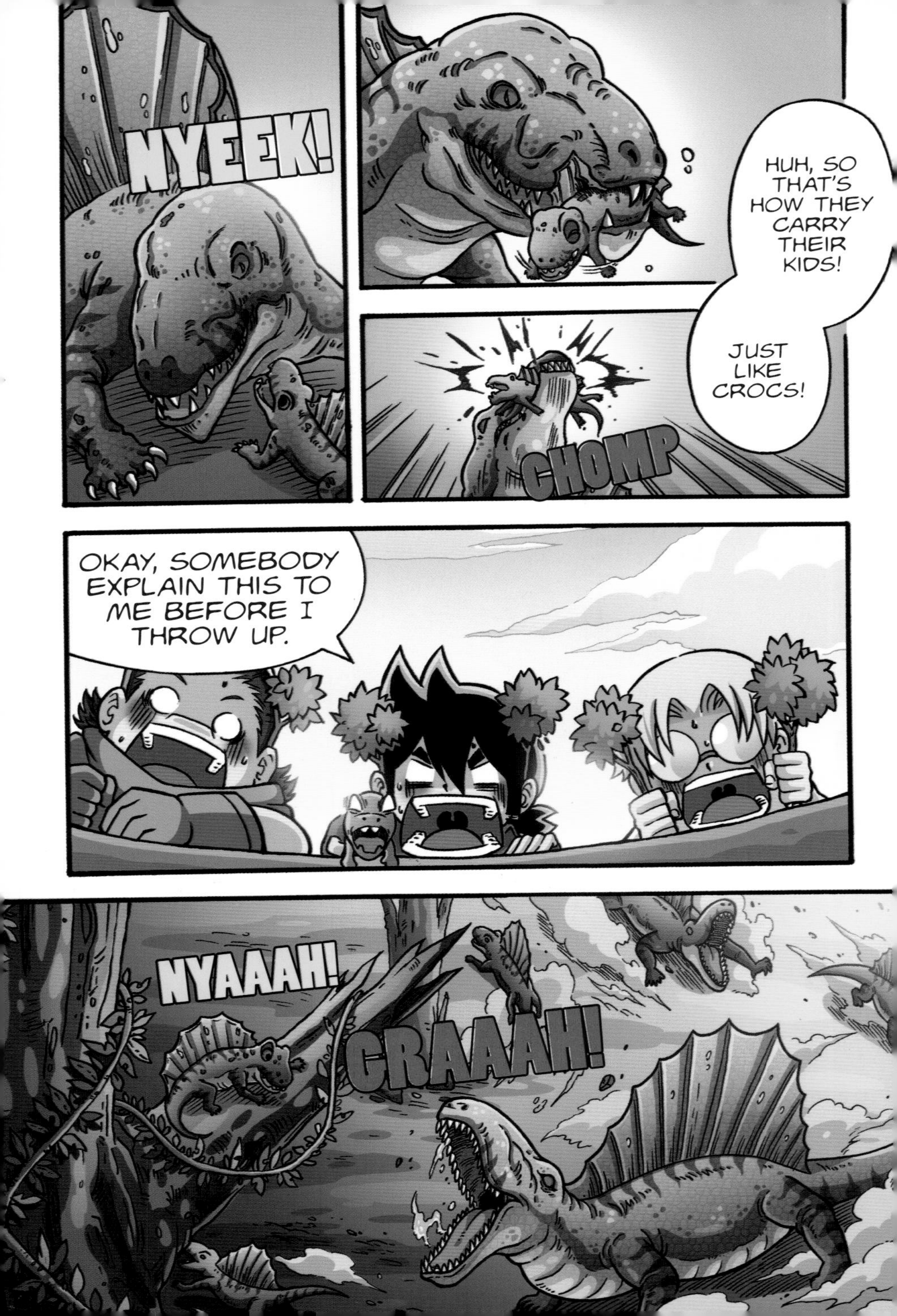
NYEEK!
HUH, SO THAT'S HOW THEY CARRY THEIR KIDS!
JUST LIKE CROCS!
CHOMP
OKAY, SOMEBODY EXPLAIN THIS TO ME BEFORE I THROW UP.
NYAAAH!
GRAAAH!

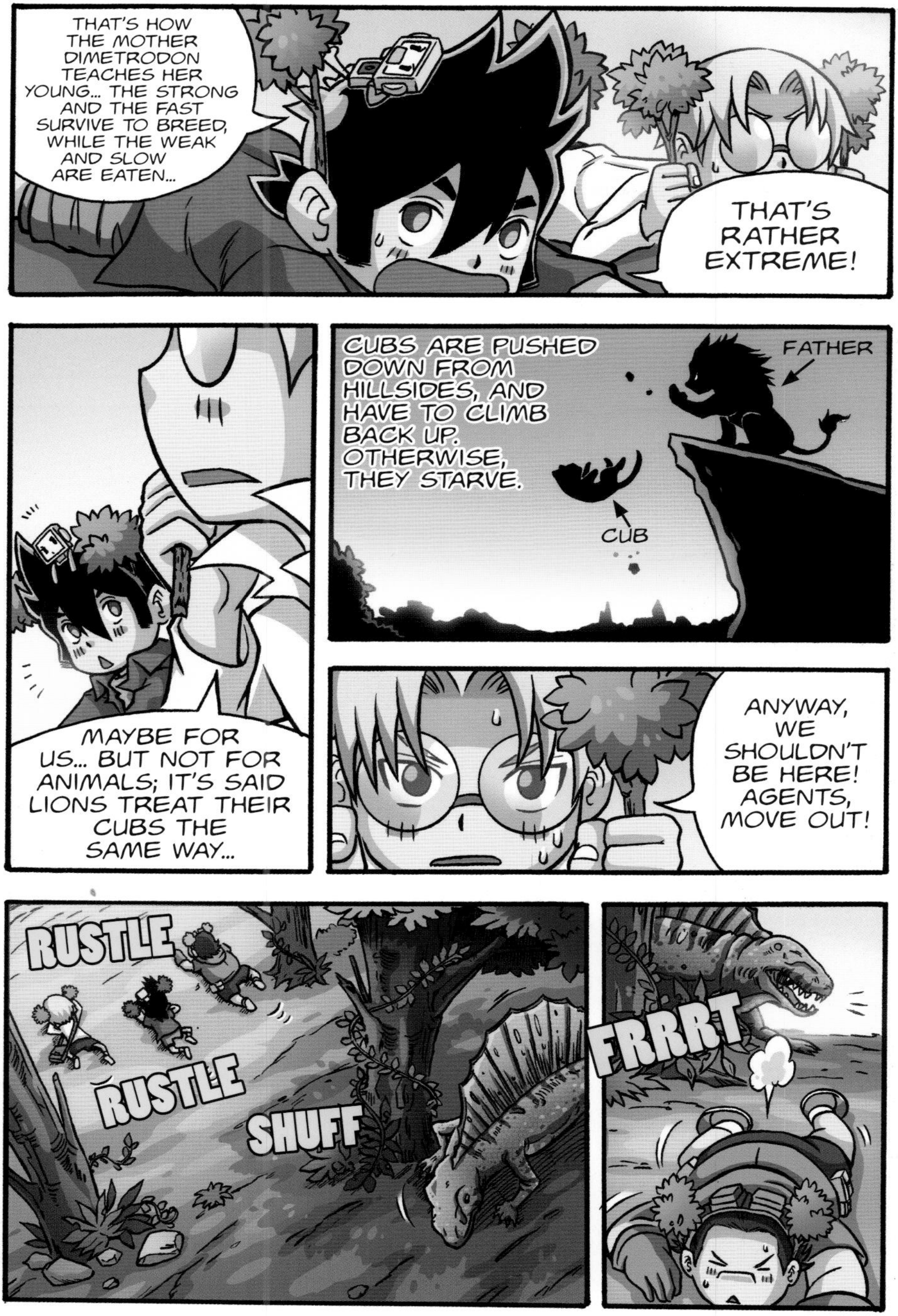
THAT'S HOW THE MOTHER DIMETRODON TEACHES HER YOUNG... THE STRONG AND THE FAST SURVIVE TO BREED, WHILE THE WEAK AND SLOW ARE EATEN...
THAT'S RATHER EXTREME!
MAYBE FOR US... BUT NOT FOR ANIMALS; IT'S SAID LIONS TREAT THEIR CUBS THE SAME WAY...
CUBS ARE PUSHED DOWN FROM HILLSIDES, AND HAVE TO CLIMB BACK UP. OTHERWISE, THEY STARVE.
FATHER
CUB
ANYWAY, WE SHOULDN'T BE HERE! AGENTS, MOVE OUT!
RUSTLE
RUSTLE
SHUFF
FRRRT

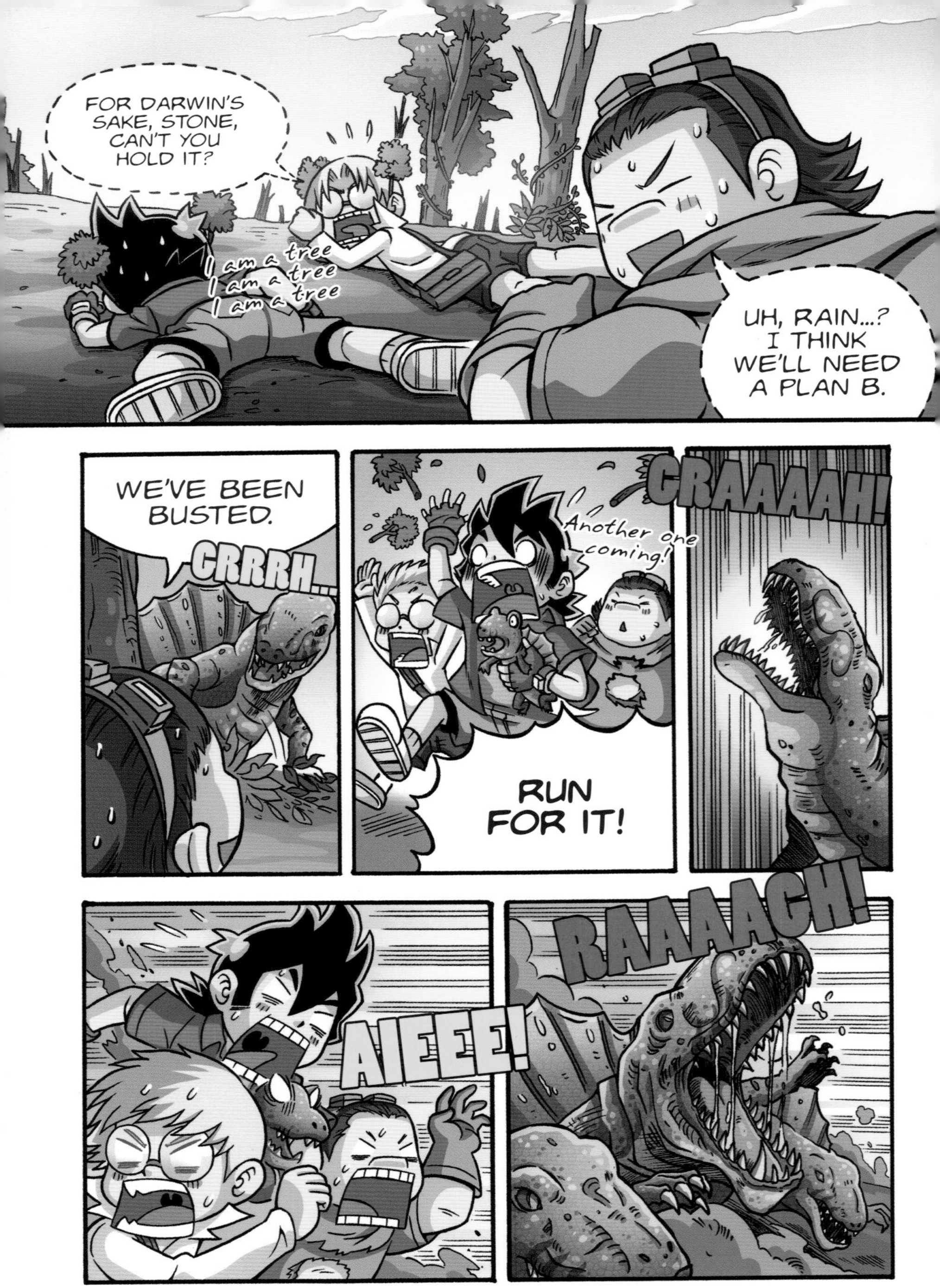
FOR DARWIN'S SAKE, STONE, CAN'T YOU HOLD IT?
I am a tree
I am a tree
I am a tree
UH, RAIN...? I THINK WE'LL NEED A PLAN B.
WE'VE BEEN BUSTED.
CRRRH...
Another one coming!
RUN FOR IT!
CRAAAAAH!
AIEEE!
RAAAACH!

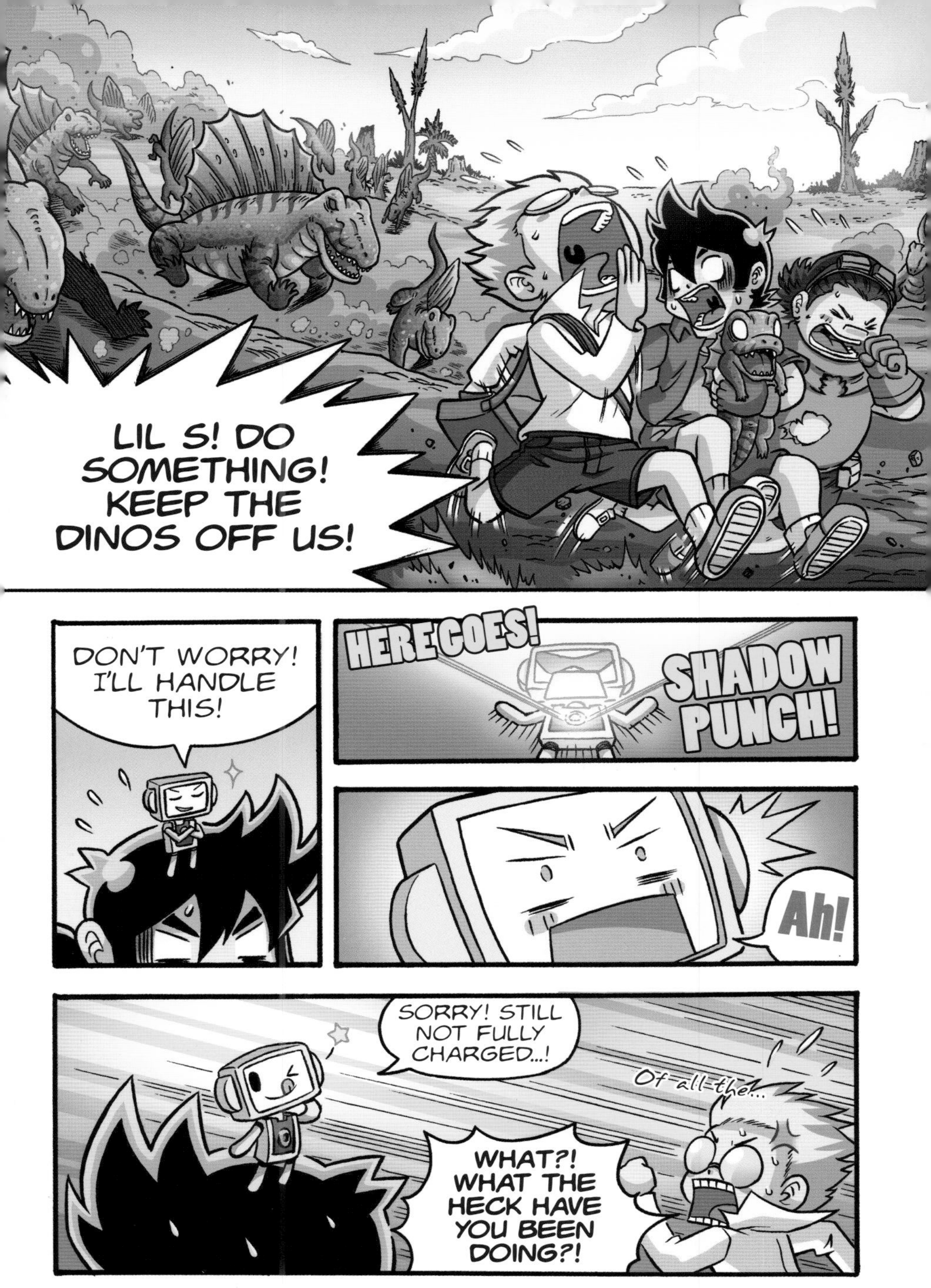

LIL S! DO SOMETHING! KEEP THE DINOS OFF US!
DON'T WORRY! I'LL HANDLE THIS!
HERE GOES!
SHADOW PUNCH!
Ah!
SORRY! STILL NOT FULLY CHARGED...!
Of all the...
WHAT?! WHAT THE HECK HAVE YOU BEEN DOING?!

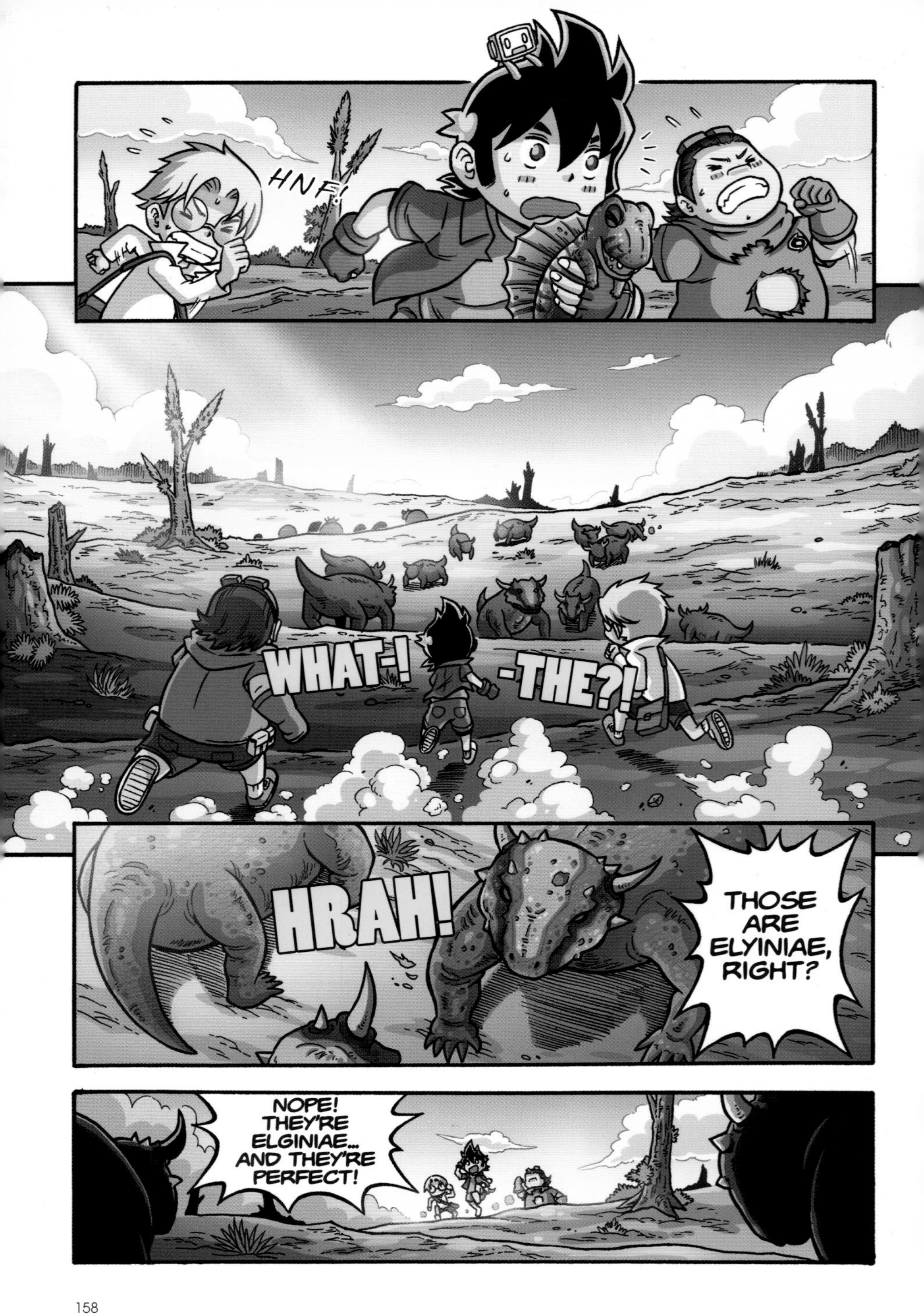

HNF!
WHAT-!
-THE?!
HRAH!
THOSE ARE ELYINIAE, RIGHT?
NOPE! THEY'RE ELGINIAE... AND THEY'RE PERFECT!

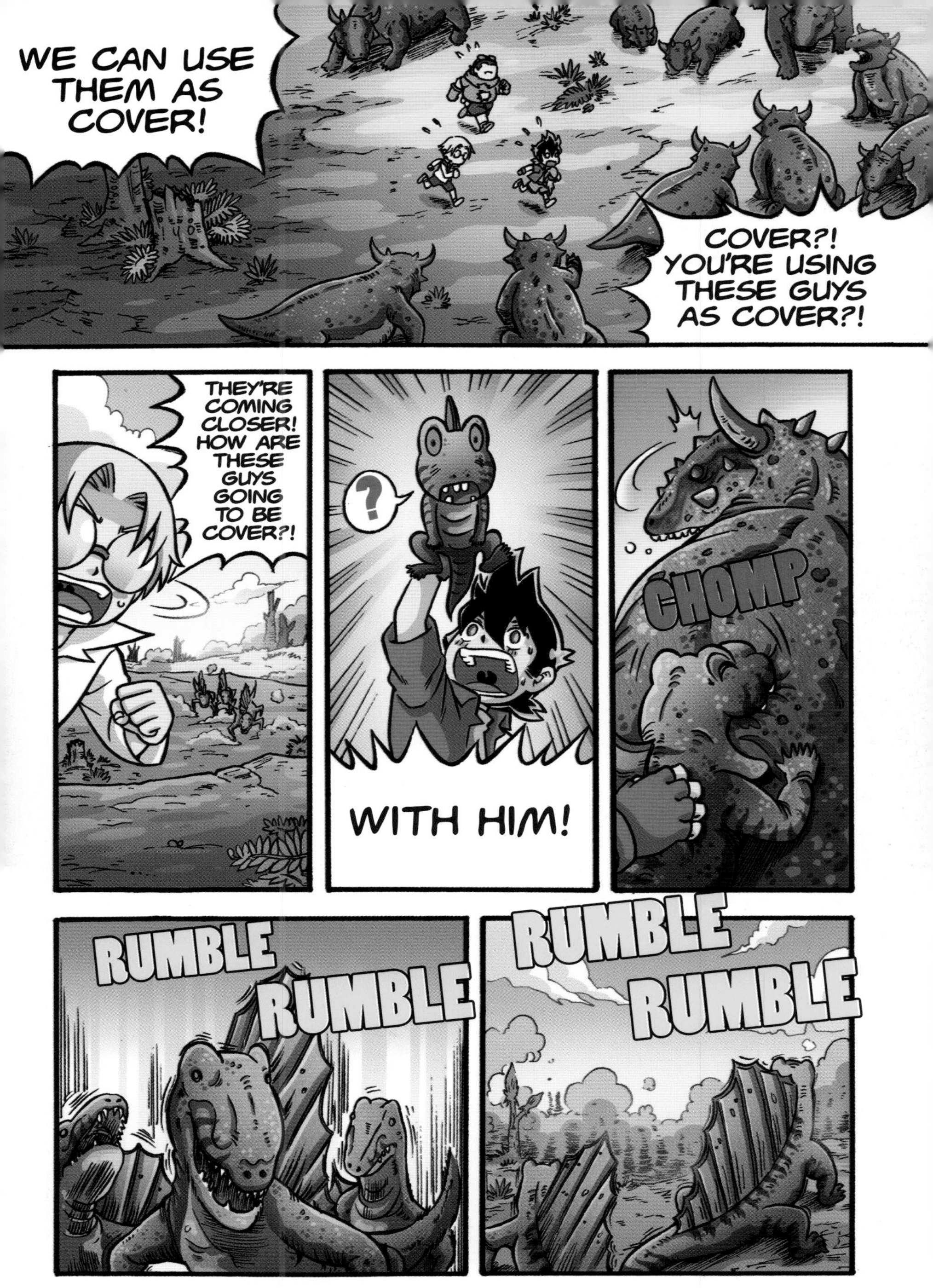
WE CAN USE THEM AS COVER!
COVER?! YOU'RE USING THESE GUYS AS COVER?!
THEY'RE COMING CLOSER! HOW ARE THESE GUYS GOING TO BE COVER?!
?
WITH HIM!
CHOMP
RUMBLE
RUMBLE
RUMBLE
RUMBLE

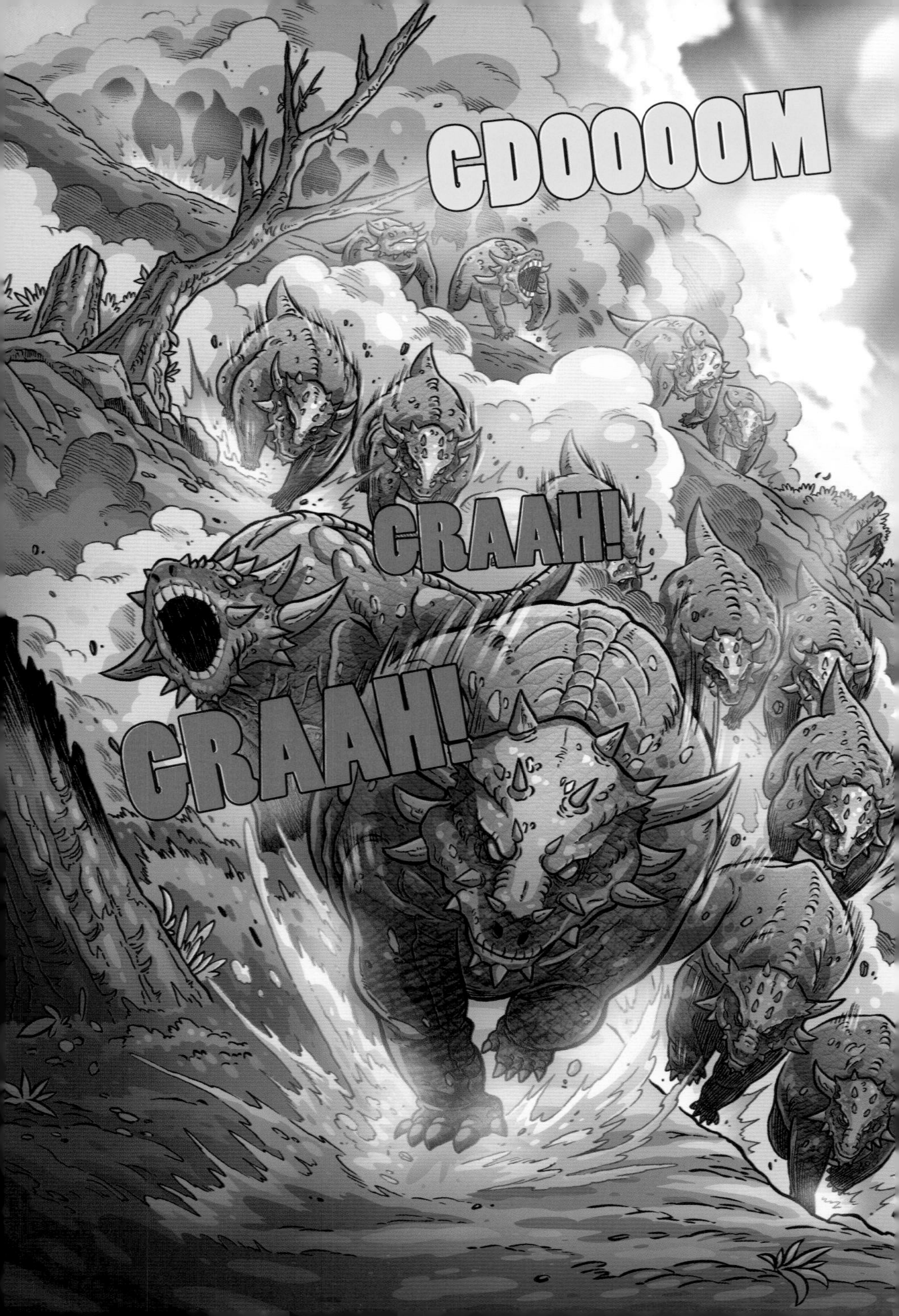

CDOOOOOM
GRAAH!
GRAAH!

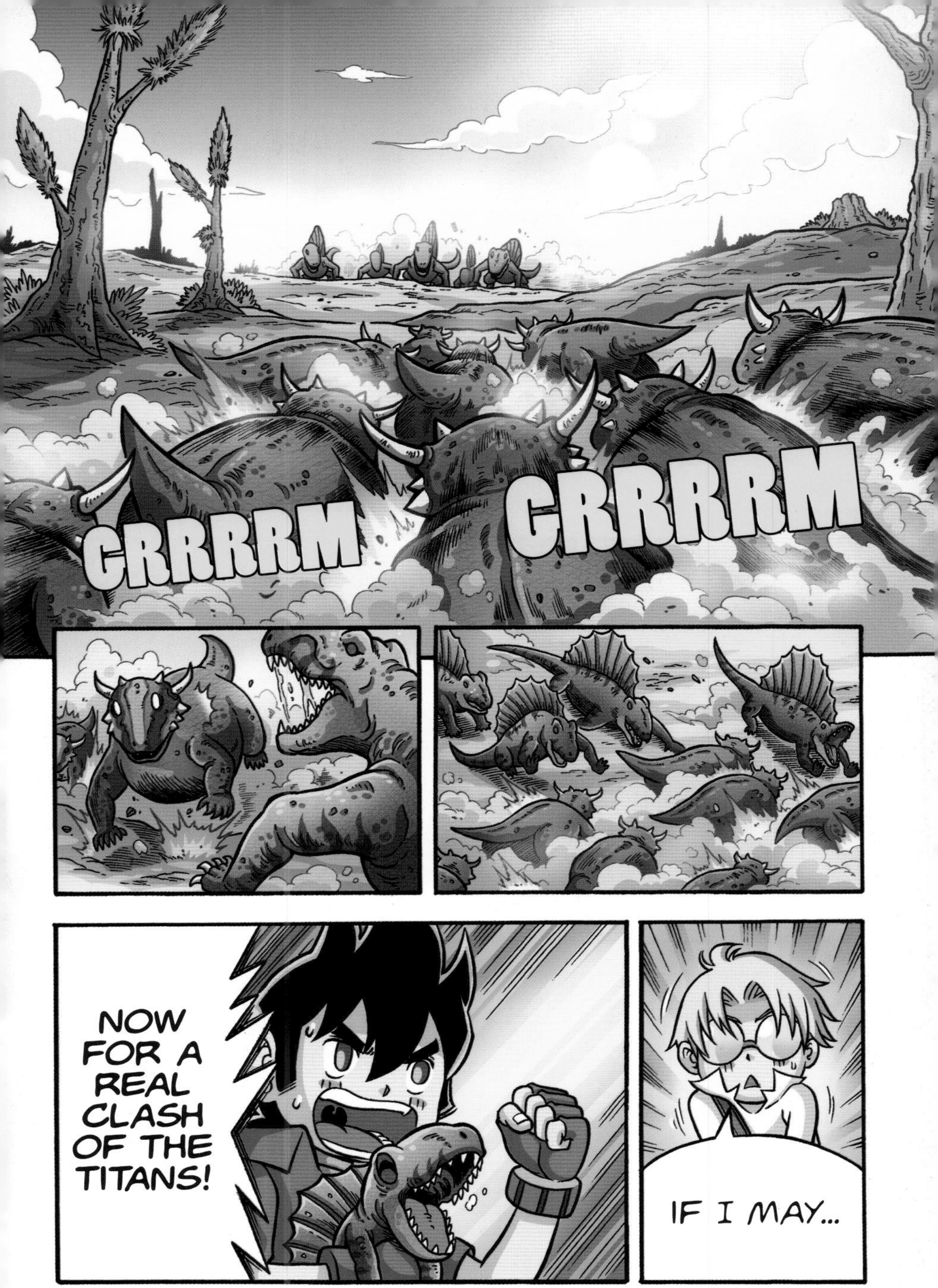
CRRRRM
GRRRRRM
NOW FOR A REAL CLASH OF THE TITANS!
IF I MAY...

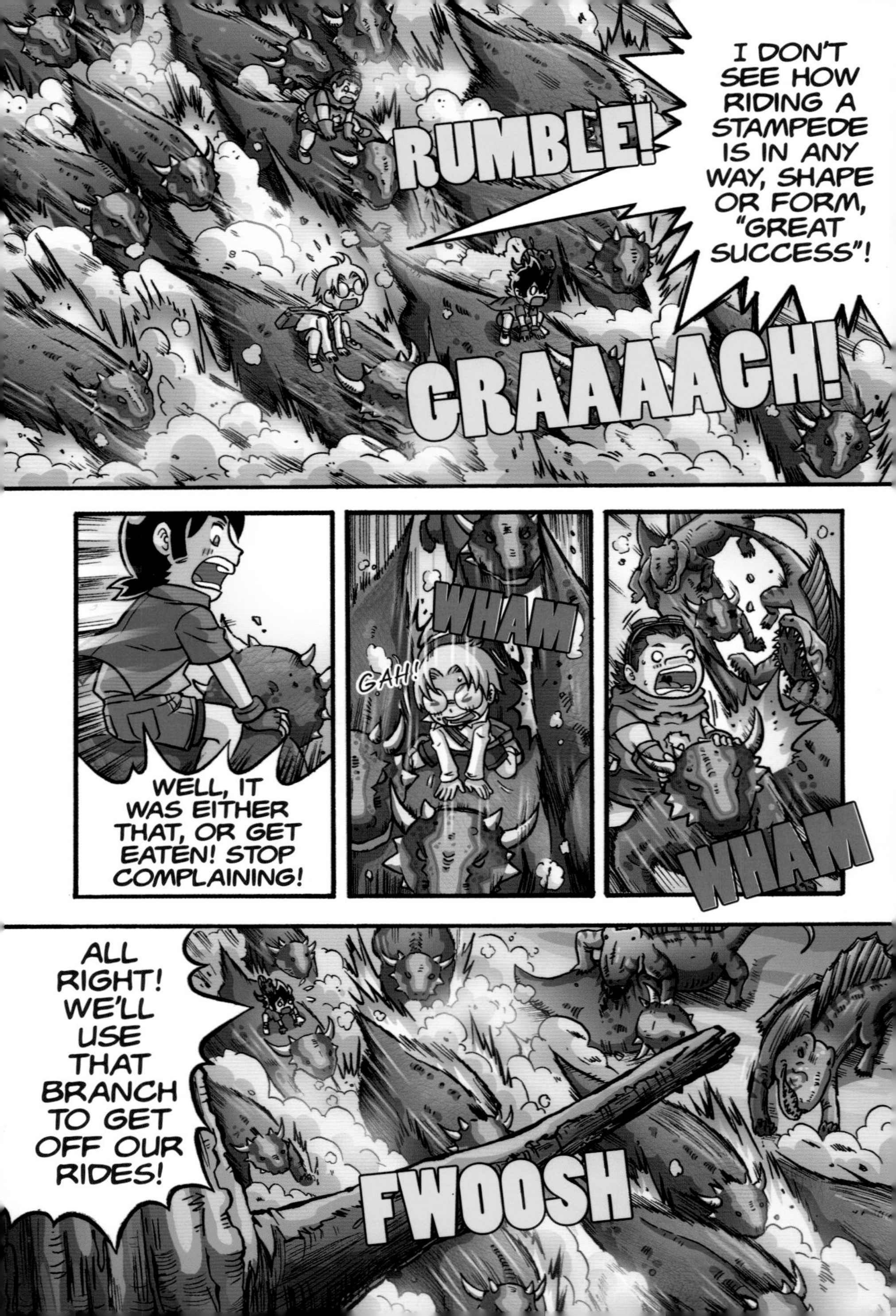
RUMBLE!
I DON'T SEE HOW RIDING A STAMPEDE IS IN ANY WAY, SHAPE OR FORM, "GREAT SUCCESS"!
CRAAAACH!
WELL, IT WAS EITHER THAT, OR GET EATEN! STOP COMPLAINING!
WHAM
GAH!
WHAM
ALL RIGHT! WE'LL USE THAT BRANCH TO GET OFF OUR RIDES!
FWOOSH

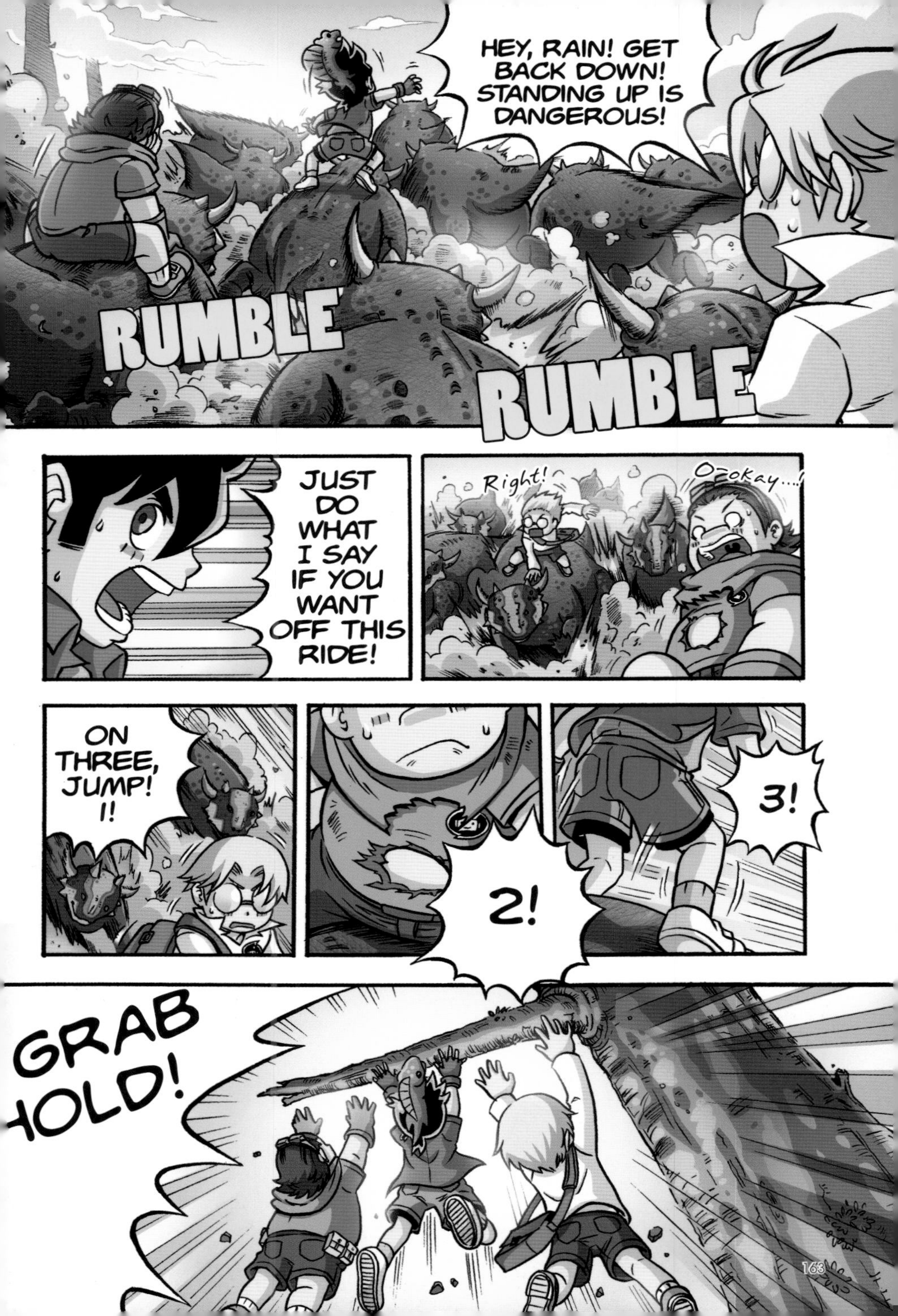
HEY, RAIN! GET BACK DOWN! STANDING UP IS DANGEROUS!
RUMBLE
RUMBLE
JUST DO WHAT I SAY IF YOU WANT OFF THIS RIDE!
Right!
O-okay...!
ON THREE, JUMP! 1!
2!
3!
GRAB HOLD!

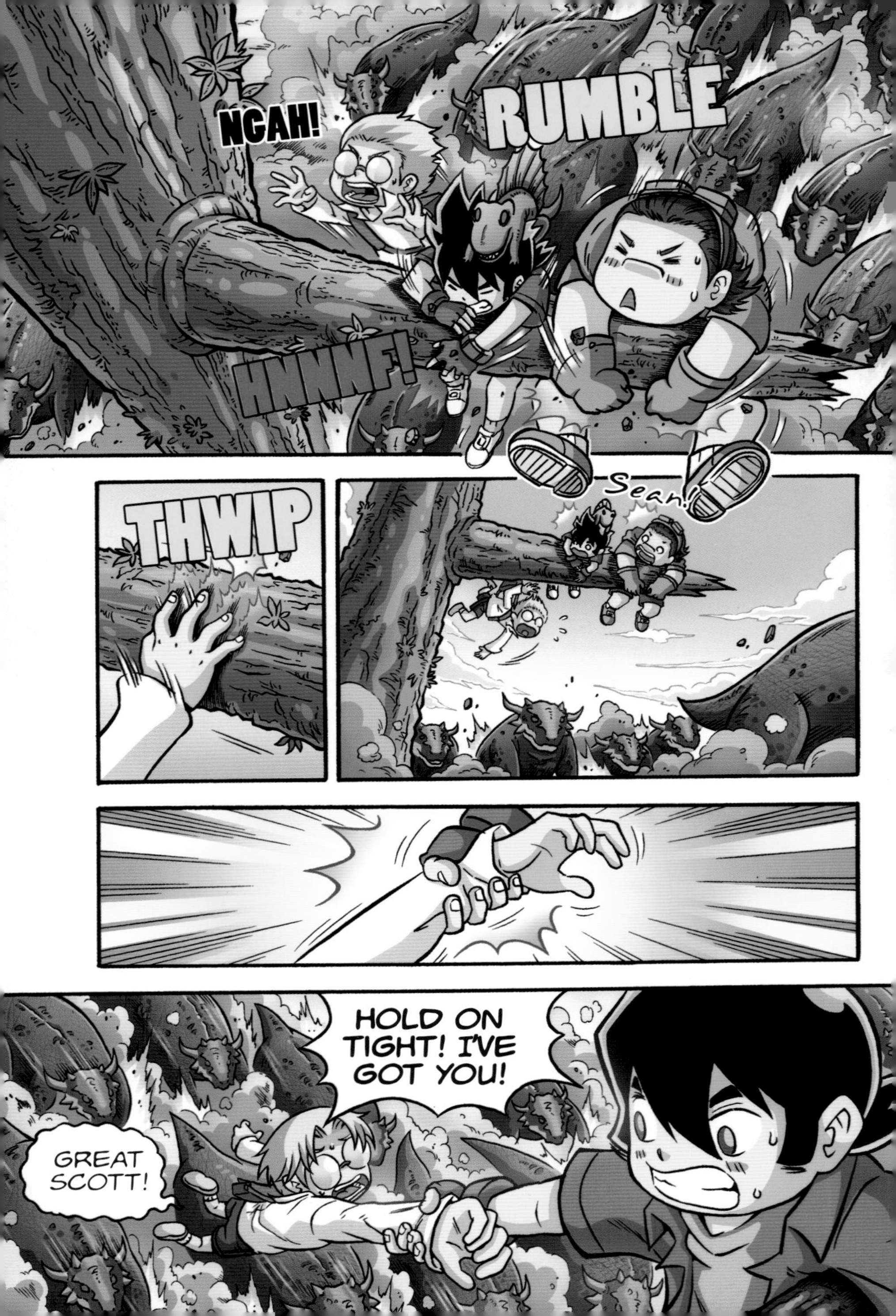
NGAH!
RUMBLE
HNNNF!
THWIP
Sean!
HOLD ON TIGHT! I'VE GOT YOU!
GREAT SCOTT!

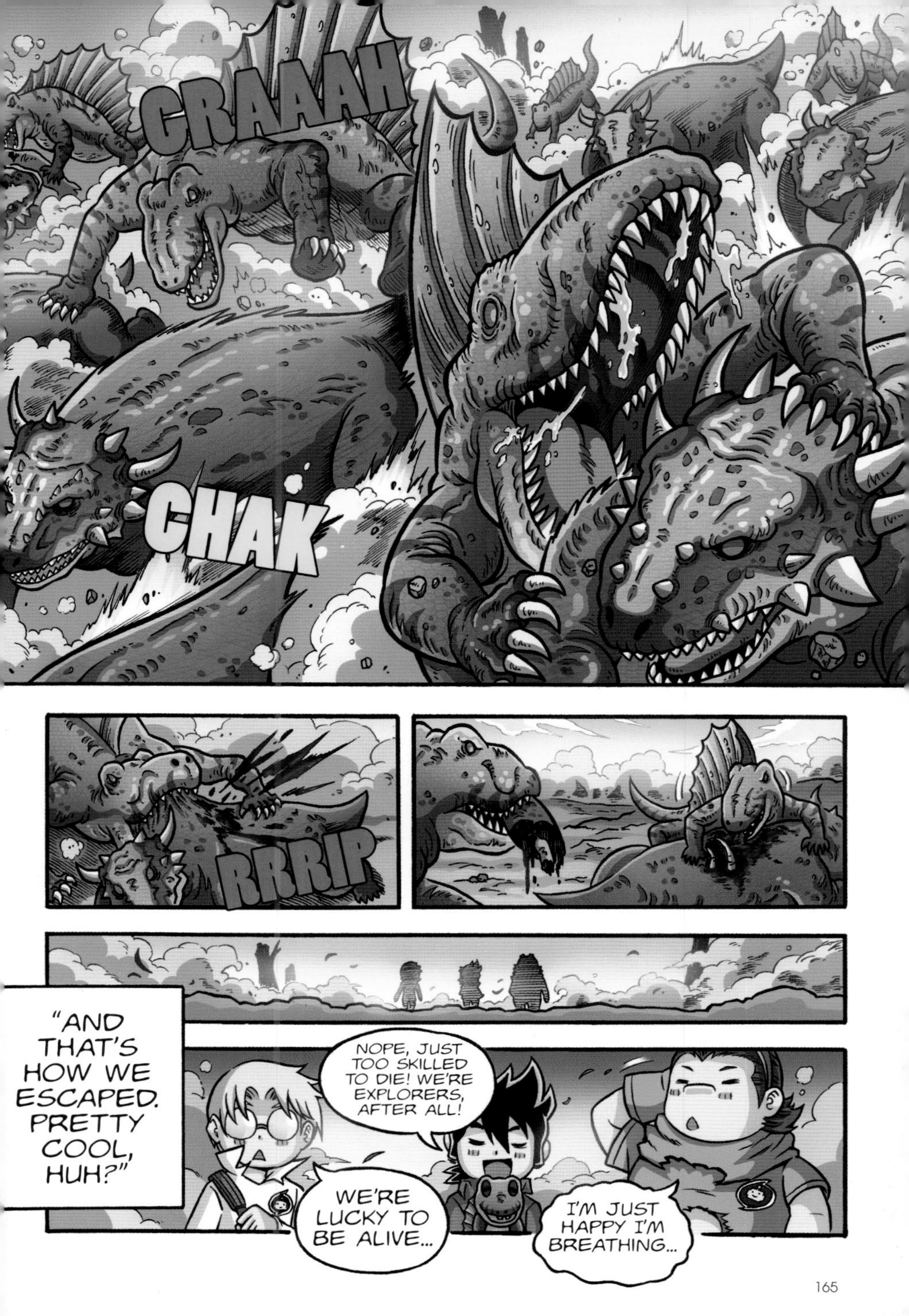
CRAAAH
CHAK
RRRIP
"AND THAT'S HOW WE ESCAPED. PRETTY COOL, HUH?"
NOPE, JUST TOO SKILLED TO DIE! WE'RE EXPLORERS, AFTER ALL!
WE'RE LUCKY TO BE ALIVE...
I'M JUST HAPPY I'M BREATHING...

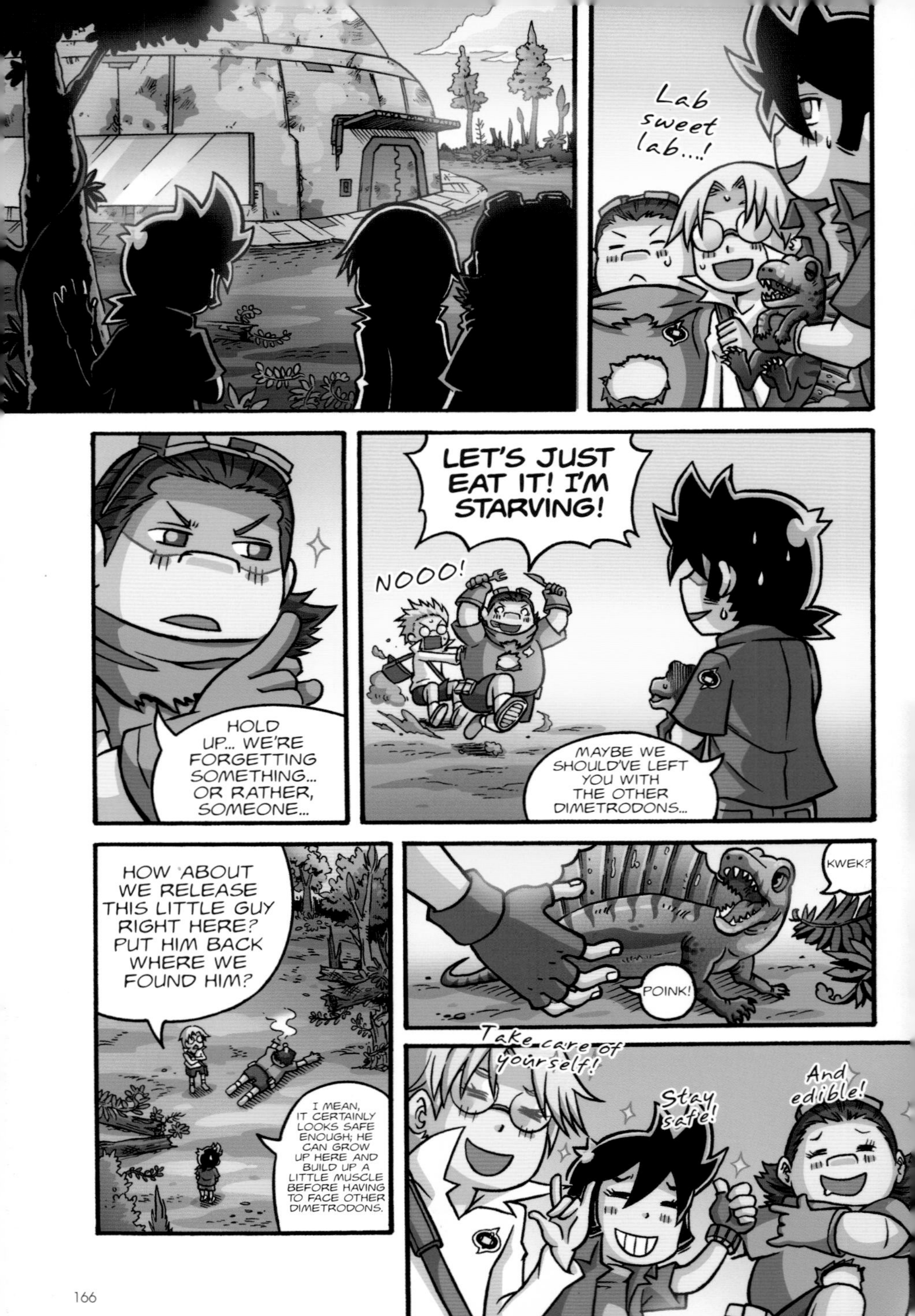

Lab sweet lab...!
HOLD UP... WE'RE FORGETTING SOMETHING... OR RATHER, SOMEONE...
LET'S JUST EAT IT! I'M STARVING!
NOOO!
MAYBE WE SHOULD'VE LEFT YOU WITH THE OTHER DIMETRODONS...
HOW ABOUT WE RELEASE THIS LITTLE GUY RIGHT HERE? PUT HIM BACK WHERE WE FOUND HIM?
I MEAN, IT CERTAINLY LOOKS SAFE ENOUGH; HE CAN GROW UP HERE AND BUILD UP A LITTLE MUSCLE BEFORE HAVING TO FACE OTHER DIMETRODONS.
KWEK?
POINK!
Take care of yourself!
Stay safe!
And edible!

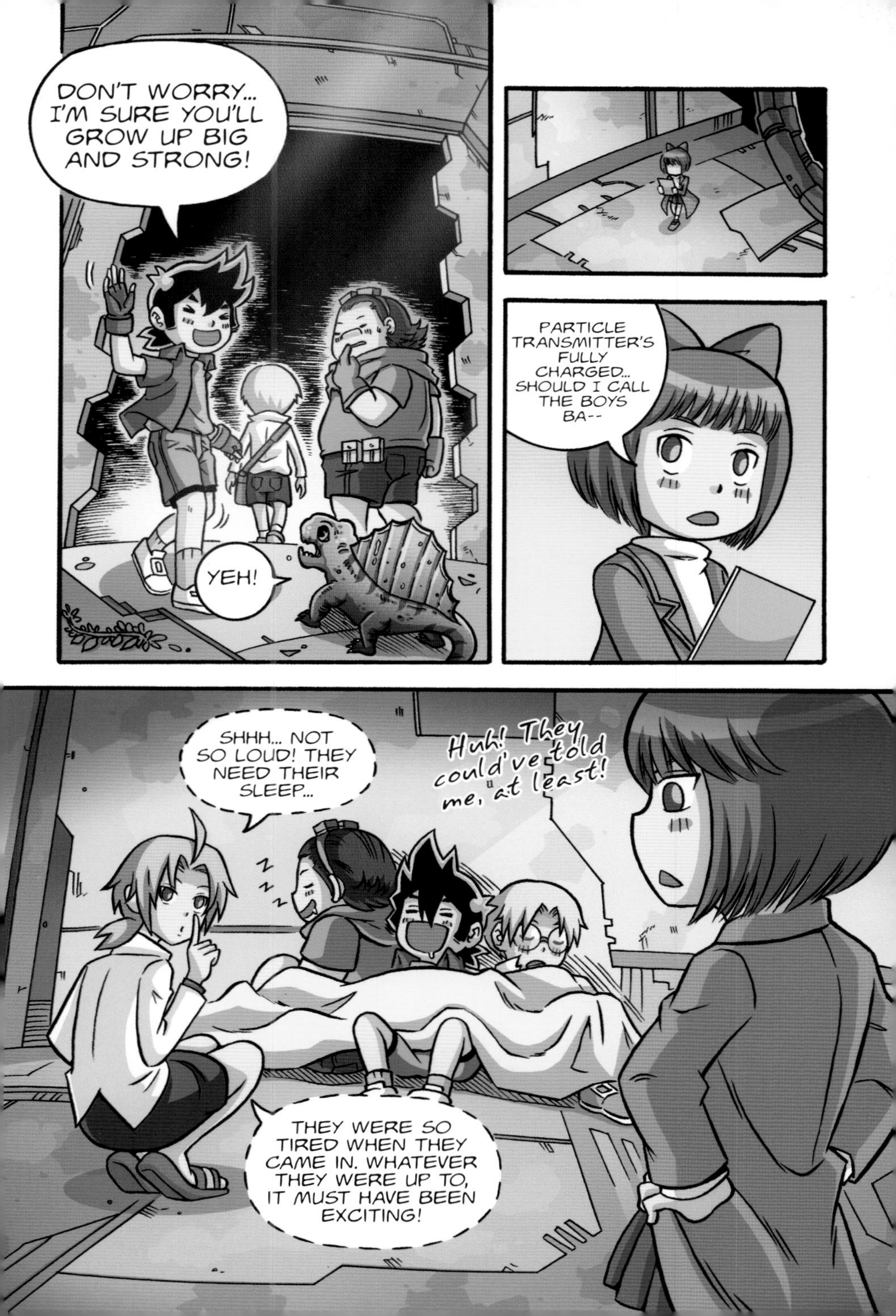

DON'T WORRY... I'M SURE YOU'LL GROW UP BIG AND STRONG!
YEH!
PARTICLE TRANSMITTER'S FULLY CHARGED... SHOULD I CALL THE BOYS BA--
Huh! They could've told me, at least!
SHHH... NOT SO LOUD! THEY NEED THEIR SLEEP...
THEY WERE SO TIRED WHEN THEY CAME IN. WHATEVER THEY WERE UP TO, IT MUST HAVE BEEN EXCITING!

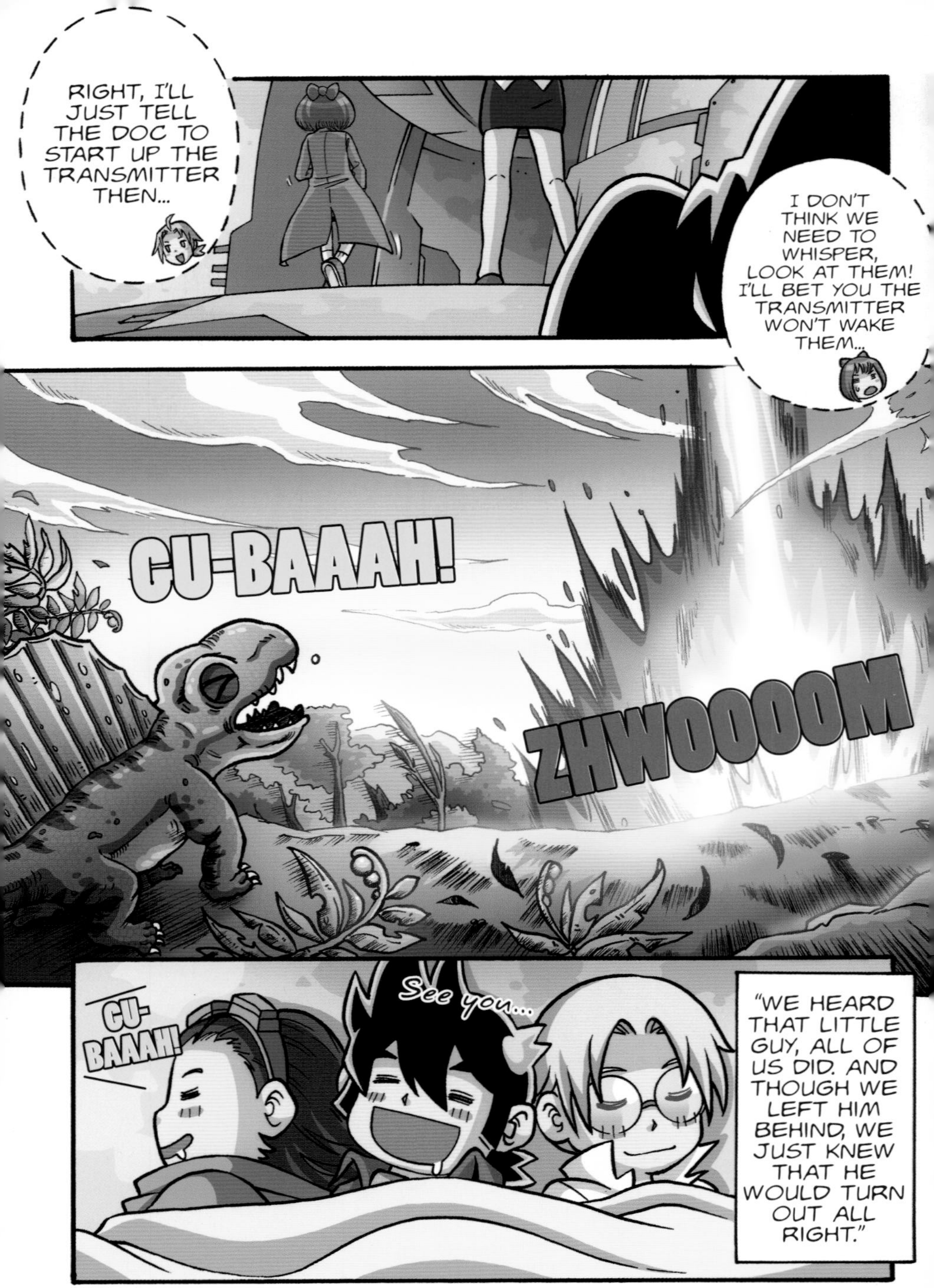
RIGHT, I'LL JUST TELL THE DOC TO START UP THE TRANSMITTER THEN...
I DON'T THINK WE NEED TO WHISPER, LOOK AT THEM! I'LL BET YOU THE TRANSMITTER WON'T WAKE THEM...
CU-BAAAH!
ZHWOOOOOM
CU-BAAAH!
See you...
"WE HEARD THAT LITTLE GUY, ALL OF US DID. AND THOUGH WE LEFT HIM BEHIND, WE JUST KNEW THAT HE WOULD TURN OUT ALL RIGHT."

SEE YOU IN THE NEXT DINOSAUR EXPLORERS!

Scutosaurus

Scientific name: Scutosaurus
Length: 8.2 feet
Diet: Plants
Habitat: Swamps and flood plains
Discovered: Eastern Europe
Era: Late Permian

The Scutosaurus was a genus of armor-covered pareiasaur. The most unusual thing about it was the heavy skull ornamented with strange knobs and ridges. It was a herd-dwelling herbivore that was well-adapted to the dry conditions which covered much of Pangaea at that time. Despite its relatively small size, it was heavy and its short legs meant that it could not move at speed for long periods of time, which made it vulnerable to attacks by larger predators.

Scutosaurus skeletal structure

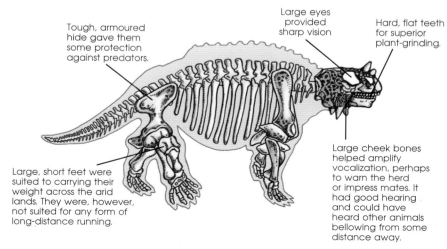

Tough, armoured hide gave them some protection against predators.

Large eyes provided sharp vision

Hard, flat teeth for superior plant-grinding.

Large, short feet were suited to carrying their weight across the arid lands. They were, however, not suited for any form of long-distance running.

Large cheek bones helped amplify vocalization, perhaps to warn the herd or impress mates. It had good hearing and could have heard other animals bellowing from some distance away.

PERUSING THE PERMIAN

Dimetrodon

The Dimetrodon dominated the Permian. This carnivorous pelycosaur possessed a spectacular sail on its back, supported by long, bony spines, each of which grew out of a separate spinal vertebra. The sail may have been a thermoregulatory structure, used to absorb and release heat. It had a large skull with sharp canines and shearing teeth. It was probably quite slow because it walked on four side-sprawling legs.

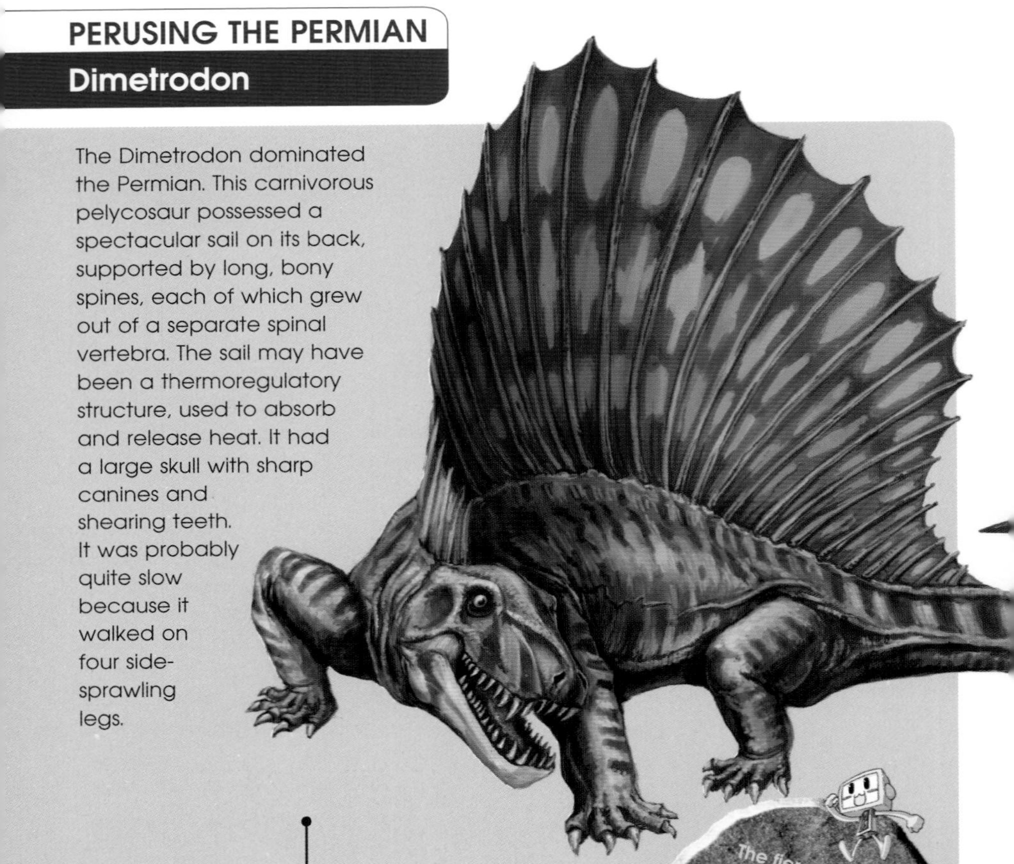

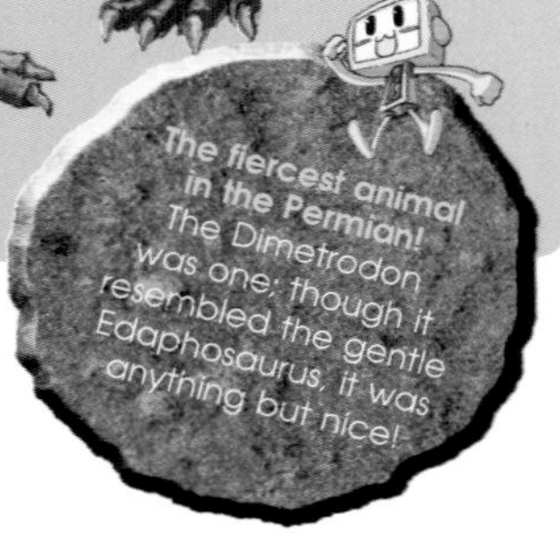
The fiercest animal in the Permian!
The Dimetrodon was one; though it resembled the gentle Edaphosaurus, it was anything but nice!

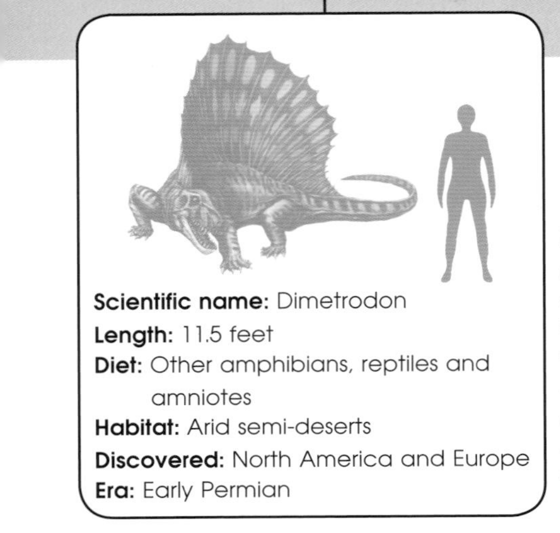

Scientific name: Dimetrodon
Length: 11.5 feet
Diet: Other amphibians, reptiles and amniotes
Habitat: Arid semi-deserts
Discovered: North America and Europe
Era: Early Permian

Dimetrodon was one of the largest and most dangerous apex land predator of its day, with an impressive average 90% kill success rate (in comparison, the best lions have ever managed is about 70%). Because of its sail-like fin, it appeared larger to other animals and along with its powerful jaws gave them the advantage over their rivals.

Reptile to mammal evolution

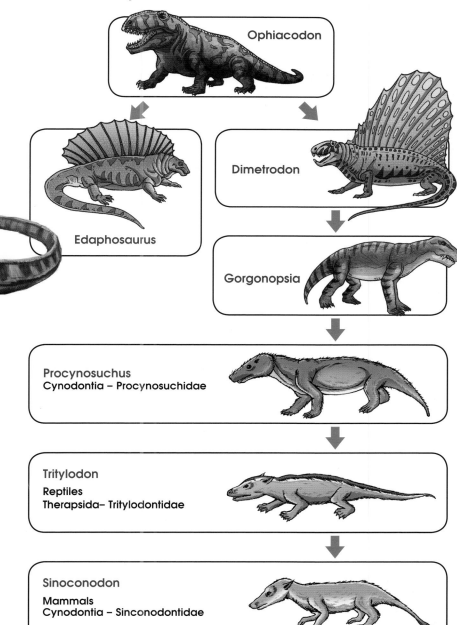

Ophiacodon

Edaphosaurus

Dimetrodon

Gorgonopsia

Procynosuchus
Cynodontia – Procynosuchidae

Tritylodon

Reptiles
Therapsida– Tritylodontidae

Sinoconodon

Mammals
Cynodontia – Sinconodontidae

PERUSING THE PERMIAN
Gorgonopsia

Gorgonopsia, meaning "Gorgon face," gets its name from the 4.7 inches long saber-like teeth. It was lightly built, with long running legs, and was a very capable dominant land predator of the Late Permian. Once it smelled blood, it had a tendency to pursue its prey at all costs. Despite its agility and fearsome teeth, it went extinct by the end of the Permian, along with most other synapsid groups.

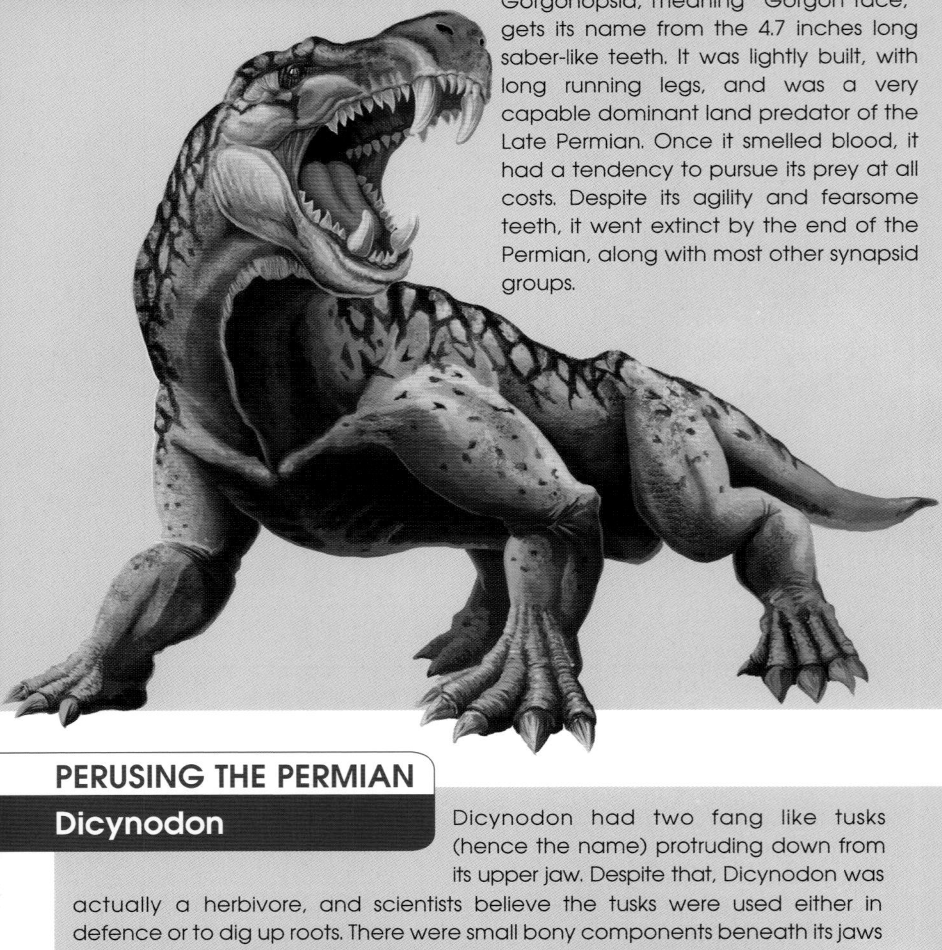

PERUSING THE PERMIAN
Dicynodon

Dicynodon had two fang like tusks (hence the name) protruding down from its upper jaw. Despite that, Dicynodon was actually a herbivore, and scientists believe the tusks were used either in defence or to dig up roots. There were small bony components beneath its jaws which helped it hear. These bony pieces later evolved into the components of modern middle ears.

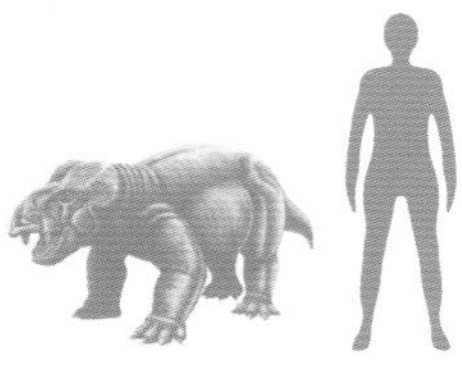

Scientific name: Dicynodon
Length: 3.3 feet
Diet: Plants
Habitat: Unknown
Discovered: South Africa
Era: Late Permian

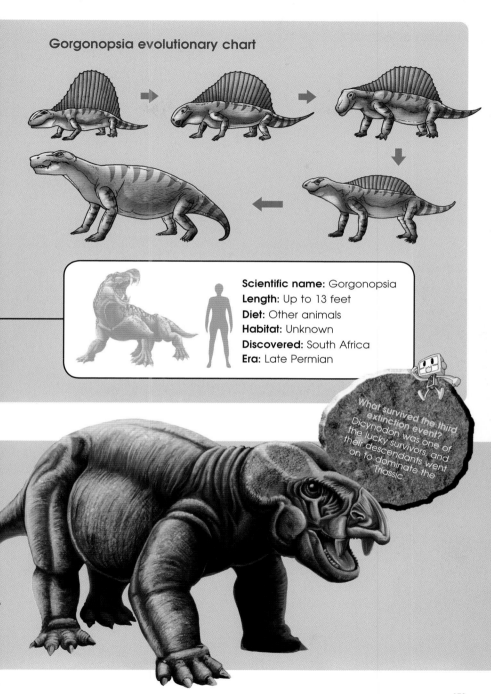

Gorgonopsia evolutionary chart

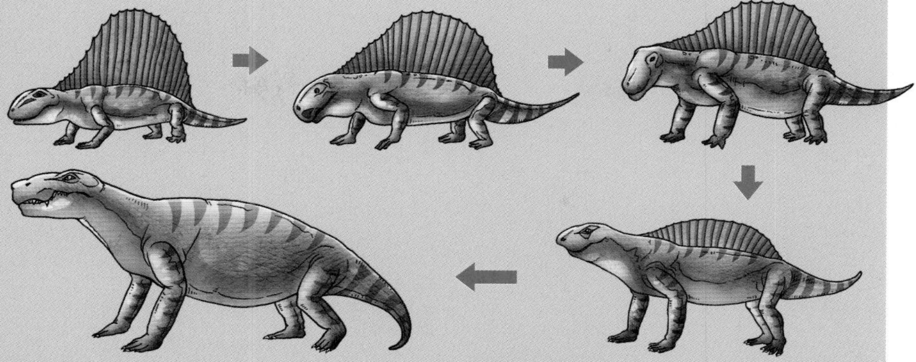

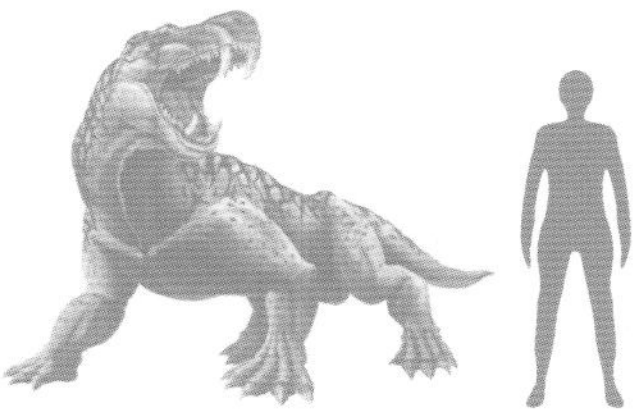

Scientific name: Gorgonopsia
Length: Up to 13 feet
Diet: Other animals
Habitat: Unknown
Discovered: South Africa
Era: Late Permian

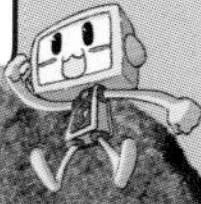

What survived the third extinction event?
Dicynodon was one of the lucky survivors, and their descendants went on to dominate the Triassic.

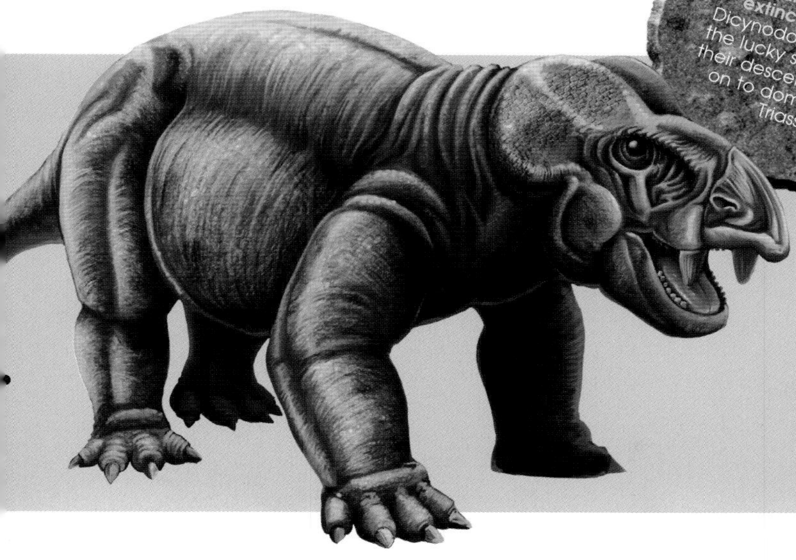

PERUSING THE PERMIAN

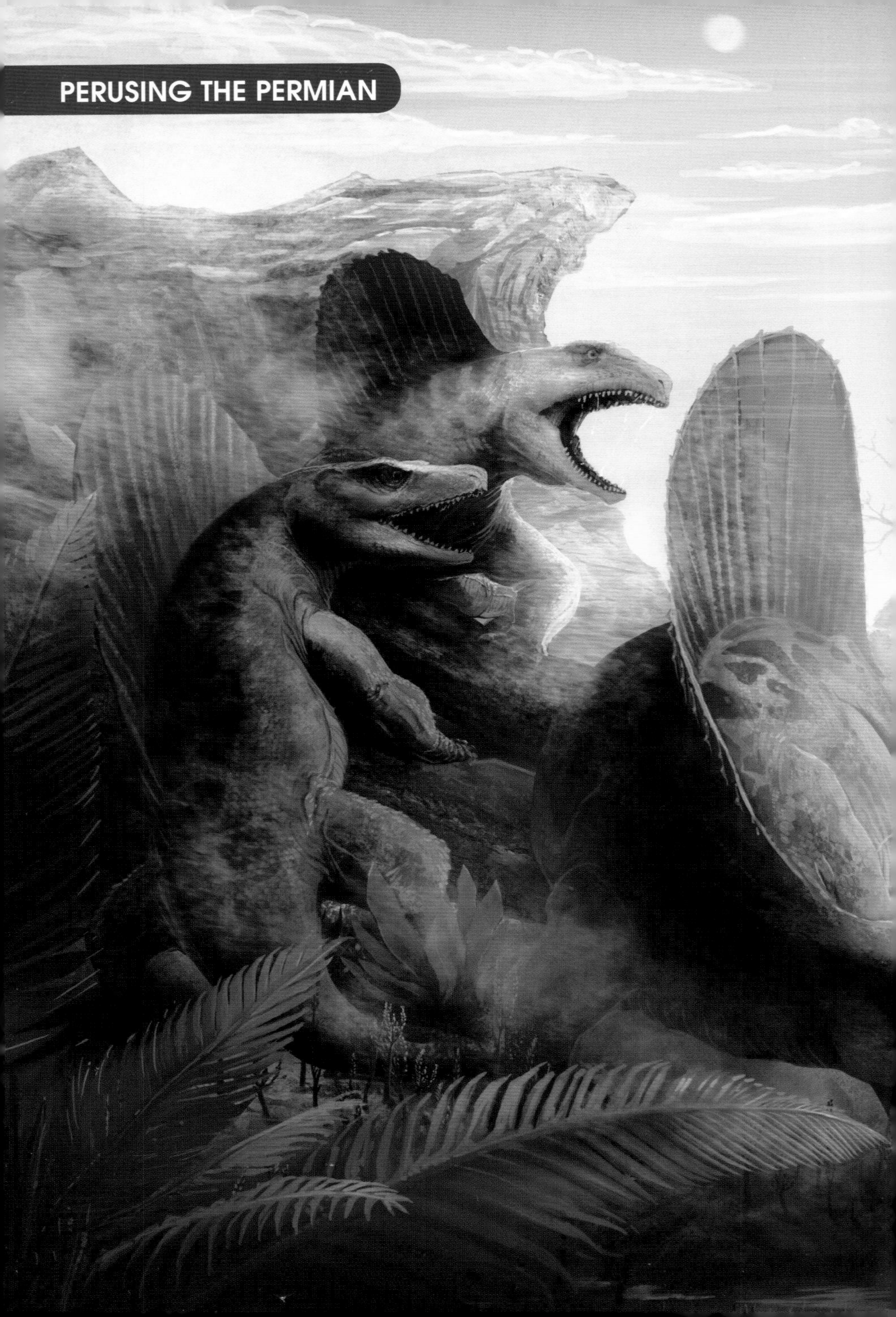

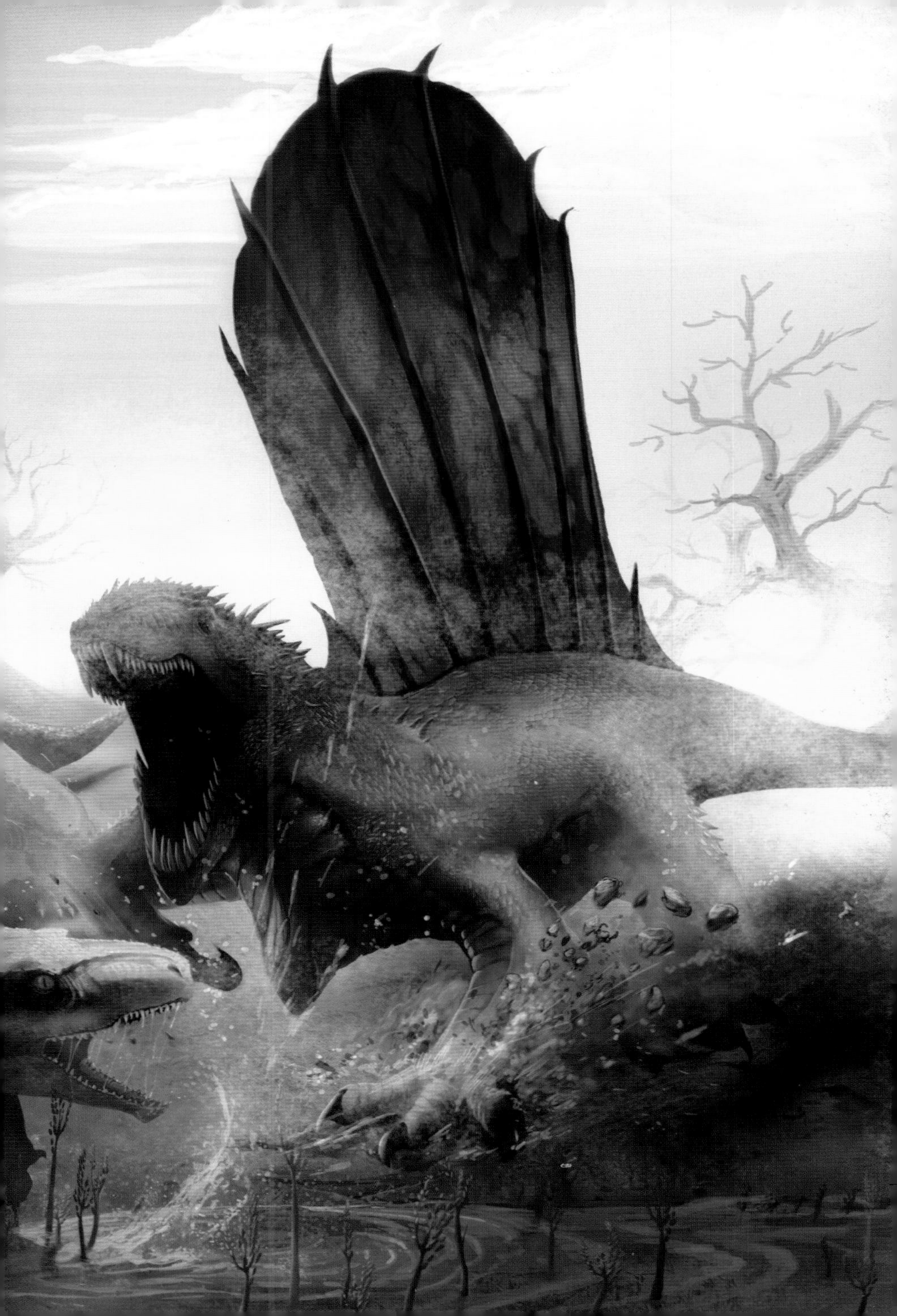

WATCH OUT FOR PAPERCUTZ

Welcome to the thrilling, thunderous, third DINOSAUR EXPLORERS graphic novel by Redcode and Albbie, writers, and Air Team, artists, from Papercutz, those Stone Age survivors dedicated to publishing great graphic novels for all ages. I'm Jim Salicrup, the Editor-in-Chief and former Fossil watch-wearer, here to let you know a bit about what's going on behind-the-scenes here at Papercutz...

The biggest news is that dinosaurs are finally in DINOSAUR EXPLORERS!

If you've picked up DINOSAUR EXPLORERS #1 "Prehistoric Pioneers" and #2 "Puttering in the Paleozoic," then you know that Dr. Da Vinci, along with Diana, Emily, Rain, Starz, Sean, and Stone have been slowly working their way back to the present after having been flung 570 million years back in time. That was so far back, that they were exploring the world BEFORE dinosaurs even existed. But our heroes have finally made it to the Carboniferous, and now they can't seem to get away from dinosaurs!

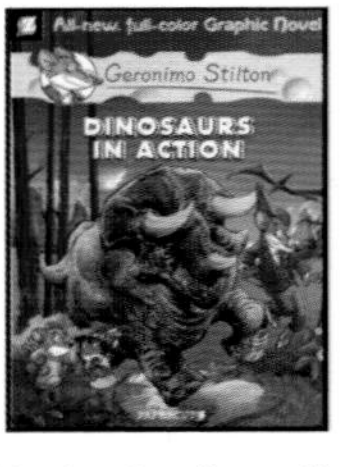
All-new, full-color Graphic Novel
Geronimo Stilton
DINOSAURS IN ACTION

Here's the deal—the Particle Transmitter, which took them into the past, can only travel so far into the future in a single trip due to the lack of sufficient energy sources. Too bad they don't have the Speedrat—they'd be back in the present by now. You're familiar with the Speedrat, right? That's the time machine Professor Von Volt invented for Geronimo Stilton and his family and friends to use to save the future from the temporal tampering of the Pirate Cats. The Speedrat has never had a problem getting back to the present from the past. Of course, you knew that if you've been following Geronimo Stilton's graphic novel adventures published by Papercutz. While GERONIMO STILTON #5 "The Great Ice Age" and GERONIMO STILTON #7 "Dinosaurs in Action" dealt with dinosaurs, most of Geronimo's time-travel adventures tend to focus on great moments in history, such as GERONIMO STILTON #1 "The Discovery of America."

Speaking of great moments in history, critics are talking about the latest graphic novel from the Papercutz imprint, Super Genius: THE ARTIST BEHIND SUPERMAN: THE JOE SHUSTER STORY. Writer Julian Voloj and artist Thomas Campi tell the true story of how writer Jerry Siegel and artist Joe Shuster came together to create the greatest superhero of all time. It's really an exciting story filled with many surprises and dramatic twists. You'd think the guys who created Superman would be incredibly rich, right? Well, the truth will shock you. But similarly to DINOSAUR EXPLORERS and GERONIMO STILTON, there are certain fantasy elements added to the story, although nothing quite so fantastic as time travel (even though Superman has been known to journey back into the past quite often), but overall, the story is based on well-documented facts about the legendary comicbook creators. Just as the information about dinosaurs in DINOSAUR EXPLORERS and the history in GERONIMO STILTON is all true as well.

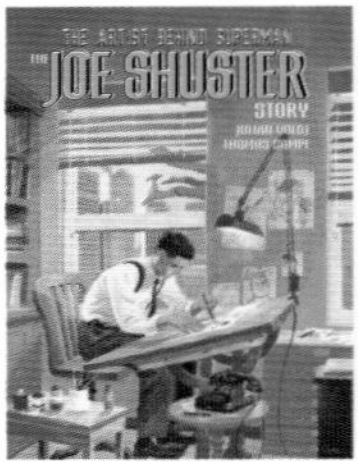
THE ARTIST BEHIND SUPERMAN
THE JOE SHUSTER STORY

Funny, we're living in age where it's tricky to tell what's fact from fiction, so maybe I should be as clear as possible. While time travel, talking mice, and super-heroes don't exist, as far as we know, dinosaurs really did exist. Paleontologists are literally digging up new information about those amazing creatures that lived on Earth centuries before we humans came along. It seems we just can't get enough of dinosaurs—new dinosaur toys, movies, and yes, graphic novels, seem to just keep popping up. For example, keep an eye out for DINOSAUR EXPLORERS #4 "Trapped in Triassic," coming your way in the not-too-distant future from your soon-to-be-recent past—and that's a fact!

Thanks,

Jim

STAY IN TOUCH!

EMAIL: salicrup@papercutz.com
WEB: papercutz.com
TWITTER: @papercutzgn
INSTAGRAM: @papercutzgn
FACEBOOK: PAPERCUTZGRAPHICNOVELS
FAN MAIL: Papercutz, 160 Broadway, Suite 700, East Wing, New York, NY 10038

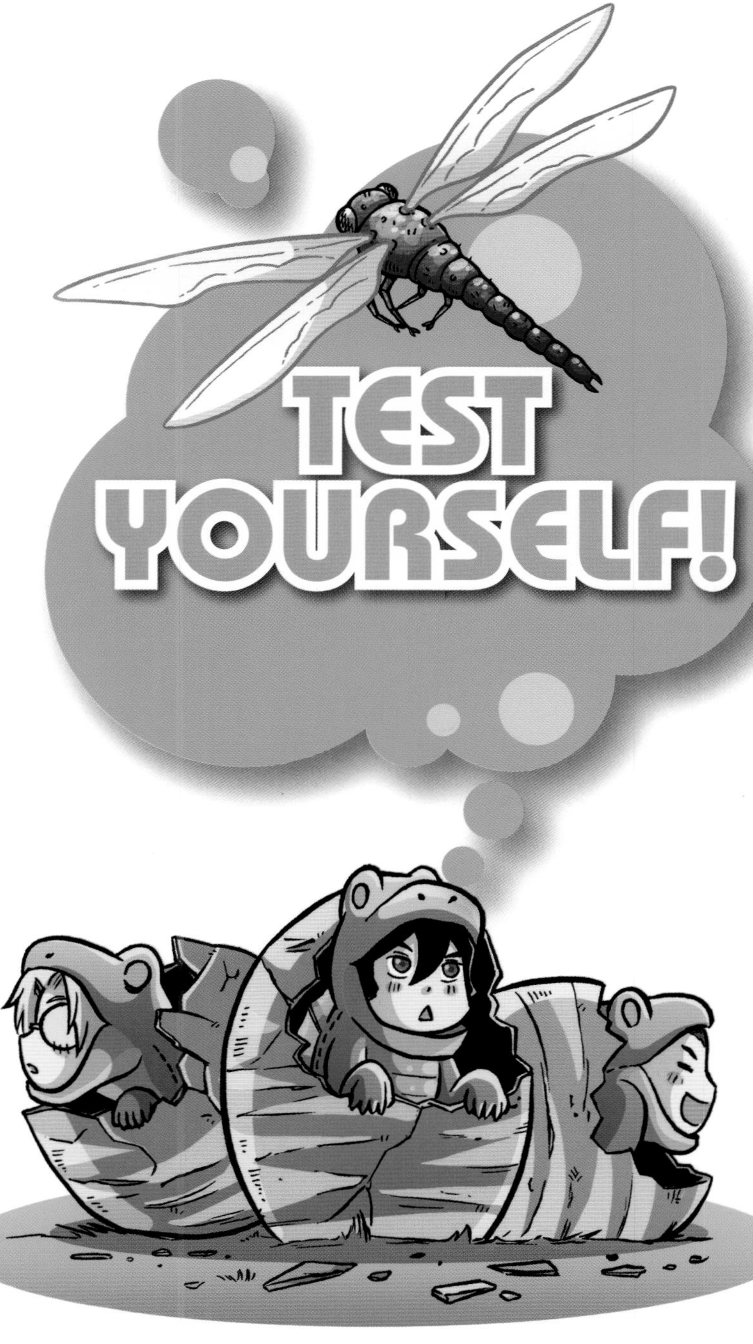
TEST YOURSELF!

QUIZNEFEROUS CARBONIFEROUS!

01 What was the dominant fish species during the Carboniferous?

A - Acanthodians

B - Agnathans (jawless fish)

C - Actinopterygii

02 What was the Blattodea?

A - A cockroach

B - A fly

C - A dragonfly

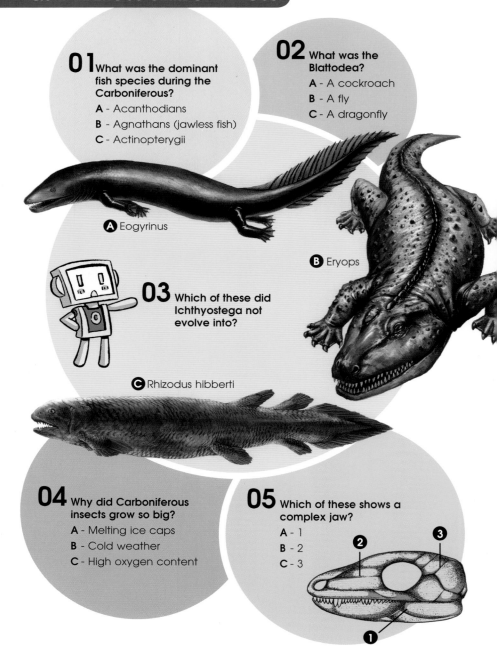

A Eogyrinus

B Eryops

03 Which of these did Ichthyostega not evolve into?

C Rhizodus hibberti

04 Why did Carboniferous insects grow so big?

A - Melting ice caps

B - Cold weather

C - High oxygen content

05 Which of these shows a complex jaw?

A - 1

B - 2

C - 3

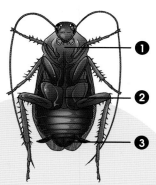

06 Which of these was an early anapsid?

A - Coelurosauravus
B - Hylonomus
C - Conolophus subcristatus

07 Which of these did the female cockroach use to carry her eggs?

A - 1
B - 2
C - 3

08 What animal's bone structure is shown in the diagram below?

A - Diadectes
B - Hylonomus
C - Ophiacodon

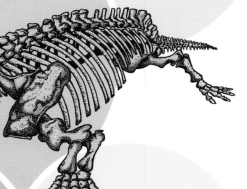

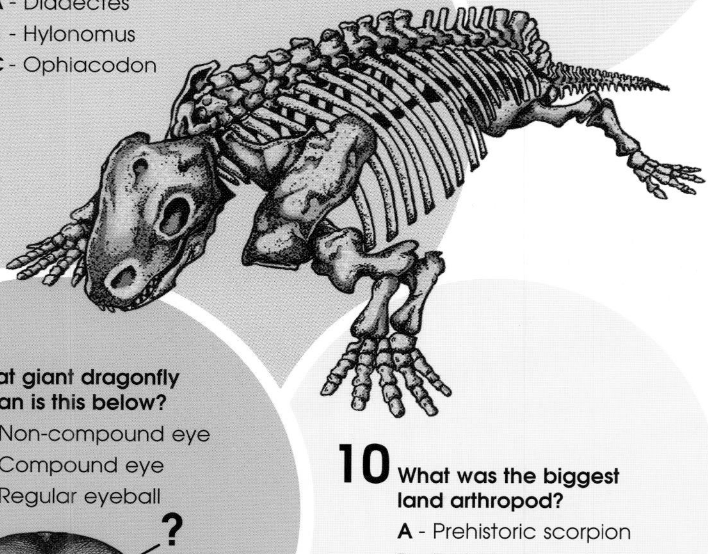

09 What giant dragonfly organ is this below?

A - Non-compound eye
B - Compound eye
C - Regular eyeball

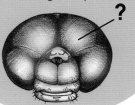

10 What was the biggest land arthropod?

A - Prehistoric scorpion
B - Prehistoric centipede
C - Prehistoric spider

PERMIAN POP QUIZ

11 **When did the Permian begin?**

A - 250 million years ago

B - 290 million years ago

C - 520 million years ago

12 **Which animal's bone structure does this diagram show?**

A - Conolophus subcristatus

B - Ophiacodon

C - Diplocaulus

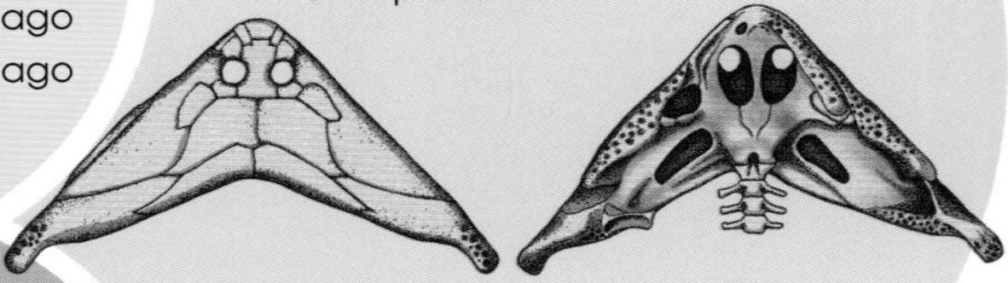

13 **What plant dominated the Permian?**

A - Psilopsida

B - Gymnosperms

C - Angiosperms

14 **Which of these is a carnivore?**

B Dimetrodon

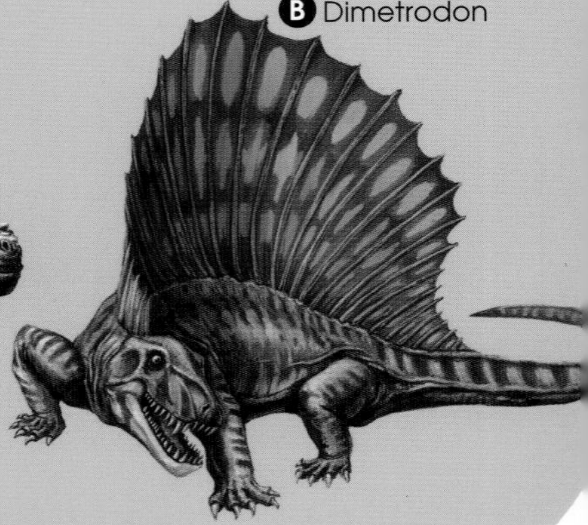

A Scutosaurus

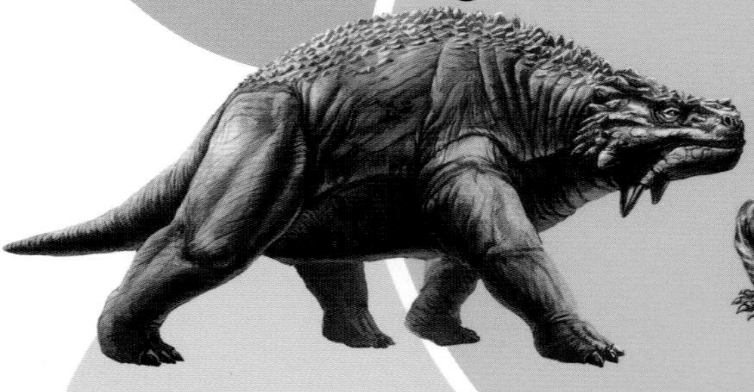

C Dicynodon

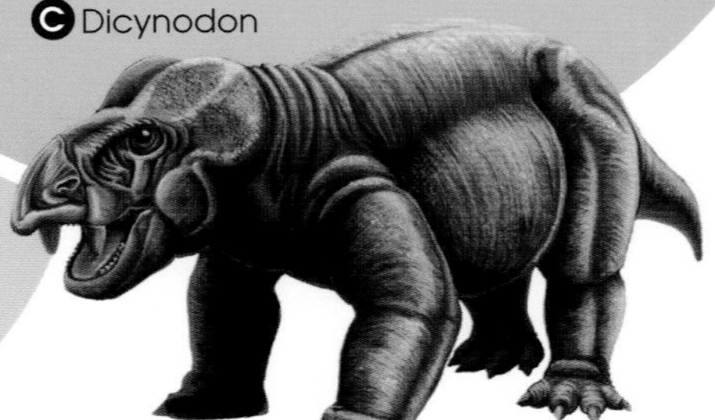

15 **Which of these was the first to have special glands?**

A - Estemmenosuchidae

B - Gorgonopsia

C - Ophiacodon

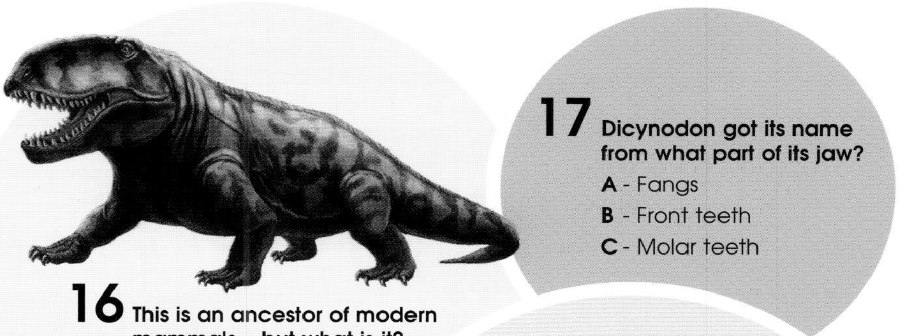

16 **This is an ancestor of modern mammals – but what is it?**

A - Hylonomus

B - Ophiacodon

C - Petrolacosaurus

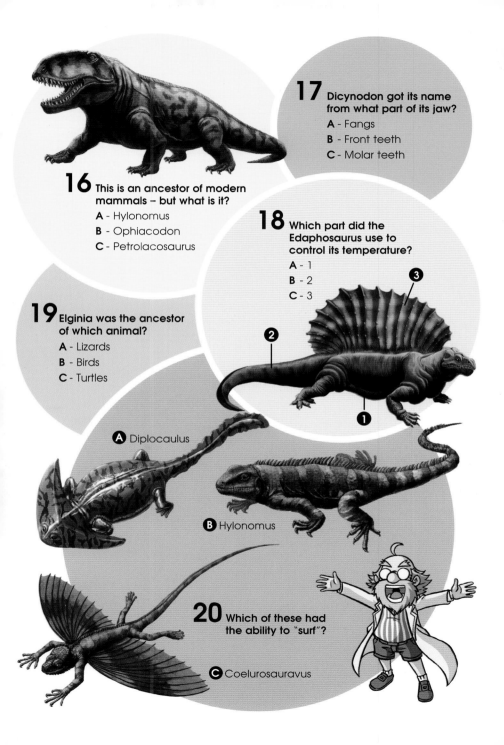

17 **Dicynodon got its name from what part of its jaw?**

A - Fangs

B - Front teeth

C - Molar teeth

18 **Which part did the Edaphosaurus use to control its temperature?**

A - 1

B - 2

C - 3

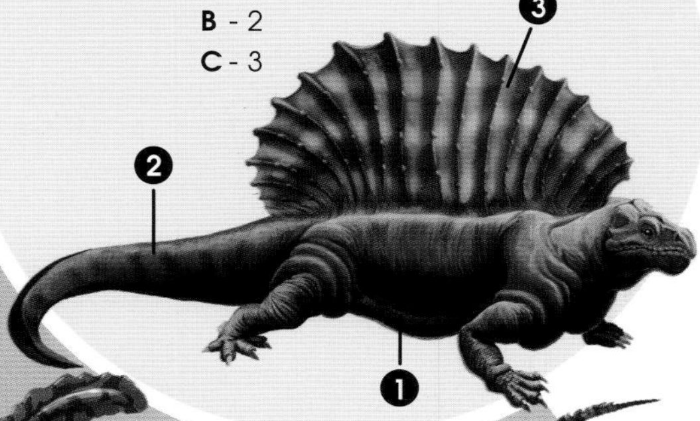
3
2
1

19 **Elginia was the ancestor of which animal?**

A - Lizards

B - Birds

C - Turtles

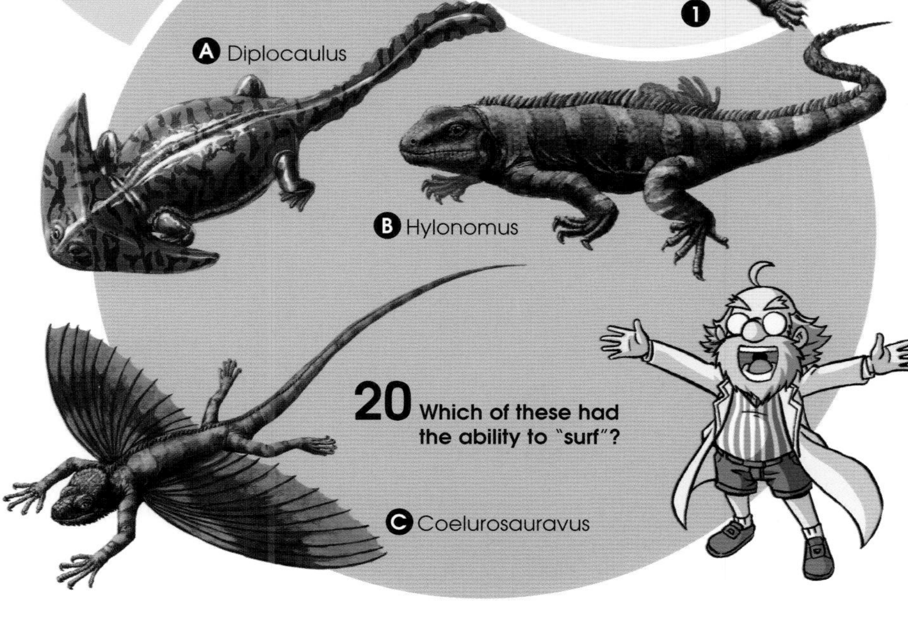
A Diplocaulus
B Hylonomus
C Coelurosauravus

20 **Which of these had the ability to "surf"?**

ANSWERS

01 C	02 A	03 C	04 C	05 A
06 B	07 C	08 A	09 B	10 B
11 B	12 C	13 B	14 B	15 A
16 B	17 A	18 C	19 C	20 C

All correct?
Congrats! You're
as smart as I am!
I think.

16 – 19 correct?
I'm actually smarter
than the Doctor!
Don't tell anyone!

12 -15 correct?
Don't just take in knowledge–
apply it to real life!

8-11 correct?
What? You're smarter
than me? Impossible!

4 – 7 correct?
Huh, looks like we both can use
some work! Let's go to the library!
Studying's better with friends!

0-3 correct?
Don't worry, you're as
S-M-R-T smart as me!

MORE GREAT GRAPHIC NOVEL SERIES AVAILABLE FROM PAPERCUTZ™

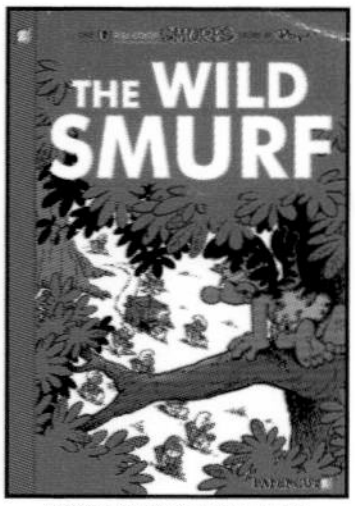
THE WILD SMURF
PAPERCUTZ
THE SMURFS #21

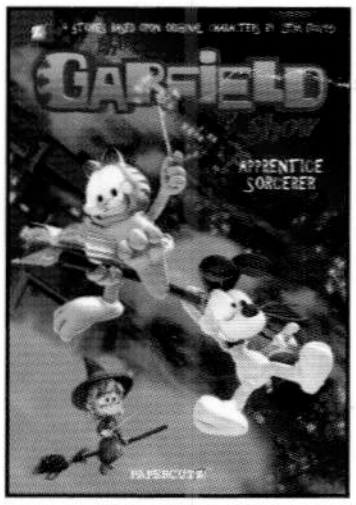
GARFIELD Show
APPRENTICE SORCERER
PAPERCUTZ
THE GARFIELD SHOW #6

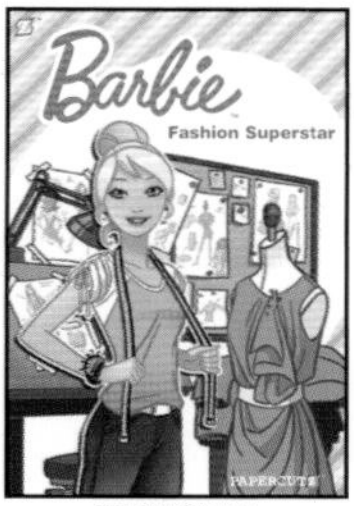
Barbie
Fashion Superstar
PAPERCUTZ
BARBIE #1

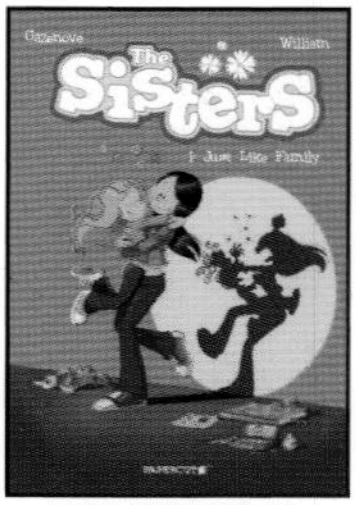
The Sisters
Just Like Family
PAPERCUTZ
THE SISTERS #1

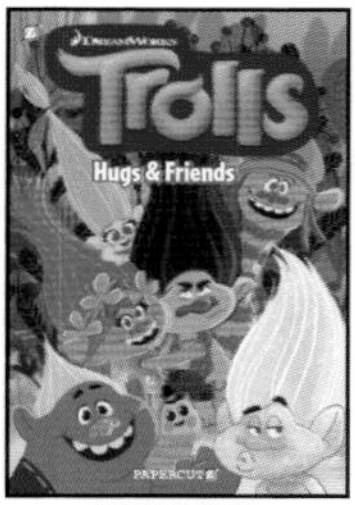
DreamWorks
Trolls
Hugs & Friends
PAPERCUTZ
TROLLS #1

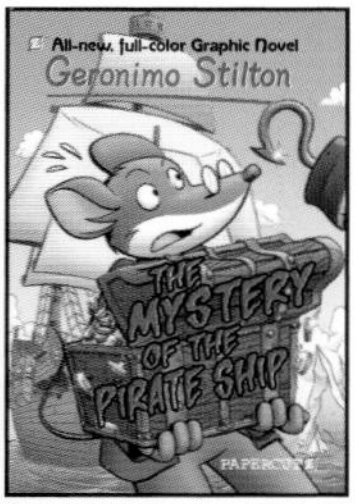
All-new, full-color Graphic Novel
Geronimo Stilton
THE MYSTERY OF THE PIRATE SHIP
PAPERCUTZ
GERONIMO STILTON #17

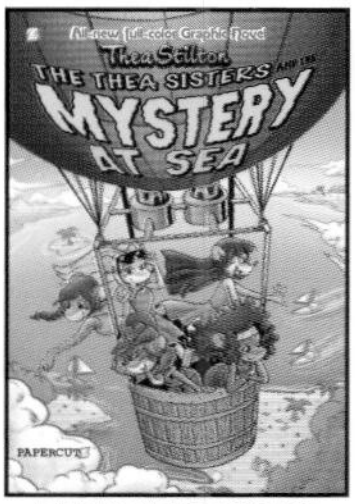
All-new, full-color Graphic Novel
Thea Stilton
THE THEA SISTERS AND THE
MYSTERY AT SEA
PAPERCUTZ
THEA STILTON #6

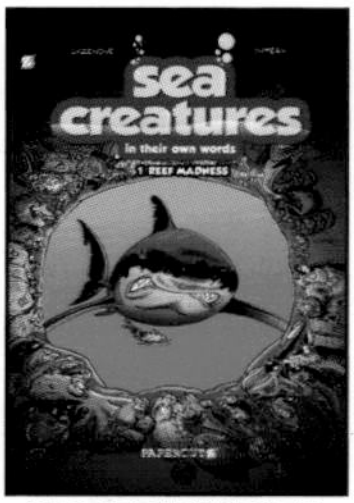
sea creatures
in their own words
PAPERCUTZ
SEA CREATURES #1

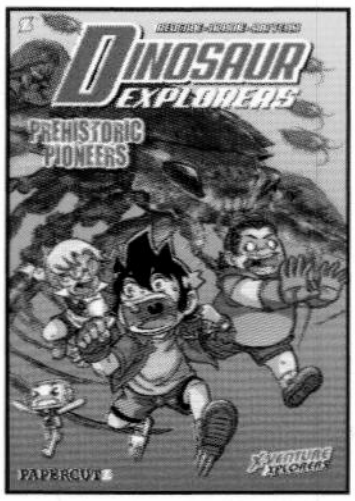
DINOSAUR EXPLORERS
PREHISTORIC PIONEERS
PAPERCUTZ
DINOSAUR EXPLORERS #1

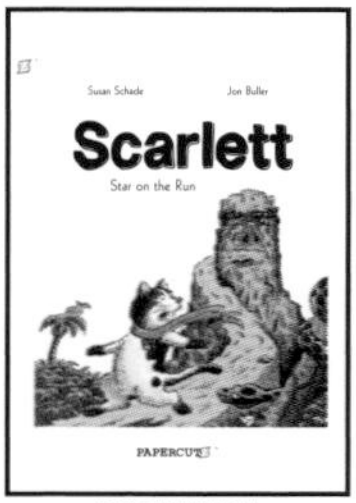
Susan Schade
Jon Buller
Scarlett
Star on the Run
PAPERCUTZ
SCARLETT

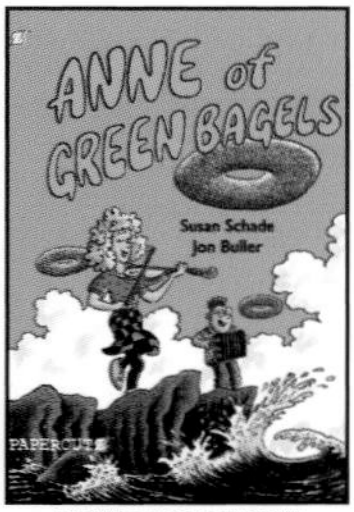
ANNE of GREEN BAGELS
Susan Schade
Jon Buller
PAPERCUTZ
ANNE OF GREEN BAGELS #1

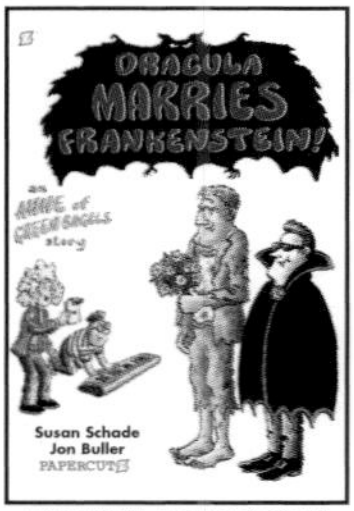
DRACULA MARRIES FRANKENSTEIN!
an ANNE of GREEN BAGELS story
Susan Schade
Jon Buller
PAPERCUTZ
DRACULA MARRIES FRANKENSTEIN!

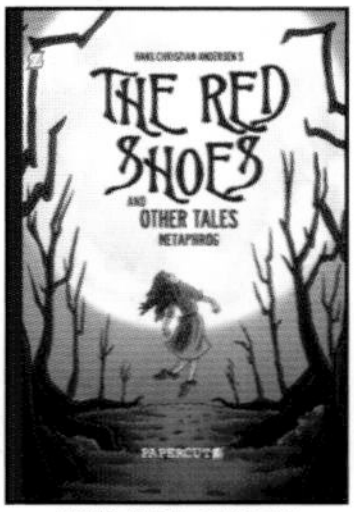
HANS CHRISTIAN ANDERSEN'S
THE RED SHOES
AND OTHER TALES
METAPHROG
PAPERCUTZ
THE RED SHOES

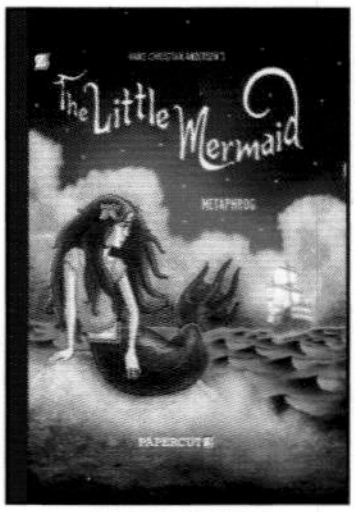
HANS CHRISTIAN ANDERSEN'S
The Little Mermaid
METAPHROG
PAPERCUTZ
THE LITTLE MERMAID

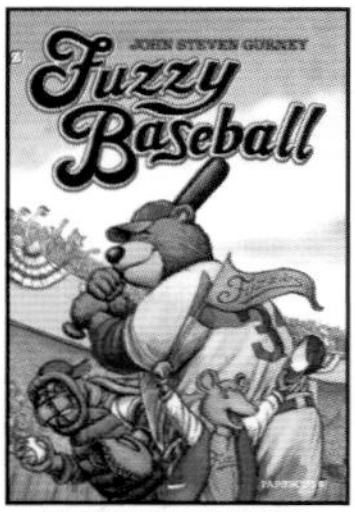
JOHN STEVEN GURNEY
Fuzzy Baseball
PAPERCUTZ
FUZZY BASEBALL

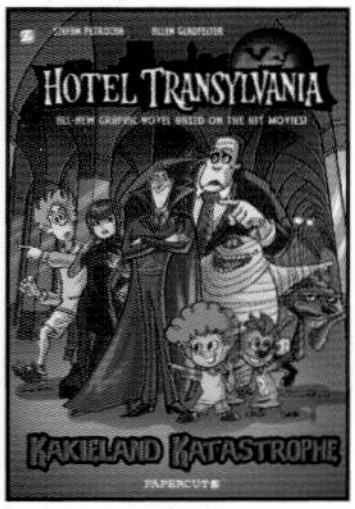
HOTEL TRANSYLVANIA
KAKIELAND KATASTROPHE
PAPERCUTZ
HOTEL TRANSYLVANIA #1

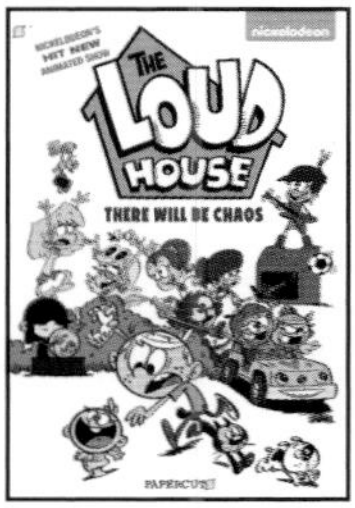
nickelodeon
THE LOUD HOUSE
THERE WILL BE CHAOS
PAPERCUTZ
THE LOUD HOUSE #1

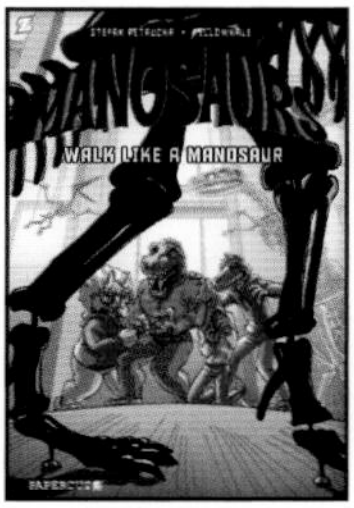
MANOSAURS
WALK LIKE A MANOSAUR
PAPERCUTZ
MANOSAURS #1

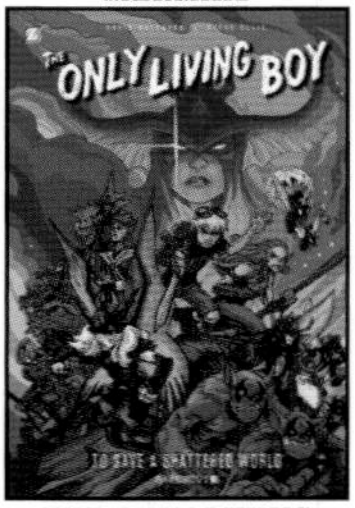
THE ONLY LIVING BOY
THE ONLY LIVING BOY #5

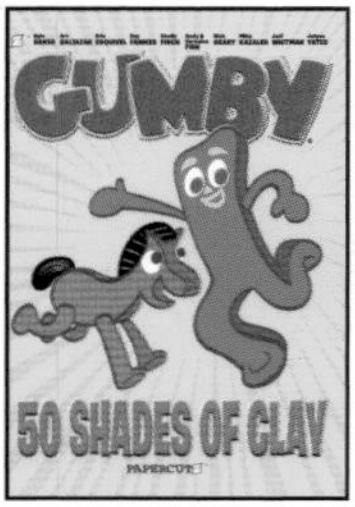
GUMBY
50 SHADES OF CLAY
PAPERCUTZ
GUMBY #1

THE SMURFS, THE GARFIELD SHOW, BARBIE, HOTEL TRANSYLVANIA, MANOSAURS, THE LOUD HOUSE and TROLLS graphic novels are available for $7.99 in paperback, and $12.99 in hardcover. THE ONLY LIVING BOY and GUMBY graphic novels are available for $8.99 in paperback, and $13.99 in hardcover. GERONIMO STILTON and THEA STILTON graphic novels are available for $9.99 in hardcover only. FUZZY BASEBALL graphic novels are available for $9.99 in paperback only. SCARLETT and ANNE OF GREEN BAGELS graphic novels are available for $14.99 in paperback only. THE RED SHOES and THE LITTLE MERMAID graphic novels are available for $12.99 in hardcover only. DRACULA MARRIES FRANKENSTEIN! graphic novels are available for $12.99 in paperback only. THE SISTERS graphic novels are available for $9.99 in paperback, and $14.99 in hardcover. SEA CREATURES graphic novels are available for $10.99 in hardcover only.

Available from booksellers everywhere. You can also order online from www.papercutz.com. Or call 1-800-886-1223, Monday through Friday, 9–5 EST. MC, Visa, and AmEx accepted. To order by mail, please add $5.00 for postage and handling for first book ordered, $1.00 for each additional book and make check payable to NBM Publishing. Send to: Papercutz, 160 Broadway, Suite 700, East Wing, New York, NY 10038.

THE SMURFS, GUMBY, THE GARFIELD SHOW, THE LOUD HOUSE, THE ONLY LIVING BOY, BARBIE, TROLLS, GERONIMO STILTON, THEA STILTON, FUZZY BASEBALL, THE LITTLE MERMAID, HOTEL TRANSYLVANIA, MANOSAURS, THE SISTERS, SEA CREATURES ,THE RED SHOES, ANNE OF GREEN BAGELS, DRACULA MARRIES FRANKENSTEIN!, and SCARLETT graphic novels are also available wherever e-books are sold.